Dear Reader,

USA TODAY bester of the romantic su books published a Daniels has lived i her love for the state sh most beloved books—inc the two favorites showcased here, *Ambushed!* and *High-Caliber Cowboy*.

In *Ambushed!*, Sheriff Cash McCall has spent the past seven years looking for his fiancée, Jasmine Wolfe. When her car is found—with blood inside—not far from his office, the evidence seems to be mounting against him. Then Molly Kilpatrick appears, claiming to be Jasmine, and if Cash can prove that she's who she says she is, he'll be off the hook. But Cash has a growing suspicion that Molly isn't Jasmine, and that whoever she is, she's running scared from something. Now Cash is fighting on all sides to exonerate himself and protect Molly, both from the past she's trying to leave behind and the dangerous situation she's walked into.

The suspense doesn't let up in *High-Caliber Cowboy*, featuring Cash's brother, Brandon. Brandon invites trouble when he decides to work for his family's arch-enemy, Mason VanHorn, whose ranch has been hit by a rash of vandalism. Brandon is out to nab the culprit… until he finds out who it is. Suddenly, Brandon is caught between family loyalties, old desires and even older secrets that someone is willing to kill to keep hidden….

Daniels hooks her readers from the very first page with edge-of-your-seat suspense that moves at a breakneck speed. Enjoy the ride!

The Editors,

Harlequin Books

B.J. DANIELS

wrote her first book after a career as an award-winning newspaper journalist and author of thirty-seven published short stories. That first book, *Odd Man Out*, received a four-and-a-half-star review from *RT Book Reviews* and went on to be nominated for Best Intrigue for that year. Since then, she has won numerous awards, including a career achievement award for romantic suspense and many nominations and awards for best book.

Daniels lives in Montana with her husband, Parker, and two springer spaniels, Spot and Jem. When she isn't writing, she snowboards, camps, boats and plays tennis. Daniels is a member of Mystery Writers of America, Sisters in Crime, International Thriller Writers, Kiss of Death and Romance Writers of America.

To contact her, write to B.J. Daniels, P.O. Box 1173, Malta, MT 59538 or email her at bjdaniels@mtintouch.net. Check out her website at www.bjdaniels.com.

USA TODAY Bestselling Author

B.J. Daniels

DOUBLE PLAY

Harlequin®

TORONTO NEW YORK LONDON
AMSTERDAM PARIS SYDNEY HAMBURG
STOCKHOLM ATHENS TOKYO MILAN MADRID
PRAGUE WARSAW BUDAPEST AUCKLAND

ISBN-13: 978-0-373-68880-7

DOUBLE PLAY

Copyright © 2010 by Harlequin Books S.A.

The publisher acknowledges the copyright holder of the individual works as follows:

AMBUSHED!
Copyright © 2005 by Barbara Heinlein

HIGH-CALIBER COWBOY
Copyright © 2005 by Barbara Heinlein

www.Harlequin.com

Printed in U.S.A.

CONTENTS

This book is dedicated to Teagan and Hayden.
Thank you, baby girls, for all the hugs and kisses.
I can't tell you what the tea parties
with you two mean to me. I love you both dearly.

AMBUSHED!

CHAPTER ONE

Tuesday
Outside Antelope Flats, Montana

THE ABANDONED BARN loomed out of the rain soaked landscape, the roof partially gone, a gaping black hole where the doors had once been.

Sheriff Cash McCall pulled his patrol car up next to Humphrey's pickup. Through the blurred thumping of the wipers, Cash could see Humphrey Perkins behind the steering wheel, waiting.

Cash cut the engine and listened to the steady drum of the rain on the patrol car roof, not anxious to go inside that barn. Hadn't he known? Hadn't he always known?

Steeling himself, he pulled up the hood on his raincoat and stepped out of the patrol car. Humphrey didn't move, just watched as Cash walked past his pickup toward the barn.

Five minutes ago, Humphrey had called him. "I found something, Cash." The old farmer had sounded scared, as if wishing someone else was making this call, that someone else had found what had been hidden in the barn. "You know the old Trayton homestead on the north side of the lake?"

Everyone knew the place. The land had been tied up in a family estate for years, the dilapidated house boarded up, the barn falling down. There were No

Trespassing signs posted all around the property, but Humphrey owned the land to the north and had always cut through the Trayton place to fish. Seemed that hadn't changed.

"I noticed one of the barn doors had fallen off," Humphrey had said on the phone, voice cracking. "I think you'd better come out here and take a look. It looks like there's a car in there."

Cash stepped from the rain into the cold darkness of the barn. The shape under the large faded canvas tarp was obviously a car. He could see one of the tires. It was flat.

He stood, listening to the rain falling through the hole in the roof patter on the tarp. Clearly the car had been there for a long time. Years.

Wind lifted one corner of the canvas and he saw the back bumper, the Montana State University parking sticker and part of the license plate, MT 6-431. The wind dropped the tattered edge of the tarp, but Cash had seen enough of the plate to know it was the one a statewide search hadn't turned up seven years ago.

He'd been praying it wasn't her car. Not the little red sports car she'd been anxiously waiting to be delivered.

"When I get my car, I'll take you for a ride," she'd said, flirting with him from the first time he'd met her.

How many times over the years since she'd disappeared had he heard those words echo in his head? "I'll take you for a ride."

He closed his eyes, taking in huge gulps of the rank-smelling barn air. Her car had been within five miles of Antelope Flats all these years? Right under their noses?

The search had centered around Bozeman, where she was last seen. Later, even when it had gone statewide, there wasn't enough manpower to search every old barn or building. Especially in the remote southeastern part of the state.

He tried to breathe. She'd been almost within sight of town? So close all these years?

Cash opened his eyes, scrubbed at them with the heel of his hand, each breath a labor. He turned away and saw Humphrey's huge bulk silhouetted in the barn door, the hood of his dark raincoat pulled up, his arms dangling loose at his sides.

"It's her car, isn't it?" Humphrey said from the doorway.

Cash didn't answer, couldn't. Swallowing back the bile that rose in his throat, he walked through the pouring rain to his patrol car for his camera.

He knew he should call for forensics and the state investigators to come down from Billings. He knew he should wait, do nothing, until they arrived. But he had to know if she was inside that car.

Rain pounded the barn roof and fell through the hole overhead, splattering loudly on top of the covered car as he stepped past Humphrey to aim the camera lens at the scene inside. He took photographs of the car from every angle and the inside of the barn before putting the camera back in the patrol car.

On the way to the barn again, he pulled the pair of latex gloves from his pocket and worked them on his shaking fingers. His nostrils filled with the mildewed odor of the barn as he stepped to one side of the car, picked up the edge of the tarp and pulled.

The heavy canvas slid from the car in a whoosh that

echoed through the barn and sent a flock of pigeons flapping out of the rafters, startling him.

The expensive red sports car was discolored, the windows filmed over, too dirty to see inside except for about four inches where the driver's side window had been lowered.

He stared at the car, his pulse thudding in his ears. It had been summer when she disappeared. She would have had the air-conditioning on. She wouldn't have put the window down while she was driving. Not with her allergies.

The rain fell harder, drumming on the barn roof as several pigeons returned, wings fluttering overhead.

He walked around the car to the other side. The left front fender was dented and scraped, the headlight broken. He stepped closer, the cop in him determined to do this by the book. Kneeling, he took out the small plastic bag and, using his pocket knife, flaked off a piece of the blue paint that had stuck in the chrome of the headlight.

Straightening, he closed the plastic bag, put the knife and bag in his pocket and carefully tried the driver's side door.

The door groaned open and he leaned down to look inside. The key was in the ignition, her sorority symbol key chain dangling from it along with the new house key—the key to the house she'd told everyone they would be living in after they were married.

The front seat was empty. He left the door open and tried the back. The rear seat was also empty. The car would have been brand new seven years ago. Which would explain why it was so clean inside.

He started to close the door when he saw something in the crack between the two front seats. He leaned in and picked up a beer cap from the brand she always drank. He started to straighten but noticed something else had fallen in the same space. A matchbook.

Cash held the matchbook up in the dim light. It was from the Dew Drop Inn, a bar in Bozeman, where she'd been attending Montana State University. Inside, three of the matches had been used. He closed the cover and put the matchbook into an evidence bag.

Shutting the back door, he stood for a moment knowing where he had to look next, the one place he'd been dreading.

He moved to the open driver's side door and reached down beside the front seat for the lever that opened the trunk. He had to grip the top of the door for a moment, steadying himself as he saw the large dark stain on the light-colored carpet floor mat under the steering wheel.

The tarp had kept the inside of the car dry over the years, the inside fairly clean, so he knew the stain on the mat wasn't from water. He knew dried blood when he saw it. The stain was large. Too large.

As he pulled the lever, the trunk popped open with a groan. He drew the small flashlight from his coat pocket and walked toward the rear of the car, the longest walk of his life.

The bodies were always in the trunk.

Taking deep breaths, he lifted the lid and pointed the flashlight beam inside. In that instant, he died a thousand deaths before he saw that what was curled inside wasn't a body. Just a quilt rolled up between a suitcase and the spare.

Cash staggered back from the car, the temporary relief making him weak. Was it possible Jasmine had been on her way to Antelope Flats? All these years he hoped she'd run off to some foreign country to live.

Instead she'd been on her way to Antelope Flats seven years ago. But why? His heart began to pound. To see him?

Or at least that's what someone wanted him to believe. Wanted the state police to believe.

He thought of the blood on the floor mat, the car hidden just miles from his office, from the old house he'd bought that Jasmine called her engagement present.

He rubbed a hand over his face, his throat raw. Jasmine wasn't living the good life in Europe, hadn't just changed her mind about everything and run off to start a new life.

He turned and walked back out into the rain, stopping next to Humphrey's pickup. The older man was sitting in the cab. He rolled down the driver's side window as Cash approached.

"I'm going to call the state investigators," Cash said, rain echoing off the hood of his jacket. "They're going to want to talk to you."

Humphrey nodded and looked past him to the barn. "Did you find her?"

Cash shook his head and started toward his patrol car, turning to look back at the barn and the dark shadow of Jasmine's car inside. All those years of trying to forget, trying to put that part of his life behind him.

He realized now that all he'd been doing was waiting. Waiting for the other shoe to drop.

That shoe had finally dropped.

Las Vegas, Nevada

MOLLY KILPATRICK CHUCKED her clothing into her only suitcase. No time to fold anything.

Since the phone call, she'd been flying around the

hotel room, grabbing up her belongings as quickly as possible. She had to skip town. It wouldn't be the first time. Or the last.

She fought back tears, trying hard not to think about Lanny. Her father's old friend was probably dead by now. He shouldn't have taken the time to warn her. He should have saved his own skin. She tried not to think about the horrible sounds she'd heard in the background before the phone went dead.

Even if the police had responded to her anonymous call immediately, they would have gotten there too late. She knew she couldn't have saved Lanny. All she could do was try to save herself.

Zipping the suitcase closed, she slid it off the bed and took one last glance around the room. She'd never owned more than she could fit into one suitcase, never stayed long in one place and made a point of never making friends. This, she knew, was why.

She'd been raised on the run, she thought, as she picked up the baseball cap from the bed and snugged it down on her short, curly blond hair.

As she passed the mirror, she checked herself, adjusting the peach-colored T-shirt over her small round breasts, tucking a pocket back into her worn jeans, glancing down at the old leather sandals before slipping on the sunglasses and picking up her purse.

She could become a chameleon when she needed to, blending into any environment. It was a talent, the one talent she'd learned from her father that she actually appreciated. Especially right now.

She didn't bother to check out since she wasn't registered anyway. For someone like her, getting past a hotel-room lock was a walk in the park.

From experience she knew that entire floors of suites

were set aside for high rollers and those rooms got little use even when rented for the night. She was always gone shortly after sunrise and even the couple of times she'd been caught, she'd been able to bluff her way out of it.

She thought about picking up her last check at the café where she'd been working. It wouldn't be enough money to make it worth the risk.

Vince and Angel would find out soon enough that she'd taken off. No reason to alert them yet. It was too much to hope that the police had gotten to Lanny's quick enough to catch the two convicted felons in the act.

No, she could only assume that Vince and Angel had not only gotten away but were looking for her at this very moment. If anything, fifteen years in prison would have made them even more dangerous.

On the way through the hotel, she stopped at one of the slot machines. It was foolish. She should be getting out of there as fast as possible. But superstition was something else she'd gotten from her father. And right now she needed to test her luck to make sure it was still with her.

She dropped a quarter into the slot machine and pulled the handle. The cylinder spun, stopping on first one bar, then another and for a moment she thought she might hit the big jackpot, but the third bar blurred past.

A handful of quarters jangled into the metal tray anyway. She scooped them up. Not as lucky as she had hoped but still better than nothing, she thought as she shoved the quarters into her jeans pocket, picked up her suitcase and headed for the exit.

As she moved through the noisy casino, she looked straight ahead but noticed everything, the hectic movement of gamblers pulling one-armed bandits, change girls stopping to hand out rolls of coins, cocktail waitresses weaving through the crowds with trays of drinks.

Goodbye Vegas, she thought as she cleared the doorless opening and stepped from the air-conditioned casino into the hot desert night. She breathed in the scents, knowing she wouldn't be back here, not even sure she would be alive tomorrow. She had no idea where she would go or what she would do but it wasn't as if she hadn't done this for as long as she could remember.

As she headed toward her car parked in the huge lot, a white-haired couple came out of their RV, a homeless man cut through the cars toward the busy street and a handful of teenagers rolled through the glittering Vegas night on skateboards.

There was no one else around. But still she studied her car under the parking lot lights as she neared it. She doubted she had to worry about a car bomb. Vince and Angel preferred the personal touch. Also, they would want her alive. At least temporarily.

She unlocked the trunk of the nondescript tan sedan, put the suitcase in and slammed the lid. As she opened the driver's side door, she surreptitiously took one quick glance around and climbed in.

Not one car followed her as she wound her way through the lot and exited on a backstreet. She headed down the strip toward Interstate 15, took the first entrance ramp, and saw that she was headed north. It didn't matter where she was headed, she had no idea where she was going to go anyway.

Keeping an eye on her rearview mirror, she left the

desert behind. But she knew she wasn't safe, not by any means. Vince and Angel would move heaven and earth to find her.

And they'd kill her when they did.

CHAPTER TWO

Wednesday
Outside Antelope Flats, Montana

SHERIFF CASH MCCALL stood next to his patrol car and watched as the last of the officers came out of the old barn. They'd been searching for hours and he knew without asking that they still hadn't found her body.

He felt himself sag. He'd hoped that Jasmine's body was in the barn, that this would finally be over. He hadn't slept, couldn't get the sight of her car with the old tarp, the dented fender, the blood stain on the driver's side floor mat out of his mind.

He rubbed a hand over his face as the lead state's investigator came toward him.

John Mathews shook his head. He was a large man with a bulldog face. "We'll continue searching the farm in the morning."

Cash knew it would take days, possibly weeks, and even using the latest equipment, there was a good chance her body would never be found, that her disappearance would never be solved, that he would have to live the rest of his life without ever knowing when or if she would turn up.

"I'm sorry," Mathews said. "We didn't find anything."

Cash nodded.

Mathews had been furious when he'd realized that Cash hadn't called him immediately upon finding the car. "That was a fool thing to do. What the hell were you thinking looking in the car before we arrived?" His tone had softened. "I know how hard this must be on you. But you were her fiancé for cryin' out loud. That makes you a suspect. Especially now that her car has been found within sight of your office."

"I had to know if she was in the car," Cash said. "I took photos. I did everything by procedure."

John had sighed. "If you're smart you'll stay as far away from this investigation as physically possible."

Cash had said nothing. He knew Mathews was right but that didn't make it any easier.

Now Cash watched Mathews look past him to the lake. "We'll broaden our search to the area around the barn. When I hear something, I'll let you know."

Cash knew that was as good as it was going to get. He took off his western hat and raked a hand through his hair, unable to hide his frustration. "You know that was the year the lake was down because the new dam was being built."

"Cash," Mathews said, a clear warning in his voice. "I like you. That's why I'm going to say this to you. Stay out of it. I realize this is your turf, you know the area, your expertise might be invaluable, but don't go telling us to look in the lake, okay? If her body turns up in the lake… You know what I'm saying."

He knew exactly what Mathews was saying. He was a suspect. He'd been a suspect from the moment Jasmine disappeared seven years ago. "I just want her found."

"We all do. But you're smart enough to know that the stain under the steering wheel was blood." He nodded. "It's her blood type. Given the dent in the right front fender, the fact that the car has been hidden in the barn all these years, the amount of blood on the floor mat and the steering wheel, we're treating this as a homicide."

Cash knew that Mathews thought Jasmine had been run off the road and then attacked, possibly hitting her head on the steering wheel, or had been struck while behind the wheel by the attacker, who had then gotten rid of her body somewhere and hidden her car in the barn. Cash knew that because given the evidence as it now stood, he would have thought the same thing.

What hit home was that Jasmine really might be dead. The hidden car, the blood, seven years without anyone seeing her. There was nothing else to surmise from the evidence. The weight of it pressed down on his chest making it almost impossible to breathe. Head wounds caused significant blood loss. He couldn't keep kidding himself that she'd somehow walked away from a blow to her head.

The facts no longer gave credence to his fantasy that she'd taken off, had been living it up on some Mediterranean island all these years.

"Even if you weren't a suspect, you're too emotionally involved to work this case anyway," Mathews said.

Cash fought to curb his anger and frustration, knowing it would only strengthen Mathews's point. "Unless her disappearance is solved, I will *always* be a suspect. You have any idea what that is like?"

"You know how this works," Mathews said quietly. "You still have your job as sheriff. You think you would if anyone believed for a minute that you had something to do with her disappearance?"

"Let me call the family."

Mathews raised an eyebrow. "Not much family left as I hear it."

"Just her stepbrother Bernard. But I'd just like to be the one to tell him," Cash said.

Mathews nodded. "Maybe he'll have some idea how her car ended up down here. But then if he knew his sister was coming down to see you, he would have mentioned it seven years ago, right?"

They'd been over this ground before. "She didn't drive down here to see me. She had plans in Bozeman. But if someone wanted me to look guilty, hiding her car in a barn outside my town would certainly do it."

Mathews nodded in agreement. "Awful lot of trouble to go to since she was living almost five hours away."

"Covering up a murder sometimes requires a lot of trouble, I would imagine," Cash snapped back.

Mathews nodded slowly. "You ought to take a few days off. Didn't I hear that you have a cabin on the other end of the lake?"

Cash said nothing.

"Fishing any good?"

"Smallmouth bass and crappie are biting, a few walleye and northern pike," Cash said, seeing where this was going. "I have some vacation time coming. I think I'll tie up the loose ends back at the office and do that. You have my cell-phone number if you hear anything."

Mathews nodded. "I suppose it is a godsend that her father didn't live to see this." Archie had died five years ago of a heart attack. Jasmine's stepmother Fran was killed just last year in a car accident. "Her stepbrother Bernard is kind of a jackass but I liked the old man and he seemed to like you. He really wanted you to marry his daughter." The investigator sounded a little surprised by that.

No more surprised than Cash, but looking back, Cash knew that was probably why he'd been able to keep his job as sheriff when Jasmine disappeared. Archibald

"Archie" Wolfe had never once thought that Cash had anything to do with Jasmine's disappearance.

Cash had expected the prominent and powerful Georgia furniture magnate to hate him on sight the first time they met—just after Jasmine had disappeared. It had seemed impossible that Archibald Wolfe would have ever wanted his Southern belle socialite daughter to marry a small-town sheriff in Montana. Jasmine had already told Cash that her father never liked any of the men she dated.

But Archie had surprised him. "You're the kind of man she needed," the older man had said. "I know she's spoiled and would try a saint's patience, but I think all she needs is the right man to straighten her up."

"Mr. Wolfe, I'm afraid you have it all wrong," Cash had tried to tell him.

"Archie, dammit. You know I disinherited her recently. I would have burned every cent I had to keep her from marrying the likes of Kerrington Landow. But once Jasmine is found and the two of you are married, I'll put her back in my will, you don't need to worry about that."

"I don't want your money, Mr. Wol—Archie, and I don't need it," Cash had said. "Let's just pray Jasmine is found soon."

Archie's eyes had narrowed. He had nodded slowly. "I think you actually mean that. How did my daughter find *you*?"

Cash had shaken his head, thinking that's exactly what Jasmine had done, found him and not the other way around. He'd tried to think of something to say. It hadn't seemed like the time to tell Archie the truth.

Archie had died a broken man, the loss of his daughter more than he could stand.

"Cash? Did you hear what I said?"

He mentally shook himself. "Sorry, John."

Mathews was studying him, frowning. "If there is anything you want to tell me that might come out during this investigation…"

Cash shook his head. How long did he have before he was relieved of his position and his resources taken away so he wouldn't be able to work the case in secret? Not long from Mathews's expression.

"There's nothing I haven't already told you pertaining to the case," Cash answered truthfully.

Mathews nodded slowly, clearly not believing that. "Let me know how the fishing is."

As Cash drove back into town, he knew he'd have to work fast and do his best not to get caught. It was only a matter of time before Mathews learned the truth—and Cash found himself behind bars.

North of Las Vegas, Nevada

THE FEAR DIDN'T REALLY HIT her until Molly lost sight of Vegas in her rearview mirror. She was running for her life and she didn't know where to go or what to do. She had little money and, unlike Vince and Angel who had criminal resources she didn't even want to think about, she had no one to turn to.

She wiped her eyes and straightened, checking the rearview mirror. In this life there isn't time for sentimentality, her father had told her often enough. That was why you didn't get close to anyone. If you cared too much, that person could be used against you. Wasn't that why the Great Maximilian Burke, famous magician and thief, had never let her call him Dad?

He'd insisted she go by Kilpatrick. He'd told her it was her mother's maiden name. Since Max and her mother Lorilee hadn't been married when Molly was born, her name on her birth certificate was Kilpatrick anyway, he'd said.

Molly had asked him once why he and Lorilee hadn't married before her mother died.

"Your mother wouldn't marry me until I got a real job," Max had said with a shrug. "And since I never got a real job…"

Her mother had died when Molly was a baby. She didn't remember her, didn't even have a photograph. Max wasn't the sentimental type. Also, he and Molly were always on the move, so even if there had been photos, they had long been lost.

All she had of her mother was a teddy bear, long worn, that Max had said her mother had given her. The teddy bear had been her most prized possession, but even it had been lost.

She wiped at her tears, tears she shed not for herself but for Lanny. She hadn't let herself think about her father's best friend. Lanny had always been kind to her and had remained Max's friend until her father's death. That was what had gotten Lanny killed, Molly was sure.

Her stomach growled and she realized she hadn't eaten. She pulled off the interstate in one of the tiny, dying towns north of St. George, Utah, and parked in the empty lot of the twenty-four-hour Mom's Home-cooking Café.

A bell jingled over the door as she stepped inside. It was early, but Molly doubted the place was ever hopping. She slid into a cracked vinyl booth and rested her elbows on the cool, worn Formica tabletop.

A skinny gray-haired waitress who looked more tired than even Molly felt, slid a menu and a sweating glass of ice water onto the table. She took a pad and a stubby pencil out of her pocket, leaning on one varicose-veined leg as she waited.

"I'll take the meat-loaf special with iced tea, please," Molly said, closing the menu and handing it to her, noticing that the waitress took it without looking at her, pocketed the pad and pencil without writing anything down and left without a word.

Molly watched her go, thinking her own life could be worse. It was a game she and Max used to play.

"You think your situation is bad, kiddo, look at that guy," he would say.

He called her kiddo. She called him Max and had since she was able to talk.

"Better no one knows we're related," he'd always said. "It will be our little secret." He told everyone that he'd picked her up off the street and kept her with him because she made a good assistant for his magic act.

There was a time she'd actually believed he was just trying to protect her by denying their relationship because Maximilian Burke had always been outside the law.

He'd raised her, if a person could call that raising a child. He'd let her come along with him. He used to say, "You're with me, kiddo, I'm not with you." Which meant she didn't get to complain, even when he didn't feed her for several days because he had no money. He would hand her a couple of single-serving-size packets of peanuts and tell her they would be eating lobster before the week was out.

And they usually were. It had been feast or famine. A transient existence at best. Homeless and hungry at worst. Her father was a second-rate magician but turned out to be a first-class thief.

She glanced out the café window, remembering late

nights in greasy-spoon cafés, lying with her head on her arms on the smooth, cool surface of the table, Max waking her when the food was served. Too tired to care, she ate by rote, knowing that tomorrow she might get nothing but peanuts.

"You have to learn to live off your wits," Max used to say. "It's the best thing I can teach you, kiddo. Some day it will save your life." That day had arrived.

The waitress brought out a plate with a slice of gray-colored meat loaf, instant mashed potatoes with canned brown gravy over them, a large spoonful of canned peas and a stale roll with a pat of margarine.

Molly breathed in the smell first, closing her eyes. This was as close to a mother's home-cooked meal as she'd ever come. What she loved was the familiarity of it. This was home for her, a greasy-spoon café in a forgotten town.

She opened her eyes, tears stinging, and picked up her fork, surprised that she still missed Max after all this time. Surprised that she missed him at all. But as much as he'd denied it, he was all the family she'd ever had.

She took a bite of the meat loaf. It was just as the meat loaf she'd known had always tasted, therefore wonderful.

After she'd finished, the waitress brought her a small metal dish with a scoop of ice cream drizzled with chocolate syrup as part of the meat-loaf special.

She got up to get the folded newspaper on the counter where the last patron had left it, opened it and read as she ate her ice cream, feeling better if not safer.

The article was on page eight. She wouldn't have even seen it if the photograph of the woman hadn't caught her eye. The spoon halfway to her mouth, the ice cream melting, she read the headline.

Missing Woman's Car Found in Old Barn.

She put down the spoon as she stared at the woman's photograph. The resemblance was uncanny. Looking at the photograph was like looking in a mirror. Or at a ghost. Molly could easily pass for the woman, they looked that much alike.

Heart pounding, Molly read the entire story twice, unable to believe it. Fate had just given her a way out. Her luck had definitely improved.

Las Vegas, Nevada

VINCE WINSLOW PULLED UP in front of the motel room and honked the horn of the large older-model car he'd bought when he'd gotten out of prison.

Vince thought of himself as a fair man. He'd been a mediator in his cell block at prison and everyone agreed he had a way with people. It was a gift. He would hear gripes and grievances, then he would settle them. One way or another. Sometimes he'd just bang a few heads together. Whatever it took.

The one thing he couldn't stand was injustice. It made him violent and that was dangerous for a big, strong man who'd spent most of his fifteen-year stint in the weight room at the prison, planning what to do when he got out.

He honked again and Angel Edwards came out of the motel room scowling at him. Vince slid over to let Angel drive.

"What? Are your legs broken? You can't get out of the car? You got to honk the damned horn?" Angel slid behind the wheel, cursing under his breath.

Compared to Angel, Vince was a saint. Angel was a hothead. Short, wiry, all energy with little brains.

"Haven't you ever wondered why I put up with you?" Vince asked in his usual soft tone. Right now he was definitely wondering that very thing himself.

Angel snorted. "I'm the best getaway-car driver in the business and you know it."

Vince couldn't argue that. Angel had lightning-fast reflexes. But since that life was behind them, Vince didn't need a getaway driver anymore.

"You also love me," Angel said without looking at him.

Vince stared over at him, realizing that was the only reason he didn't take Angel out into the desert and put a bullet through his brain. Angel was his half brother. Blood was everything, even if your mother had no taste when it came to men.

"Damn, it's like a refrigerator in here," Angel complained, reaching over to turn off the air-conditioning. "You tryin' to kill me?"

All those years of being locked up in the same cell block had made Vince even more aware of his brother's shortcomings. Not that it had ever taken much to set Angel off, but now, once angry, Angel was nearly impossible to control. That had proved to be a problem. On top of that, now that Angel was out of prison, he had unlimited access to sharp instruments and a fifteen-year fixation on getting what he had coming.

"We need to talk," Vince said.

"What is there to talk about?" Angel demanded, glaring over at him. "We find the bitch. We get what's coming to us. This ain't brain surgery."

"My fear is that when we find her, you will go berserk like you did with Lanny and kill her before she tells us what we want to know," Vince pointed out calmly. "If I hadn't gotten you out of there when I did last night, we would be on death row right now. We almost got caught because you can't control your temper."

"You were going too easy on Lanny. I had him talking. He was just about to tell us. If he had lived just another few seconds…"

Vince groaned. "When we find Molly, you have to refrain from that kind of…persuasion, or we will never get the diamonds."

"If she hasn't already fenced them," Angel snapped.

"She hasn't," Vince said for at least the thousandth time. These particular diamonds couldn't be easily fenced—they were too recognizable. And Vince had his sources on the outside watching for them. There was no way Molly could have tried to fence the uncut stones without him knowing about it.

Angel shifted in the seat, his left cheek twitching from a nervous tic. "Okay, okay. So why are we still sitting here? Let's find the bitch."

"I found her before I found Lanny. She's working at a greasy spoon off the Strip," Vince said.

"You've seen her?" Angel asked, his voice high with excitement and suspicion. "Why didn't you take me with you?"

Vince raised a brow as if to say, "Isn't it obvious?"

"You wouldn't try to cut me out of my share, would you?" Angel asked, going mean on him. Angel didn't trust anyone, but still Vince took it as an insult.

"You're my *brother*." As if that meant anything to Angel. Vince reached into the backseat and picked up the latest in laptop computers. Opening it, he booted it up.

"What? You going to check your email?" Angel snapped.

"Patience. She isn't going to get away," Vince told him calmly. "I put a global positioning device on her car."

"What?" Angel swore. "You were close enough to her to put some damned gadget on her car but you didn't grab her? Are you crazy?"

"Like a fox," Vince said.

"So where is she, Mr. Smart Guy?"

Vince studied the screen and smiled. "She's running for her life."

CHAPTER THREE

Antelope Flats, Montana

WHEN CASH GOT back to his office, he found his sister Dusty sitting behind his desk. She leaped to her feet like the teenager she was and ran to him, throwing her arms around his neck.

"Did they find her?" she asked stepping back from the quick hug, a mixture of hope and fear in her expression.

He shook his head and stepped around behind his desk.

Dusty was dressed in her usual jeans, western shirt, boots and a straw cowboy hat pulled low. A single blond braid trailed down her slim back. She was a beauty, although she seemed to do everything possible to hide the fact that she was female. Cash wasn't sure if it was because Dusty was raised pretty much in an all-male household or because she actually loved working on the ranch more than doing girl stuff.

"You're going to keep looking though, aren't you?" She sounded surprised he was here rather than out with the other officers searching the Trayton place.

"I'm off the case, Dusty," he said dropping into his chair. His sister had been only eleven when Jasmine disappeared. He doubted she understood the implications of Jasmine's car being found so close to town, but she would soon enough, once the Antelope Flats rumor mill kicked in. He wanted to be the one to tell her, but still the words came hard.

"I was her—" he paused, the word coming hard "—fiancé and with her car found near here, I'm a suspect in her homicide." He waved a hand through the air, knowing there was more that would come out but no reason to open that can of worms until he had to.

"Homicide?"

"A sufficient amount of her blood type was found in the car to change her disappearance to a probable homicide," he said.

"How could anyone think *you* would hurt her?" Dusty cried. "She was the love of your life—*is* the love of your life. She can't be dead. She's probably in Europe just like you thought. She'll come back once she hears about her car being found and, when she sees you again, she'll remember what you shared and she'll be sorry she stayed away and she won't ever leave again."

He smiled up at her, surprised that his tomboy sister was such a romantic and touched that she cared so much. He didn't have the heart to tell her how wrong she was. "What are you doing in town? I thought you were helping with branding?"

"Shelby sent me in to check on you and tell you that you're expected at dinner tomorrow night." Dusty rolled her eyes. "Who knows what big bombshell she's planning to drop now."

Shelby was their mother, but it was complicated as all hell. Just a few months ago, out of the blue, Shelby Ward McCall had shown up at the ranch. What made that unusual was that Cash thought his mother had died when he was just over a year old.

Shelby had not only announced that she was alive, but that she and their father Asa had cooked up her demise. It seemed they had thought it would be better for Cash and his three brothers to believe she had died rather than just left. Shelby and Asa couldn't live with each other and didn't want the children to have the stigma of divorce hanging over them.

At least that was their story and they were sticking to it. But to make matters worse, he and his brothers had always thought that their little sister Dusty was the result of an affair their father had nineteen years ago. Asa had brought Dusty home when she was a baby with some cock-and-bull story about her being orphaned. He'd legally adopted her and Cash guessed he thought his sons didn't notice how much she looked like them.

Turned out that Dusty was the result of Asa and Shelby getting together years ago in secret to "discuss" things.

Well, now Shelby was back at the ranch and tongues were wagging in four counties. Cash was trying to keep both of his parents from going to prison for fraud and Dusty was hardly speaking to either parent.

His family had always been the talk of the town for one reason or another. Cash knew that was partly why he'd become sheriff. He was tired of being one of the wild McCall boys.

"Say you will come to dinner," Dusty pleaded. Dusty had taken the betrayal the hardest. It didn't help that she looked so much like her mother. She'd also been the closest to their father and felt betrayed by him. But she was especially angry with her mother. While Dusty could possibly understand how Shelby might walk away from four sons, she couldn't forgive her mother for giving up a daughter.

Since Shelby's astonishing reappearance, the family undercurrents were deadly. She never had explained why she'd returned to the living. But it was obvious a lot more was going on between her and Asa than either had let on. Cash had seen the looks that had passed between them, seen Shelby crying and Asa hadn't been himself since she'd come back. Their father, a cantankerous, stubborn, almost seventy-year-old man who'd alienated all four of his sons on a regular basis, was actually trying to be nice.

It worried the hell out of Cash.

So it was no wonder that the last thing he wanted to do was attend one of the McCalls' famous knock-down-drag-out family dinners—especially now.

But he knew that an invitation to a family dinner was really a summons to appear. If he sent word back that he wasn't coming, Shelby herself would drive into town to try to change his mind. He didn't need that.

"I'll be there." He hated to think what new surprises might be sprung at dinner tomorrow night.

Dusty sighed in relief at his acceptance. "I think the dinner is probably about Brandon. You know he's been acting weird lately."

Cash had noticed a change in his brother, but didn't think it weird. Brandon, at thirty-three, seemed to have finally grown up. He'd taken on more responsibility out at the ranch, had really seemed to have settled down. He was talking about attending law school next fall and, according to their older brother J.T., had opened an account at the bank to save for it. "Isn't it about time Brandon grew up?"

Dusty didn't seem to be listening. "He comes in really late at night. I think he has a girlfriend, but he denies it."

Cash laughed. "If you're right, he'll tell us when he's ready."

She made a face at the "if you're right" part. It was a given that a McCall was always right, especially a female one. "Aren't you even curious why he would try to keep a girlfriend secret?"

"No, we're a family of secrets," Cash said, realizing just how true that was. He thought of his own secret, pushed for years into some dark corner of his heart.

The problem with secrets was that they didn't stay that way. It was only a matter of time, now that Jasmine's car had been found, before his came out.

Somewhere outside St. George, Utah

AFTER LEAVING THE CAFÉ, Molly found a newspaper stand and bought a copy of the paper. She ripped out the article and sat behind the wheel of her car, studying the photograph of the missing woman.

On closer inspection, the woman didn't look that much like her. The resemblance was in the shape of the face, the spacing and color of the eyes, the generous mouth. The hair was different, long, straight and white-blond compared to Molly's curly, short, darker blond locks.

But with some makeup, a few highlights in her hair and the right clothes… The clincher was that the woman was close to her age—just a year and a half older—and about her height—an inch taller and ten pounds heavier.

As Molly looked into the woman's face, she felt a chill at just the thought of what she was thinking of doing. Talk about bad karma.

According to the article, Jasmine Wolfe was last seen at a gas station on the outskirts of Bozeman seven years ago. The clerk at the station had noticed a man approach the blond woman driving the new red sports car. The man was about average height wearing a dark jacket, jeans and cap. The clerk didn't see his face or note his hair color.

When the clerk had looked up again, the man was holding the woman's arm and the two were getting into the car. They appeared to be arguing. The clerk hadn't thought much about it, just assumed they were together, until she'd read about the search for the missing woman and remembered Jasmine, the new red sports car and witnessing the incident.

It was speculated that Jasmine had been abducted by an unknown assailant who had forced her into her car at possibly knife- or gunpoint. That theory was heightened a month later when a man was arrested outside of Bozeman trying to abduct a woman at another gas station in the same area.

The man was sent to prison and, while he never admitted to abducting Jasmine Wolfe, he was believed to have been involved in several other missing persons' cases in the area, including hers. The man had committed a murder in prison and was still serving time there with little chance of parole.

That was good news. But not as good news as who Jasmine Wolfe was—the daughter of Archibald Wolfe, a furniture magnate from Atlanta, Georgia. Archie, as he was known to his friends and employees, had offered a sizable reward for any information about his daughter. The reward had never been collected.

Molly let out a low whistle. "You've just hit the jackpot, kiddo," Max would have said. "All you have to do is convince the sheriff that you're the missing woman, then the family will be a snap. Seven years. People change a lot in seven years."

Maybe, she thought. But Antelope Flats Sheriff

Cash McCall would definitely be the one she'd have to fool. Jasmine had been engaged to him, according to the newspaper. A man would know his former fiancé. Except if she kept him at arm's length, which shouldn't be that hard to do. There was no photograph of the sheriff but Molly could just imagine some backwoods local yokel.

She reached into the backseat for her old road atlas. Antelope Flats, Montana, was on the southeastern corner of the state just miles from the Wyoming border. Bozeman, where Jasmine Wolfe had been a graduate student at Montana State University, looked to be a good five hours away.

Antelope Flats had to be tiny, really tiny, since it appeared to be no more than a dot on the map.

No one would ever look for Molly there. Especially if she were someone else altogether. She knew she'd go crazy within a week in a place like that. But a week might be long enough.

Molly's original plan had been to run, just keep one step ahead of Vince and Angel. But as she stared at Jasmine Wolfe's photograph, she knew this plan—bad karma and all—was her best bet.

She opened the container she'd brought from the café. Chocolate-cream pie. It was about as homemade as the rest of the meal had been, but just as familiar.

And, she thought taking a big bite of the pie, she would need to put on a few pounds if she was going to Antelope Flats, Montana. She could do a lot with makeup, a change in her hair color and style. She could become Jasmine Wolfe, she was sure of it.

But what if Jasmine Wolfe's body turned up. State investigators were searching the abandoned farm. Or even Jasmine herself, alive and in the flesh after seeing the article? And even if neither happened, still Molly would have to pull off a major magic act with the sheriff.

But, no thanks to her father, Molly had been performing from the time she could walk. And like her father, she'd always believed in omens as well as in luck. Just when she had two killers after her and needed a place to disappear, she'd seen this article. If that wasn't a sign, she didn't know what was.

Also, she was a realist. She had only a little money saved. It wouldn't last long. If she hoped to stay alive, what better way than becoming someone else for a short period of time?

She wasn't worried about Vince and Angel seeing the article and putting two and two together. Even if they could add—or read—she doubted either had ever read a newspaper in their lives.

If by chance Vince and Angel saw the story in a newspaper, she didn't think they would notice the resemblance between Jasmine Wolfe and her. Neither man had seen her since she was fourteen and she'd changed a lot. And while she thought her resemblance to the missing woman was uncanny—it was the little touches she would make in her appearance that would convince others she was Jasmine.

Going to a pay phone, she made another anonymous call to the Vegas Police Department. Vince and Angel hadn't been picked up yet. But someone else had called in and given a description of a car leaving the scene of the murder.

She gave a description of each man as if she'd seen them leaving the murder scene as well. She told them that she'd heard the big one call the little one Angel, the one who looked like he had a prison tattoo on his neck.

It shouldn't take long for the police to put it all together. The day Max, Vince and Angel had pulled off the big heist in Hollywood, they'd returned to Lanny's house where Lanny and Molly had been waiting. It was there that the police had arrested Vince and Angel. It was there that Max had shown up in a separate vehicle and, seeing the police, had tried to make a run for it and was shot down in the street.

Molly tried not to think about that day, about her father dying in her arms in the middle of the street.

As she hung up the phone, she didn't kid herself. It could take a while before the two recently paroled felons were caught. Once they were, she was sure the police would find something on the two to send them both back to prison—even if it couldn't be proved that Vince and Angel had killed Lanny.

Still, her best bet was to stall for time.

Hiding was always preferable to running. With luck, she could pull this off. And if she played her cards right, there could even be some money in it. She cringed at how much she sounded like Max. But taking money from Jasmine's family was no worse than pretending to be her, was it?

And if anyone could pass herself off as someone else, it was Molly Kilpatrick. She'd pretended to be someone else for so many years that she had no idea who the real Molly Kilpatrick was anymore.

The decision made, she folded up the clipping and put it in her purse. She would follow the story as she headed to Montana. There was always the chance that Jasmine Wolfe would turn up before she got there.

Meanwhile, she had a few tricks up her sleeve, thanks to her father the Great Maximilian Burke, magician and thief.

Antelope Flats, Montana

CASH PICKED UP THE PHONE the moment Dusty left and dialed Bernard Wolfe's number. Bernard was about Cash's age, thirty-five, four inches shorter, stocky like a weight lifter, with rust-colored hair, small dark brown eyes and a cocky arrogance that seemed to come with the Wolfe fortune. Cash had disliked Bernard from the get-go and vice versa.

"She's just playing you to drive our father crazy," Bernard had said to him when they'd met for the first time. "It's what she does. Plays with people. Our father cut off her money so now she's going to make him pay by threatening to marry you. You are one of many in a long line. She'll tire of you and this game—if she hasn't already."

It had taken all of Cash's control not to slug him.

After Jasmine's disappearance and Archie's death, Bernard had taken over the furniture conglomerate, a business that had put him in the top five hundred of the nation's wealthiest men.

"Wolfe residence," a man with a distinct English accent answered.

Cash made a face and told himself he shouldn't have been surprised that Bernard would have an English butler.

"I'm calling for Mr. Wolfe. My name is Sheriff Cash McCall of Antelope Flats, Montana. Would you please tell him it's important. It has to do with his sister—step-sister," he corrected. "Jasmine."

As sheriff of the county, he'd had to make a lot of calls like this, some worse than others. They were never easy. He wondered how Bernard would take the news. Did Bernard even give a thought to his missing stepsister?

"Yes?" Bernard said when he came on the line a moment later. "What is this about?" He had only a touch of cultured Southern drawl, unlike his father. Bernard was Oxford educated, that probably explained it.

Cash had not talked to him in almost seven years. He cleared his throat. "This is Sheriff Cash McCall. I wanted to let you know that Jasmine's car's been found."

Silence, then what sounded like Bernard pulling up a chair and sitting down. "Where?"

"Just a few miles from Antelope Flats. The car was discovered in an old abandoned barn on a deserted farm north of the lake. It had been covered with a tarp."

"Was Jasmine…?"

"No." Cash waited to hear relief in Bernard's voice but heard nothing. "The investigators are searching the farm. They found blood and are treating the case as a homicide."

"They aren't letting you near the case I hope."

Cash clamped down his jaw, then took a breath and let it out. "I wanted to be the one to call you."

"Why is that?"

"Personal and professional courtesy. It's often hard on family members to get this kind of news."

Bernard made a rude sound. "I'll fly out as soon as I can." He hung up.

Cash stared at the phone in his hand. What had he expected? He wasn't sure. There was no doubt that he'd hoped to rattle Bernard, shake him up a little, maybe even get him to make a mistake when it came to his story from seven years before.

Bernard had said he'd been hiking up in the Bridger Mountains the day Jasmine disappeared. His alibi was his friend and Jasmine's former fiancé, Kerrington Landow. Supposedly the two had been together, which provided them both with alibis.

Cash had always suspected that the man the clerk had seen with Jasmine at the gas station was Bernard. He fit the description—just like the man who'd been arrested for an attempted abduction in the same area. A man who had refused to confess to Jasmine's abduction even when offered a deal.

As Cash hung up the phone, he knew Bernard would call Kerrington and tell him about Jasmine's car being found. Cash had heard that Kerrington had married Jasmine's best friend and former roommate, Sandra Perkins.

After seven years and marriage to another woman, what would Kerrington do? Come to Antelope Flats? Cash wouldn't be surprised. Kerrington and Bernard were both so deep in Jasmine's disappearance that neither would be able to stay away.

Somewhere south of Montana

MOLLY STOPPED at a computer store and used the internet service to access everything she could find about Jasmine Wolfe and her disappearance. Because of her prominent old Southern family, the story had been in all the major newspapers.

Molly read every article she could find, becoming more excited as she did. This could definitely be the answer to her problems.

The sheriff was the drawback though. That and the fact that Molly hadn't pulled any kind of "magic trick" since her father had died fifteen years before. She'd given up that way of life and had promised herself that she would never go back to it.

For years she'd never stayed in one place long, knowing that Vince and Angel could get out on parole at any time. At least that's what she told herself. In truth, the one thing she hadn't been able to cast off was the transient lifestyle of her childhood or the fear that Max had been right—that fraud was in her blood.

No matter how hard she tried, she found she got restless within weeks and would quit her job, move somewhere else and get another mediocre job. Fortunately she had an assortment of skills that lent themselves to quick employment and she'd never been looking for a "good" job since she'd be moving on soon anyway.

But Vince and Angel were out of prison now and after her. She hadn't seen anything in the papers about Lanny Giliano. She could only assume he was dead and she was next. She had to do a disappearing act, and maybe Max was right. Maybe fraud was in her blood and just waiting to come out.

On a hunch, she found an online video of Jasmine giving a speech at some charity benefit. The father had put the video online at the time of Jasmine's disappearance, saying he thought his daughter might be suffering from amnesia and hoped someone would recognize her and call.

Molly watched the video a half dozen times online until she could mimic Jasmine's gestures, her way of speaking, her facial expressions. Mimicking was something Molly had learned at an early age, a gimmick she and her father used during his act when he pretended to read minds in the audience.

Molly would secretly pick someone from the audience while her father had his back turned. Then he would read her mind and point to the person she'd picked. It amazed the audience. But the trick had been quite simple. She would just mimic the expression and body language of the person and her father would spot it and match it with the right person. Magic!

It amazed her how quickly all that training came back. Her mind was already working out the details. Not that she wasn't aware of the danger. Identity fraud. Fortunately, there was little record of her life the past fifteen years since her father's death or, for that matter, the fourteen years before that.

All of her "jobs" with her father hadn't involved paperwork, and few of her jobs had since. She preferred work where she was paid "off the books" in cash. Jobs where she didn't have to provide a social security number or an address. Much safer.

And there were enough employers who wanted to avoid paying taxes that it hadn't been hard to find menial work. She had pretty much remained invisible over those years, but she knew that wouldn't protect her from Vince and Angel. They would turn over every rock to find her. And they wouldn't stop until they did.

The way Molly saw it, only one person—the person who put Jasmine's car in that barn—would know that she really wasn't Jasmine. And that person was in prison serving time for his other crimes.

Which was good, since Molly already had two killers looking for her. That was sufficient.

CHAPTER FOUR

Atlanta, Georgia

KERRINGTON LANDOW never thought he'd be relieved to have the phone ring in the middle of a meal. But if he had to listen to one more of Sandra's lies...

"Let the maid get it," Sandra said with impatience.

He ignored her as he shoved back his chair and gave her one of his this-isn't-over-by-a-long-shot glares. Throwing down his napkin, he turned and stalked out of the dining room to take the call on the hall phone.

"Hello," he snapped, surprised how furious he was. In truth, he didn't care if Sandra was cheating on him or not. No, what made him angry was that she seemed to think he was so stupid he didn't know what she was up to.

"Jasmine's car's been found."

He went rigid.

"Did you hear me?" Bernard Wolfe demanded.

"Yes. I heard you." But still he couldn't believe... "What about—?" He looked up. Sandra had followed him. She was watching him from the dining room doorway, frowning, definitely interested in whom he was talking to.

"They haven't found Jasmine's body. Not yet anyway," Bernard was saying. He sounded upset.

The same way Sandra would be when she heard. He

had purposely not said Jasmine's name in front of her for that very reason. Sandra had thrown Jasmine up to him for years.

"I know I was your second choice," she said whenever they had a fight. "Do you have any idea what it's like living in that woman's shadow? It was bad enough when Jasmine was alive. But now I have to contend with her ghost?"

He had tried to reassure Sandra but the truth was, he'd never gotten over Jasmine and doubted he ever would. And now her car had been found.

"What is it?" Sandra asked coming down the hall. She was looking at him as if she'd seen him pale, had noticed the tremor in his hand clutching the phone. Sweat broke out under his arms. He worried she could smell the fear on him.

"They found her car in an old barn near Antelope Flats," Bernard was saying on the other end of the line.

Kerrington said nothing. He'd checked out the town when Jasmine had told him her plans to marry the sheriff. He'd laughed in her face. He'd known she would never go through with it.

"*What?*" Sandra demanded. She was standing directly in front of him now, her eyes locked on his face as if she could see through him, always had been able to.

Sometimes he forgot that Sandra had known Jasmine probably as well as anyone. She and mousy little Patty Franklin had been Jasmine's roommates at Montana State University in Bozeman. Jasmine had gone there on a whim after she'd already worked her way through all the men at several other universities, he thought bitterly.

Sandra had been the opposite of Jasmine, tall and slender, her hair dark like her eyes. She'd been available and he'd needed someone to use to make Jasmine jealous. Jasmine would never have believed it if he'd dated Patty the Pathetic, as Bernard called her.

"What?" Sandra demanded again, practically spitting in his face.

"They've found Jasmine's car," he said, knowing it would be impossible to keep something like this from her.

He'd expected the green-eyed monster to rear her ugly head. Instead, Sandra seemed stunned. She leaned against the wall, her face stony and remote.

"Sandra is there?" Bernard said with obvious disgust.

Where else had Bernard expected her to be? She was his wife, although Kerrington couldn't even guess where she'd been spending a lot of her time lately. He was hit with the most ridiculous thought. That the man Sandra had been seeing behind his back was Bernard. The two deserved each other, no doubt about that. But they couldn't stand to be in the same room together.

He rubbed a hand over his face and turned his back to Sandra to look in the hall mirror. He felt a need to assure himself and he'd always been reassured by what he saw in the mirror, as long as he didn't look too deeply.

Jasmine used to say he was classically tall, dark and handsome. Only she'd made it sound as if he were a cliché. He'd even overheard her and her brother Bernard refer to him as her "mindless pretty boy."

He shook off the memory, replacing it with a more pleasant one. Jasmine naked and in his arms begging for more.

"I'm flying out tonight," Bernard was saying. "I think

you and I should talk before I go, don't you? The cops are going to be asking a lot more questions. I think we need to get our stories straight so we tell them the same thing we did seven years ago."

Kerrington swore softly under his breath. It had been so long, he'd thought all of this was behind them. He should have known Jasmine's car would eventually turn up. Wasn't that what he'd hoped? Just not now, not after all this time.

"I'm going, too," he whispered into the phone as he caught movement out of the corner of his eye. Sandra had gone into the living room and sat down, her sour hatred of Jasmine almost palpable.

"You should just stay home and take care of your wife," Bernard said.

"Never mind what I should do," Kerrington growled. Had Bernard heard something about Sandra? Is that why he was suggesting Kerrington take care of his wife? Or was that earlier thought of Bernard and Sandra closer to the truth than he'd wanted to admit? It would be just like Bernard.

"I'm flying to Montana as soon as I can get a flight," Kerrington said, keeping his voice down, his back to Sandra and the living room. "We can talk there."

"That's not a smart thing to do."

"She was my girlfriend," Kerrington argued.

"The one who *dumped* you."

"Who knows who she'd be married to now if she were still alive."

Bernard made a scoffing sound on the other end of the line. "Assuming she's dead." He hung up.

Assuming she's dead. Kerrington stood holding the phone. Did Bernard know something? It had been Bernard who'd come to him with the offer of an alibi.

"If you need to, you can say you were with me," Bernard had said two days after Jasmine disappeared—just before the cops arrived to question them. "I was hiking in the Bridger Mountains. Took my gear and camped up there. Didn't get back home until well after dark the second day."

Kerrington had been so grateful to have an alibi at all that he'd gone along with Bernard's. It wasn't until later that he realized he'd also given Bernard an alibi.

He hung up the phone, then turned, bracing himself for the mother of all arguments he knew he was about to have with Sandra.

But Sandra was gone.

Antelope Flats, Montana

NEWS TRAVELED AT the speed of light, even in a county where there was little or no cell-phone service and ranches were miles apart.

The news about Jasmine's car being found had given Shelby McCall's return-from-the-dead story a rest. For hours Cash had been able to avoid his mother's call, but when the phone rang shortly after he'd hung up from talking to Bernard Wolfe, he knew before he answered who was calling.

"Cash? Are you all right?"

He wanted to laugh. He was so far from all right…. "I'm fine."

"I think you should move back home so you are close to your family during this time."

That did make him laugh. This coming from a woman who'd been gone for thirty years? Where was his mother when he'd needed advice about Jasmine? Being raised in an all-male household had left him pretty clueless about women. Dusty hadn't counted since she was just a kid. He really could have used a mother during those years.

"I'm sorry, Cash."

Sorry that Jasmine's car had been found and searchers expected to find her body in some shallow grave on the old farm at any time? Or sorry that she'd never been a mother to him and it was too late to start now?

"I know what you must be going through."

"Do you?" he said, then could have kicked himself.

"Obviously you loved her or you wouldn't have asked her to marry you."

He said nothing, afraid of what would come out.

"Let me know if there is anything I can do." She seemed to be waiting for him to say something. When he didn't, she hung up. She didn't mention dinner. Must have realized it would have been a bad time to ask for anything.

When he looked up, his brother J.T. was standing in his office doorway.

"Mother? She means well," J.T. said, closing the door behind him as he came in.

Cash grunted.

J.T. stood, looking uncomfortable. That was the problem with being raised by a bad-tempered man like Asa and a disagreeable ranch foreman like Buck. The brothers had grown up believing that softness was a weakness. So they sure as hell knew nothing about comforting each other.

Even Dusty was more tomboy than girl.

But J.T.'s rough edges had been smoothed a lot since Regina Holland had come into his life last fall. Cash had seen the change in him and approved. Reggie, as J.T. called her, was perfect for his brother, strong and yet soft in all the right ways. She was like a ray of sunshine in J.T.'s life and it showed in his older brother's face. Cash had never seen J.T. so happy.

"Is there anything I can do?" he asked now.

Cash shook his head, figuring Reggie had sent him. "The state investigators took over the search. I'm supposed to go fishing."

J.T. nodded. "You're not going to though, are you?"

Cash smiled. His brother knew him too well.

"Reggie said if you need someone to talk to…"

Cash laughed. He *knew* Reggie had sent J.T. His brother looked too uncomfortable for words. "Tell her thank you."

J.T. nodded, looked down at his boots, then up at Cash. "I'm sorry."

Cash nodded. "Maybe it will finally be over." He knew that was what his family had hoped for, that he'd be able to move on once he knew what had happened to Jasmine. If they only knew the truth. He feared though that before this investigation was over, they *would* know. Everyone would.

After J.T. left, Cash picked up the phone and dialed the number for Jasmine's car insurance company, which he'd found in her glove box. He knew Mathews would find out soon enough that he was doing some investigating on his own and all hell would break loose.

But all hell was going to break loose eventually anyway and he couldn't just wait for the state boys to call and tell him they'd found Jasmine's body and they had some questions for him.

Atlanta, Georgia

BERNARD WENT THROUGH the motions. He called to have the company jet readied, instructed George, his

English butler, to pack for him, and told the chauffeur to stand by to take him to the private airstrip later tonight.

Bernard had held it together fairly well he thought. Even when he'd had to deal with that jackass Kerrington. It was just like the fool to fly to Montana.

But he'd wanted to be the one to tell him. He didn't want Kerrington seeing it on the news and doing something stupid. And it would be hitting the news, if it hadn't already. He seldom paid any attention to more than the financial news.

He thought about ringing George and having the bottle of champagne he'd asked to be chilled brought out and opened. But he could wait.

He'd waited seven years so he could have Jasmine declared legally dead. Before their father had died, Archie had put aside part of his estate for Jasmine, still holding onto the ridiculous hope that she would turn up one day.

Bernard deserved that money. He'd spent his life "watching out" for his stepsister. "Keep an eye on her, won't you, Bernard," Archibald Wolfe would say. "Take care of your sister."

He wished he had a dollar for every time he'd heard his stepfather say those words.

His mother had married Archie when Bernard was four. Jasmine had been just a baby, her mother having died in childbirth.

Bernard had seen his stepfather struggle with trying to love him as much as he did Jasmine. There had been times when Bernard had felt loved, felt like he really was a Wolfe, not just adopted because his mother had married Archie.

But then Jasmine had grown up, been a wild teenager

and an even wilder adult. Keeping her out of trouble had proved impossible. She had loved to upset their father, hadn't cared that she got Bernard and herself into trouble, had rebelled at every turn as if it were her birthright. The Wolfe money had meant nothing to her. She was Daddy's golden girl and she'd known he would never disinherit her. At least not for long.

Bernard had never felt that secure as the stepson.

When Jasmine had decided to get another degree in a long line of degrees, this time in Montana, Archie had asked Bernard to go with her. "Just keep an eye on her. Make sure she's all right. Be there if she needs you."

Bernard had wanted to laugh. Jasmine hadn't needed him, hadn't even liked him, and he'd resented the hell out of his role as protector of his precious stepsister.

But Bernard had known he'd had no option. Archie had set him up in a condo near the university with unlimited spending and nothing really to do other than ski and party—and of course try to keep Jasmine out of trouble.

Jasmine had reverted to form and had enticed Kerrington to come to Montana so they could be together, except for those times when she was bored with him. Archie had heard about it and had been furious with Bernard, but even more furious with Jasmine. This time Archie had done more than threaten to disinherit her, he had done it.

Kerrington had been beside himself, begging Jasmine to make up with her father. He and Jasmine had argued and the next thing Bernard knew, she had announced that she was engaged to some cowboy sheriff from Antelope Flats, Montana. Kerrington had been inconsolable. He'd been dating Jasmine's roommate Sandra to make Jasmine jealous. It apparently hadn't worked.

Bernard had pretended to reason with his sister, but with her out of the will, he would get everything. Jasmine had never listened to him anyway. He hoped she would marry her cowboy sheriff and live in some dinky town in Montana, but he knew her better than that. Jasmine had just been playing them all.

Then Jasmine had disappeared. Archie had never said outright that he blamed Bernard, but Bernard knew he did. It had taken a while, but Bernard had finally gotten close to his stepfather before Archie died.

He'd worked hard to take over the Wolfe Furniture conglomerate, proven himself worthy in so many ways. In the end, he'd felt as if Archie respected him, maybe even loved him. Then Archie had died and Bernard's mother Fran had been killed.

Bernard was left alone—with everything—except for the chunk that had been left to Jasmine.

In just a few weeks, Bernard could have had her declared legally dead. And now this. Jasmine's car turning up, stirring it all up again. It was as if Jasmine was plotting against him from the grave. As if she couldn't stand for him to be happy.

Now he would have to fly to Montana or it would look suspicious. He would have to act as if he gave a damn. He just hoped it wouldn't take long. He'd always resented Jasmine, often disliked her. But right now he hated her.

His cell phone played "Dixie" in his suit pocket. He didn't have to look at the number to know whom it was. He also knew what she would want. "Yes?"

"I need to see you. Where are you?"

"At home getting ready to leave for Montana." He'd been waiting for her call. Had the champagne chilling for the two of them.

"Don't move." She hung up.

He smiled and snapped his phone shut as he thought of her and what she would want him to do to her. It was warped, twisted in ways he didn't even want to think about. It was also dangerous. But worth it.

He checked to make sure George was finished with his packing, then rang the kitchen and asked for the champagne to be brought up to the master bedroom.

She would be here soon. He was already aroused just thinking about the pain he would inflict on her. Maybe this wouldn't be such a bad day after all.

Las Vegas, Nevada

"ARE YOU CRAZY?" Angel demanded for the hundredth time. "You let Molly get away."

"She knows we're after her," Vince assured him again. "I was counting on Lanny calling her. She'll lead us right to the diamonds. It's all part of my plan."

"You'd better hope this works," Angel said.

Vince heard the threat in his brother's tone. "I thought you might like to gamble while I get everything ready before we go after her."

Angel's eyes lit because he knew Vince would also provide the money. Angel had already blown what little he'd had.

Four hours later, Vince found Angel at a blackjack table in the casino where he'd left him earlier. From Angel's expression, he'd lost all the money Vince had given him and was in a foul mood. Nothing new there.

"Come on," Vince said.

"I hope to hell we're finally going to do something," Angel snapped as they left the casino and headed for the car. "I'm sick of waiting around."

Vince slid into the passenger seat as Angel got behind the wheel. He sat tapping the steering wheel as if he couldn't sit still. With each passing day, Angel had become more tense. Sitting next to him was like being next to an electrical wire in a thunderstorm. Vince wasn't sure how much longer he could keep Angel under control.

"I told you. We needed to give her a head start," Vince said, knowing this wasn't what Angel wanted to hear.

Angel swore as he pulled out of the casino parking lot in a screech of tires. He pushed his foot hard onto the gas pedal and roared out into the traffic.

"We've waited fifteen years," Vince said patiently. "We can wait a little longer. She's still moving. I want to wait until she lights."

Angel shot him a look and almost rear-ended the car in front of them. He slammed on the brakes. "Did you ever consider that she's gotten rid of the car and you're tracking the wrong person?"

"She won't get rid of the car. She has no reason to."

"You should have let me handle it," Angel argued. "If you'd let me wait for her outside the café where she worked it would be over by now."

Vince didn't doubt that. "Like you handled Lanny? You would have killed her before we found out where the diamonds were and where would that've left us?"

"You've never given me enough credit," Angel complained, slamming his fist down on the steering wheel as the traffic began to move again. "You think I couldn't do this without you?"

Vince felt himself go cold.

Angel seemed to calm down. "You're sure this GPS thing will work, we'll be able to find her?"

"Global positioning system."

"I know what the hell it is," Angel snapped. "I just don't like the idea that she's taken off and we might not be able to find her again."

"We can pinpoint her location down to the street number," Vince said. "Once she stops running, I can even pull up a map that will show us exactly how to get there." He could see that Angel was dubious. Angel hadn't been interested in learning about computers or electronics while in prison.

"She thinks she's gotten away, that she's safe. That's why I don't want to crowd her."

Angel muttered something under his breath.

Vince groaned and glanced in his side mirror. "We agreed we would do this together," he said to Angel as he felt a headache coming on. "Or we don't do it at all."

Angel shot him a look. "What the hell is that supposed to mean?"

Vince didn't answer. He spotted a black-and-white behind him, the patrol-car light bar gleaming in the desert sun. Vince glanced over at the speedometer then up the street. "Watch your speed."

Vince figured he would have to give Angel more money to lose gambling. It would be the only way to keep his brother from getting into trouble while they waited.

Angel let up on the gas. They cruised through the intersection.

Vince looked in the side mirror again. The cop in the patrol car had pulled in two cars behind them. Vince looked ahead and saw another cop car turn into the motel where he and Angel had been staying.

"Trouble," he said as yet another patrol car fell in behind them.

"What?"

"We've been made," Vince said.

Angel's gaze darted up to the rearview mirror.

"Another car just turned into our motel," Vince said.

Angel swore. "Who would put the cops on us?"

"Who do you think?"

As Angel drove on past their motel, Vince saw yet another patrol car coming toward them. The cop hit his brakes. "They know our car. He's spotted us."

The cop made a U-turn in the middle of the street, flashing lights and siren coming on.

Angel hit the gas and ran the next red light. Brakes screeched, horns blared and a wail of police sirens took up the cry behind them. Vince was glad Angel was behind the wheel. Angel loved this. He cornered hard and accelerated, driving Vince back against the seat.

So Molly wanted to play hardball? Vince was surprised. He still thought of her as a fourteen-year-old little girl. This changed his perception of her.

Another cop car joined in the chase and Vince thought he heard a helicopter overhead. As Angel wheeled around corners, racing along the backstreets of Vegas to the scream of sirens, Vince shook his head. He was not pleased with Molly. How could she call the cops on them after it had been cops who'd killed Max, the man who had picked her up off the street and been like a father to her? Did the woman have no loyalty at all?

He sighed, unable to understand that kind of thinking. He had planned to cut Molly some slack in respect for Max. He might have even let her live after she gave them the jewels. Or at least he would have told Angel to kill her quickly.

But now she'd left him little option. He would let Angel use the knife on her, keeping her alive until she gave them the jewels and apologized for betraying them.

First though, they had to escape the cops. Then there would be no more waiting. They were going after Molly.

Atlanta, Georgia

KERRINGTON POURED HIMSELF a stiff drink and sat down in his empty living room. He couldn't believe Sandra had left without a word—not after they'd just been arguing about her recent disappearances.

He'd checked the garage, not surprised to find her car gone. She wasn't even trying to hide her affair. Did she really believe he was going to put up with this? The woman must think him a complete fool.

He took a gulp of his drink. The expensive Scotch sent a wave of warmth through him. A thought floated past on the boozy warmth. What if it wasn't an affair? He couldn't imagine what else Sandra would be sneaking behind his back about if not sleeping around. He realized he had no idea what she did all day. Or with whom.

He finished the drink and poured himself another, the booze calming him. He was almost relieved Sandra had left. She would have been looking for a fight if she'd stayed.

"What do you care if Jasmine's car's been found?" she would have demanded. "Like she gave a damn about you." Sandra always threw it up to him that Jasmine had broken the engagement.

"She *dumped* you," Sandra was fond of reminding

him. "After that big article on the society page. How did that make you feel?"

Sick. But he'd never told Sandra that. Sandra thought he had been embarrassed, made to feel like a fool. What Sandra didn't know was that when you lost someone like Jasmine all you thought about was getting her back. Once you got over the initial shock and that feeling of being sick to your stomach.

Jasmine had a way of making nothing matter but her. She was like a drug you needed to survive. You would do anything to have her.

Unfortunately, Jasmine knew it. She made you crazy, until you felt that if you couldn't have her, no one else would either. Hell, he'd followed her to Montana and she would have changed her mind and married him if it hadn't been for her father cutting her out of the will.

He sipped his drink, eyes narrowing at the thought of Jasmine. If she were alive, she would have come to her senses and realized he was the only man for her. How different his life would have been. Her father would have come around. Archie would have never denied Jasmine her legacy if he truly believed she had married the right man. And Kerrington was the right man.

And he would never have married Sandra. Even when she told him she was pregnant with his baby. She blamed Jasmine's disappearance for her miscarriage. Bernard had always said Sandra wasn't even pregnant and Kerrington had been a fool to buy in to her story without demanding proof.

All water under the bridge, he thought putting down his drink. He picked up the phone and called the airport for a flight west. If he hurried, he could get out right away and be there by tonight. Let Sandra come home to an empty house and wonder where *he* was for a change.

Across town

FROM HIS HOT TUB on the master-bedroom deck, Bernard told George to send his guest up when she arrived. The water was hot, the jets relentless. He was sunk up to his neck, eyes closed. It wasn't long before he caught a whiff of her perfume. Opening his eyes, he found her framed in the doorway. He closed his eyes again, knowing when he opened them she would be waiting in the bedroom.

He took his time. He liked to make her wait. He dried himself and, breathing in her scent, moved through the large master bedroom, expectation arousing every nerve fiber.

She lay on her back across the end of his king-size bed, buck naked, her eyes closed. He watched her chest rise and fall, her nipples already hard nubs. Her legs were long and shapely, her body as close to perfect as money could buy.

He let the towel wrapped around his waist drop to the floor.

She turned her head to look at him, watching him with a mixture of excitement and fear in her expression. He liked that about her.

He picked up the belt from where he'd left it on the chair near the end of the bed and looked down at her, their eyes locking.

Then slowly, he raised the thick leather belt, saw her tense, her eyes widening but never leaving his.

He brought the leather down sharply across her thighs. She let out a cry, arching her back. He lay the leather across her belly, her breasts. He had never wanted to hurt her as badly as he did tonight.

She didn't stop him, just as he knew she wouldn't. This is what she came here for.

To the sound of her soft whimpers, he finally tossed the belt aside. She was watching him again, almost daring him to do whatever he wanted with her.

"Tell me Jasmine is dead," she whispered as he rolled her over.

"Jasmine is dead."

CHAPTER FIVE

Antelope Flats, Montana

MOLLY WAS SICK of sagebrush. She'd been driving on two-lane blacktop highways for what seemed like days, passing through tiny dying towns and miles and miles of barren landscapes.

Not far inside the Montana state line, she saw what appeared to be a small cluster of buildings on the horizon. A mirage in the middle of nowhere. A few miles up the road, she spotted the city limits sign: Antelope Flats.

She couldn't believe her eyes. She'd expected small, but this town was even smaller and more isolated than she'd imagined. She'd expected it would be backwoodsy, but not to this extent. The western town seemed trapped in another time, the buildings straight out of an Old West movie.

She drove through town. It didn't take long. Then she turned around, stopping to shake her head and laugh. Well, she'd wanted to disappear in a place where Vince and Angel would never think to look for her. And it appeared she'd gotten her wish.

Getting into her role, Molly had put on at least five pounds, changed her makeup, lightened her hair and bought herself some conservative clothing, something she thought a woman like Jasmine Wolfe might have worn. Coming from the South and a wealthy Atlanta family, Jasmine had to have a whole lot of conservative in her background.

Molly had watched the newspapers as she worked her way toward Antelope Flats. Jasmine Wolfe's body hadn't been found as of yesterday. Nor had the woman turned up.

As Molly drove back into town, she couldn't help but wonder why a woman with Jasmine Wolfe's money and background would want to live here, let alone marry the sheriff.

The town seemed even smaller this time around. If she had blinked, she would have missed it. She pulled up in front of the small brick building on the edge of town with the sign Sheriff out front. It was late and she'd worried that she might not catch him before he left for the day.

But as she turned off her car engine, she noticed a car marked Sheriff was parked in front. No other cars were on the street except for a few muddy pickups at the other end of town outside the Longhorn Café.

She glanced toward the front window of the sheriff's office but the slanting sun was shining on the glass, making it more like a mirror. She took a breath and re-minded herself that she was the daughter of Maximilian Burke. Even rusty from lack of sleight-of-hand practice, she could do this.

But she didn't kid herself, she would have to give the performance of her life to pull this off. If she blew it, she had a lot worse to worry about than attempted fraud charges.

Taking her purse and the first newspaper article and photo, she got out of the car and walked to the door of the sheriff's department. Tentatively she tried the door.

Unlocked. She pushed the door open, sliding a little too
easily into the other woman's skin, a little too easily into
that former life of lies, as she stepped inside.

BY LATE AFTERNOON Cash had made a half dozen calls
as well as copying Jasmine's case file. He was surprised
that he hadn't been relieved of his job yet. He knew it
was only a matter of time.

Cash had covered his tracks as much as possible and
was just finishing up when the phone rang. He picked it
up, afraid it was going to be Investigator Mathews with
bad news.

It was Jasmine's insurance company calling back.

"It took a while for me to find the policy," the agent
told him. "This particular policy was canceled almost
seven years ago due to the car being stolen?"

Something like that. "I need to know if an accident
claim was filed. In September seven years ago? It would
have been right after she bought the car." Cash listened
to the shuffle of papers.

"None that I can see. September? Sorry. No claim."

He raked a hand through his hair, leaning back in
his chair, letting go of the breath he'd been holding. So
Jasmine hadn't filed a claim or reported the accident.
He thanked the agent and hung up.

Now all he could do was wait. But he'd been waiting
for either a call that Jasmine's body had been found or
that he was being suspended until the investigation was
completed.

But neither call had come. Everyone in the city offices next door had gone home for the day.

He got up from his desk, too anxious to sit any longer.
He should go home. If Mathews caught him in his office… He moved to stand in the back doorway. Here he
could catch the faint breeze in the pines out back. The

spring evening was hotter than normal and his office had no air-conditioning. Hell, few places in Montana had air-conditioning.

He didn't want to leave just yet. He was waiting for a call back from the Dew Drop Inn, a bar on the outskirts of Bozeman. He knew Mathews would eventually check on the matchbook found in Jasmine's car. Cash hoped to beat him to it. Mathews would be furious, but Cash would have to deal with that when it happened.

Right now, he needed answers, answers he should have gotten seven years ago. All these years he'd pretended Jasmine was alive. He couldn't pretend anymore. At any moment, Mathews would call to say her body had been found in a shallow grave on the farm, that she'd been murdered.

For years, he'd put his life on hold, unconsciously waiting for that call. Now, it seemed the wait might be over.

Behind him he heard his office door open. He turned. His heart seized in his chest, all breath gone, all reason evading him as he stared at the woman standing in the doorway.

"Jasmine." Her name was out before he could call it back.

She looked startled, as if she hadn't seen him standing at the back of the office.

His heart lodged in his throat, his senses telling him something his mind refused to accept now that her car had been found. Jasmine was *alive?*

"I…I…" She started to turn as if to leave and he finally found his feet, lunging forward to stop her, half-afraid she was nothing more than a puff of smoke that would scatter the moment he touched her.

She took a step back, seeming afraid, definitely startled. He stopped just feet from her, struggling to rein himself in, fighting to believe what was before his eyes. My God, could it really be her? Jasmine? Alive? He could only stare at her. How was this possible?

She stared back, her green eyes wide. "I was looking for Sheriff Cash McCall," she stammered, still angled as if she might bolt at any moment.

He cleared his throat, confused. "I'm Sheriff Cash McCall," he said, realizing with a start that there was no recognition in her expression.

"I'm…I'm—"

"Jasmine, Jasmine Wolfe," he said, the cop in him thinking of the blood found in her car, the seven years no one had seen her or the fact that she didn't seem to know him from Adam.

She shook her head and held up what appeared to be a newspaper clipping, the edges torn, the print smudged as if she'd spent a lot of time looking at it. "I'm not sure, but I saw this and I thought…"

He took the clipping she held out, glanced away from her just long enough to recognize the Associated Press story about the discovery of her car.

"The woman looked like me…." She stopped. "This was a mistake." She reached behind her for the door-knob.

"No." He hadn't meant to speak so sharply. "Please, don't go." He took a breath, tried to slow his racing pulse, tried to make sense of this. He'd been expecting a call that her body had been found, not this.

He stared at her, unable to take his eyes from her. Somehow Jasmine had survived. True, she looked different in ways he couldn't put his finger on. But one thing was perfectly clear, she was more beautiful than even in his memory.

But where had she been all these years? And why was

she looking at him as if she'd never seen him before and was as shaken by what she saw?

He stared into her eyes. She'd didn't remember him.

Or maybe she did and was only pretending not to.

All he knew for sure was that if Jasmine had escaped the grave, then she would be back after only one thing. Vengeance.

MOLLY KNEW SHE WAS GAWKING but she couldn't help it. To say Sheriff Cash McCall was nothing like she'd imagined was a major understatement. And it wasn't just because he was drop-dead gorgeous. Which there was no denying he was. Tall, broad-shouldered, blond and blue-eyed but rugged looking. He wore western-cut jeans, boots and a short-sleeved, tan uniform shirt. A blue jean jacket hung over the back of his desk chair and close at hand was a pale gray cowboy hat.

It wasn't his looks that surprised her. It was the feeling that she'd been headed here her whole life. As if everything else had just been time spent waiting for this moment.

She met his gaze and quaked inside at the rush of feeling. There was some powerful chemistry here that drew her to him and at the same time, warned her to be careful. Very careful.

"Jasmine," he said again in his deep voice. "I can't believe this."

The sound of his voice seemed to echo in her chest, a drumming like that of her pulse. She tried to steady herself. *Calm down. This is working.* Just as she'd thought, she looked enough like the woman with the changes she'd made to fool even Jasmine's fiancé. As Max would have said of one of his magic tricks, "This definitely plays."

The talent required to perform magic or a con was showmanship. Only a small percentage of the act was the actual *trick*. It was amazing what could be done with a little misdirection.

She shook her head and backed away, using everything Max had taught her. "This was a mistake. I'm sorry."

He closed the distance between them, his fingers clamping over her wrist. He was strong but she cried out more in surprise than actual pain.

He quickly released her. "I didn't mean to hurt you. Please. Don't go."

She had him. So why did her instincts tell her to run? The "tricks" with her father hadn't been this up-close-and-personal. She could see the combination of hope and naked relief in his eyes. He loved Jasmine.

Molly knew what it was like to lose someone she'd loved. Clearly, Sheriff Cash McCall had never gotten over that loss. She hadn't considered that after seven years he might still be in such pain. She didn't have to look to know that there was no wedding band on his left hand. She doubted there was even a woman in his life. But what guy would wait around for a woman seven years knowing she might be dead or just never coming back?

Sheriff Cash McCall obviously.

He seemed to be staring at her in a kind of bewildered amazement. "If there is any chance that you're Jasmine—"

"There isn't," she said.

"Please. Something made you come here."

Right. Two killers and the need for a place to hide.

"Please," he said again. "Sit down for a moment. What do you have to lose?"

She didn't even want to think about that. She must have been out of her mind. Her father's genes obviously coursed through her veins because she'd latched on to this idea without thinking it through. She hadn't expected to feel like this.

He smiled reassuringly and stepped back, giving her space. "Won't you sit down? Please."

There was a kindness in his voice, a calmness in his movements, although she could see how badly he needed her to be his fiancée.

All she had to do was *load* the hat—slip in the rabbit that she would later pull out as if by magic. She had him right where she wanted him. So why did she feel so miserable about it?

And even more alarming, why did she feel like he had *her?*

Either way, she couldn't walk away now. She was in too deep. She had no choice but to stay and play this through. She couldn't admit that she'd known all along she wasn't the missing woman, whereas if she stayed, he would realize eventually she wasn't his lost love. He would be hurt. She would feign disappointment, sorry that she'd gotten his hopes up. No harm would have been done.

Right, you just keep telling yourself that.

She gave him a tentative smile and took the chair he offered her. He pulled up one next to her rather than go behind the desk. She could see that he didn't know what to do with his hands. They were large, the fingers long and finely sculpted, tanned from the sun, callused from some type of manual labor and definitely strong.

She shifted her gaze to his eyes, the same pale blue as summer skies. There was something so appealing about Cash McCall....

"Why do you think you're not Jasmine?" he asked quietly.

That one was easy. But she could hear Max saying, "Don't be a fool. Have you forgotten Vince and Angel and what they'll do to you if they catch you? Stall for time. You're safe here. And there just might be a pot of gold at the end of the rainbow, kiddo."

She felt sick and realized she was more like Max than she'd ever admitted. She had only thought of herself. And now she was in trouble. So like Max.

"I know I look like her, but I can't see how…" She made a motion with her hand, swallowed and looked around the office. It was sparsely furnished. A gold-framed photograph on his desk caught her eye.

"Your family?" she asked, indicating the photo of a group of blond, blue-eyed people standing at a wide porch railing.

"Shelby insisted on a family portrait," he said, looking uncomfortable. "She also insisted I put it on my desk. Shelby's my mother. She's a bit…bossy at the moment, probably always has been." He shook his head before she could ask what that meant. "It's a long story." He leaned forward a little, obviously trying to relax. Or at least make her think he was relaxed. "Tell me about *you.*"

Going in, she knew she couldn't lie about her name or her past—at least the past seven years of it because he was bound to check. There was no reason to anyway, since those years had been innocuous enough and her pattern of living would suggest that she'd been unsettled, lost, searching for something.

"For as long as I can remember, I've traveled from one place to another," she said honestly. "My name is Molly Kilpatrick. At least that's what I've been going by." She'd learned at an early age that it was always best to blend as much truth as you could with the lies. It made keeping the lies straight that much easier. You just had to be careful that you didn't start believing your own lies.

Meanwhile, she needed to make it clear that as far as she knew, she was Molly Kilpatrick and any confusion on her part as far as her resemblance to Jasmine Wolfe was innocent. Even if he found out that she was the daughter of Maximilian Burke, she figured her father's death could easily explain her alleged lapses of memory.

"I've always had the feeling that something happened in my past, something traumatic that I want to forget, and that's why I can't remember," she continued. She described her life pretty accurately, at least the years since her father died.

When she finished, she saw that the sheriff was studying her intently. Magicians called it "the burn" when someone is watching you with an unblinking stare, looking behind your words and sleight of hand to see the "trick."

Cash felt like pinching himself. Jasmine. He couldn't have been more shocked or relieved. While she was saying she didn't believe she was Jasmine, he was looking at her face, the color of her hair, the sound of her voice, her mannerisms. All Jasmine. Only just different enough to account for the fact that she'd been lost for seven years.

"This is amazing," he said when she stopped talking. The cop in him told him he should be paying more attention to her story, but the man in him could only stare in wonder. Somehow Jasmine had survived—and found her way back.

To him, he realized with a start.

He would have expected her to contact her family. Or her old roommates. Except Sandra Perkins was married to Kerrington Landow now and who knew where Patty Franklin was.

He just found it hard to believe that she could come to him. Not after the last time he'd seen her. But maybe she really couldn't remember what had happened between them any more than she could remember him.

He tried to concentrate on what she was saying as she told her story haltingly, stopping occasionally to lick her lips. He tried to remember that mouth. It had been so long. Would it be the same if he kissed it?

When he'd thought of Jasmine over the years, the memories had been sharp and painful. Now though, as he studied her, he realized he'd forgotten how he'd felt, that initial first attraction, or how she'd tasted when he'd kissed her.

She stopped talking, then added, "That's why when I saw the article about Jasmine Wolfe…" Her eyes met his.

He remembered that pale green color. Only he'd remembered it as reminding him of cool jade, not warm tropical waters as it did now.

"You're not sure how many years you've lost?" he asked, trying to pay more attention.

She shook her head, catching her lower lip in her teeth. It was something he couldn't remember Jasmine ever doing.

"When I read that there was a search going on for her, I thought that if there was even a chance that I was…" She stopped, licked her lips again. "I didn't want people to keep looking for her if… I didn't want her family to…" She shook her head. "You must think I'm a fool to come here."

Jasmine had *never* been a fool. Nor could he imagine her thinking herself one. "No, you're no fool," he said studying her. "Can you remember anything about the day you disappeared?"

She shook her head slowly and let out a small laugh. "I didn't even know I'd...disappeared."

He smiled realizing that, from her perspective, that was probably true. "Have you seen a doctor about your memory loss?"

She nodded. "He said sometimes a blow to the head can cause it. I would imagine that's where I got this." She lifted a lock of her blond hair away from the left side of her forehead.

The scar was shaped like a crescent moon, pale white and about an inch and a half long. He drew in a breath and let it out slowly. Head wounds bled a lot. That would explain all the blood in her car.

He felt a wave of relief. Not that she didn't look and act like Jasmine, but the cop in him had questioned how she could be alive given the large amount of blood that had been found in her car. The blood loss, the head injury, couldn't those both contribute to memory loss? And couldn't that explain why she'd just *disappeared* for seven years?

"You don't know how you got the scar?" he asked.

She shook her head. "It was just there one day when I looked in the mirror."

He could see that the scar had scared her. He tried to imagine just looking in the mirror one day and seeing a scar and not knowing when or where you'd gotten it.

It should have scared her, he thought. It certainly did him, just trying to imagine how she'd gotten it.

She absently touched the scar with her fingers. "I

think I came here hoping to find…myself." Her voice broke a little and tears glistened in her eyes.

He'd never seen Jasmine vulnerable before. That he did remember. It took everything in him not to pull her into his arms. But he was a stranger to her. And she was clearly scared. The last thing he wanted her to do was bolt.

"I realized when I saw the photograph that I've put my life on hold for years waiting for something I didn't understand." She frowned. "Does that make any sense to you?"

He wished it didn't. He'd done the same thing and hadn't consciously realized he was doing it. With a start, he remembered that Bernard would be flying in. "Your brother—stepbrother—Bernard is on his way here. If he's not already here."

Her eyes widened in alarm. She shook her head. "But what if I'm not Jasmine? I don't want to get his hopes up."

Cash doubted Bernard's hopes would be raised by the thought of Jasmine being alive. Bernard had inherited everything when Archie had died, as far as Cash knew. And knowing even as little as he did of Bernard, Cash couldn't see Bernard wanting to share it with a stepsister back from the dead.

"It would be like him losing his sister all over again," she was saying. "And I couldn't bear to think I had a brother only to have him snatched away if I'm right and I'm not Jasmine."

Losing Bernard wouldn't break anyone's heart, Cash thought. "You don't have to see him if you'd rather not."

Her relief was almost palpable. "It's not that I don't want to see him. Later. If I really am Jasmine. Isn't there some way we can keep this quiet until we know for sure?"

He hated to tell her how impossible that would be in a town the size of Antelope Flats. He had to tell State Investigator John Mathews. But he had no way of reaching him at this hour. Cash couldn't see what it would hurt to wait. Mathews would do everything he could to keep the story from blowing wide open, but he would want to question Jasmine—and in her state, Cash feared she would take off again.

Cash knew he was just making excuses.

What he needed was time. Before anyone else got involved, he had to be sure in his own mind that she really was the woman he'd spent seven years trying to forget.

"Maybe there is a way to keep it quiet," he said, watching for her reaction. "I can take your fingerprints and send them to the FBI. They have Jasmine's on file."

"How long will it take to get the results?" she asked without even a blink.

He would send them to his friend in the FBI. With luck he would know by tonight, but he didn't tell her that. "It usually takes a week. Maybe more."

She seemed relieved rather than upset by that news. He got the feeling that things were happening too fast for her.

"I'll just stay in a motel out of sight until then."

"Your brother will be staying at the only motel in town."

She looked surprised, then worried. "What can we do?"

We? A sliver of doubt embedded itself under his skin. He told himself he was just being a cop. She had come to

him, she needed his help. Of course, she would say "we."
So why was he suddenly suspicious of her motives?

Because she'd involved him so slickly into a conspir-
acy to keep her existence a secret. It worked perfectly
into his plan to have her to himself until he could decide
if she was really Jasmine—and what she wanted.

But he had to wonder if it also worked perfectly into
some plan she had.

"If anyone finds out that I came to you before we
know for certain if I'm Jasmine... Can you imagine
what would happen if the newspapers got hold of this
story?"

He could well imagine. His life had been blown wide
open for months after she'd disappeared. But she didn't
need to sell him any further on hiding her. "There might
be a way to keep you hidden until we have proof that
you're Jasmine." He let the words hang in the air for a
few moments, not wanting to act too eager. "You can
stay with me."

Her surprise almost seemed genuine. "Oh, I
couldn't."

"I have a large house. There is plenty of room. It is
the only way to stay hidden in a town this size. Unless
you'd rather not, under the circumstances."

She frowned. "Circumstances?"

"The general assumption was that you were abducted
by a man at the gas station who is now in prison," Cash
said. "But for several reasons I don't think that was the
case."

"What reasons?" she asked, sounding more curious
than worried.

"First off, the man serving time in prison right now
was offered a deal if he told them what he'd done with
you. He didn't take the deal. I don't think he was the one

the station clerk saw get into your car." He was watching her, not exactly sure what he was looking for, just a feeling that he should be leery of her. Especially if she was Jasmine.

"Secondly," he continued when her expression didn't change. "You would never have gotten into your car with a stranger even if he was holding a gun on you. You'd been taught what to do because kidnapping was a real threat given your family's wealth. The only reason you would leave with the man at the station was because you weren't afraid of him."

That last seemed to finally get a reaction out of her. "You think I *knew* the man who abducted me?"

He nodded slowly. "A man who left you for dead seven years ago."

"You're telling me that if I'm Jasmine Wolfe, I'm lucky to be alive."

"Oh, I think you got *very* lucky. The problem is, if I'm right, your assailant won't be happy to hear you're alive and can identify him."

"But I can't! I don't remember anything about that day."

"My point exactly. You could be in the room with a killer and not even know it. Until it was too late."

She bit her lower lip as if considering that she might be in danger. "I guess the safest place I could be now is with the town sheriff," she said with a nervous laugh. "Right?"

He cleared his throat and met her eyes. "Right." Unless, of course, she was going home with the prime suspect in Jasmine's disappearance and attempted murder.

CHAPTER SIX

MOLLY COULDN'T BELIEVE how easy it had been as she watched Cash prepare to take her fingerprints.

She'd come away *clean* without getting caught with any cards up her sleeves. As Max used to say when he'd fooled someone in the front row of the audience with one of his magic tricks, "I could have gone south with an elephant in front of that guy!"

Not only did the sheriff buy her as Jasmine, he'd also agreed to keep the news quiet—and was taking her home to his house. She couldn't have asked for a better place to hide out.

There had only been that one surprise. Cash seemed to think Jasmine had known her attacker, that the person was still at large, that her attacker had left her for dead. And now with Jasmine back, Molly's life was in danger.

It was her karma and the risk that went with stealing a dead woman's identity, she thought bitterly. Wasn't it bad enough that she already had two killers after her?

She hoped that Cash was just being cautious. He seemed a cautious man. Of course he could also just be trying to scare her. If he knew she wasn't Jasmine, what better way than to make her think she was in danger from a killer if she continued this charade.

No, she thought, studying him. He believed she was Jasmine because he wanted to. Maybe he really was worried about her safety. Maybe the man now in prison for abducting those other women really hadn't picked up Jasmine at that filling station.

Good thing she wasn't planning to stay in this gig long. And there was always the chance that Cash was wrong. The cases were too similar not to have been the same man—even if the man now in prison hadn't confessed to Jasmine Wolfe's abduction.

"Yes?" Cash said. He was looking at her, studying her again as if he saw her struggling with her thoughts.

She shook her head. "Nothing. This must come as a shock to you." Her prints weren't on file anywhere. That was one reason she hadn't been able to get a job at a Vegas casino. Casinos took all employees' fingerprints as a matter of course. But still, she felt a little anxious to think he was about to send them to the FBI. Did that mean they would be on file from now on? Good thing she was going straight again after this.

He reached for her hand. His fingers were warm and she felt a small thrill ripple over her as he began to take her fingerprints. She mentally kicked herself as he raised a brow at her reaction. Cash McCall didn't miss much.

"Am I anything like her?" she asked grabbing hold of every magician's best defense—misdirection and patter. Talk about anything. Just draw the audience away from what you're really doing. "I mean other than the way I look?"

He took her fingerprints, carefully getting a perfect print from each finger. He didn't look at her as he worked. "You sound like her and some of your mannerisms remind me of her," he said after a few moments.

"Were we close?" she asked shyly.

His gaze came up to meet hers. There was heat in it and although it had been a while, she recognized the look for what it was: desire.

"We were engaged, weren't we?" He looked back down.

"I know this must be hard on you," she said. "I'm sorry I don't remember...us."

He finished taking the rest of her prints before he looked up again. "Here, you can clean the ink off with this," he said, handing her a towelette.

"Thank you." She scrubbed at the ink, still watching him out of the corner of her eye. When she'd asked about their relationship, he'd grown quiet, almost pensive. There was something he didn't want to tell her.

"I'll send these in," he said, getting up, turning his back to her.

"I'm sorry."

"What do you have to be sorry about?" he asked over his shoulder as if surprised.

"All these questions. But I don't know much about Jasmine. Just what I've read in the papers...." She pretended to hesitate. "And there are so many questions that only you can answer."

He took a breath and let it out slowly as he finished taking care of the prints. "What do you want to know?"

She shrugged. "Anything you can tell me. How did you meet?"

He took his chair behind his desk, giving her his full attention. "I was teaching a class in criminology at Montana State University in Bozeman. We ran into each other in the hall." He shrugged. "The next day you were waiting for me outside my classroom."

Jasmine hadn't been a shrinking violet, had she?

"How long did we…you date?"

"Not long. The engagement was kind of…sudden." He smiled a little as if embarrassed and met her eyes. "I'd never met anyone like…you."

And she'd thought he was a cautious man. Probably was. Except when it came to women. Or at least one woman. She felt a prick of jealousy and wondered what kind of lover he'd been. And Jasmine?

Cash was smiling. "You had another question?"

She really had to watch herself. He seemed to be reading every expression. "I was wondering about… our relationship, that is, yours and Jasmine's."

He laughed. It was a wonderful sound. "You want to know if we were…*intimate?*"

The word was so old-fashioned. Like Cash. She suspected he followed some Code of the West. "It's just if I'm going to stay with you…" She wasn't really blushing, was she?

"Are you worried about your virtue?" he asked.

There was an edge to his voice that surprised her. Had her question upset him because it was so personal? Or was it something to do with Jasmine?

"I know it's none of my business," she said quickly. "I shouldn't have—"

"We never slept together."

She tried not to look surprised by that—or the flash of anger she'd seen in his expression. Obviously their not sleeping together hadn't been his idea.

"Oh" was all she could think to say. She was no authority on relationships, since she never stayed long enough in one place to have anything long-term. And her idea of a short-term relationship was a dinner or a movie date. At almost thirty, she had never even been in love.

But any woman who wouldn't want to go to bed with Cash McCall needed her head examined. Her gaze fell on his hands, and desire stirred within at just the thought of those hands on bare skin.

"Her loss," she added ruefully and then could have bit her tongue.

He cocked his head at her as if taken aback by her comment. Not half as much as she was. The idea was to distract the audience during a trick—not shoot yourself in the foot.

An awkward silence fell between them, which she didn't dare try to fill. Who knew what she'd say?

"We should see about getting you to the house. I thought you could drive your car and follow me. It's only two blocks. We can put your car in my garage."

She glanced toward the open back door of the office. She could smell the sweet scent of pine coming from the growing darkness. "You're sure it won't be an imposition?"

"Having second thoughts?" He smiled but this time it didn't reach his eyes.

He's angry at Jasmine and he thinks I'm her. "Are you sure you're all right with this?" She wasn't sure she was.

His gaze flickered as if he hadn't expected any concern from her—and it touched him. "Don't worry about me. I can't promise that I can keep you a secret for long. But I will try until we get the fingerprint results."

"Would you mind calling me Molly?"

He nodded slowly.

"It's just that…"

"You don't have to explain," he said. "You're still not comfortable with the idea of being Jasmine."

She nodded. And it wasn't something she intended to get comfortable with. All she'd done was buy herself a little time. "Thank you. For everything. I appreciate you letting me stay at your house."

"Have you had dinner yet?"

She shook her head.

"I haven't been to the grocery store but I do have some leftover pot roast with vegetables from my garden."

She laughed. The man had a garden and he cooked. Unbelievable. "I *love* pot roast," she said, relaxing a little. There was nothing to worry about. He didn't suspect anything. She had to quit questioning her luck. Obviously, it had changed for the better.

But when she looked at him, he was frowning. "What is it?" she asked, realizing that she'd done something wrong.

He shook his head, quickly replacing the frown with a smile as if she'd caught him. "Nothing. It's just your... laugh. I'd forgotten...how much I've missed it."

She felt her stomach churn, but she forced herself to smile. Fear reverberated through her.

He had just lied to her.

And a few moments ago she would have bet anything that he wasn't the lying type.

Maybe she was wrong about him. Maybe she hadn't fooled him. With a shudder, she realized that she'd talked her way into staying at his house, alone with him, her car hidden in his garage. And he was the only person in town who even knew she existed.

Suddenly, that nagging feeling—that she would regret this—was back again, stronger than ever.

"Ready?" he asked from the doorway.

She started toward the door.

"Just follow me," he said. "It's the last house at the edge of town."

Of course it was.

"You can't get lost," he added.

She'd been lost her whole life. Right now she just wanted to run. Running was easy, she realized. That was probably why Max had been so good at it.

Cash looked at her as if he sensed her thoughts and had no intention of letting her out of his sight. "Don't worry. We'll figure this out together."

She walked to her car, unlocked it and climbed in. There were a few more pickups parked down Main Street in front of the Longhorn Café but other than that, the town was dead. As she inserted the key and started her car, he got into the patrol car. If she took off, he would come after her. Now how stupid would that be on her part?

He backed up and she followed him the two blocks to where he parked the patrol car in front of a large old house surrounded on three sides by huge pine trees. The house was at the edge of town, just as he'd said, no other house close by.

She pulled into the driveway in front of the separate garage and looked up at the monstrous place in the fading light. She'd never liked old houses. They were cold and rambling, smelling of age, often haunted with the lives of those who had lived there before, those hard lives worn into the steps, carved like scars into the walls, their lives still echoing in the high-ceilinged rooms.

She sat in her car and watched him get out of his and open the garage door. Now or never. She started to reach for the key when he appeared at her side window and motioned her to pull into the now open garage. She hesitated, but only a moment and drove inside. She turned off the engine, she pulled the key out and opened her door.

He smiled as if to reassure her.

She tried to smile, but realized she was ridiculously nervous. Max must be rolling over in his grave. She'd played it just right. She'd gotten what she wanted. What she needed. But if she didn't get control of herself she would blow it.

"What do you think of the house?" Cash asked. "I bought it for you as an engagement present. It was a surprise. Unfortunately, you never got to see it."

She didn't know what to say. He bought a rich woman an old house?

He was studying her, expecting a reaction. She could only nod at him and blink as if fighting tears.

He got her suitcase from the backseat and led the way up the steps. She braced herself as he opened the door and stepped aside for her to enter.

"THIS IS IT," CASH SAID as he reached in and turned on a light. Over the years, he'd thought about remodeling the house. He'd thought more about selling it. The house stood as a constant reminder of Jasmine and he guessed that's why he'd kept it. He never wanted to forget.

In the end, he'd done nothing. He'd been locked in a holding pattern, unable to move on with his life, unable to decide what to do with the white elephant, no desire anymore to fix it up.

He watched her come through the door wavering between his conviction that she was Jasmine and a nagging feeling that things weren't as they seemed. What had really brought her here? Not him. He was almost certain she'd come for something else. Whatever it was, he was determined to find out.

He was no fool. He'd seen the way she'd gotten him to invite her to stay here at the house. Well, she was here. Now what?

"It needs a little work," he said as he watched her take in the worn hardwood floors, the faded walls, the paint-chipped stair railing.

Her green eyes widened as she looked around. "It's… it's…"

He watched her struggling to find the words as he fought the urge to laugh. She hated it. He could see it on her face. She was horrified. Any doubts he had that she might not be Jasmine went out the window.

"I bought the house planning to restore it but I just haven't gotten around to it," he said. "I thought you, that is Jasmine and I would do it together."

"Oh? Well, it has all kinds of possibilities," she said, moving from the foyer to the bottom of the stairs.

"You think?" he said behind her.

"Definitely. It will be a lot of work but…" She turned and met his gaze, nodding. "Definite possibilities."

"I was hoping you would like it," he said and waited.

"Oh, I do. I'm sure Jasmine would have loved it, too."

He smiled at that.

"Buying her a house… Why, that's so…romantic," she said as if she needed to fill the silence.

"Romantic?" He couldn't help himself. He laughed.

She seemed surprised at first, as if not sure how to

react, then she laughed with him. "I'm sorry, I just can't imagine anyone buying *me* a house."

He stopped laughing and looked at her. "I don't remember you being such a romantic."

"I'm sure I've changed," she said.

Boy howdy, he thought.

She looked so unsure of herself, he stepped to her, thinking only of comforting her, taking away that frightened, confused look in those green eyes. He cupped her face in his hands and felt the reassuring throb of her pulse, telling himself not to question this. Jasmine was alive—and he was off the hook.

She didn't pull away, her eyes locking with his and he felt himself diving into all that warm tropical sea-green. He leaned toward her, wanting to feel his mouth on hers, to taste her, to reassure himself.

But he caught a whiff of fragrance, something expensive and rare. The memory wasn't a pleasant one and not of Jasmine directly, but it was enough to make him jerk back, suddenly queasy.

She seemed surprised. Maybe a little disappointed. But also relieved? She straightened as if she had been leaning toward him as well. Now she looked away to brush invisible lint from the sleeve of her blouse as if embarrassed.

"I should show you to your room," he said, his voice sounding hoarse even to him as he picked up her suitcase and turned on the ancient chandelier overhead, throwing a little light on the stairs.

She was still standing in the foyer, looking as if she were shaken by what had almost happened moments before. He knew the feeling. Kissing her had been the last thing he'd planned to do and yet for a moment, he'd felt something so strong between them….

He shook his head at his own foolishness as he started toward the steps.

"Cash?" she said behind him.

It was the first time she'd said his name. The sound pulled at him like a noose around his neck, dragging him back to the first time he'd seen her. He stopped, one foot on the bottom stair, his heart pounding.

Slowly, he turned, not sure what he expected. The way she'd said his name, the sound so familiar, he thought she might say she'd suddenly remembered everything including the last time she saw him seven years ago.

That was why he wouldn't have been surprised to turn and see a weapon in her hand. He'd already seen murder in those green eyes.

But her hands were empty, her purse strap slung over one shoulder. She wasn't even looking at him, but staring through the doorway into the dark living room.

He followed her gaze, his eyes taking a moment to adjust with the shades drawn, and froze. Someone was sitting in his living room.

Las Vegas, Nevada

"I'M NOT GOING BACK to prison," Angel said as he cornered hard again.

Vince grabbed the door handle and held on. The car came down hard as Angel straightened it out and hit the gas, driving him back into the seat.

Horns blared, brakes screeched. Behind them, sirens wailed. Overhead, the dark shape of a police helicopter blocked the desert sun for a moment before Angel cut between two buildings, sending a crowd of pedestrians scattering, their screams dying off under the roar of the engine. Vince could almost hear the sound of a prison-cell door closing behind him.

"Did you hear me?" Angel yelled over the noise.

"I heard you. You'd rather die than go back to prison."

Angel jumped a curb, the car coming back down with another jarring slam. Vince closed his eyes. This was not the way he'd hoped his life would end. He thought of Max and how Max had made a run for it the day of the jewel heist. Foolish, very foolish. Going out in a blaze of glory. Only there was no glory; there was only blood and pain.

Not that Vince could convince Angel of that. He opened his eyes again as Angel cut through a casino parking lot, then another, then another until the sound of cop cars diminished just a little and there was no sign of the helicopter overhead.

Angel whipped into an underground parking garage and threw on the brakes. He was out of the car before it came to a complete stop. Vince got out too, his legs rubbery. He was getting too old for this.

He heard the shatter of glass, then the soft pop of a door opening. A moment later, an engine roared to life. Vince stumbled over to the vehicle, leaned against the side of it as Angel took off the license plates and switched them with another car in the lot.

Vince could hear the sirens growing closer. He thought about telling Angel to hurry, just for something to do, but Angel was good with his hands, quick, his movements efficient in ways his brain had never been.

The sirens grew louder and louder. He waited for Angel to get into the car and open the passenger side. All Vince wanted right now was to lie down in the back, close his eyes and trust that Angel would get them out of this—just as he had on numerous other occasions.

"You're going to have to get into the trunk," Angel said over the top of the car. He reached inside. Vince heard the soft click and whoosh as the trunk came open.

Angel was grinning, face flushed, eyes too bright. It was that feeling again of standing under a power line to be even this close to him. Angel loved this. And that frightened Vince more than the sound of the approaching sirens.

"The trunk?" Vince said dumbly as he watched Angel knock the rest of the glass out of the side window and reach in the back for a cap that had been lying on the rear seat.

Angel put the cap on his head, adjusted it in the side mirror. "I would suggest you hurry."

All the other times Vince had just slid down in the front seat or hidden lying down on the backseat, but he could see that Angel was determined to have it his way this time—and there wasn't time to try to reason with him.

Vince moved to the gaping open trunk. The sirens were so close he could almost feel the handcuffs on his wrists. He climbed into the trunk, scrunched up to fit his large body into the cramped space. He hated tight spaces. And darkness. It reminded him of when his stepfather used to lock him in the root cellar.

Angel slammed the trunk lid, the snap of the latch deafening in the pitch-black, musty darkness.

CHAPTER SEVEN

Antelope Flats, Montana

MOLLY HEARD AGAIN the soft rattle of ice in a glass, the same sound that had drawn her attention to the dark living room—and the man sitting there—in the first place.

She caught her breath as the faceless dark figure rose from the chair and moved toward her slowly, almost awkwardly.

Vince? He couldn't have found her. Not this quickly. Her pulse thundered in her ears. Run, her mind was screaming, but her feet seemed rooted to the floor.

As the man reached the light from the hallway, Molly saw with relief that he wasn't Vince. But the look on his face made her take a quick step back anyway. She heard Cash swear.

"Jasmine," the man whispered. "My God. You're alive." His face was ghastly white, his fingers holding the drink glass in his hand trembling, the ice in his drink rattling softly.

"What the hell are you doing here?" Cash demanded, stepping in front of Molly as if to protect her.

"The door was open," the man said vaguely as he peered around Cash to stare at her. He was soap-opera-star handsome dressed in chinos, a polo shirt and deck shoes. But next to Cash, he looked like a cardboard ad cut out from a fancy men's magazine.

"So you just made yourself at home?" Cash demanded.

The man was obviously shaken, deathly pale with beads of sweat breaking out on his upper lip. Molly thought he might be either drunk or dazed. Or both.

She wondered how he knew her. That is, Jasmine.

"Who the hell do you think you are?" Cash snapped.

Yes, Molly thought, who are you? And how did you know Jasmine? One thing was clear, Cash didn't like him. Nor did the man like Cash.

The man seemed to drag his gaze from her to look at the sheriff. "I needed to talk to you," he said, glancing down at the drink in his hand as if surprised to find it there. "I called the state investigator. He said I might find you here since you wouldn't be at your office. The door was unlocked so I helped myself to your Scotch."

Cash stood ramrod straight, his hands balled into fists at his side, anger in every line of his body. "We don't lock our doors in Antelope Flats," he said biting off each word. "Normally we don't have to. What do you want, Kerrington?"

"Kerrington?" Molly repeated in surprise, recognizing the name from one of the articles she'd read about Jasmine's disappearance.

"The *first* man you promised to marry," he said, scowling at her. "As if you don't remember."

"She *doesn't* remember," Cash snapped. "She's suffering from some kind of memory loss."

Kerrington stared at her. "Right," he said and let out an unpleasant laugh. As if playing along, he held out his hand. "Kerrington Landow." His hand was damp and cold from the glass he'd been holding, his grip too firm, as if he thought he could feel the truth in her pulse. "Still want to pretend you don't know me?"

"I'm afraid I don't know you," she said. "I'm sorry." But she wasn't. She didn't like the man.

He glared at her. From his expression, she couldn't tell if he was glad Jasmine might be alive or just the opposite.

Cash cleared his throat. "Now if you don't mind…" He grabbed for Kerrington's arm as if to show him out.

"I'm not leaving until you tell me what the hell is going on here," Kerrington said, drawing back out of his reach. "I thought the state investigators were still looking for her body out at that farm?"

"They are," Cash said. "She might not be Jasmine."

"So the state investigator doesn't know she's alive?" Kerrington said.

Molly decided the man was both drunk and dazed. And dangerous. She stepped in quickly. "Sheriff McCall, I don't want Mr. Landow going away with the wrong impression." She had to convince Kerrington that he couldn't believe his eyes before he blabbed this all over town. She was counting on being long gone before it hit the newspapers.

"I know I resemble Jasmine," she said reasonably.

Kerrington nodded and looked smug as if he were finally going to get the truth out of her.

"There is a lot about my past that I can't remember," she said. Or don't want to remember. "So I came here looking for answers. The sheriff has been kind enough to send my fingerprints to the FBI to be compared to

Jasmine's. I'm staying here, out of sight, until we know for sure who I am."

"*You're* hiding her?" Kerrington said and shot a look at Cash, who groaned. "You think I don't know about the fight you had with Jasmine? And now her car turns up just a few miles from town…. I think the state investigator needs to know what you're up to."

"I'm not up to anything," Cash said between gritted teeth. "What are you doing in town, anyway? Jasmine isn't your concern. Or is she? I never bought your alibi, Landow."

Kerrington jerked his head back as if Cash had slugged him. "I didn't kill her. I have an alibi. And anyway she's alive, right?" He looked at Molly. "You're just trying to confuse me, aren't you. Make me say something you can use against me."

"I think we're all getting upset here for nothing," Molly said quickly. "Let's just wait for the fingerprint report to come back from the FBI. I don't believe I'm Jasmine Wolfe. My name is Molly."

"Molly," Kerrington said, nodding, but she could tell by his expression that he didn't believe her. "You look just like Jasmine. You sound just like her."

She wished now that she hadn't gotten Jasmine's voice and mannerisms down quite so well. She'd been able to copy Jasmine's faint southern accent flawlessly from the videotape. Jasmine's inflection, mannerisms and tone had been easy for someone who'd learned to mimic from the time she was a child.

"It would be a mistake to assume I was Jasmine, though," Molly said. "I don't want anyone looking like a fool because of me. If you were to tell people…" She saw Kerrington reconsider, just as she knew he would.

She'd learned to read people. His worst fear would be to look like a fool.

"When will you get the results on the finger-prints?"

"At least a week, probably two," Cash said, sounding as if he hoped this didn't mean that Kerrington would stick around that long.

Molly could see Kerrington considering his options. "This isn't some kind of a trick?"

And to think Kerrington hadn't looked that percept-ive, she thought darkly. "Why would I lie to you?"

He suddenly looked drunker, as if the Scotch he'd poured for himself was one of many he'd already had today. "That's what I'm trying to figure out." He looked at the drink in his hand again, must have thought better of finishing it and handed the half-full glass to Cash. "I should go."

"I agree," Cash said. "I hope you're walking, other-wise I'm going to have to drive you."

"I walked," Kerrington said straightening. "I'm stay-ing at the motel. The only one in this damned town." He seemed about to say something but changed his mind as he looked at Molly for a long moment, then left without another word.

"He'd *better* be walking," Cash said, going to the door to look after him. Kerrington was. Otherwise Cash would have seen his car parked out front. Molly figured Cash probably knew what everyone in town drove.

He closed the door, locked it and turned to look at her. His jaw was clenched, his body still rigid with anger. "I can't believe that jackass."

She wanted to ask him why he disliked Kerrington as much as he obviously did. Was it just jealousy? Kerrington had been engaged to Jasmine first. But Cash didn't seem like the jealous type.

"He's going to tell, you know," Cash said.

"Do you think he'll go to the press?"

Cash shook his head. "He'll tell your brother though. Jasmine's stepbrother Bernard," he amended. "That means Bernard will have to see for himself whether or not you're Jasmine."

"Is that bad?" she had to ask.

Cash swore under his breath. "It's not good."

She smiled and saw some of the tension uncoil from his body. "You don't like Kerrington."

He shook his head. "Sorry."

"I'm the one who's sorry. There is no way I could have been engaged to that man."

Cash's smile was tight. "Apparently he never got over you."

"Over Jasmine," she said, wondering more and more about the woman who had two men she'd promised to marry and both hadn't let go even after seven years. She must have been *some* woman.

"He's married to Sandra Perkins." He seemed to hesitate, waiting for a reaction from her. "She was your—Jasmine's roommate. They got married just a few months after you disappeared. I'd heard she was pregnant. Must not have been. They have no children that I know of. Doesn't act like a married man, does he?"

Molly felt for Kerrington's wife. "You think she's here in town with him?"

Cash shook his head. "I doubt she even knows he's here. And what the hell is he doing here, anyway?"

Kerrington would tell Jasmine's stepbrother Bernard

Wolfe. But would either of them chance going to the press before the fingerprint results came back?

She had no way of knowing. She still believed she could pull this off. Not that she had much choice. But she'd learned from Max long ago that a magician stayed with the trick—even when he realized the rabbit was no longer in the hat.

Las Vegas, Nevada

VINCE TRIED TO SLOW his breathing, afraid he would run out of air in the car trunk before Angel stopped and let him out.

The car moved at a snail's pace. He could hear other traffic. He was cramped and couldn't move, the darkness seeming to close in on him. He tried not to think about it or how much air he had left.

He thought instead about Molly and what he would do once they found her. He could understand her fear—especially if she'd heard what had happened to Lanny.

He could even understand her running. It was calling the cops that had him mystified. She obviously didn't understand the concept of honor among thieves and that disappointed him more than he wanted to admit.

He felt the car speed up and tried to relax. It wouldn't be long now before Angel pulled over and let him out. He took a breath of the hot musty air, feeling lightheaded. He guessed they were on the interstate now, gauging the speed and the smoothness of the road. It was getting hotter in the trunk, closer, tighter.

He was sweating profusely now, the smell of fear filling the tight space. His muscles were starting to cramp, he was having trouble catching his breath and just the thought of being trapped in the trunk brought on a panic attack.

What if Angel had made him get in the trunk for another reason besides hiding him? What if he planned to take him out in the desert and kill him?

Unlike him, Angel had never held much store in the fact that they had some of the same blood coursing through their veins. Angel wasn't the sentimental type. Angel would have killed his own grandmother if there were something in it for him.

Vince stiffened as he felt the car decelerate. The tires left the smooth pavement for a bumpy road that jarred every bone in his body. Why didn't Angel stop and let him out? Where the hell was he taking him?

After an interminable amount of time, Angel finally stopped.

Vince held his breath and listened. He could hear the tick-tick-tick of the motor as it cooled. A car door opened and closed, no sense of urgency in the movements. The door opened again. Vince heard the scrape of the key in the trunk lock. That was strange. Why hadn't Angel just pulled the trunk lever before he got out of the car?

The trunk lid rose slowly.

Antelope Flats, Montana

CASH LED THE WAY up the stairs to the bedroom where Molly would be staying, cursing to himself.

Kerrington. He should have known the moment he caught that fragrance. The memory of Kerrington's cologne was now all tied up in his memories of Jasmine.

Cash knew he should call State Investigator Mathews and inform him about this latest possible development before Kerrington did. Still, he hesitated. He would know about the fingerprints by tomorrow at the latest. The call could wait until then.

And maybe he would get lucky and find out what she wanted, whomever this woman was whom he'd invited to stay in his house.

Her reaction to Kerrington had certainly surprised him—and Kerrington as well. Not just a complete lack of recognition on her part, but she didn't seem to like him. It could have been an act, he supposed. It could all be an act. But at least Cash wanted to believe her dislike for Kerrington was real.

He couldn't put his finger on what was bothering him about her. Part of him acknowledged that she was different from the Jasmine he remembered—the memory loss aside. He told himself that seven years and not knowing who she was would make her different. Not to mention whatever had happened to her before her car ended up in that barn.

As she'd said, she felt something horrible had happened to her. Any change he thought he saw in her could be directly related to that. And she had the scar to prove it.

Or she could be lying, just as Kerrington had accused her, the scar from some other accident. Cash hated that he and Kerrington might ever agree on anything, but there was something about Molly Kilpatrick, something that warned him to be wary whether she was Jasmine— or a complete stranger.

When had he become so suspicious? He knew the answer to that one as he turned to look back at her. She had stopped at the top of the stairs and appeared to be studying an old photograph of the ranch.

"Is this your family's ranch?" she asked.

The photograph was of the original homestead, the old hewn-log cabin, a herd of longhorns grazing in a meadow behind it.

"Yes." And no, he thought. But the photo was the essence of the ranch, how it had all begun. If she was curious about what his family ranch was now worth... well then that was something else.

"It's the Sundown Ranch. My great grandfather drove a herd of longhorns up from Texas to start it."

She nodded as if she didn't know what else to say and he saw that she seemed nervous.

"If you'd be more comfortable at the motel..."

She shook her head. "No, it's just..." She waved a hand through the air and looked into his eyes. Hers were a warm Caribbean sea-green in the hall light, as inviting as a kiss. He remembered almost kissing her earlier with no small regret. "You don't know me and yet you offered me a place to stay. I could be a total stranger."

"Could be." He smiled ruefully. For strictly personal, selfish reasons he wanted Jasmine to be alive. Didn't want her disappearance hanging over him the rest of his life. He wanted her to remember everything. No matter who it hurt, himself included.

"I might not be the man you think I am," he warned her.

She met his gaze. "Or me the woman you hope I am."

"I'm not worried," he said, knowing that wasn't entirely true. "Are you?"

Slowly she returned his smile and shook her head. "No. I know it's the safest place for me to be right now."

Or so she thought, he mused. "Your room is right down here."

He led her to the door of the master bedroom and opened it. It was a large, bright room. Fortunately, the house had come with some furniture. The high, white iron bed frame was one of the pieces.

When the house was built, the room was wallpapered in a tiny flower print of yellows, greens, blues and pinks. The print had faded some but was still intact. This room had always seemed too large, as if it demanded double occupancy. That's why he'd opted for a smaller bedroom down the hall. He kept this one made up for the times Dusty or one of his brothers stayed over.

"There's a large bath in here," he said, stepping past her to push open the door.

She let out a cry of delight at the sight of the huge claw-foot bathtub.

"I guess it was made special, that's why it's so large." Large enough for two, he thought ruefully.

"I love it," she said as if she could see herself sunk in the tub.

He had to smile. "So does my sister. She left an assortment of bubble bath. Help yourself."

"Thank you." Her gaze came back to him. Her smile was shy, uncertain, her mouth turning up a little higher on one side. He didn't remember Jasmine ever smiling like that, but he'd forgotten so much…. And some things he would never forget.

He tried to swallow the lump in his throat as he put down her suitcase. "If you need anything just let me know."

He hurried out of the bedroom, the large room suddenly feeling claustrophobic.

Who *had* he invited to stay with him?

"Come down when you're ready," he called back. "I'll just heat us up some dinner."

By this time tomorrow, he should know. Twenty-four hours. And every moment of it he would be looking for Jasmine in this woman. And waiting. Waiting to find out the real reason she had come to him.

Atlanta, Georgia

THE WOLFE COMPANY JET was winging its way across the Midwest when Bernard got the call.

He checked caller ID and felt his pulse jump. Stay calm. He'd recognized the name on the caller ID. Patty Franklin, Jasmine's former roommate. Seemed she hadn't married. Or if she had, she'd kept her maiden name.

He took a breath, not wanting her to hear anything in his voice that might give him away. "Wolfe here."

"Bernard?" Patty sounded tentative. She always sounded tentative. Didn't take a brain surgeon to figure out why Jasmine had befriended *her.* Can you say *door-mat?*

"Yes?" He pretended he didn't recognize her voice. Hell, it had been almost seven years since he'd heard from her. He wondered how she'd gotten his cell-phone number.

"It's Patty. Patty Franklin?" she said. "Your sister's former roommate?"

"Patty." He tried to make that one word say, "Why are you bothering me after all this time?"

"I'm sure you've heard about Jasmine's car being found," Patty said.

The story he'd found out had gone national. *Everyone* had heard. "Of course."

"I've been so upset. Is there any more news?"

No, and there is no more money to keep your mouth shut either. "No, I'm afraid not."

"Well, I didn't mean to bother you," she said. "I just wanted to see if there was anything I could do. I've never forgotten her. She really was one of a kind." He couldn't argue that. "I guess you're coming to Montana."

Patty just happened to still be in Montana? He waited for her to make her pitch for more money and said nothing. Force her to ask this time.

"I know how hard this must be for you," she said hesitantly. "I should let you go. I just wanted to say how sorry I am and how much I appreciated your kindness when we lost Jasmine."

"Thank you for calling, but I have to keep the line open in case there is any news," he said and disconnected, turning off his cell phone just in case she called back and wanted another fifty thousand in kindness.

And what was that about "when *we* lost Jasmine"? Patty hadn't meant anything to Jasmine and she sure as hell meant nothing to him. Why had she called?

He wondered if he'd made a mistake by not offering her more money. She'd never really *blackmailed* him. At least not outright. She'd just made a point of mentioning how she would never tell the police anything that might make him look guilty because she knew he couldn't hurt Jasmine. And the next thing he knew he was paying for her college education. Jasmine would have liked that, he'd told Patty and she'd cried and agreed. What a dummy he'd been.

HE SWORE NOW AND LOOKED at his watch. He couldn't wait to get to Montana and get this over with. He tried to forget Patty. He hadn't heard from her in seven years, so maybe her call had been just what she'd said it was.

Maybe by the time he got to Montana, Jasmine's body

would have been found and he could finally put Jasmine to rest.

"Amen," he said, but Patty's phone call was still bothering him. He contemplated how far he'd go to get rid of her if she tried to extort him again. One thing was certain. He wasn't giving her another cent.

Antelope Flats, Montana

MOLLY WAITED UNTIL SHE HEARD Cash's footfalls die off down the stairs before she let herself relax. What a day this had been!

She'd bought herself a little time. She should have been relieved. But Jasmine's brother would be in town soon, if he wasn't already. Cash was convinced that Kerrington would tell Bernard. How would she avoid *that* bullet?

Knowing that Cash would try to protect her made her feel all the more guilty. That and seeing how much he wanted her to be Jasmine, how much he'd obviously loved the woman.

She looked around the room and tried to tell herself that she was safe and that was all that mattered. No way could Vince and Angel find her. But was that all she had to worry about? Could Cash be right about Jasmine's abductor being someone she knew, someone who wasn't going to be happy to see her alive?

She couldn't worry about that now. She'd just had two close calls. Running into Kerrington and an even closer call with Cash. She'd almost kissed him. Had wanted to kiss him. If he hadn't pulled back—

He was already suspicious. Kissing him would have been stupid. Something had happened back at his office, she'd done something wrong. She still didn't know what it was but she remembered the doubt she'd glimpsed in his face.

The only thing that had saved her was his desperation to believe she was Jasmine, she thought with a chill as she glanced around the room. He'd bought this house for Jasmine? And kept it for seven years untouched? Had he expected her to turn up one day just as Molly had done?

He hadn't moved on with his life, that much was clear. But why, she wondered. Because he'd loved Jasmine too much to let go? Or for some other reason?

She remembered what Kerrington had said about a fight between the two of them. And her car turning up just a few miles from town. Was he insinuating that Cash had something to do with Jasmine's disappearance?

She shook off the bad feeling that came with the thought. Cash had loved Jasmine. He wouldn't have hurt her.

And yet he was hiding something from her. She'd seen it in his face when she'd asked about their relationship.

She took a breath and let it out slowly. *Don't borrow trouble. You're safe. At least for a while. With luck, Vince and Angel have been arrested by now.* She still hadn't heard anything about Lanny Giliano. She would call tonight. Maybe somehow he'd gotten away.

This would be over soon and she would be gone. Like it or not, she would again be Molly Kilpatrick, daughter of the Great Maximilian Burke, magician extraordinaire and thief.

It would be a far cry from the daughter of Archibald Wolfe and the Wolfe furniture fortune. A far cry from being the woman Cash McCall had loved, she thought.

She looked around the master bedroom. If Jasmine

really were alive, Cash would be sharing this room with her.

With a shudder, Molly hurried downstairs, feeling as if she'd just walked across the woman's grave.

CHAPTER EIGHT

Outside Las Vegas, Nevada

AT FIRST ALL Vince saw was darkness as the trunk lid swung upward, then a blinding light. He recoiled, drawing back into the tight space, covering his head with an arm, gasping for what he feared would be his last breath.

When something touched his shoulder, he cried out.

"What's wrong with you?" Angel demanded. "You get sunstroke or something in there?"

Vince peered out from under his arm. He'd expected to see a knife in Angel's hand. But all Angel held was a flashlight. "You blinded me."

Vince could see his brother frowning. "You need help out or what?"

Vince shook his head. He'd just spent fifteen years in prison with murderers and worse, but he'd never been as frightened as when that trunk lid had swung open. It made him sick that he could even think his half brother would kill him. What kind of man was he?

"My legs are asleep."

"Here, take my hand," Angel said. Awkwardly, Vince crawled out of the trunk with Angel's help.

"So?" Angel said as Vince stood and tried to get feeling back into his limbs. Just as he'd suspected, Angel had driven out to an isolated part of the desert. He could see lights in the distance on the interstate and hear the distant hum of the traffic. His chest ached, heart still pounding too hard. He sucked in the hot desert night air and tried to calm himself.

"I'm okay," he said as if trying to reassure himself.

"That's all you have to say?" Angel sounded disappointed, angry. "I got us out of Vegas with dozens of cops chasing us. You think that was easy back there?"

Vince shook his head. "You saved us. You're the best. Thanks."

Angel nodded. Clearly he'd hoped for more but Vince wasn't up to it right now.

"Yeah, well, don't forget it. You need me."

Vince put a hand on his brother's shoulder. "I do need you," he said, his voice breaking with emotion.

"You sure you're all right?" Angel asked again, eyeing him.

"Fine. Great. I'm great."

"Then let's get the hell out of here," Angel said, slamming the trunk.

Vince walked around to the passenger side and threw up in the sagebrush before climbing into the car.

"Where to?" his brother asked, sliding behind the wheel.

With still-trembling fingers, Vince took the laptop from the backseat where Angel had put it. He booted up the program and waited for the GPS tracking device to tell him exactly where they could find Molly. It was time.

Antelope Flats, Montana

MOLLY SAID SHE *loved* POT ROAST, Cash thought as he put the leftover roast and vegetables in the microwave.

Was she just being polite? He didn't think so. She'd almost seemed impressed. He smiled at the memory. If she was Jasmine, she was definitely an improved version.

The Jasmine from seven years ago had been the pickiest eater he'd ever known. She ate like a bird, always worrying about her weight, but also very finicky about what she ate. She would have turned up her nose at pot roast. Her tastes ran more to expensive restaurant cuisine, takeout, anything that came in white boxes or fancy-shaped foil impressed *her*.

The doorbell rang. Cash swore. He wasn't up to seeing Jasmine's brother Bernard. Not now. And he didn't want to put Jasmine-Molly-whoever she was through another scene.

He moved to the door and looked through the peephole, already deciding that if it was Bernard, he wouldn't let him in.

It wasn't. It was Shelby, his mother. And she knew he was home and, therefore, wouldn't give up until he opened the door.

He swore under his breath and glanced up the stairs as she rang the bell again. Molly was still in her room. Now if she would just stay there until he could get rid of his mother. He opened the door before she could ring the bell again. "Shelby."

"I know I should have called first," she said as she stepped past him and into the foyer. "I wanted to see how you were."

"I told you—"

"I know what you told me," she said, stopping in the center of the hallway to turn back to look at him. "I'm worried about you." She sniffed the air and smiled. "At least you're eating. But I hate the idea of you eating alone."

"I've been eating alone for years." He hadn't meant to say it so sharply. "I'm fine. Really." He needed to get rid of her before Jasmine came down.

She was eyeing him as if she didn't believe he was fine. "I'm so glad you're coming out for dinner tomorrow night."

He'd completely forgotten he'd agreed to that. What would he do with Jasmine? He couldn't leave her. "Listen, Shelby, about that—"

But his mother wasn't listening. She was staring at Jasmine's pale pink jacket. He'd hung it by the door when he'd brought in her suitcase.

"You have company?" she asked, sounding surprised.

At just that moment, Jasmine appeared at the top of the stairs. She stopped, almost stumbling as she saw that he wasn't alone.

"Jasmine?" Shelby whispered, grabbing hold of Cash's arm to steady herself, a look of horror on her face.

CASH STARED AT HIS MOTHER. Not only had Shelby recognized Jasmine, she also sounded stunned to see her and not the least bit pleased. What the hell?

"You know Jasmine?" he asked, a little stunned himself. He'd just assumed his mother hadn't known or cared what was happening in Antelope Flats during the time she'd been pretending to be dead. He'd thought she and Jasmine had that in common.

"We've never met, if that's what you mean," Shelby said. "I just…know about her."

He stared at his mother, amazed that she continued to surprise him. Clearly she knew a lot more about Jasmine—and his relationship with her—than he would have guessed. Possibly more than anyone else knew.

Jasmine cleared her throat and looked to him as if waiting for an introduction—or an explanation for this woman's obvious shock and thinly veiled animosity.

"Forgive my manners," he said and motioned her down the stairs. "This is Shelby, my mother."

Jasmine smiled warmly as she came down the stairs.

Shelby clutched his arm tighter. He could feel her trembling and frowned as he realized it could be from fear. Or rage. "You're even more beautiful than you were seven years ago."

His mother's words echoed in his head. She'd seen Jasmine seven years ago? Just how much did his mother know? He felt sick. Was it possible she knew his secret?

"I thought you were dead," Shelby said. "I mean, we all did."

"You do have that in common," Cash remarked, hating the anger and bitterness he heard in his voice but at the same time wanting to defend Jasmine. Or at least this version of her.

His mother shot him a reproachful look as she let go of his arm. "When were you going to tell us that Jasmine was alive?"

"I'm not Jasmine, I'm Molly." She looked to Cash as if for help. "That is, I don't think I'm Jasmine."

Cash sighed and said, "She's been going by the name Molly Kilpatrick." He filled her in, giving Shelby the short version of how she'd seen the article and the photo and had come here to find herself.

"We won't know for certain until the fingerprint results come back in a week or so," Cash finished. Except he planned to know a whole lot sooner than that.

Jasmine held out her hand. "In the meantime, please, call me Molly."

Shelby took Jasmine's hand in both of hers. "All right, Molly." She sounded as if she didn't believe for an instant that this woman was anyone but Jasmine Wolfe.

Cash watched his mother, seeing not the woman who'd been trying to ease her way back into their lives but one who, like the grizzly sow, was ready to fight to the death to protect her cub.

He wasn't sure what surprised him more. The fact that his mother had known about Jasmine or her apparent fear for him and need to protect him.

"We need to keep Molly a secret until the fingerprint results come back," Cash said. "If word got out, the press would have a field day." Asa had somehow managed to keep Shelby's return out of the papers, but hadn't been able to stop this part of the state from talking about it. The Longhorn Café had been abuzz for weeks.

"Trust me, I won't breathe a word," Shelby said, meeting his gaze. "And I think you know how good I am at keeping secrets."

"Oh yeah."

"You have to bring Jasmine to dinner tomorrow night," Shelby continued.

"Molly," Jasmine insisted.

"Yes, Molly," Shelby said, her smile anything but inviting. "You will come to dinner out at the ranch, won't you?"

It was clearly an order. "That would not be a good idea," Cash said. It was bad enough that his mother knew about her. He didn't need his whole family knowing. And then there was whatever was going on between his mother and Jasmine.

"Don't be ridiculous," Shelby was saying. "Of course you'll bring her. The ranch is the safest place for her. I will swear the family to secrecy."

Cash groaned. "Our family has enough secrets."

His mother shook her head as if he was wasting his time arguing with her. "You can't leave Jasmine here alone and you've already promised to come to dinner. It isn't as if you can keep her locked up in this house for weeks while you wait for the fingerprint results."

He realized she wasn't going to take no for an answer. Nor could he tell her in front of Jasmine that he had no intention of keeping her here for weeks. Just until he got the fingerprint results. Or until he knew on his own whom she really was.

And then what?

He'd cross that bridge when he came to it.

"Come out about six," Shelby said, then gave Jasmine a forced smile and said she was looking forward to seeing her at dinner, before turning back to him. "Walk me to my car, will you, dear?"

Shelby Ward McCall wasn't the type of woman who needed a man to walk her anywhere.

"Okay," he said and shot a look at Jasmine. "I'll be right back."

"Nice meeting you," Molly said.

"What was *that* about?" Cash asked Shelby the moment he closed the front door behind them.

"You're sure she's Jasmine?" his mother asked, an edge to her voice that took him aback.

"If I was sure, why would I send her fingerprints to the FBI?"

"Cash…" Shelby gripped his arm, an urgency in her voice. "Don't trust her."

He laughed. "If I didn't know better I'd think you were being one of those no-woman-is-good-enough-for-my-son mothers." Except that she had happily welcomed both Cassidy and Regina into the family when Rourke and J.T. had brought them home.

"If that woman in there is Jasmine, she's dangerous," Shelby said.

He felt himself go cold inside just as he had earlier. "Why would you say that? If you know something, Mother—"

She didn't seem to notice that he'd called her *Mother*. "Don't pretend with me. Whatever you once felt for that woman, don't turn your back on her until you find out what she wants."

"This might surprise you, but I know what I'm doing."

She let go of his arm and gave him a tentative smile, worry in her eyes. "I'm sorry. But she fooled you once before. She'll try again." With that, she walked to her car with the stride of a woman half her age.

Cash watched her go, filled with a sense of regret that he hadn't known her all those years when she'd been pretending to be dead. She was a tough old broad, he thought with a smile.

But how much did she know? He hated to think.

Molly felt a chill the moment the front door closed behind Cash and his mother. The woman hated her. Molly had seen it in Shelby McCall's expression, felt it in her handshake.

"What have you gotten yourself into?" she whispered

as she folded her arms to rub her shoulders, trying to fight off the icy dread that filled her. Being Molly Kilpatrick hadn't been any picnic, but being Jasmine Wolfe was turning out to be even worse.

What kind of trouble had Jasmine gotten herself into at the end? Something that had gotten her killed, Molly was pretty sure of that. Apparently, Jasmine had her share of enemies. And possible lovers. Unless she hadn't slept with Kerrington either.

She glanced toward the front door, wondering what Cash's mother was telling him about her. Not her. Jasmine. Being Jasmine was becoming more of a pain than she ever could have imagined. And possibly more dangerous as well.

The front door opened and Cash came back in. He frowned. "Are you all right?"

"Fine. Just a little chilly." *Kind of like that reception I got from your mother.*

"Here." He took a fleece jacket from the coat rack by the door, instead of her jacket. "It might be a little big but it's warmer than yours. The house can be a bit drafty."

"Thanks." She pulled on the soft fleece. The jacket was huge on her. He took one sleeve. She watched him roll it up, could feel his gaze on her face as he did.

"Your mother seems nice," she said.

He stopped rolling the second sleeve to look at her. He must think she was a complete idiot not to notice his mother's negative reaction to her. But he said nothing and after a moment, he finished rolling up the sleeve. "There. Warmer?"

She nodded. "Were they close? Your mother and Jasmine?"

"I had no idea my mother even knew you. You have no memory of her?" he said.

Molly shook her head. He was referring to her as Jasmine again. Isn't that what she'd hoped originally? That he and everyone else would think she was Jasmine?

"Hungry?" he asked.

Her stomach rumbled as if in answer.

"Let's get you fed before anyone else shows up at the door," he said and led the way into the kitchen as if nothing were wrong.

But Molly could see the change in him since his mother's visit. He seemed even more wary of her—if that were possible. What had his mother said to him?

Molly had hoped to gain his trust. But she realized there were some large key pieces of the Jasmine puzzle missing—just as if she really *did* have amnesia.

Why wouldn't he be suspicious of a woman who'd vanished into thin air and suddenly turned up on his doorstep, so to speak, seven years later?

But she knew it was more than that. There were undercurrents here that she didn't understand. Something to do with him and Jasmine. And his mother seemed to know about it.

Molly could feel Cash pulling away from her and the irony was he seemed to be doing it not because he suspected she wasn't Jasmine—but because he thought she *was*. "Are you sure I can't help with dinner?"

"Thanks but I've had it warming," he said and motioned her to a chair at the table as he took a large casserole dish from the microwave.

As he lifted the lid, she caught a whiff of dinner and everything but food was pushed from her mind. The casserole dish was filled with thick, juicy slices of pot roast surrounded by lightly braised carrots, potatoes and onions—and if that didn't smell heavenly enough, he also retrieved warm rolls from the oven and a plate of real butter from the fridge.

"Oh, that smells *so* wonderful." She breathed in the scents as if she hadn't eaten in days. It *had* been hours. At the moment, she didn't care if he knew what she was up to or not. She didn't care that everyone she'd met who'd known Jasmine besides Cash seemed to hate her. And what had been going on with Cash and Jasmine was still to be determined.

The woman had been his fiancée. He'd put his life on hold since her disappearance. But there was more to the story. Much more, she suspected. She thought about what Kerrington had said and was reminded of that old adage: If you've never thought about murdering someone, you've never been in love.

Cash handed her a large serving spoon. "Dig in," he said, taking the chair across from her.

She did, ladling the rich gravy over several luscious slices of pot roast, lightly browned small red potatoes, slivers of golden carrots and whole baby onions.

"May I?" he asked as he buttered himself a roll and offered to do the same for her.

"Please." She took a bite of the pot roast and one of the small onions, closing her eyes as she let the amazing flavors fill her senses. So this was *home cooking*.

"You like it?" he asked.

She opened her eyes. "I *love* it."

He handed her the buttered roll and watched as she took a bite. She felt the melted butter dribble down her chin. She licked her lips, laughed again without thinking and reached for her napkin. Too late.

He leaned across the table and touched his napkin to

the edge of her mouth, then her chin. Her eyes locked with his. Her breath caught in her throat.

Then he drew back, looking embarrassed.

She wiped her mouth with her napkin, shaken. It had felt as if he were seeing *her*—not Jasmine. And for that instant, he'd looked at her with…desire—as if he could feel the chemistry bubbling between them and was as surprised about it as she was.

She dropped her gaze to her plate. "You're a good cook." It was the only thing she could think to say.

"Thank you."

He took a bite of his own meal and she did the same. They ate for a few minutes in silence. And she soon lost herself again in the food. She couldn't remember a meal that had ever tasted so wonderful and told him so.

"I'm happy to see you enjoying it," he said smiling, but from his tone she knew she'd made another mistake, that he'd seen the card up her sleeve.

She should have been worried. But the meal was too good and she was too hungry.

"Tell me about Jasmine's brother Bernard," she said as she took the second buttered roll he offered her. Misdirection, a magician's best friend. "What is Bernard like?" she asked, pretty sure if Cash didn't like him, she wouldn't either.

"Spoiled, arrogant, superior." Cash looked up at her. "I'm sorry. I shouldn't have—"

"No, I appreciate your honesty," she said quickly.

Cash looked down at his plate, took a bite, chewed, swallowed, then said, "I suppose you should know. Your brother thinks I had something to do with your disappearance." His eyes locked with hers. "As a matter of fact, he thinks I killed you."

CHAPTER NINE

Antelope Flats, Montana

THE MOMENT KERRINGTON got back to his room at the Lariat Motel, he dialed Bernard's cell-phone number. Not that Bernard had given it to him. The two hadn't talked in years. They didn't even like each other anymore. Maybe they never had. He'd had to copy the number from his caller ID before he left Georgia.

"Jasmine is alive," he said after the beep to leave a message.

"You hear me? Jasmine is *alive*. Call me." He left his cell-phone number and disconected, wishing he'd called from the motel land line so he could have at least slammed down the receiver. He wanted to smash something. Jasmine was alive and staying with the sheriff. How in the hell? He couldn't imagine this being any worse.

On top of that, he was trapped in a motel room that was smaller than his bathroom in Atlanta. What was he going to do? Just sit around and wait for Jasmine to remember?

He wished Bernard would call him back. He was so desperate to talk to someone that he'd even take Sandra. He'd never liked being alone. If Sandra were here, he would have made a joke about the antelope print hanging on the wall and possibly even gotten a smile out of her.

Not that he was in the mood to joke. Nor would Sandra have been thrilled about this motel or staying in Antelope Flats. And she would have hit the roof when she heard that Jasmine was alive. He counted his blessings that she was in Atlanta. Nothing could get Sandra out here. Not after growing up in the West.

It was Jasmine's fault that he'd ever even met Sandra, let alone married her. He'd only started dating Jasmine's roommate to make her jealous. Instead, he'd gotten Sandra pregnant and ruined everything with Jasmine.

He groaned at his own stupidity, opened his cell phone and dialed his home number. The phone rang and rang. Either Sandra wasn't there or she wasn't picking up. Maybe she hadn't returned home, didn't even know he'd left.

He swore as he snapped the phone shut. He had worse problems than Sandra, he thought, rubbing his neck. Jasmine had looked right at him and hadn't known him. Or at least pretended she hadn't.

The sheriff had said she couldn't remember anything. What if it wasn't an act? He knew amnesia was rare, but he supposed...

No, this was Jasmine. Wasn't it just like her to return from the dead and pretend she didn't know any of them, jerk their chains for a while and then go in for the kill?

He couldn't stay in this motel room waiting for Bernard to call or he'd go crazy. What he wanted to do was go back to the sheriff's house and confront Jasmine without the cop being there, but he knew that wasn't going to happen.

Jasmine was no fool. She knew exactly what she was doing by staying with the sheriff—and worse, McCall believed her act. What a fool.

Kerrington grabbed up the motel-room key and slammed out of the room, got into the SUV he'd rented and started the engine, belatedly realizing he didn't have any idea where he was going. It wasn't like there was anything to do in this town. Billings was hours away. He was stuck here.

He remembered a bar on his way in. The Mello Dee. He drove to the edge of town, just outside the city limits, and pulled under the flashing neon. The place needed a good coat of paint among other things. A small hand-printed sign said it was under new ownership. He didn't care, just as long as it was open and it served strong mixed drinks.

As he got out, he noticed there were only two other cars in the lot. A country song twanged on the jukebox as he opened the door. A couple was playing pool at one end of the large open room. Several older guys were sitting at the far end of a long, scarred wooden bar.

Everyone turned to look at him as he took a stool at the opposite end of the bar from the old guys. The patrons lost interest in him quickly and went back to what they were doing. The bartender, a woman with a head of spiky dyed red hair, was bent over the sink washing glasses.

The moment the woman looked over at him, Kerrington realized he'd just made a horrible mistake.

CASH SAW FEAR FLICKER in her green eyes before Molly said, "Bernard thinks you were responsible for Jasmine disappearing? That's ridiculous." She said it with almost enough conviction that Cash believed she meant it. "You *loved* her. You wouldn't have hurt her. Anyway, if her brother knew you, he'd know you aren't that kind of man."

Cash had to smile. "Thanks for the vote of confidence. You almost sound as if you've known me longer than a few hours."

"I'm a pretty good judge of character," she said. "Anyway, you had no reason to hurt her."

He didn't correct her. Instead, he slid the pot roast closer to her. "Well, with you alive, I guess that proves I'm innocent at least of killing you. But it remains to be seen whether or not I had something to do with your disappearance. Too bad you can't remember that day."

She helped herself to seconds while he buttered her another roll and one for himself—and said nothing.

There was no way Jasmine would have eaten even a small plate of pot roast, let alone two, and there was no way she'd have even touched a roll dripping with butter. Jasmine had been off bread long before the low-carb craze.

He felt the prick of a memory, Jasmine making a scene at a café when served iceberg lettuce. He tried to swallow down the bad taste the memory left in his mouth. He'd forgotten how much he'd disliked eating with her because she always picked at her food and complained.

So how could this woman who looked so much like Jasmine actually be her? He told himself that losing her identity, her money, possibly almost her life and being forced to live a hand-to-mouth existence could change a person. But Jasmine Wolfe?

He couldn't see her changing even if she were homeless and starving. He had a flash of Jasmine digging in a garbage can saying, "Iceberg lettuce? You have to be joking. I'd rather starve."

He studied the woman across the table from him. Was it possible that the Jasmine he'd known and this woman really were the same person?

Jasmine *had* been one hell of an actress, playing any role she thought would get her what she wanted. But she wasn't *this* good.

He watched her clean her plate as if she'd never tasted anything so good. Watching her eat with such relish, such passion, he started to think of her as Molly—the last thing he wanted to do. "Would you like a glass of milk?"

She seemed surprised, as if she'd been lost in the meal. She smiled and nodded. "That would be nice."

Jasmine wouldn't touch milk, he thought as he went into the kitchen to the fridge. He brought back a tall glass of whole milk—not even two percent—and watched her chug half of it then smile and lick her lips. "Thank you. That was delicious."

He nodded. If she was Jasmine, he liked the changes, he thought, then realized he'd thought *if.* What if she wasn't Jasmine? He wanted her to be Jasmine even more desperately than he had earlier. He wanted her to be alive. Needed her to be alive. And he would have gladly taken this Jasmine over the last one.

But more and more, he realized he found himself thinking of her as Molly. Either way, his instincts warned him that it would be a mistake to misjudge this woman, whomever she was, but especially if she was Jasmine, didn't really have amnesia at all and had come back for blood. His.

"I was thinking about what might jar your memory," he said.

She looked up, swallowed and waited, her green eyes wide with innocence and interest.

"The only thing I could come up with was your prized possession. You waited months for it, special ordered it loaded." He shook his head. "I know it cost a small fortune at the time. If you'd like to see it, I might be able to pull a few strings."

Her expression was priceless. "Jasmine's *car?*"

"Your car quite possibly," he said.

She swallowed again. Clearly the car was the last thing she wanted to see. She looked…scared. He felt a start. Was it possible she wasn't faking her amnesia and she was afraid to go out to that barn because a part of her remembered the horrible thing that had happened in the car the day she disappeared?

And if she wasn't Jasmine? Why would a total stranger be afraid to see Jasmine's car?

THE MUSIC BLARED in the Mello Dee as the bartender smiled at him and, drying her hands on her apron, moved down the bar toward him.

Kerrington watched her, wanting to run. Maybe if he just turned around and left—but it was too late.

"Hi." She put a cocktail napkin down in front of him and smiled. "I know you, don't I?" she said, cocking her head to one side as she studied him.

"No. I'll take a martini."

She arched a brow at him.

"Sorry. I've had a bitch of a day."

"Haven't we all." She wore flip-flops, blue jeans and a halter top, four inches of her midriff bare above the waist of her jeans. She wasn't bad looking, about his age and she beat the hell out of the alcohol-less motel room, except for the fact that he'd recognized her.

She put the drink on top of the cocktail napkin without spilling a drop. "I never forget a face. I just can't put my finger on where I know you from, but it will come to me. It always does." She held out her hand. "Name's Teresa Clark but everyone calls me T.C."

"Bob. Bob Jones." He lied but wasn't even sure why, since he didn't think she'd ever known his name. Just his face. Now if she would just go away so he could enjoy his drink and a little peace and quiet. With luck, Bernard would call and give him an excuse to leave without making her suspicious.

"Bob Jones," she repeated.

He picked up the drink and turned on the stool to watch the couple playing pool, hoping she'd take the hint and go away. The first sip burned all the way down.

The alcohol buzz he'd had going earlier was gone. He needed a drink and then he would get out of here. So what if she remembered who he was? But he knew the answer to that one.

"It's driving me crazy," she said behind him. "I've been told I have three talents. I never forget a face, I'm great in bed and I make the best damned margaritas this side of Mexico. Do I know you from Seattle? I spent five years out there."

"Sorry, never been there," he said without turning around. He drained his drink and slid off the stool, turning to put the glass on the bar while he dug in his pocket for his wallet.

"Wait a minute!" T.C. cried. "I've got it. You used to come to the Dew Drop Inn outside of Bozeman with that snotty blonde." Jasmine. "And her uptight brother. Oh hell, she's the one I saw in the paper. The one whose car was found near here." Then her eyes narrowed and Kerrington knew what she'd remembered. The last time she'd seen him with Jasmine.

North of Las Vegas, Nevada

"WELL? DOES THE STUPID THING work or not?" Angel demanded, looking over at the computer screen on Vince's lap.

"It works," Vince said, more relieved than he wanted to admit. If he'd lost Molly, he wasn't sure what Angel would have done. He was beginning to wonder if he had the stomach for this anymore.

"So where is she?" Angel snapped.

"She's in Montana."

Angel looked over at him. "What would she be doing in Montana?"

Vince shrugged. "Her car isn't moving."

"You sure she hasn't dumped the car?"

He wasn't sure of anything right now. "She's in Antelope Flats, Montana." Or at least her car was.

"So we're going to Montana."

So it would seem. Vince hoped he was right about Molly not finding the tracking device and ditching her car.

"We'll have to pick up another car," Angel said. "This one is too hot. I'm thinking a car lot. Might not be missed for a while. We'll have to borrow more plates, too."

Vince nodded. He left all of that to Angel. His job was to find Molly. And now that she'd set the cops on them, they wouldn't be safe anywhere. They had to find her fast, get the diamonds and get out of the country.

"Molly wouldn't have run unless she had something to hide," Angel said. "And she wouldn't have called the cops on us."

"She's scared," he said. He knew scared.

"Well, when we find her, she's mine."

Vince looked over at him, imagining what Angel had in mind. It made him sick to his stomach, but he tried not to show his disgust. Angel was on edge, all that nervous tension back in his movements as he drove north.

"Once we have the diamonds, we'll get out of the country." Vince could tell his brother wasn't listening.

Angel had his head cocked to one side, hearing another voice, one that seemed to be getting stronger, a voice Vince now knew he wouldn't be able to override.

Antelope Flats, Montana

"YOU'VE CONFUSED ME with someone else," Kerrington told the bartender as he slapped money on the bar and turned to walk out.

"No way," she called after him. "I never forget a face."

The door closed behind him and he grabbed the wall to hold himself up. T.C. had recognized him, remembered that he'd been with Jasmine at the Dew Drop Inn. What else did she remember?

"Oh hell," he groaned. What was he going to do?

He hurried toward his rental SUV, wanting to get away from the bar in case she followed him outside.

She didn't seem like the type to just let it go. He couldn't believe how badly he'd handled that. He should have admitted the truth. No big deal. Instead he'd pretended he wasn't the guy.

What would she do now? Call the sheriff? He groaned at the thought.

His cell phone rang, making him jump. He fumbled it from his pocket and snapped it open as he climbed into the SUV. "Landow."

"What the hell kind of message did you just leave on my phone?" Bernard barked. "If this was supposed to be some kind of joke—"

"Jasmine's alive. I saw her less than an hour ago."

"Are you drunk?"

"Sober as a judge. She's staying with the sheriff." He

could hear Bernard's breathing increase and knew he had his undivided attention *now*. "She calls herself Molly and is pretending she has amnesia, but believe me, it's Jasmine and I'm afraid she knows exactly what she's doing."

Silence.

"You still there?" He rolled down his window, needing air. He looked back at the Mello Dee, thinking of T.C. "That's not all. Remember that bartender at that out-of-the-way place we used to go to up by Bozeman? The Dew Drop Inn?"

"What?"

"That bar where we used to meet up with Jasmine," Kerrington said. "Remember the bartender who called herself T.C.? She had that line about she was only good at three things: never forgetting a face, great in bed—"

"And she made the best margaritas this side of Mexico," Bernard finished.

"She's working at a bar here in Antelope Flats."

Silence. Then, "What is it you think Jasmine's up to?"

"I don't know. Why are you taking this so calmly?"

"Because it can't be Jasmine," he said. "There's no way. And who the hell cares if a bartender from seven years ago is working in Antelope Flats."

"She recognized me and put me with Jasmine."

"I told you not to go up there," Bernard said. "You should have just let me handle it."

"Yeah? Like you did seven years ago?"

"What is that supposed to mean?" Bernard snapped.

"You're the one who came to me for an alibi."

"That's right, Kerrington. And I never asked you why you so readily lied to give me one."

Kerrington said nothing into the silence.

"Why, after seven years, would Jasmine show up now?" Bernard finally asked.

"She says she saw the story about her car being found, saw her resemblance in the photograph and had to find out who she was."

"What about all that blood the cops found in her car? When the sheriff called me, he said the cops were treating it as a homicide. I doubt they would do that if there was any chance—"

"I don't know, all right? You didn't see her. I did. It's Jasmine. The sheriff sent off her fingerprints. He's waiting for the results. He didn't even want me to tell you that I saw her."

"Who else have you told?" Bernard sounded strange.

"No one. Just you. Who the hell else would I tell?" He thought of Sandra. Is that who Bernard had meant?

Bernard covered the phone and said something Kerrington couldn't hear.

"There someone with you?" Kerrington asked.

"I was talking to my pilot as if it is any of your business," Bernard snapped. "Jasmine mention where she's been?"

"I just saw her for a few minutes before the sheriff threw me out."

"Where are you staying?"

"You know there's only one motel in town. The Lariat." He felt depressed and told himself Sandra wasn't with Bernard. He'd been stupid to think she'd been with him in the first place. And what did it matter if she was?

She'd pretty much tricked him into marrying her. Maybe she would go after Bernard. Would serve him right.

But if she *was* with Bernard, she was on her way to Montana.

"The sheriff ask you any questions about Jasmine's disappearance?" Bernard asked.

"No. Why would he with her being alive?"

"Because this isn't over. Maybe Jasmine is alive. Maybe she's faking amnesia. Or maybe not. Either way, you think the sheriff is going to stop looking for the person who hid her car in that barn? And now you've got some bartender after you?"

"Not just me. The bartender remembered you, too."

"We'll talk when I get there. The sheriff said the state investigators were still searching the farm."

"They are. I saw lights out there as I was driving here, to the bar. They don't know that Jasmine is alive yet."

"Go back to the motel and stay there. You've done enough damage for one night." Bernard hung up.

Kerrington thought he couldn't feel any worse. He wished he hadn't called Bernard, hadn't told him a damned thing. He wished he had a drink. He wished he'd worn a coat. He was cold. And depressed as hell. He rolled up the window. It was colder here than in Georgia.

He tried his home number, left a message for Sandra to call him on his cell and hung up, wondering if she was on the plane with Bernard. Or if she was sitting in the living room refusing to pick up the phone.

He had no choice. He'd have to go back to the motel. Idly he wondered what time T.C. got off work and what would happen if he was waiting for her in the parking lot.

Somewhere over the Midwest

"What's going on?" Sandra said, putting down the magazine she'd been reading as Bernard came back into the airplane cabin.

She was sitting in one of the comfortable chairs, her long legs crossed, that same rabid-dog look on her face that she'd had when he'd boarded his company jet and found her waiting for him.

"I'm going with you," she'd said.

"What are you going to tell Kerrington?"

"I don't give a damn *what* you tell him. I'm hitching a ride. Plain and simple."

Nothing was ever plain and simple when it came to Sandra. He'd wanted to argue, list all the reasons this was a really bad idea. But he'd seen by her expression that she was going. He could have had her thrown off, but he wasn't stupid enough to think that wouldn't have massive repercussions.

"That was Kerrington who called you, wasn't it?" she said eyeing him. "Why else would you leave the room?"

Business. A woman. Any number of reasons. But he wasn't up to arguing with her.

"Good news," he said sarcastically. "Kerrington says he just saw Jasmine." He knew the effect that would have on her. He took a sick pleasure in it when Sandra turned the color of skim milk.

"What?"

"He says she's alive."

"How is that possible?" Sandra asked, her voice a hoarse whisper.

Bernard shook his head and considered telling her the rest. But bringing up a bartender from a place where

Kerrington met Jasmine in secret didn't seem the wise thing to do. Not if Bernard wanted any peace and quiet on this trip.

Sandra already looked stunned from the other news. He decided to leave well enough alone.

But as he sat back down, he gritted his teeth just thinking about Kerrington. The damned fool had done more stupid things in his life than anyone Bernard had ever known, starting with marrying Sandra.

Now he had a bartender who could place him with Jasmine on the day she disappeared. A bartender who had also seen Bernard that day.

Antelope Flats, Montana

CASH WANTED HER to see Jasmine's car?

Molly swallowed, trying to think of a good reason it would be a bad idea. Wasn't it bad enough to steal the woman's identity—even temporarily and for a good cause? Molly was pretty sure that Jasmine had died in that car. Talk about bad karma.

"Is there some reason you wouldn't want to see the car?" Cash asked.

Molly nodded and put down her fork, her appetite suddenly gone. "I'm afraid."

"Of remembering?"

"Just the thought of seeing the car terrifies me," she said truthfully. "But if you feel it's necessary…"

He shook his head. "It can wait. Maybe we'll go out to the ranch early tomorrow. Do you know how to ride a horse?"

Had Jasmine? She hesitated. "I love horses and have ridden some." At once she saw his surprise. Wrong answer?

"You didn't ride seven years ago. In fact, you said you didn't like horses," he said, studying her.

She raised a brow. "More proof I'm not Jasmine. Or maybe I changed my mind."

"Maybe. But it's good that you ride. We have several gentle mares and we wouldn't go far. From horseback is the best way to see the ranch."

"I'm looking forward to it," she said truthfully.

From what she had gathered, the Sundown Ranch was a good ways outside of town. Which meant there was little chance of running into anyone she was supposed to have known.

He smiled. "Good. Let's just have a nice day tomorrow and not worry about anything. How does that sound?"

"Heavenly. Thank you." She wondered why he'd let her off the hook so easily. It didn't matter. She felt as if she'd been given time off, but maybe that's exactly what Cash *wanted* her to think.

She'd felt him studying her during the meal and several times caught him frowning. Tomorrow could be a trap. She'd be a fool to let down her guard. And then there was his mother.

Still, she thought even Shelby McCall was a better bet than Jasmine's brother Bernard. She hoped to put off that encounter as long as possible.

"Did you have enough to eat?"

She nodded and groaned. "Are you kidding? It was the best meal I've ever had."

He laughed, not realizing she really meant it as he shoved back his chair and began clearing the dishes.

She stood as well and took her plate over to the sink. "Dinner was amazing. Thank you again."

He didn't look at her as he began to rinse the dishes and put them in the dishwasher. The old-fashioned kitchen felt cozy and warm, rich with the wonderful smells of dinner. She noticed that he'd made some improvements in here, unlike the rest of the downstairs.

Her gaze lit on his face and she experienced a jolt. Was that a guilty conscience she'd felt? Whatever it was, it made her uncomfortable. She dropped her gaze.

He put soap in the dishwasher and started it. "I could make us some coffee…."

"Not for me, thanks."

"Don't you drink coffee?" he asked.

Immediately she saw that this was a test. Jasmine must have loved coffee.

Well, too bad. She hated coffee and she wasn't drinking it. "I don't like the taste."

"Jasmine didn't like coffee either," he said, surprising her. "At least not unless it was a latte or something that hid the actual taste of the coffee."

Molly said nothing, feeling as if she'd just dodged a bullet.

"I didn't ask you if you'd like dessert. I have some fudge brownies—"

"Please. Don't tempt me." She grinned, licked her lips just thinking about brownies and realized he was staring at her mouth and frowning. "So was it love at first sight?" she asked quickly, wondering if there was something about her mouth that was giving her away.

"What?" He jerked his gaze up to her eyes.

"You and Jasmine, was it love at first sight?"

"Something like that," he said. His gaze settled over her, making her feel too warm. "You must be tired."

She nodded. "It's been quite the day."

"Why don't we talk tomorrow on the way out to the ranch?" he said. "It's been quite the day for me as well."

"I'm sorry I have so many questions."

He shook his head. "It's understandable. I can't imagine what it must be like for you, not knowing who you are."

She nodded, feeling more like a fake than ever. "You're right, I *am* tired."

"I put some towels out in the bathroom," he said.

Suddenly the option of sinking into that claw-foot tub up to her neck in bubbles was all she could think about. "Thank you. For everything." She met his pale blue eyes. They reminded her of bright sunny mornings, clear blue skies and the short periods she'd felt happy in her life.

"My pleasure. Please let me know if you need anything." He seemed to hesitate. "Good night…Molly. I can't tell you how glad I am that you saw that photograph in the paper and came here."

She smiled, wondering if he would feel that way when the fingerprint results came back. "Good night."

But as she started to turn away, she saw him move toward her. Her body anticipated his touch, warming, skin instantly hypersensitive, pulse pounding, a breath catching in her throat.

His fingers brushed her arm, turning her back to face him. He looked into her eyes and she felt something inside her melt as if touched to a flame.

She'd promised herself she wouldn't let him kiss her. A lover's kiss would give her away faster than fingerprint results from the FBI.

But she couldn't move, couldn't breathe, couldn't bear the thought that he might change his mind.

He cupped her cheek with one hand, his eyes never leaving hers as he drew her closer. His other arm slipped around her, pulling her to him.

She looked into all that blue, lost in the wonderful

feel of being sheltered in his arms. She could feel the thump of his heart beneath the soft fabric of his uniform shirt as he drew her closer.

He leaned toward her. She should have drawn back. She should have stopped him.

His mouth dropped to hers. There was nothing tentative about his kiss. It was a lover's kiss, full of pleasure and passion, desire and heat. Her lips parted, opening to him, her body alive with sensation.

It felt so right being in his arms that she forgot who she was. Forgot her promise not to let this happen. Forgot that he thought he was holding Jasmine, the woman he'd loved, not her. Not Molly Kilpatrick.

She pulled back. She was starting to believe her own lies, starting to care for a man who was in love with a ghost. "I…I'm not Jasmine." Her voice broke and she felt hot tears. What was wrong with her?

"No," he said, his voice rough with emotion as he let go of her and stepped back. "You're Molly. Molly Kilpatrick."

She stared at him, her eyes burning with tears. At that moment she would have given anything to be Jasmine. She swallowed, realizing the horrible mistake she'd made. He had to have known that she wasn't the woman she was pretending to be. The kiss had given her away.

"I'm sorry," he said.

No sorrier than her. She waited for him to call her on her lie. He knew now that she wasn't Jasmine, didn't he?

"I promised myself I wouldn't do that," he said.

She nodded slowly, unable to speak.

"Please say you'll still go with me out to the ranch tomorrow. I won't kiss you again."

He still wanted to take her to his family ranch?

"I wanted you to kiss me," she said.

He raised a brow.

"I had hoped it might trigger a memory," she said quickly. She was tired. And foolish. And she couldn't remember the last time a man had kissed her like that.

"But the kiss didn't trigger anything?"

She shook her head, waiting for him to say something about the kiss. He didn't.

"Good night again," he said instead. "Let me know if you need anything. I'm just right down the hall."

"Good night." She hurried to her room before he could see how shaken she was.

The kiss had stirred surprising emotions in her. She didn't want to feel anything for Cash McCall. It was bad enough what she was doing to him by pretending to be Jasmine. She didn't want to start liking the man. Or worse.

Too late for that. Who wouldn't have liked him? He was a nice guy.

All the more reason not to get any more involved than necessary.

She'd known it wouldn't be easy, pulling this off. But she hadn't expected Cash McCall. Not this gentle, loving cowboy who'd waited seven years for the woman he loved.

She could just hear her father saying that Cash was nothing but a small-town sheriff. How wrong her father would be. There was more to Cash McCall than any man she'd ever met. And he was in love with the woman she was pretending to be. Just her luck.

And as luck would have it, he was also the kind of man who wouldn't take being duped lying down.

CASH WASN'T SURE what had awakened him at first. He'd had a terrible time getting to sleep, unable to forget the kiss and the emotions it had evoked.

He'd thought once he kissed her, he would know for certain whether or not she was Jasmine. Instead, the kiss had only further confused him. He hadn't expected to *feel* anything. Not after seven years. Not after everything that had happened.

But he'd *felt* more than just something. The kiss had knocked him off his feet. He had never felt anything like it. Certainly not with Jasmine.

But if this woman *was* Jasmine, what kind of sense did that make? Even more to the point, what if she was a complete stranger who evoked this kind of passion with her kisses like no woman he'd ever known?

He heard a floorboard creak outside his door. Old houses settled constantly. He'd come to know the house's unique sounds. This wasn't one of them.

He quit trying to identify the woman he'd kissed and slipped on his jeans. Whomever she was, she was up, walking around his house.

This woman had…passion. He realized that was the word that best described her. She not only had passion, she also stirred it in him. That made her very dangerous, he realized.

Another floorboard creaked. She was headed down the hallway. He stood perfectly still, listening as the footsteps retreated down the hall toward the stairs.

He waited until he heard the third stair from the top groan, then moved quietly to the door. Carefully, he opened it and looked out just in time to catch a glimpse of her blond head in the moonlight from the window over the stairs.

Maybe she was going downstairs to get a drink of water. Or find those brownies he'd told her about earlier.

Or maybe she was looking for something.

He sneaked down the hall in the dark, trying to avoid the spots on the floor that creaked.

A lower step creaked under her weight. He slowed at the top of the stairs and waited for her to finish her descent. From where he stood out of the light, he could see her dark shadow creeping down the remaining steps as if trying hard to be quiet.

He waited to see which way she went next, hoping she would head for the kitchen and the brownies.

Instead she moved down the hall to his den.

He frowned. Maybe she was sleepwalking and didn't know where she was going.

Right.

She opened the den door and quickly stepped inside. He descended the stairs, stepping over the creaky ones. A thin gold line of light shone under the den door by the time he reached it.

He didn't think sleepwalkers turned on lights or closed doors or made phone calls. He could hear her dialing the phone. She either didn't have a cell phone or it didn't work in Antelope Flats.

He listened but heard only the click of the phone as she hung up.

The light went out under the door. He hurried back down the hall to duck into the dark living room, flattening himself against the wall where he had a view of part of the hallway, the opening to the dark kitchen and the stairs.

She stopped at the entrance to the kitchen as if undecided about something. He heard her say, "No," firmly, then start up the stairs.

He held his breath, afraid she would turn and see him, knowing he would have no explanation for sneaking around in his own house. Her call could have been innocent. Uh-huh.

She didn't get far up the stairs when she stopped, sighed, looked down at her feet and shook her head, then turned and came back down the steps. She disappeared into the dark kitchen.

The light came on. He heard her opening and closing cabinet doors, obviously trying to be quiet. She was looking for the brownies.

He smiled in spite of his concern about the phone call. He heard her find the brownies and the silverware. He heard her open the fridge, pour a glass of milk, close the carton and pull out a chair at the kitchen table.

He peeked around the corner. She was sitting at the kitchen table, her back to him. He eased his way out of his hiding place and crept up the stairs, the sight of her branded into his memory.

Molly sitting cross-legged on the chair in her baby-doll pajamas, her blond hair still wet from her bath, her feet bare, her toes painted with pale pink polish, her legs tanned and long. Nothing about her reminded him of Jasmine just then. And he was surprised that it didn't upset him.

The cop in him reminded that she'd just sneaked down to make a phone call in the middle of the night. His smile faded. The woman had a secret. Probably more than one.

He hurried to his room. A few minutes later, he heard her return to hers. He could assume she was in for the night. He picked up the extension in his bedroom and hit Redial.

A long-distance number came up on the caller ID screen. He waited as the number rang.

"You've reached the answering machine of Lanny Giliano. Can't come to the phone right now. Leave a message. I'll get back to you."

He hung up and checked the area code. Las Vegas, Nevada. That's where she'd said she'd been most recently.

And apparently she'd called a man there. Of course there would be a man in her life, he thought ruefully. Especially if she was Jasmine.

CHAPTER TEN

MOLLY WOKE TO the smell of fresh-perked coffee and cinnamon rolls and the sound of a soft tap on her door after the best night of sleep she'd ever had.

It helped that she hadn't had to get up early to evacuate the room so she wasn't caught by some energetic hotel maid. The brownie and glass of milk she'd eaten in the middle of the night hadn't hurt either.

But her call to Lanny had produced no news. Had the police found him? Was it possible he was still alive?

She'd climbed into the bed last night, the sheets smelling of sunshine, after soaking in the claw-foot tub and had dropped right off. Her last thought before she'd fallen asleep was Cash, followed quickly by the admonition, *Don't get used to this.*

Then she'd woken in the middle of the night thinking about Lanny. Needing to know what was happening. Last night though, she'd just hung up, afraid she'd made a mistake calling Lanny's again.

She sat up now, pulling the covers to her chin. "Come in," she called. Her heart took off at the memory of their kiss, but she rounded it back up. *Remember, he thinks you're Jasmine.*

The door opened and he came in with a tray. A cup of

coffee for himself, a large glass of milk for her and two huge warm cinnamon rolls cut in slices and buttered. There was also a small bouquet of flowers.

She couldn't help the smile that burst out at the sight of him—and the tray of food and flowers. No one had ever brought her breakfast in bed. Certainly no one who ever looked like Cash McCall. This was like a dream she never wanted to wake up from.

He dragged up a chair. "Sleep well?"

She nodded eagerly, feeling only a little guilty about her middle-of-the-night phone call. She wanted to tell him the truth, hated that she was deceiving him. But she couldn't chance that Vince and Angel were still on the loose and looking for her. And she didn't want to leave here. Not yet.

He handed her the glass of milk and she helped herself to one of the slices of cinnamon rolls. She groaned, closing her eyes and licking her lips. She heard his soft laugh and opened her eyes again.

"My sister-in-law Cassidy made those," he said of the cinnamon rolls. "She owns the Longhorn Café. Best cook around."

She heard the admiration in his voice. "She's married to your brother…."

"Rourke. They just got back from their honeymoon." He looked down into his coffee cup as if uncomfortable. If Jasmine hadn't disappeared he would have been married now too.

They ate in a companionable silence. It felt odd having a man in her bedroom. Probably because it had been so long since she'd even had a date. And then there was that kiss they'd shared last night. She'd sworn she'd seen fireworks.

She studied him from under her lashes, worried that after the kiss last night he knew she wasn't Jasmine.

But as they finished the rolls and he drained his coffee cup, he rose and said, "I thought we'd head out to the ranch this morning as soon as you're ready." He seemed shy, hesitant.

She flashed him a smile. "Thank you for breakfast. It was wonderful. I've never had breakfast in bed before." She caught herself. "At least not that I can remember."

He smiled. "I'll see you downstairs. Wear something comfortable."

When she was dressed in jeans, a shirt and tennis shoes, she went down. "Cash?" No answer. "Cash?"

As she passed the closed den door, she heard him in there on the phone. She wanted to get a hat she'd left in her car. The garage was separate from the house, so she opened the front door and stepped out.

The day was beautiful, the sky crystalline blue, the mountains in the distance snowcapped. Closer, a breeze stirred the boughs of the pines around the house. From here, she couldn't even see another house, and only the glimpses of other buildings toward town through more trees.

She walked out to the garage and had just started to open the door when she heard someone behind her.

Turning, she came face-to-face with Kerrington. She hadn't seen his car. But she should have smelled his cologne. It was a nauseating scent that had mixed with his sweat. He looked as if he had either slept in his clothes or hadn't been to bed at all.

"We need to talk," he said gruffly. "The sheriff isn't here, so you can drop the act." He glanced toward the house, then grabbed her arm and pulled her to the side of the garage, away from the house under a large old pine.

Beyond the trees there was nothing on this side of the house but open land to the west, red sandy bluffs, sagebrush and a few dark pines against the horizon. A thought sped by: could Cash hear her in the house if she screamed?

"What did you tell him?" Kerrington demanded, her unease growing at the agitated look in his eyes.

"What?" Cash would have no idea where she'd gone. And Kerrington was scaring her.

"I didn't sleep at all last night," he said as if it were her fault.

She'd slept like a baby, once she'd put the kiss out of her mind. And once she'd had that brownie and milk. "What is it you want?"

"When are you going to tell him?"

"I don't know what you're talking about."

"About us," he snapped.

Us? "I told you. I'm not Jasmine and I don't know what you're talking about." He was obviously angry and she didn't like being alone with him. She started to step past him but he grabbed her arm and jerked her to him. She slammed into his chest, his grip on her arm tightening.

"You and I both know your...engagement to Cash McCall was a sham and not the romantic love story that's been in all the papers," Kerrington said with a sneer. "You were seeing me behind the sheriff's back. You love *me*."

Jasmine had been having an affair with Kerrington while engaged to Cash? "I don't believe you," she snapped, jerking her arm free and stepping back from him.

"There is no one here but the two of us," he said, almost pleading now. "What's going on. Please, Jasmine." His gaze met hers and Molly saw pain there. He really had loved Jasmine. Was it possible Jasmine had felt the same way about him? "You can't have forgotten what we had together."

An affair. Behind Cash's back. That part she saw wasn't a lie. She felt sick with the knowledge. "I'm not Jasmine. Now, let me pass."

"You're making a big mistake," he said through gritted teeth as he stepped closer.

"You're the one making the mistake," said a rough-edged male voice behind Kerrington.

Kerrington whirled around, his face blanching at the sight of Sheriff Cash McCall behind him. He stepped back, obviously seeing the fierceness in Cash's eyes, the set of his jaw, the clenched fist.

"Jasmine and I were just…talking," Kerrington said.

"Really? It almost sounded as if you were threatening her," Cash said. A muscle jumped in his jaw and Molly could see that it was taking every ounce of restraint in him not to attack Kerrington physically.

He shot her a glance. "Are you all right?"

She nodded, but he would have been a fool not to see that she was shaken. And Cash McCall, she was learning, was no fool. She wondered how much of the conversation he'd overheard. And hated the thought that he might have heard about the affair.

Cash turned to Kerrington again. "I think you'd better leave."

Kerrington nodded in agreement and shot her a look

she couldn't read. She just knew she didn't want to meet him in a dark alley. He turned and walked down the street toward Main Street without looking back.

A silence fell between her and Cash. She didn't know what to say. But she could see that he was still angry. She prayed he hadn't overheard all of their conversation. He'd loved Jasmine. Hadn't been able to move on with his life even after all this time. She couldn't bear the thought of him being hurt. Especially by Kerrington.

She couldn't help but think about what Cash had said about Jasmine leaving the gas station with someone she knew. Kerrington? Had he gotten away with murder?

If that was the case, no wonder he was so upset at seeing a woman he thought was Jasmine.

Molly was beginning to realize the danger she'd put herself in. Kerrington believed she was Jasmine. Was it possible that if he'd thought he'd killed Jasmine, that he might do just as Cash had feared and try to finish the job before she remembered?

She shivered, remembering the look in Kerrington's eyes.

"Are you ready?" Cash asked, none of the usual warmth or concern in his voice.

With a shock, she realized he was angry with her. He thought she was Jasmine. How much had he heard? She wanted to deny everything, deny she was Jasmine, but she realized right then he wouldn't have believed her even if she had confessed everything.

"I just need to get my hat out of my car," she said, feeling sick with shame for an affair she'd never had, for hurting a man she found herself caring about more and more all the time.

"I'll get it for you," he said and disappeared into the garage.

She leaned against the garage wall, miserable with what she'd learned. Cash had definitely fallen in love with the wrong woman. Is that why his mother had reacted to her the way she had? Did she know about Jasmine's affair with Kerrington?

And now they were headed out to the ranch. Molly groaned inwardly. She'd put herself in danger on all fronts. What did she expect pretending to be another woman? This had turned out to be even more reckless than she'd first thought. And heartbreaking as well, she thought as Cash came out with her hat.

CASH WAS STILL SHAKING with anger as he loaded a small picnic basket into his newer model red pickup. He tried not to think about Kerrington or the phone call he'd had just moments before that.

He'd wanted to hit Kerrington. But it wasn't the first time and he doubted it would be the last.

He hadn't heard Jasmine leave the house. He'd been on the phone with State Investigator John Mathews. Mathews had called to tell him that he was being relieved as sheriff pending the conclusion of the investigation.

"You're taking this better than I expected," Mathews had said.

Cash had wanted to tell him that Jasmine might be alive. But he heard himself say, "Not much I can do about it. With luck, the case will be solved soon."

Mathews had cleared his throat and Cash had known there was more coming. He had held his breath, afraid Mathews would tell him that they'd found Jasmine's body.

"There was a murder. Coroner puts it at about 4:00 a.m. The bartender out at the Mello Dee."

With a shock, Cash had realized he hadn't been called. So he'd been relieved of his duties yesterday and Mathews just hadn't told him.

"Name was Teresa Clark. You know her?" Mathews had asked.

For a moment, Cash had wondered if he was a suspect in her murder, too. Then he'd realized that the question was a normal one given that he was from here and Mathews was out of Billings, hours away.

"No, but I heard the Mello Dee had sold and was under new management," he'd said.

"We'll be investigating the murder, along with still searching the farm for…remains." Remains.

Cash had said nothing, waiting for what had to be coming next.

"That blue paint chip you took from Jasmine Wolfe's car," Mathews had said. "The lab says it's from a Ford pickup. I believe you drove a blue Ford pickup seven years ago."

Cash had closed his eyes. "A lot of people drove blue Ford pickups seven years ago. It must have been their most popular color."

Mathews had said nothing. "Where can I reach you if I need to talk to you?"

"Just give me a call on my cell phone. I'm not going anywhere."

Mathews had sounded relieved to hear that.

As Cash had hung up, he'd caught a glimpse of Kerrington through the window. By the time he reached the front door, Kerrington was dragging Jasmine around the side of the garage.

Cash raked a hand through his hair now and swore, remembering what he'd overhead.

Molly came up behind him. He didn't turn. Didn't want to face her right now. What he'd heard between her and Kerrington had him too upset and he didn't want her to see that. Didn't want her to know what he was feeling right now.

"Cash?"

He felt her hand on his back, the heat coursing through him to his core. He took a breath and let it out slowly before he finally turned and forced himself to smile. "We couldn't have picked a more beautiful day for a horseback ride around the ranch."

MOLLY TRIED TO RELAX as she climbed into the front seat of Cash's pickup. They wouldn't be taking the patrol car. She was thankful for that, thinking this way they would attract less attention.

Cash was still upset. He was trying to hide it, but she'd been reading people for too much of her life not to see it. She was torn with a need to warn Cash that she believed Kerrington might have killed Jasmine—and yet not give herself away.

"I was thinking about what you said yesterday about Jasmine not getting into a car except with someone she knew," Molly said carefully.

He shot her a look. "You think she got into the car with Kerrington."

"He is so angry."

Cash didn't drive downtown, but seemed to wander the gravel backstreets, coming out on the edge of town on Main Street, as if he didn't want to be seen. Didn't want her to be seen.

Molly slumped down a little in the seat, not wanting another confrontation this morning. If they could just get out of town—

"He does seem awfully angry with Jasmine," Cash said without looking at her. "Any idea what that is about?"

Not a clue since she wasn't Jasmine.

"I just thought I should warn you," she said.

He looked over at her and smiled. "Thanks for your concern."

She couldn't tell if he was being sincere or not. She shut up and looked out the window, worried what Kerrington would do next.

As Cash turned onto the main highway, Molly looked up and saw a car driving slowly into town. She spotted the Nevada license plates first. Her gaze flew to the two men behind the windshield. Vince and Angel.

Her heart dropped. They'd found her? She flung herself forward, pretending she'd dropped something, as the car slowly passed them. Had they seen her?

"Are you all right?" Cash asked.

"Fine. I just dropped my…lipstick on the floor." Vince and Angel were in town. It was impossible. Even if they'd followed her…. Not that it mattered. All that mattered was that they'd found her—and she had to disappear and quickly.

She had a tube of lip gloss in her purse. Bent over, she did a sleight of hand, and straightened, the gloss in her fingers. She held it up, smiled foolishly. "Got it."

As she leaned back, she checked the side mirror. The car had turned in to the Longhorn Café.

"Darn," Cash said. "I forgot. I need to run one quick errand before we go out to the ranch. You don't mind do you?"

SHE DID MIND. Cash could see fear in her expression, the same fear he'd seen when she'd spotted the car. Her skin had blanched white under her tan. She looked as if she'd seen a ghost or worse. Nor had he been fooled by why she'd ducked down as the two men had driven by. Nevada plates. Didn't she say she'd been in Las Vegas?

He'd quickly glanced in his side mirror and memorized the license plate number as she'd bent to retrieve her lipstick. He hadn't seen where she'd pulled it from, but he was positive she hadn't dropped it.

"I just need to talk to my sister-in-law for minute," he said, swinging the pickup around. The two men had gotten out of the car with the Nevada plates and were headed into the Longhorn Café. One was big, the other short and wiry-looking. "I told you she owns the only café in town."

He thought Jasmine might have a heart attack.

"The café?" she said a little breathlessly, looking down the street as the two men disappeared inside the café. That was definitely fear in her expression. No mistaking it. Who were the men? And why was she was so frightened of them?

"Why don't I drop you by the house," he said. "I'm not sure how long this will take. I'm sorry."

She was so relieved, he almost felt guilty for letting her think he was taking her to the café where the two men had gone. Almost. What was she hiding from him? Something to do with the men. Well, he would find out soon enough.

He stopped in front of the house. "The door's open. I won't be long. I promise."

She smiled and got out. "Don't hurry on my account."

Would she try to take off while he was gone?

"Oh, shoot, I need to get something from the garage first." He got out. "Make yourself at home." He waited. She stood for a moment on the sidewalk then headed for the house. He waited until she was inside before he stepped into the garage to make sure her car wasn't going anywhere.

MOLLY COULDN'T QUIT SHAKING. Vince and Angel were in town. How could they have found her? Not that it mattered. She had to get away. *Now.*

She hurried upstairs, threw her few belongings into her suitcase and carried it downstairs. Peering out the front window, she saw with a sigh of relief that Cash hadn't returned. She felt awful running out on him like this. She would call him when she was far enough away he couldn't find her. Not that he'd come looking for her—once she told him the truth.

Opening the door, she stepped out with her suitcase and turned to close the door behind her.

"Going somewhere?" asked a voice behind her.

CASH PARKED HIS PICKUP behind the Longhorn Café and hurried in through the back door. His sister-in-law's office was just inside. He stepped into it and waited to catch her attention, motioning her to join him.

"Two men just came into the café. I need their prints," he said without preamble. He'd known Cassidy his whole life. He'd always thought of her as a sister, which was fortunate since she'd been in love with his brother Rourke since the two were kids.

Cassidy smiled and lifted a brow. "Okay. Nice to see you too, Cash. The honeymoon? Oh, it was wonderful. Your brother Rourke? He's fine."

"Sorry. I don't have much time."

"It's okay." Her smile faded. "I heard the news about Jasmine's car being found. I'm sorry."

He nodded.

"So let me guess which two men you want prints on," she said. She described the two who'd just come in. "Both look like they've had some time to lift weights not to mention the prison tattoos."

Cash wasn't surprised. "Get me their prints if you can on anything they touch. I'll stop by later. Thanks. I really appreciate this. I wouldn't ask but—"

"No need to explain. We're family," she said. "Any time you need *anything...*"

He smiled. "Thanks." He couldn't wait to get back to Jasmine but he had to make one more stop. His office. There was a chance Frank might have sent him the fingerprint results.

He rolled down his window, needing the fresh air to collect his thoughts as he drove the few blocks to his office. He wanted to rush back to the house and make her tell him about the men at the café. And the phone call she'd made last night. He wanted to demand answers. But part of him was afraid she would tell him that she wasn't Jasmine, and that was something he didn't want to hear. Not yet.

One thing was clear. Whomever this woman was, she was in some kind of trouble. But was she in trouble because she was Jasmine? Or because she wasn't?

MOLLY SPUN AROUND TO SEE a tall, slim woman with long dark hair pulled back from a pale, narrow face. Beside her was a smaller woman with mousy-brown hair done in a style much too old for her. She seemed to be standing back as if almost afraid.

"Well," the taller of the two said on a hasty breath. "You really *are* alive."

Molly couldn't miss the knife edge to her voice. "I'm sorry, do I know you?"

The woman laughed. "I heard you were having trouble remembering. I'm Sandra. Your best friend."

The way Sandra said it, Molly assumed Sandra and Jasmine had been anything *but* best friends.

"And this is Patty Franklin," she said dismissively. "We were your roommates."

Molly looked at Patty, then Sandra. "I'm afraid you've gotten the wrong impression…."

"Cut the crap and invite us in," Sandra said and looked toward the door to the house. "You're not going anywhere."

Molly looked into Sandra's face and saw that she would do whatever it took to keep her from leaving. Picking up her suitcase from where she'd set it on the porch, Molly pushed open the door, seeing no way to avoid this. Telling the women she wasn't Jasmine wouldn't do the trick. No one believed her. Molly had done too good of a job becoming Jasmine.

Once in the living room, Molly motioned to the bar and Sandra poured herself a drink, then lit a cigarette. Patty stood, looking nervous and unsure. Molly hurried to find something Sandra could use as an ashtray. If she could get rid of the women before Cash returned—

"Okay, let's have it," Sandra snapped, then took a

drag on her cigarette, glaring at her through the smoke as she exhaled.

"I beg your pardon?" Molly said.

"What is it you want? Kerrington? He's yours. Half Bernard's money? Get a good lawyer, but I'm sure you can have that, too. What else can we give you?" Sandra sounded close to tears, which surprised Molly.

"I don't want anything."

Sandra laughed again, a sharp painful sound. "Oh, you *always* want something. Usually something someone else has."

Molly looked over at Patty. "Did you all hate Jasmine that much?" She couldn't hide her surprise or horror.

Sandra narrowed her gaze again. "Are we back to you pretending you're not Jasmine again?"

"I know I look like Jasmine but my name is Molly. Molly Kilpatrick."

Sandra sneered at her. "Can we just be honest with each other for a minute? It's just us girls."

"Okay," Molly said. "Why don't you start with telling me why someone would want me dead?"

Sandra laughed. "You don't know? You play with people's lives for your own amusement."

"Kerrington," Molly guessed.

Sandra stiffened. "You don't love him. You never did. You just didn't want me to have him."

"I'm sorry."

Sandra's eyes were bright and hard with tears. She shook her head as if she didn't believe her.

"Look, the sheriff sent off my fingerprints so they can be compared with Jasmine's," Molly said. "We'll know in a week or so if I'm Jasmine. But I can tell you right now, I'm not. I don't expect you to believe me," she continued before Sandra could argue the point. "But you have nothing to fear from me. I don't want Kerrington or Bernard's money or…" She looked at Patty, having almost forgotten about her. The woman looked scared and Molly wondered what she feared Jasmine might want from her. "Or to hurt any of you."

"If what you say is true, and these fingerprint results will be back in a week and prove you aren't Jasmine," Sandra said, "then where are you taking off to in such a hurry?"

"I have some personal business I need to take care of, which has to do with me being Molly Kilpatrick—not Jasmine Wolfe," she said honestly.

"Right. Whatever you're up to, Jazz, we aren't going to let you destroy our lives," Sandra said. "Not anymore. Don't try to leave town. We're going to finish this before any of us leave, understand?"

Sandra's threat might have scared her if Molly didn't have two felons after her—one who loved to cut up people.

"Let's go, Patty," Sandra said. Patty hadn't uttered a word the entire time.

As the women left, Molly heard Cash's pickup pull up out front. She groaned and hurriedly stashed her suitcase behind the couch.

As Sandra and Patty left, Molly saw them pass Cash on the walk. He turned to watch them get into a silver rental sedan and drive away, then turned to see her standing on the porch.

"I guess the word is out," he said. "You all right?"

She nodded. What did it matter if everyone found out about her now? Vince and Angel had already found her. "Sandra and Patty, roommates of Jasmine's, just wanted to stop by for a talk."

"And?" He looked worried.

"They think I want something from them. They just don't know what yet."

His look said he thought the same thing. "Ready to go? It's about ten miles out to the ranch," he said, as if he suspected there was nothing she wanted more than to distance herself from here right now.

"Great," she said. "I'm ready." This wasn't what she'd planned when she'd packed her suitcase, but at least she would get out of town for a day. Then tonight, when Cash was asleep, she would retrieve her suitcase from behind the couch and leave.

CHAPTER ELEVEN

MOLLY ROLLED DOWN her window as Cash had done,
letting the wind whip at her short hair. She closed her
eyes and tried to breathe. The late morning air chilled
her. She tried to calm down, to think.

Vince and Angel were in town. They'd found her. Or
at least found out what town she was in—and given the
size of Antelope Flats, it wouldn't be long before they
knew where she was hiding.

She couldn't believe what a mess she'd made of
things. Antelope Flats was the one place she'd never
expected to be found. Nor that she was jeopardizing
Cash's life just by being with him. She had to leave as
soon as possible.

She thought about telling him the truth. But why
would he believe her? He was convinced she was Jasmine. As sheriff, he could keep her from leaving, thinking he could protect her. She wouldn't endanger his
life. Even Cash McCall was no match for Vince and
Angel.

"That's the Tongue River Reservoir," Cash said as
the pickup climbed a long hill.

She looked in the direction he'd pointed and saw the
pool of blue against the red rock bluffs. "It's beautiful."

"The legend is Native Americans named the river
the Tongue because of the way it winds."

Like a forked tongue, she thought, as the rolling countryside blurred past. The air smelled of summer and water, sage and pine. Wild grasses ran bright green to silver sage. On the rocky bluffs, dark green pine trees stood against the clear blue of the summer sky.

She tried to relax. They would be safe at the ranch, then tonight as soon as Cash was asleep—

"Those are the Bighorn Mountains," Cash said, pointing in the other direction.

The mountains were the same snowcapped ones she'd seen from his house this morning. They stretched across the horizon, deep purple except for the snow-covered tips.

"We run our cattle on summer range up there," he said as he turned onto a dirt road.

"How many cows do you have?"

"That's something you never ask a rancher."

"I'm sorry," she said quickly and he laughed.

"It's all right. I don't mind. We run about a thousand head and still keep longhorns mostly just for tradition since they were what the ranch was started with. Our main herd is Herefords."

She heard the pride in his voice. "I'm surprised you became a sheriff instead of staying on the ranch."

"Oh, I still help ranch. It's in my blood," he said. "But I needed to do my own thing." He was silent after that.

She stared out at the land. What could keep a person here where there was little more than rocks and trees? Just inertia. That's what Max had always said kept most men in one place. Laziness or inertia. "They just don't know or want any better."

Not that moving around had seemed to make her life better or her father's. But it did fight boredom. She feared she would grow stagnant if she stayed too long in one place. But then she didn't seem to belong anywhere.

Dust boiled up behind them as the road trailed alongside a sparkling creek. The water rushed in a tumble of white spray through large boulders, pooling dark in eddies, hedged in by bright red bushes.

"That's Rosebud Creek," Cash said. "Those are wild rosebushes growing along the edge. The taller trees are cottonwoods and willows."

"What are those?" she asked.

"The red? Dogwood. The other bushes are chokecherry trees. By the end of August the branches will be heavy with fruit."

She looked over at him, hearing a kind of reverence in his voice. "How long have you lived here?"

He laughed. "I was born here. So was my father. As I mentioned last night, my grandfather brought one of the first herds of longhorn cattle to Montana from Texas. The minute he saw this land, he knew he'd found his home."

What was it like to have roots that ran that deep? As she looked out at the countryside, she tried to imagine being one of the first white men to see this. The landscape looked inhospitable to her. She couldn't imagine fighting to tame even a small part of it for a home.

"Was your grandfather married?" she asked, unable to see a woman wanting to live this far away from civilization even now let alone a hundred years ago.

Cash laughed at her question. "Not at the time." He was smiling at her.

"What?"

"You're trying to imagine why anyone would live out here."

She started to deny it, then laughed. "Sorry. I've always lived in cities."

"At least the part of your life you remember," he said.

She realized her mistake. "Yes."

As they came over a rise, he said, "There's the ranch." He drove under a huge log entry that read: Sundown Ranch.

She remembered the old cabin she'd seen in the photograph last night in the hallway at his house. But what she saw instead made her catch her breath. A cluster of buildings, the barns red-roofed, the house at the center rambling and huge, scattered across a grass carpet.

The ranch house was built of logs, just like the first homestead, but these logs were massive and golden in the sun. There was a tan rock chimney that towered up one side and a porch that ran across the entire front of the house.

She remembered the photograph she'd seen on Cash's desk, the one of his family, and knew it had been shot on that very porch.

The memory, like the ranch house, sparked a yearning she'd never felt before. Not for the ranch or the beautiful home. But for the family. Tears burned her eyes.

She hurriedly wiped at them. "I had no idea it was so…" She waved a hand through the air, unable to find the right words.

"My father built the house. It's nothing like the places you've lived."

He was right about that—just not in the way he meant, she thought as he pulled into the yard and cut the engine.

She stared at the sprawling two-story, log ranch house with its red tin roof and tried to imagine what it would be like to grow up here, to be raised in a large family like that. It was beyond her imagination.

Through the big window, she could see the wide staircase, almost feel the homey, inviting warmth of the furnishings. She was hit again with that sense of yearning. It felt a lot like the emotion she'd experienced last night when Cash had taken her in his arms and kissed her.

The need to run practically made her throw open her door and take off at a trot. She was just beginning to realize what she'd gotten herself into. Even if Vince and Angel hadn't come to town, she needed to leave. Even if Jasmine's enemies didn't want to kill her again, she needed to distance herself from this place, from these people. She'd thought she would be safe here. She'd been wrong on all counts.

Nothing was safe about getting this close to Cash. Or his family. Her very thoughts weren't safe, let alone the emotions Cash evoked in her. She would leave him a note confessing everything. He wouldn't come after her. She was sure of that. He would be too disgusted.

He had climbed out of the pickup and gone around to open her door for her. She'd been so wrapped up in her thoughts that she'd hardly noticed. But now she felt shy, as if they were on a date, and anxious about meeting his family and seeing his mother again. If she could just get through this day—

"I should warn you," Cash said as he led her up the steps to the porch. "My family can be—" The front door flew open. Molly could hear raised voices as a young woman emerged from the house, slamming the door behind her, then halting in surprise to see them on the porch.

"—a little much," Cash finished. "Dusty?"

The young woman was pretty, dressed in western

attire with blond hair pulled back into a ponytail, no makeup, and even paler blue eyes than Cash's.

"Dusty?" he said again.

The young woman's eyes widened at the sight of Jasmine. Obviously Shelby had warned the rest of the family.

"This is Molly," Cash said, as if purposely not calling her Jasmine.

Dusty continued to stare.

Molly could see that Cash's sister was both curious—and protective of her brother.

"But Shelby said—"

Cash made a strangled sound. "She looks like Jasmine but we haven't verified that she is yet. So for simplicity's sake, let's call her Molly."

Molly felt a surge of gratitude toward him. He was trying to protect her. Maybe especially from his mother, and whatever Dusty and Shelby had been just fighting about.

Dusty seemed to make up her own mind. She threw her arms around Molly's neck.

Molly stiffened for a moment in surprise, then raised her arms and embraced the young woman, looking over her shoulder at Cash in surprise.

He groaned again. "Dusty, you're embarrassing her."

Dusty pulled back, her eyes full of tears. "I just know how much my brother loves you, how much he's missed you. Whatever happened in the past, it doesn't matter. The two of you belong together."

Molly felt the full weight of the young woman's words. "Dusty, I might not be Jasmine—"

Dusty smiled and cut her eyes to her brother. "Don't

you think Cash would know his own fiancée? The love of his life?"

It would seem so, Cash thought, looking over at Molly. She seemed different today. In fact, when he looked at her, he wondered what had made him so sure she was Jasmine. She was so different from the woman he'd known.

But like Jasmine, this woman had secrets. And that alone almost convinced him she was Jasmine. That and the fact that he needed Jasmine to be alive for strictly selfish reasons.

And by tonight, his friend at the FBI would have called with the fingerprint results.

"What's going on?" he asked Dusty, indicating whatever he and Molly had interrupted.

"*Shelby,*" Dusty said, as if that explained it all.

"I thought the two of you were closer after working on Rourke and Cassidy's wedding," he said.

Dusty rolled her eyes. "Like one wedding is going to change everything?"

He realized it was a subject best dropped as his father appeared in the doorway. Cash tried to see Asa McCall through Molly's eyes. A large, still solid man, his blond hair graying at the temples, his eyes a blue much like Cash's. There was strength of character in his weathered face and in his ramrod-straight posture.

Cash had always respected his father. Not that he wasn't acutely aware of his faults.

"This is my father, Asa McCall," he said, feeling a sense of pride that surprised him.

Molly stepped forward, her hand outstretched. "Please call me Molly. It's an honor to meet you, sir."

Asa seemed amused. "My pleasure."

Shelby appeared then. Clearly, she had intended to ignore Jasmine.

"It is so nice to see you again," Molly said extending her hand.

Shelby had no choice but to take it. Her expression seemed to change from cool indifference to a scowl. Cash promised himself he wouldn't leave here without finding out why his mother hated Jasmine so.

"I feel like we got off on the wrong foot," Molly was saying to Shelby. "I know I look like Jasmine but I don't feel like her. I have little knowledge of her. I'm finding out things about her though that are very disturbing. Especially her behavior before she disappeared."

Shelby's eyes narrowed at such frankness.

"If I'm Jasmine, I'm very sorry if I hurt your son," Molly said. "I can't imagine a woman who wouldn't appreciate everything about Cash. He's a wonderful man who deserves to be happy."

Shelby seemed to thaw right before his eyes. Cash had never seen anything like it.

"We're going for a ride around the ranch," he said into the uncomfortable silence. "We'll be back in plenty of time for dinner."

"I would like to help," Molly said. "I'm not used to being waited on." She blushed. "At least not during any of the life I can recall."

"Come into the kitchen when you return," Shelby said. "I'm sure I can find something for you to do."

Molly smiled. "I'll do that."

Cash quickly ushered her out of the house. It wasn't until they were headed for the horse barn, out of earshot of the house, that he looked over at her. "How did you do that?"

She seemed surprised. "What?"

"Shelby. My mother. You completely turned her around in there. How did you do that?"

Molly laughed. He could no longer remember how Jasmine laughed, no longer cared. More and more, this woman was becoming Molly to him. Jasmine would never have handled his mother like that. Jasmine would have gotten mad, done her I'm-superior-to-all-of-you-people routine and made an enemy of his mother for life.

Molly's laugh hung for a moment in the clear morning air. "I don't know what you're talking about," she said, head held high as she headed off across the field ahead of him.

He watched her for a moment, thinking he didn't know this woman but he wanted to.

Molly smiled when Cash caught up to her. He chuckled softly as he walked beside her, realizing how much he liked her. He found himself half hoping she wasn't Jasmine, even knowing that would mean he'd still be a suspect in Jasmine's murder.

MOLLY GLANCED OVER at the man beside her as they fell into a companionable silence. She refused to think about tomorrow. She would enjoy this day, enjoy Cash and take the memory with her.

"See that tree," Cash said. "I fell out of it when I was five and broke my leg. It was J.T.'s fault. He said I couldn't climb as high as he could."

"But you did," she said, smiling over at him.

He laughed. "Oh yeah."

The day was bright, the sky a clear, deep blue, the cool morning air filling her lungs, filling her with…happiness.

The word surprised her, but she realized she *was*

happy, a word she wouldn't have used to describe most of her life.

Cash made her feel good. So did his family. She'd even made progress with his mother. She knew none of that should have mattered. She had to leave tonight. She would never see any of them again.

But for today, she'd let herself be happy. She'd enjoy being a part of his family. She was safe. She wouldn't think about tonight. Or tomorrow. For today, she wasn't running anywhere.

"I thought you might like to ride Baby," Cash said as he pushed open the barn door and led her to one of the stalls.

The mare raised her head, blinked big brown eyes at Molly and came over to nudge her hand on the gate. Molly heard Cash's intake of air.

"She likes you," he said.

Molly rubbed the white star between Baby's ears, surprised by the connection she felt. She'd never had a pet as a kid. Not with her and Max moving all the time. Not as an adult for the same reason. The horse was spotted brown and white and reminded her of western movies she'd seen. "What is she?"

"A pinto."

"She's beautiful."

"She's yours. As long as you're here," he added and looked embarrassed.

No one had ever offered her something so wonderful and with such generosity. She felt tears spring to her eyes as she stared at him. "No one has ever given me..." Her voice broke. He'd meant this horse for Jasmine. Not for the first time, she wished she *was* Jasmine. To be loved by this man... "Cash, thank you. That's so..."

"Romantic?" He laughed softly and touched her cheek.

The truth was like a stone in her throat. "But I'm not—"

"I know, you're Molly." He smiled. "Baby's very gentle. I broke her myself. You ready to ride her?"

Molly nodded. She was touched that she would get to ride her because she knew Jasmine never would.

She stood back and watched him as he saddled Baby and another larger horse named Zeke. She liked watching Cash's hands, the way they touched the horses, the way they worked. She understood the calluses she'd seen on those hands, this rancher, cowboy sheriff.

They rode behind the ranch house through deep wild grass up into the stands of aspens, the leaves rustling in the morning breeze.

"You ride well," Cash commented.

She had ridden horses when Max had been involved with a traveling Wild West show for a while. She felt at ease on Baby, felt even more at ease with Cash.

She watched his face, saw a peace in his expression that she hadn't seen in the time she'd known him. This was his home. This land. She envied him the way she had never sought money or fame. She envied him this place that made him so content.

The air smelled of pine as they rode higher, until they were on a bench overlooking the ranch. Cash dismounted and lifted Molly from Baby. The sun burned down on them. She walked to the edge of the bluff and looked out across the land. McCall land. She felt a lump in her throat. What it must be like to have a connection to all of this, a history, a future. "It's so peaceful."

"I thought we could have lunch by the creek," Cash

said as he took off his saddlebag and motioned toward an outcropping of rocks and trees.

She could hear water running as she neared the trees. As she wound her way through the huge boulders, she came upon a picturesque creek. The water pooled among the rocks before tumbling down the mountainside.

Molly stepped to a flat spot at the edge of one of the clear blue pools, the water gurgling around the smooth boulders. "It looks so inviting," she said, already reaching down to unlace her tennis shoes.

Cash spread the blanket he'd brought under a huge pine and set down the picnic lunch he'd packed. When he turned, the last thing he expected was to see her with her shoes and socks off and stepping into the creek.

"The water is deeper than it looks and the rocks are slip—"

He didn't get his warning out before she slid into the pool and disappeared beneath the water. Hell. Did she know how to swim? Did she even know if she knew how to swim?

He raced to the edge of the creek, ready to jump in, clothes, boots, hat and all, when her head burst out of the water in a shower of droplets.

She was laughing, the water droplets glistening around her in the sunlight, her green eyes dancing and that wonderful laugh of hers hanging in the air.

He rocked back, taken completely off guard by the rush of feelings at just the sight of her. She looked like a drowned rat and couldn't have been more beautiful, soaking wet and laughing in that blue-green pool of water.

She also couldn't have looked less like Jasmine.

He put out his hand to help her out. She took it, still laughing. "I only meant to get my feet wet."

He shook his head. "I thought I was going to have to dive in and save you."

She came out of the water and shook her blond head, sending spray into the air. Her hair was curly now, not straight like she'd been wearing it. It cupped her face, making her green eyes seem larger, definitely brighter. The makeup she'd applied that morning had washed off.

He noticed for the first time that she had a sprinkling of light freckles across her cheeks and nose.

"Boy was *that* refreshing," she said grinning at him.

He caught his breath as his eyes locked with hers. This woman wasn't Jasmine. The shock rattled through him. He didn't need fingerprint results. He knew, soul deep. He grabbed her, gripping her upper arms, turning her to face him.

Molly saw his expression change an instant before he grabbed her. He looked as if he were about to say something, but then his mouth dropped to hers.

It was so unexpected, her breath caught, her lips parted and she kissed him back.

The kiss didn't last half a minute before Cash pulled back.

"Cash, there is something I have to tell you," she blurted out. "I'm not—"

His mouth was on hers again, his kiss overpowering her senses. She resisted at first. He thought he was kissing Jasmine. Not her. She desperately wanted to tell him the truth. She wanted him to kiss *her*. Molly Kilpatrick. She wanted his desire to be for her. Not the ghost of Jasmine Wolfe.

But his mouth was hot and unrelenting and she gave in to it, passion sparking and catching fire between them. She circled his neck with her arms as he grabbed her waist and drew her against him, wet clothes and all. She felt his need in the kiss, in the strength of his hands pulling her closer, in the hardness of his body.

She wanted him. It didn't matter who he thought she was. He was kissing *her*. Wanted *her*.

He drew back to look into her eyes. His fingers trailed along the side of her cheek, dipping to the open neck of her shirt, across the lace of her bra, across one already hard nipple.

His large hands cupped her breasts, warm fingers teasing her nipples, sending shafts of heat to her center. She groaned as those hands explored her body, his touch setting fire to her chilled skin as he stripped her naked, tossing each piece into the boughs of the pine tree to dry.

He stared at her, caressing her body with his gaze, making her skin tingle and ache. She closed her eyes as he kissed her neck, then dropped lower, taking one aching nipple in his mouth. Heat shot to her center. She groaned, cradling his head in her hands.

"Cash, oh Cash."

He stopped.

She opened her eyes.

He seemed surprised and overpowered by that desire, as if he hadn't expected this. Knew it was the last thing he should be doing with her. "Say you want me as much as I do you," he said, his voice breaking.

His words enflamed her. "I *want* you like I have never wanted anything in my life."

He dragged her to him with almost a sob as his mouth found hers again. They staggered over to the warm nest of pine needles where he'd spread the picnic blanket. And under the wide, sweeping, green branches of the tree, he stripped. She watched until there was nothing between them and he was on the blanket with her, his body as hot as her desire.

Their naked bodies glistened in the morning sun as they clung to each other with a passion like none Molly had ever dreamed.

Cash had never known anything like it. She was more beautiful naked than he could have imagined. She opened to him and he thought he would die if he didn't have her.

"I love your hands," she breathed against his mouth.

He cupped her breasts and looked into her eyes. Molly. She was Molly, the woman who loved food, laughed joyously, thought even the silliest of things were romantic. Molly.

At that moment it didn't matter why she'd come to Antelope Flats. Or who she'd called last night. Or why she was so afraid of the two men back in town.

Nothing mattered but her.

He kissed her, deepening the kiss as his hands touched her everywhere. He wanted to know her body as intimately as he knew her laugh. He wanted her, his desire so strong that nothing could stop it.

The cop in him told him he had no business making love to her. Even now that he knew she was Molly, he could still get his heart broken. Or worse. And what about her? What would she do once he told her he knew.

"Molly." He pulled back again to look at her. "Molly," he repeated.

She smiled, tears swimming in all that green.

He made love to her, the first time in a frenzy of need, the second time slowly, gently, lovingly on the blanket under the wide sweeping boughs of the pine tree, to the sound of the creek moving through the rocks.

She seemed to blossom under his fingers, her body a woman's, full and lush.

When they were both finally spent, they lay under the shade of the huge pine, the breeze stirring the branches over their heads, the soft whinny of the horses ground tied nearby, the gentle rise and fall of her breasts, her eyes closed, her lips turned up in a smile of contentment.

He smiled too as he pushed himself up on one elbow. Just looking at her filled him to overflowing. How had he lived without this woman?

How could he live without her when she left?

The thought startled him. Why would she leave?

Because she wasn't Jasmine.

He sat up abruptly and reached for his clothes.

She must have felt the movement. He heard her stir behind him.

"What is it?" she asked.

He didn't look at her. "It's getting late. We should get back."

She touched his shoulder and he turned to look at her. She'd pulled her blouse from a low pine bough and held it with one hand in front of herself as if to cover her beautiful breasts.

Just looking at her made him catch his breath again. She reached for him and the next thing he knew she was in his arms. He held her tight to him, wanting to make love to her again. And yet afraid of what he was feeling for her. A woman he couldn't trust. A woman he didn't know.

"Jasmine?" he breathed against her hair and felt her

tense. He'd called her Jasmine to remind himself of her lie. And remind her as well.

This time she was the one to draw back. "You're right. We should get back. I promised your mother I would help with dinner."

He dressed, his back to her, pretending to give her some privacy, when in truth he knew he would take her in his arms again if he looked at her and confessed that he knew she wasn't Jasmine. His desire for this woman was boundless. Inexhaustible.

But now more than ever he needed to know who she was. Who he was falling in love with.

CHAPTER TWELVE

THEY RODE BACK to the ranch, saying little. The air felt hot and close, and Molly was glad to get off the horse in the cool barn.

"Go on in. I can take care of this," Cash said without looking at her.

She stared at his broad back, wanting to touch him, wanting to say something. But telling him the truth now seemed the worst thing she could do. *Get through this family dinner. Then leave the first chance Cash gives you tonight. A clean break. No harm done.*

But even as she thought it, her heart broke at the thought of never seeing him again. No harm done, like hell. But she reminded herself that it wasn't her he'd made love to, but Jasmine.

You were so good at pretending you were Jasmine that you fell in love with her fiancé. But if he knew who you really were…

She entered the cool, elegant ranch house and stood for moment. Earlier she had wanted to be a part of this family so badly and had felt it for those few minutes. But she didn't belong here. She never had. Jasmine would have fit in, Jasmine with her wealth, her privileged upbringing.

"There you are."

Molly turned to see Cash's mother.

"Is everything all right?" Shelby asked.

Molly nodded quickly and smiled. "Wonderful. The ride was…amazing. It just got hot out there." She couldn't help but look sheepish. "I fell in the creek."

"I like your hair better that way," Shelby said. "It suits you."

Molly wiped at her forehead, fighting back tears at the memory of being in Cash's arms under the sweeping pine.

"Freshen up in the bath down the hall, then come into the kitchen," Shelby offered. "I'll pour you a large glass of lemonade. You look like you could use it."

In the bathroom, Molly washed up, the cool water feeling good on her flushed, sweaty skin, the same way Cash's hands had felt hot on her cold skin. She touched the scar on her forehead. She'd told Cash the truth. She didn't know how she'd gotten it. The scar had just been there for as far back as she could remember. Max had said he didn't know when she'd gotten it or how. She knew he had to be lying. Wouldn't it have bled horribly?

She shut off the water. She could still smell Cash on her skin, still feel his touch. She closed her eyes trying not to cry. Then, getting control, she headed down the hall to find the large functional kitchen.

Shelby smiled when Molly came in, then handed her the promised glass of lemonade. The glass was cold and wet. She put it against her forehead for a moment, then took a sip of the lemonade inside.

"Thank you. It's delicious." She looked around. "What can I do?"

Shelby seemed to study her, then nodded. "Would you like to make the salad?"

"I would love to," Molly said with relief. She needed

to keep busy. She needed not to think about Cash. Or the lie that had put her in this unbearable position.

CASH COULDN'T BELIEVE his family that night at dinner. Everyone was there, Rourke and Cassidy with news of their honeymoon—and the construction of their new house up the road in a corner of the ranch; J.T. and Reggie and their upcoming wedding plans, as well as the construction of their home; even Brandon and Dusty seemed in good spirits.

Cash looked around the table at his ever-growing family and felt a sense of pride in them tonight. He caught Asa and Shelby exchanging what could only be called intimate looks. They loved each other. There was no doubt about that.

"How was your horseback ride?" Reggie asked Molly.

"Reggie's been taking lessons," J.T. added. "Hasn't been bucked off in what? Hours?"

Everyone laughed, even Reggie. "You wait. I'm going to be a ranchwoman yet. You'll see."

"Even if it kills you," J.T. said, but with obvious pride.

"So how was your ride?" Reggie asked Molly again.

Molly had been avoiding looking at Cash during dinner. Not that he could blame her. He'd wanted to distance himself from her and calling her Jasmine up on the mountain had definitely done it. He swore at his own foolishness. He'd made love to Molly. Not Jasmine.

Now she glanced over at him as she answered. "The ride was wonderful. Everything about it was incredible. I've never experienced anything like it."

The room was suddenly silent as he locked eyes with

her, sparks arcing between them. Then she seemed to sense the quiet and added hurriedly, looking down at her plate, "The ranch is so beautiful."

Cash saw the exchange of knowing smiles around the table and hoped to hell his face wasn't as red as Molly's.

"So when will your house be done?" he asked Rourke, trying to change the subject. But he could feel his mother's eyes on him. She hadn't missed the exchange between him and Molly.

The rest of the meal passed without incident. Just as the family housekeeper and cook Martha was about to serve dessert, the phone rang. Martha answered it and announced it was for Cash.

"I need to take this," he said rising. "I'm sorry. If you'll excuse me." He headed for his father's office and closed the door, knowing it was the call he'd been waiting for.

"Cash?" said the voice on the other end of the line. "It's Frank. Sorry I couldn't get back to you any sooner."

Cash had sent an email to Frank with the fingerprints saying it was urgent he get the results. Frank had emailed right back while Molly had been cleaning the ink from her fingers to say he could have them in twenty-four hours.

"You said you needed these ASAP," Frank said.

"You have no idea. I can't thank you enough."

Frank sighed. "I hate to disappoint you, but they don't match Jasmine Wolfe's. But there is something interesting—"

"You're sure?" Cash interrupted, hearing only that Molly Kilpatrick's prints didn't match Jasmine's. She wasn't Jasmine. He'd known, of course, but now it was confirmed. He felt a swell of relief, then a deep sense of regret. Jasmine was likely dead. But he'd known that, too, hadn't he?

So who was Molly? She looked so much like Jasmine. When she wanted to, he realized. Molly was nothing like her. Especially now, after her dip in the creek, without makeup, her short blond locks curly, her face flushed from the sun. She looked very different from the woman who had come into his office the evening before.

With a jolt, he remembered how she'd rolled down the window in his pickup. Jasmine would never have done that because of her allergies. He swore. Jasmine might have changed over seven years, but she couldn't have overcome her allergies.

He should have seen it earlier, felt it the moment he touched her, let alone kissed her.

"Definitely no match but as I was saying, the interesting thing is that the prints you sent me did come up in another matter."

Frank's words finally registered. "You have Molly Kilpatrick's prints on file?" Cash sat down hard at his father's desk, his heart in his throat. That meant she was wanted for something.

"Not on file, but a red flag came up on them. I'm going to have to track 'em down," Frank said. "I'll call you as soon as I have something. Meanwhile, you want me to send what I have to you?"

"Sure." He thanked Frank, then hung up and waited for the email with the report.

He thought about when he was taking Molly's prints. She hadn't known hers were on file or she would never have agreed to it. What the hell was she wanted for? He shuddered to think.

One thing was clear: she had to know she wasn't Jasmine Wolfe. So who was she?

And maybe more important, why was she pretending to be Jasmine?

Archie Wolfe's fortune? What else? But how did she hope to pull that off once her fingerprints didn't match Jasmine's? Did she hope to get money out of Bernard before the print results came back?

Good luck with that.

Cash scrubbed a hand over his face as he pulled up the report, his dread growing. He couldn't let on that he knew she wasn't Jasmine. Which might work out, since he needed her to be Jasmine. Desperately needed her to be alive—until he could find out who killed her. Until he could clear his name.

He heard the door open behind him and turned, expecting it would be Molly. His mother came in, closing the door firmly behind her.

Oh boy. He knew what was coming. If he'd learned anything about his mother since she'd come back from the dead, it was how perceptive she was. He'd seen her watching them all, learning things they thought they kept hidden. Hidden from most people anyway.

"If this is about Molly—"

"Of course it's about Molly," his mother snapped. "I'm worried about you."

"Didn't we already have this discussion last night? I told you I know what I'm doing."

She made a face as if she knew better. "You've fallen in love with this woman."

"That is old news. I think you know I was engaged to Jasmine seven years ago."

"No, not Jasmine," Shelby said with obvious irritation. "Molly. You're in love with Molly."

He stared at his mother. Did she know that Molly

wasn't Jasmine? Given the way she'd treated Molly last night compared to tonight… "You lost me."

"I really doubt that," she said. "This woman isn't the woman you knew seven years ago."

No kidding.

"Stop looking for that woman and appreciate what's right in front of your eyes," she said, sounding angry.

He laughed. "Whoa, wait a minute. Last night you told me not to trust her."

"Last night I thought she was Jasmine."

He stared at his mother.

"Don't give me that look. Jasmine hurt you. Get over it. This woman isn't Jasmine. She's…Molly."

His mother meant well but she had no idea what she was talking about.

"We're all waiting on you before we have dessert," Shelby said and turned on her heel and left the room.

"Oh, she's Molly all right, but who the hell is Molly?" he said to himself as he followed her back toward the dining room, stopping to print out the report and stuff it into the pocket of his jacket hanging in the hallway.

MOLLY WONDERED what important phone call Cash had gone to answer and why it was taking him so long. She tried not to watch the door, tried not to look anxious for his return.

Had Jasmine's body been found? Or Jasmine herself?

Right now, it would have been a relief to have this all end. She needed to leave one way or the other. Earlier, she'd tried to tell Cash the truth but he hadn't wanted to hear it. He wanted her to be Jasmine. Not Molly Kilpatrick.

A few minutes ago, Cash's mother had excused herself and disappeared down the hall, obviously going to check on him. Molly had wanted to go as well. As time passed, she felt herself growing more anxious.

She looked up. Shelby came back into the room. Cash wasn't far behind. He didn't meet her eyes as he sat back down.

"I'm sorry. It was official business," he said.

"Is everything all right?" his father asked.

Cash took a bite of his dessert as if stalling for time. He was different. And it wasn't her imagination. She'd been trained to read people. Cash was upset, shaken. What had the phone call been about?

"The bartender at the Mello Dee was killed last night," Cash said after a moment. "Teresa Clark." He glanced at his youngest brother Brandon. "You haven't been going out there have you?"

Brandon shook his head. "I thought the place was closed."

"Was she murdered?" Dusty asked.

"Can we please talk of more pleasant things?" Shelby interrupted. "Cassidy, didn't you have something you wanted to say?"

Everyone looked down the table at Cassidy. She blushed then nodded as she reached for her husband's hand. "Rourke and I are expecting!"

There were cheers and applause. Molly found herself in tears and hurriedly wiped at them, offering her congratulations. Cassidy looked so happy and Rourke, who looked like all the McCall men—blond, blue-eyed and handsome—beamed.

Of course none of the McCall boys was as handsome as Cash, Molly thought as the meal wound down and Cash announced that they had to leave. "I need to pick up those cinnamon rolls you have for me," he said to Cassidy.

"I left them at your office. I thought that would be handier for you," Cassidy said.

Molly watched the exchange. Cash was picking up more cinnamon rolls? How odd, she thought, remembering how he'd had to stop by the café before they came out to the ranch. If it was just to order more cinnamon rolls, he could have called or waited to see her once they got to the ranch.

Molly didn't want to leave here and go back to town. She'd felt so safe on the ranch with Cash and his family that she'd put Vince and Angel out of her mind for a while. The men would be looking for her back in town. Could be waiting for her in the shadows around Cash's house. She couldn't jeopardize his life by not warning him.

To her surprise, Shelby hugged her as they were leaving. Molly saw Cash's surprise—and the frown when Dusty also hugged her. He didn't want her getting any closer to his family, she realized. Why was that?

Did he regret their lovemaking? Or was he just keeping her at arm's length until he knew who she was, afraid of getting involved with a woman who might be…say, the daughter of a known criminal, she thought ruefully.

Cash said little as they left the ranch. She debated what to tell him. His silence scared her.

"I need to tell you something," she said as they neared town. She had to tell him the truth. She had to warn him about Vince and Angel.

"Can it wait?" he asked as he pulled up in front of the sheriff's office. "I just need to run in here for a minute, then we can go back to the house. We can talk there, all right?"

He didn't give her a chance to argue. He hopped out of the pickup. She watched him unlock his office and step inside, the light coming on behind the blinds.

ONCE INSIDE HIS OFFICE, Cash sat down at the computer and typed in a description of the men, suspecting there might be a warrant out on them since Molly's prints had come up on the FBI's radar.

Still, he was surprised when he got a hit. There was an APB out on two men matching their descriptions. Their names were Vince Winslow and Angel Edwards, and both were wanted for questioning by the Las Vegas Police Department in the murder of a man named Lanny Giliano.

"Lanny?" That was the name of the man Molly had called last night. Cash put his head in his hands. What the hell was Molly mixed up in?

There was no reason to run the prints of the two men. Vince Winslow and Angel Edwards were in Antelope Flats. Nor did it take much to figure out why. They were here because of Molly.

He picked up the phone and called the Las Vegas Police Department, got the detective in the Lanny Giliano case on the line and told him he'd seen Vince and Angel.

As the detective filled him in, Cash stared out through the blinds at his pickup and Molly. He could see her dark silhouette in the front seat.

A few minutes later, he hung up, opened his desk drawer and took out his gun. Officially, he'd been re-lieved of duty by Mathews. He'd have to work around that small problem. As he strapped on the gun, he thought about the chilling news the Vegas homicide detective had given him.

Vince and Angel were dangerous monsters who'd mutilated a man in Vegas before they killed him. Lanny Giliano. A man who'd been in on a diamond heist with them fifteen years ago.

The same man Molly had tried to call last night from the phone in Cash's den.

He sat for a moment, stunned by what he'd learned. As he started to rise from his desk, he saw that he'd gotten a message while he was on the line with the detective. He hurriedly retrieved it.

"This is Greg at the Dew Drop Inn near Bozeman? You left me a message? I had to go through my records but I can tell you who was working the night you asked about seven years ago." The man sounded pleased that he kept such good accounts. Not half as pleased as Cash.

The guy cleared his throat and continued. "The bartender on duty that night was Teresa Clark. Everyone called her T.C. Last I heard she was out in Seattle. Hope that helps you." The message ended.

Teresa Clark. The woman who was murdered at the Mello Dee.

He picked up the phone and called State Investigator John Mathews.

MOLLY SLID DOWN IN THE SEAT a little. Main Street was empty. No cars cruised by. But still she cracked her window so she could hear if anyone approached the truck on foot. She wished Cash would hurry. She watched the light in his office, could see his shadow moving around inside. She was anxious for him to return, anxious to end this.

"Why won't you let me tell you the truth?" she asked, staring at his shadow through the blinds.

She knew now that she couldn't just leave tonight without telling him about Vince and Angel. She couldn't leave him here without knowing that he was in danger. She had led Vince and Angel here. They could find out that she'd been staying with the sheriff. They would think he knew where she was.

She shuddered as she imagined what they might do to him. Whether Cash wanted to hear it or not, she was going to tell him everything.

She hated to think how he would take finding out that she wasn't Jasmine, wasn't the woman he'd loved and lost, especially after their lovemaking today.

She watched the street, her anxiety growing. *Hurry up, Cash.* If he didn't come out soon, she was going in. He would listen to her. She would make him.

She shivered and looked over, noticing Cash's jean jacket on the seat between them. She picked it up. He wouldn't mind if she put it on. One of the pockets bulged. She remembered him in the jacket earlier that morning on the ride. The pockets had been empty then.

Curious, she pulled the folded paper out. Did this have something to do with the urgent call he'd received during dinner about the murder at the Mello Dee?

Even in the faint light coming through the blinds of his office, she could read the words *FBI* and *fingerprints*. Her heart stopped. Cash had gotten the results. That's what the phone call had been. He'd said it would take at least a week. Maybe two. He'd lied to her?

He knew she wasn't Jasmine! When was he going to tell her? And what would he do now?

She didn't need to read the report. She knew she wasn't Jasmine Wolfe and that her fingerprints wouldn't

match. She started to refold the piece of paper, not realizing Cash had come out of his office.

She looked up. He was standing at the driver's side
window looking in at her. Her heart stopped. He opened
the door and she saw that he had a small box of cinnamon rolls in his hands and was wearing a gun.

CHAPTER THIRTEEN

CASH LOOKED FROM her to the paper in her hand.

"Why haven't you said anything?" Her voice came out a whisper.

He took the report from her hand, angry with himself for leaving it in the truck. Had he wanted her to find it? "Did you read it?"

"I didn't have to," she said. "I tried to tell you earlier. You stopped me."

He looked over at her as he put the key into the ignition and started the pickup. "I didn't want to hear that you weren't Jasmine." He saw the effect his words had on her and wished he could rein them back in. "I'm sorry, what I meant was—"

"You don't have to apologize. I know how badly you wanted me to be Jasmine," she said. "I'm sorry I disappointed you. I can see how much you loved her, how much you wanted her back."

He shut off the engine and raked a hand through his hair. "Look, I know about Vince Winslow and Angel Edwards. I know you tried to call Lanny Giliano last night from my phone in the den. I know about the Hollywood diamond heist fifteen years ago with another man, Max Burke. Max got killed. Vince and Angel got fifteen years. They just got out. I know Lanny is dead—"

"He's dead?"

"Sorry," he said seeing her eyes well with tears.

"I knew he was dead. I was just hoping…"

"Why are Vince and Angel in town?"

"They're looking for me. They plan to kill me—after I tell them where the diamonds are from the heist. They think I know."

"Why would you know?"

"My father was the third man in the heist, Max Burke, better known as the Great Maximilian Burke, magician and thief."

"Do you have the diamonds?"

She shook her head. "I don't have any idea where they are, but Vince and Angel won't believe that. My father had the diamonds after the heist. I was the last person to see him alive. But he didn't live long enough to tell me what he did with them. Vince saw Max say something to me but it had nothing to do with the diamonds. All Max said was, 'I'm sorry, kiddo. I'll try to make it up to you.' Then he died."

"I'm sorry."

Molly looked over at him. "My father was shot down by police in the street when he tried to get away. He died in my arms. I was fourteen." She looked away, but nothing could hide the pain. "I'm the daughter of a thief. Now you know."

How could he have ever thought she was Jasmine? This woman felt so much, so deeply. "That must have been horrible for you. What about your mother?"

"She died when I was a baby."

"What did you do after your father died?"

"I ran." She looked over at him. "That's what I've been doing the past fifteen years—running. I knew Vince and Angel could get out at any time. That's what I was doing when I came here, running from them. When I saw the photograph and story in the newspaper about

Jasmine and saw the resemblance… I needed a place to hide for a while until Vince and Angel were picked up. I knew they murdered Lanny even though the police wouldn't tell me anything when I called." Her eyes filled with tears. She wiped at them, biting her lower lip in a way that he knew Jasmine never had. "I hated lying to you."

"We've both been lying to each other," he said and pulled her into his arms, holding her tightly. Her story matched what the Las Vegas police had told him. He would have believed her even if it hadn't. Whatever reason her prints came up on the FBI's system, it must have something to do with her father. He pushed it out of his mind. All that mattered was keeping her safe. For the moment.

"Let's talk about this at home," he said. Home. He'd actually called that rambling old house home?

"No," she said, grabbing his arm. "Vince and Angel could be there. You don't know these men. They wouldn't hesitate to kill you."

He smiled. "I called Mathews. He's got highway patrol looking for them right now." She was worried about getting *him* killed now? "Vince and Angel aren't waiting for us. This morning when I fixed your car so you couldn't leave I found a global positioning device on it."

"That's how they found me? I didn't think they were that smart."

"Prison is a great crime school."

Her eyes widened. "They could have killed me in Vegas. Why track me?"

"They must have thought you would lead them to the diamonds."

"Instead, I led them to you," she said, tears in her eyes as she looked over at him.

"I put the GPS on a coal car heading south and sent Vince and Angel on a wild-goose chase until I could find out why you were so afraid of them. I couldn't help but notice your reaction when you saw them."

"They'll be back," she said, looking afraid. "Only now they'll be even more angry and they'll come to the last place they tracked me. You." She groaned. "You shouldn't have done that. You don't know what these men are capable of."

"You don't know what I'm capable of," he said. "There's an APB out on them. They'll get picked up."

She looked skeptical.

"Or I'll deal with them." He drove toward the house. "I want you to get your things. I'm taking you to the family lake cabin. Vince and Angel won't be able to find you there."

"You know they'll come back to the house, that's why you want to get rid of me. You think you'll lay a trap for them. Well I'm not leaving you alone to face them."

He glanced over at her, ready to more than argue the point, but he was distracted at the sight of an SUV parked in front of his house. A rental. He parked behind it with a curse. "Stay here."

As he stepped out of the pickup, he heard the squeak of the porch swing. Bernard Wolfe was sprawled on it as if he'd been waiting for some time. Behind him, Cash heard Molly open her door and get out.

Cash swore under his breath. He had to get Molly out of town and right away.

"I WANT TO TALK TO MY SISTER alone," Bernard said, getting to his feet and coming across the porch to meet them.

Cash started to tell him it would be a cold day in hell before that happened.

"Could you leave us alone?" Molly asked. "Please. I really do need to talk to my stepbrother."

Cash saw Bernard's jaw tighten at the word *stepbrother.* Cash looked over at Molly. He wasn't leaving her alone with Bernard. What the hell was she thinking?

"Please," she said. "Bernard looks like he could use a drink. You don't mind if I show him to your bar, do you?"

Hell yes, he minded and she knew it. What was she up to? Whatever it was, he didn't like it. But he also couldn't keep her from talking to Bernard, short of locking her up in his jail. Even then, he figured Bernard would spring her.

"I'll be right here if you need me," Cash said, crossing his arms, feet planted on the porch. "Make it quick."

MOLLY OPENED THE DOOR to the house, amazed Cash still hadn't bothered to lock it when they'd left. She hoped Vince and Angel hadn't gotten wise to the wild-goose chase and doubled back already. She worried that Cash would underestimate Vince and Angel. It would be his last mistake.

She stepped inside, turning on the lights as she led Bernard to the living room.

All the color had drained from his face. "Jasmine. It really is you."

She didn't correct him. Something about his demeanor put her on guard even though she couldn't believe he would try to hurt her, not with Cash right outside the door.

"When Kerrington told me you were alive..." He

shook his head as if he still couldn't believe it. "I really could use that drink."

She motioned toward the bar. As Bernard poured himself a drink, she noticed that his hands were shaking. She declined when he offered to make her one as well.

He was visibly nervous. She watched him look around the room, then at her. "Kerrington says you have amnesia."

"You seem nervous, Bernard," she said mimicking Jasmine's voice. "Are you worried that I'm going to remember what happened the day I disappeared?"

He froze. "You remember?"

Molly thought about the woman whose life she'd stepped into. Didn't she owe Jasmine? Karma-wise no doubt about it. But the truth was, Molly couldn't walk away and let Cash continue living under this veil of suspicion. She owed him. If she could find out what happened to the woman he'd loved, she had to try. And as long as the people who'd been closest to her still thought she was Jasmine...

"You didn't want me marrying the sheriff," she said.

"You weren't going to marry him," Bernard said scowling at her as he took a drink.

"I loved him."

Bernard's laugh cut her to the quick. "You made fun of the fool with me and Kerrington. Maybe you really don't remember, but the three of us used to go to that bar where you and Kerrington hung out all the time. You would tell stories about your cowboy. Hell, you were sleeping with Kerrington. The only reason you said you were engaged to the sheriff was to piss off your father. And drive Kerrington crazy. If the sheriff found out what you were really up to..."

"Someone tried to kill me."

"Like I said. If your sheriff found out what you were really up to…"

"Cash didn't try to kill me."

"Well, don't look at me."

"You had the most to gain. You stood to inherit everything with me out of the way."

He took another sip of his drink. "I'll admit I haven't missed you. All those years of trying to keep you out of trouble. But you're barking up the wrong tree if you think I was the one who did this to you." His laugh was self-deprecating. "Hell, Jazz, I was half in love with you myself. But I'm sure you know that."

Her shock must have shown.

"Or maybe not. Even though we weren't related by blood, you never thought of me as anything more than a brother." He sounded bitter. "You ridiculed me behind my back as badly as you did everyone else, didn't you?" He nodded. "I suspected as much. But that's all water under the bridge since you don't remember it," he said sarcastically.

"I'm sorry." Jasmine had obviously hurt him badly. And not just him. Kerrington, too. Sandra and Patty. And Cash?

"Sorry?" Bernard said, as if he'd never heard the word come out of Jasmine's mouth. "You're sorry?" He drained his glass and put it down a little too hard on the bar. "What are you sorry for, Jazz? Sorry that you hurt people? Or sorry that for seven years we've been free of you and your games?"

She held her ground. He was inches from her now, his dark eyes hateful.

"Or are you sorry that one of us finally had enough and tried to kill you?" he asked, his voice hoarse with emotion. "Any one of us wanted you dead at one point or another. Kerrington. Sandra. Patty. Me. I just never had the stomach for murder."

"Really?" She played the card up her sleeve. "My memory is starting to come back, Bernard. It's just a matter of time before I know which one of you did it."

His face went ashen, his breath coming hard. "It wasn't me. I'll give you half of everything. But if you try to take it all by trying to frame me, I warn you I'll—"

"What will you do?" Cash asked from the doorway.

Bernard swung around in obvious surprise, as if he'd forgotten about Cash. "Just a little family matter," Bernard said and gave Molly a knowing look as he brushed past her and left.

Molly realized she was trembling uncontrollably. She'd thought by telling him that she remembered the day she disappeared, he would be frightened. Instead, he was furious, thinking she would try to frame him?

"What the hell are you trying to do?" Cash grabbed her by her upper arms. "Get yourself killed?"

She was too shocked to speak. She'd never heard him raise his voice, let alone seen him this furious. His fingers were biting into her flesh.

Bernard's words rang in her ears. *If your sheriff had found out what you were really up to...*

Cash saw the fear in her eyes and quickly let go. "I'm sorry. But do you realize what you've done, telling Bernard that your memory is coming back?" He swore. Just the sight of her reminded him of their lovemaking up on the mountain overlooking the ranch. He was angry with her for lying to him, but at the same time he wanted to pull her into his arms and make love to her all over again. "Aren't you in enough danger? Molly, why in the hell would you do that?"

"I owe it to Jasmine for stealing her life."

"What are you talking about?" he demanded. "You don't owe Jasmine anything." He caught one of her short blond curls between his fingers. "You're more beautiful than she was in so many ways."

"I owe it to you," she said, sounding close to tears.

He let go of her hair. He wanted to shake some sense into her. "Me?"

His face was stone. In it, Molly saw nothing of the man who'd made passionate love to her earlier on the mountain. She feared she might never see that man again.

"I'm sorry, Cash. When I came up with this plan, I hadn't met you, I never thought…" Never thought that she might fall in love with the sheriff of Antelope Flats. Isn't that what she was going to say? "I'm sorry. I didn't mean to hurt you."

"Hurt me? You think that's what I care about? You're nothing like Jasmine. I should have known right away and put a stop to this."

She felt as if he'd slapped her. "I know how much you loved her…." She turned away, unable to face him and say the words. "Let me help you find her killer—"

He spun her around to face him. "Listen to me. She wasn't the love of my life. I won't have you lose *your* life for something that wasn't true."

She stared at him. "You were engaged to be married."

He raked a hand through his hair and shook his head.

Fear squeezed her heart like a fist. He'd been keeping something from her about him and Jasmine. She'd
known it. "Tell me," she said, her voice a whisper.

He shook his head again, but she'd already seen the
answer in his face.

"You knew," she said on a breath. "You knew about
her and Kerrington."

He didn't move, didn't speak, his face frozen in a
mask of ice.

Her body went cold. "I know you didn't kill her," she
said, fear compressing her lungs, making it hard to catch
her breath. But she also knew he'd done something,
something he'd been hiding. "I know there's something
you aren't telling me."

His face seemed to melt, his expression going from
anger to pain. He slumped, turning away from her.

She reached out, touched his shoulder, felt the warmth
of his body beneath her fingers. She wanted to wrap her
arms around him and tell him everything was going to
be all right, but she feared that was a lie.

He turned slowly to look at her. "I *wanted* to kill
her."

"But you didn't. You couldn't."

His smile held no humor. "How can you be so sure
of that?"

She shook her head. She didn't know how, just
that her heart promised her it was true. "You aren't a
killer."

He looked down at the floor, then up at her. "Jasmine
and I were *never* engaged. She told everyone we were.
I went up to Bozeman the day before she disappeared
to find out why she'd done that. Jasmine and I dated a
couple of times. I was flattered. Jasmine had a way of

making you feel like you were the most important thing in her life." He sighed.

"You found her with Kerrington," Molly guessed.

He nodded. "They didn't see me."

Molly held her breath.

"I waited until she was alone." He raked his fingers through his hair. "It got ugly. She admitted that she was just using me in some game she had going with Kerrington and her father. I demanded she call off the newspapers who'd been hounding me about this stupid engagement. I had avoided the press, not wanting to embarrass Jasmine. I wanted her to call them back and tell them we weren't engaged."

He walked over to the front window, his back to her. "I found out that she'd even gotten a key to the house I'd just bought and was telling everyone it was my engagement present to her. I demanded it back. She jumped into her new little red sports car and took off. I ran my pickup into her car, denting the side, taking out a headlight."

Molly couldn't help her startled expression. There would be evidence of an accident on Jasmine's car.

"I was sorry at once and offered to have it fixed. She was livid. Damaging her car was the ultimate sin. If she had had a weapon, she would have shot me on the spot. I know I should have told the state investigators as soon as I heard Jasmine was missing…"

So that's what he'd been hiding.

"I thought it was a stunt, her being missing. That she *wanted* me to look guilty, that she was trying to take away the one thing that meant anything to me, being a sheriff. The accident had happened the day before she disappeared. It didn't seem relevant. Then, once it appeared she really was missing, it was too late." He raked a hand through his hair again as he turned to look at her. "I kept waiting for her to turn up. I refused to believe she was dead. Then when you walked into my office…"

"I'm sorry."

"I can't tell you how much I hoped you were Jasmine," he said. He must have seen her change of expression. "Not because I loved Jasmine but if she was alive, then I was off the hook."

"You believe she's dead?" Molly asked.

"If Jasmine was alive, she wouldn't have waited seven years to come back and seek her revenge."

"What does she have to be vengeful about?"

"Jasmine didn't need a reason. Her father had just disinherited her. She was angry." He shook his head. "The irony is, after she disappeared Archie and I finally met. He liked me, said he would have been proud to have me for a son-in-law, thought I would be good for his daughter. It was Kerrington he didn't want her marrying. And Archie would never have left Jasmine penniless no matter what she did. It was just this battle between the two of them. He left part of his estate to Jasmine always holding out hope that she was still alive. Another reason Bernard must be beside himself thinking you're Jasmine."

"Why do you think she was driving down to Antelope Flats?"

"It wasn't to fix things up with me, I can tell you that. Maybe she wasn't driving down here at all. Whoever hid her car in that barn might have done it to frame me for her murder."

"Jasmine seems to have had a few enemies," Molly said.

He laughed. "That's putting it mildly. That's why we have to let them know that you aren't Jasmine. If I'm right, one of them killed her, possibly left her for dead. That person can't let Jasmine remember what happened that day." She shivered and he pulled her to him. "The sooner we make the announcement the better."

She smiled up at him. He was so trusting. Deception came hard to him and because of that he would never understand the world she came from. "Cash, her killer is just going to think you're trying to protect me until I remember and you can arrest him. We have Jasmine's killer right where we want him. If we work this together—"

He started to argue but she put a finger to his lips.

"It's too late to do anything else and you know it." She met his pale blue eyes and felt a jolt. His look sent heat straight to her center, making her ache for him. His mouth dropped to hers in a kiss that curled her toes.

Sweeping her up into his arms, he headed for the stairs. "Don't you want to hear my plan?" she asked.

"No," he said. "I want to make love to you."

The doorbell rang. He ignored it and started up the steps. The doorbell rang again and a deep voice said, "It's Mathews. Open up."

CHAPTER FOURTEEN

WITH OBVIOUS RELUCTANCE, Cash set Molly down on her feet with a curse as Mathews pounded on the door.

"Sounds like I'd better tell you my plan quickly," Molly said.

"Just a minute!" Cash called to Mathews and Molly told him her plan.

Cash swore again and went to open the door. "Come on in," he said to a steaming John Mathews.

"What took you so long?" Mathews demanded, then saw Molly and stopped dead in his tracks. "Jasmine? What the hell, Cash?"

"Come on in. Wanna drink?" Cash asked.

"Am I going to need one?" Mathews asked.

"It might not hurt. State Lead Investigator John Mathews meet Molly Kilpatrick."

Mathews frowned, his gaze going from Molly to Cash and back again. "Not Jasmine Wolfe?"

"No, I just look like her," Molly said, holding out her hand.

He shook it. "Cash, I thought I told you to stay away from this investigation. In fact, I relieved you of your duties as I recall."

"Look, John—"

"I want to help you catch Jasmine's killer," Molly interjected. "I've already started the ball rolling, so to speak."

"I think I will take that drink," Mathews said.

Cash led him into the living room. Molly perched on the edge of one of the chairs. Mathews lowered his large frame into a chair opposite her as Cash made them all drinks.

"I came over because of the Teresa Clark murder," Mathews said, taking the drink Cash offered him.

When Cash had called him from his office, he'd told Mathews what he'd learned about the bartender and the matchbook found in Jasmine's car.

"I thought you'd like to know that Teresa Clark talked to one of her regulars here in Antelope Flats, Charley Alberta, before she was killed. She said she knew the woman who's car was found. And that the last time she saw Jasmine Wolfe was the night Jasmine disappeared seven years ago. It seemed Jasmine came into the Dew Drop Inn all the time with two different men. Based on her descriptions of the men according to Charley, one was her brother Bernard. The other was Kerrington. It seems Bernard had a fight with Jasmine the night she disappeared and he left the bar. Then Kerrington came in and got into it with her, even following her outside, still arguing."

"On the day Bernard and Kerrington both said they were hiking and camping in the backcountry together?" Cash asked.

Mathews nodded. "Teresa Clark could have blown apart both of their alibis. Had she lived. Guess who had a drink at the Mello Dee the night Teresa Clark was murdered? Kerrington, only he lied and said he didn't know her, even gave her a fake name."

"Kerrington," Cash said like a curse.

Mathews nodded. "I came by to tell you before I go pick him up at the motel and to tell you that if you continue to butt into my case I'm going to throw your ass in jail."

"Then you probably aren't going to want to hear about the plan Molly came up with," Cash said. "But I think you should hear her out. As much as I don't like it, it's a damned good plan and it might put an end to this once and for all."

Mathews took a gulp of his drink and looked to Molly. "There's probably a good reason you look so much like Jasmine Wolfe."

"There is, but that's not important right now. I think I know how we can catch Jasmine's killer. By using me as bait."

"And you think this is a *good* idea?" Mathews said. "You got a death wish?"

HOW COULD MOLLY EXPLAIN that she'd fallen in love with Cash and wanted to help him? That she owed this to Jasmine because she'd stolen the woman's identity to save herself?

Cash filled Mathews in on how Molly had seen the story in the newspaper and noticed the remarkable resemblance.

Mathews raised one heavy brow. "And what did you hope to gain by pretending to be her? Jail time?"

"Time." Molly filled him in on Vince and Angel.

Mathews whistled and shook his head. "And that's when you got this harebrained idea that you could catch her killer?"

She nodded, ignoring the harebrained part. "By then I'd met Jasmine's former fiancé, Kerrington Landow, her stepbrother, Bernard, and her two former roommates, Sandra Perkins Landow and Patty Franklin. Any one of them could have killed her."

"I agree on that account, anyway," Mathews said.

"Today, I told them that I was starting to remember what happened the day I disappeared," Molly said. "The killer won't come after me—until he or she knows for certain that I'm Jasmine. There is only one way the killer can be sure of that. Dig up my grave."

Mathews drew back as if she'd hit him.

"But the killer can't check the grave because you have men out there looking for it yourself," Cash put in.

Mathews was nodding. "Let me guess. I pull off my men, stake out the farm, catch the killer."

"Pretty much," Cash said.

"Except you need to let the suspects know it is believed that I'm Jasmine, that there is a chance my memory is returning and the search of the farm has been called off until the fingerprint results come back," Molly said.

Mathews shook his head. "You think the killer will go to her grave tonight to make sure she's there."

Cash nodded. "I think the only reason he hasn't gone there already is that the farm has been crawling with investigators twenty-four-seven since her car was found."

"I suppose I could have my men stake out the farm—"

"No," Cash said. "We don't know which way the killer will access the farm. I know the area. I know a place where I can see most of the farm. And if your men don't leave, the killer will know in a town this size."

"Cash, if you think I'm letting you go alone—"

"You don't still think I'm the one who killed her?" Cash said in obvious frustration.

"I've never thought that. But I need to cover my behind—and yours. Don't forget, you've been relieved as sheriff."

Cash started to argue but Mathews cut him off. "You have a point, though, about the stakeout and you do know the property. You can go in with me. I'll deputize you."

"What about Molly?" Cash asked.

"I'll put three of my best men on the house," Mathews said.

"Wait a minute, don't I have some say in this?" Molly protested.

"No!" they both said in unison.

"It was my idea. I want to be there when the killer is arrested," she complained.

"Not a chance. You'll stay here in the house with guards right outside so I know you're safe until we get back," Cash said. "No argument. Otherwise John has the authority to lock you up in jail."

"That's not a bad idea," Mathews said. "I'm definitely going to want to ask you more about the two men after you and that little issue of identity fraud, so don't get leaving into your head."

"I'm not going anywhere," she said. "Not with three men guarding the house."

Cash looked as if he wished she had a half dozen or more guarding her.

"How soon can we do this?" Cash asked.

"I'll set everything in motion. I guess we're on for tonight. If I were the killer I'd want to find out just as quick as I could," Mathews said as he got to his feet. "I'll go let Bernard, Kerrington, Sandra and Patty know. They're all staying at the Lariat. On my way here, I noticed that they had all returned from dinner."

"You've had them under surveillance?" Cash asked in surprise.

"Isn't that what you would have done if you were still sheriff and not involved in this case?" Mathews said with a smile. "I just wish I had put a tail on them before Teresa Clark was killed."

Molly listened as Cash and John Mathews worked out the details. She couldn't help but be anxious. Cash was going out by the lake to trap a killer.

Mathews used Cash's phone in the den to make the call to the motel. She heard Cash in the kitchen, then upstairs. What was he doing? Searching the house, she thought. Making sure she was safe.

"Are you sure you'll be all right here by yourself?" he asked when he joined her in the living room.

"I won't be by myself," she reminded him. "It's you I'm worried about." She cupped his warm cheek in her hand. His face was rough with stubble. He had never looked more handsome. "Be careful?"

He smiled and nodded.

Mathews came back into the room. "It's all set. My men are here. I'll have them stay outside out of sight."

"Lock the door behind me," Cash said to her. "Don't let anyone in, no matter what."

"Don't worry. I'll be fine. There's still brownies in the cupboard, right?"

He smiled, his gaze locking with hers, and for just a moment she thought he would tell her that he loved her. The daughter of a known crook? Not likely.

"Ready?" Mathews said behind him in the now-open doorway.

Cash nodded, pulling her to him and kissing her hard. "I'll be back as soon as I can." And then he was gone.

She waited until the sound of the car engine died away in the distance, still reeling from the kiss. Going to the door, she peered through the peephole. She couldn't see anyone. But then that was the way it was supposed to work.

Locking the door, she turned to look at the old house. It needed so much work. She'd been delighted to hear that he hadn't bought the house for Jasmine. It didn't sound like she was the kind of woman who would want to strip all this woodwork. Same with the hardwood floors.

Molly squinted, imagining the house with a fresh coat of paint, something bright and cheery for the kitchen and maybe a nice sage green for the living room. As for the foyer—

She stopped herself cold, surprised at her train of thought. She hated old houses. And it would take months if not years to remodel this one. She'd never stayed that long in any one place in her life.

She heard a creak upstairs and froze, waiting to hear it again. Nothing. Suspicious noise was the reason she'd never liked old houses. Right now she didn't like being alone in this one without Cash. Vince and Angel could break into this house way too easily. The men were professionals.

But her real worry was for Cash. She knew she wouldn't be able to sit still until he came back. Just let him be safe. Let him catch the killer. Let him finally be free of Jasmine. Let Vince and Angel be caught. Let this be over.

But then he will also be free of you.

Right.

She told herself he would be back soon. In the meantime what she needed was brownies. She started to go into the kitchen to find them when she heard another creak of a floorboard upstairs.

Could it be one of the cops Mathews left to protect her? Cash had searched the house and if she knew him, had double-checked to make sure all the doors and windows were locked.

Unless someone had been in the house and he'd missed them. After all, he had been looking for two men: Vince and Angel.

She listened and heard nothing. It was an old house. Old houses creaked and groaned. She was just being paranoid. Still, she waited. Not a sound.

Brownies. She needed brownies. And a glass of milk. Comfort food. She glanced at the clock and prayed Cash would be back soon. In only a few days everything had changed for her. Where she had once always loved the idea of not knowing where she was going or what she would do when she got there, that life now had little appeal.

She didn't feel the need to hit the road. In fact, dreaded the thought of leaving here. Leaving Cash.

What would he do when she was gone? Start over. Just as she would have to do.

She wandered into the kitchen, not surprised to find the brownies on the counter, covered in plastic with a note taped on top.

"Thought you might need these. Take care of yourself until I get back. Cash."

"Don't you even think about crying," she warned herself as she cut a brownie, took a bite, then put it down to open the fridge to get the milk.

The note made her feel better. That and the brownie.

As she pulled the milk carton from the fridge, she heard the sound of a footfall.

Only this time it wasn't upstairs. This time, it was right behind her.

She spun around with the milk carton in her hand, two thoughts crowding together. *Run! Scream!*

But she didn't get the chance to do either. The milk carton hit the kitchen floor, burst. Milk pooled on the floor like fresh blood as she stared at the barrel of the gun pointed at her heart.

"Don't make a sound or I'll kill you."

THE ROAD OUT TO the old Trayton place seemed farther than usual. Cash couldn't think about anything but Molly. He hated leaving her. Even with three armed guards. It was all he could do not to tell Mathews to turn the car around and take him back. He had a bad feeling, one he couldn't shake.

"You all right?" Mathews said with a sideways glance.

"Just worried about Molly," he said.

"She's in good hands. Anyway, I have a feeling that is one woman who can take care of herself."

Cash fell silent. He didn't doubt Mathews's words. But the past few days he'd fallen into the habit of taking care of her. It was a habit he didn't want to break.

He remembered that he hadn't heard back from Frank. Molly could be wanted for just about anything. She could be facing criminal charges and a long prison term. He closed his eyes to the thought.

He felt Mathews turn off on the back road, one that the killer shouldn't know about. The old barn wasn't far off the main highway, easily seen by anyone looking for a place to hide a car. Or a body.

The patrol car slowed, then stopped. Mathews turned off the engine and the lights. They sat for moment in the darkness, then Cash heard him pop the trunk. He opened his door and got out, Mathews doing the same.

They were on the far side of the farm, hidden by a small hill. From here they would walk.

Cash followed him around to the trunk. Mathews reached in and took out two shotguns. He handed one to Cash along with a look. He was touched by Mathews trust in him—but if things went badly tonight, heads would roll.

After tonight, he would tell Mathews everything. He just hoped he wouldn't lose his job over it. But with luck, Jasmine's killer would be behind bars after tonight. Her body recovered and laid to rest. His name cleared. And Molly? He just prayed that she would be safe until he returned. And she would be as long as Vince and Angel didn't realize they'd been duped and doubled back.

With any luck, a highway patrolman already had the two men in custody.

Cash took the shotgun Mathews handed him. He also had his service revolver.

"Ready?" Mathews asked.

He nodded and Mathews softly closed the trunk.

They walked up over the hill through the dark night. Clouds scudded overhead covering the moon. A few stars glittered through the clouds. They moved quickly, taking advantage of the lack of moonlight.

Below them, the lake's surface was hammered pewter. Cash could smell the water. A restless breeze rustled the cottonwoods as they moved along the north shore.

Ahead, he could make out a dark smudge on the horizon, beyond it, the broken, jagged roof of the old barn where Jasmine's car had been found.

Cash heard the sound of the vehicle at the same instant Mathews did. They both stopped to listen, their gazes meeting in the darkness. Someone was coming up the road toward the old farm. Someone driving with his headlights off.

Cash moved quickly toward the stand of pines from where they would have a good view of the barn and the rest of the farm. Overhead, the clouds parted. A shaft of moonlight beamed down as they ducked into the darkness of the pines, disappearing from view.

The sound of the engine rumbled as the vehicle drove along the bumpy road. Every once in a while, Cash would catch the flicker of brake lights as the driver slowly moved on the rutted road.

Mathews looked over at him as he heard the vehicle stop, the sound of the engine dying into silence. The night settled around them. Cash could see the dark shape of the car but couldn't tell the make.

He realized he was holding his breath. A car door opened and then closed quietly. Someone stepped away from the vehicle, just a shadow of a figure moving through the darkness, headed directly toward them. A man. He was carrying a shovel.

CHAPTER FIFTEEN

MOLLY DIDN'T FEEL the milk carton slip from her fingers, didn't hear it hit the floor and burst open, didn't notice the spray soak the hem of her jeans.

She stared at the gun in Patty Franklin's hand, her mind telling her *This isn't happening.*

Jasmine's former roommate smiled. "Surprised to see me, Jasmine?"

"Patty, I'm not—"

"Don't even bother. You might be able to fool the others but remember me? What did I hear you tell Bernard one time, that I was 'dumb as dirt and just as interesting'? But there is an advantage to being invisible. No one notices me so I hear and see things, Jasmine."

Molly's mind raced. It didn't make any sense. Molly had been so sure that the killer would go to the farm, check Jasmine's grave, not chance another murder until he was sure. Cash would never have left her if he thought there was any chance the killer would come here.

Because Patty wasn't the killer. She'd just come here, angry at Jasmine. But how had she gotten past the three men guarding the house?

Patty smiled as if reading her mind. "I was in the house all the time. Your boyfriend didn't even see me.

Another benefit of being small and mousy. I practically blend into the wallpaper."

So she hadn't even heard about the search being called off at the farm. Had she heard about the plan? "Cash and the state investigator will be back soon."

Patty smiled. "I don't think so. I would imagine they're out at the farm waiting for Jasmine's killer to show them where she's buried."

So she had heard the plan. She knew Cash and Mathews wouldn't be back, probably for a long time. "But there are three men outside," Molly said.

"And if you try to alert them I will kill you before you and I have our talk," Patty said. "And in case you really do have amnesia and don't remember, I'm an exceptional shot with a gun. I'm just not as good with a rock."

A rock? Shock rippled through her. Molly's blood ran cold at the thought of Jasmine's head injury. "*You* killed Jasmine?"

"I'm starting to believe that you don't remember what we said to each other that night in the Dew Drop Inn parking lot before I killed you the first time," Patty said.

Distracting Patty would be next to impossible. The woman seemed unshakable. Time might be the only chance Molly had. Maybe Cash and Mathews could come back for some reason. "I told you I don't remember because—"

"Because you aren't Jasmine. You even fooled the sheriff and the state investigator. I saw you with your suitcase earlier. You just got rid of them so you could take off again."

Molly groaned. Nothing she could say to Patty would convince her she wasn't Jasmine. She saw it clearly now, the reason Patty hadn't gone out to the grave. Patty wanted her to be Jasmine, wanted her to be alive—so she could kill her again.

That's why she wasn't worried about the three men outside. The moment Patty pulled the trigger they would come busting in here. She couldn't possibly get away with this. But she didn't care.

Patty's expression was that of a woman about to commit murder. There was little emotion in the single-minded way Patty held the gun. No wavering. She didn't even seem nervous. What she seemed was determined. Patty had come here to kill her. Plain and simple.

"It's over," Patty said. "But at least this time I will make sure I take you with me. This time you're going to *stay* dead."

"Jasmine *is* dead, Patty. You're making a terrible mistake. You killed her the first time. If you kill me it will be for nothing. Jasmine's wherever you buried her."

"I didn't bury you," Patty said. "I just left you behind the steering wheel of your car. I checked your pulse. I was so sure you were dead."

Molly stared at her. "Then how did the car end up in a barn outside of Antelope Flats?"

"I have no idea. Why don't you tell me? Didn't you put it there to frame the sheriff?"

Molly's head was spinning. None of this made any sense.

"I wish I'd pushed your car off a cliff instead of just leaving it in front of the bar," Patty said. "It would have made things so much easier."

"What bar?"

"The Dew Drop Inn, of course." Patty cocked her head. "Don't tell me you can't remember what we fought about."

"In case you really care, my name is Molly Kilpat-rick." Molly tried to remember what was on the kitchen counter behind her. "My father was killed after a dia-mond heist in Hollywood." Back when she worked with her father she could have recalled everything that was there in the proper placement. But she was out of prac-tice. "I'm pretending to be Jasmine because there are two killers after me."

"I heard that story when I was listening on the stairs," Patty said.

"It's true." Molly inched back toward the kitchen counter, praying there was something she could use to defend herself. But she couldn't imagine what, especially against a gun. "My father hid the diamonds and now his partners just got out of prison and think I know where the diamonds are. They plan to kill me."

"They aren't going to get the chance if you move again," Patty said, no emotion in her voice. "Even if these two killers existed, I will shoot you first."

Molly froze, seeing she meant it. "So tell me what it was you and Jasmine fought about the night you killed her."

Patty smiled. "I have some things to say to you, Jas-mine. Last time you did all the talking until I shut you up with that rock. This time, I'll do the talking." Patty glared at her. "Since you don't remember...I was wait-ing for you when you came out of the bar. You'd just had a big fight with someone. Either your brother or Kerrington since I knew you'd been with them. Who-ever it was had shoved you. You'd hit your head. It was bleeding. You were in one of your foul moods. I noticed when I was waiting that one of the headlights on that new car you were so proud of was out and when I got closer, I saw that the right front fender was smashed. I asked you what had happened, but you said you didn't have time for my 'mindless prattle.'"

Patty took a breath, shifted from one foot to the other, her eyes a little glazed as if lost in the past. But Molly knew that before she could move, Patty could get off several shots at this close range.

"You were furious because the sheriff had crashed his pickup into your brand new expensive car," Patty continued. "I *loved* it. Finally someone had stood up to you. He'd caught you with Kerrington. All your games with him were over. He threatened to go to your father if you didn't take back that announcement you'd made about being engaged to him. You were beside yourself. No one walked away from you. You'd get him back. You'd show him. Then you'd break him. And Kerrington, too. You'd found out that Kerrington wasn't just dating Sandra but that he'd gotten her pregnant and was going to have to marry her. You were going to destroy both of them, too."

Molly felt sick. Had Jasmine really been that vicious? "Jasmine must have been nice some time. Otherwise, why did any of you put up with her?" For a moment Molly didn't think she was going to answer her.

"You were nice at first. You did these little thoughtful things like buy us a pair of earrings or bring us a latte. You seemed to care." Her voice took on a bitter edge. "You got us to tell you our deepest, darkest secrets, things we'd never told anyone, and later, when you turned on us and used those secrets against us, *you* always managed to come off as the victim, the one who was so hurt that we would think you would ever do anything like that."

Molly felt a cold chill skitter up her spine. What horrible thing had she done to this woman to push her to this point? "What did I do to you?"

"I loved him." Patty's voice broke. It was the first emotion Molly had seen and she knew she'd hit a nerve.

"Kerrington?"

Patty's headed snapped back in surprise. "No. Bernard."

"Bernard?" Molly couldn't have been more shocked.

Patty was looking at her strangely. "You *really* don't remember." She gripped the gun a little tighter. "You said you would talk to him about me." Her eyes shone brightly in the kitchen light. "You said you would tell him the good things about me."

Molly could see what was coming.

Patty's eyes brimmed with tears. "When he asked me out, I was so excited. You did my hair and makeup. You said I looked beautiful. You said he wouldn't be able to resist me, once he saw me, once he got to know me."

Molly felt her own tears. She didn't want to hear anymore. "I'm so sorry, Patty."

But Patty wasn't listening. She was reliving the humiliation of that night, a humiliation Molly didn't even want to imagine.

A sob escaped Patty's lips. She choked back another. "It was all a joke. On me. A big laugh for you."

Molly saw her fingers tighten again on the gun and knew she didn't have much time now. Could one of the men outside get in fast enough to save her if she screamed and dove for the door?

Something moved behind Patty. A stealth shadow.

Cash had come back? Or maybe one of the guards had come in to check on her?

Except the doors were all locked. So were the windows. Whoever had come in either had a key. Or…Molly felt her pulse jump. Or had broken into the house.

The shadow moved closer just behind Patty, drawing Molly's attention. Patty saw Molly's eyes dart to a spot over her shoulder. She swung, trying to bring the gun around, but before she could fire a shot, Angel was on her, wrenching the gun from her hand.

Patty cried out and dropped to her knees. Angel stuck the weapon into the waist of his pants and put a knife to Patty's throat, but his eyes were on Molly as if daring her to move.

"Looks like it was a good thing we came back when we did, Vince," Angel said.

FROM THE STAND OF PINES, Cash froze as he watched the figure move through the darkness toward them, carrying the shovel.

Cash could sense Mathews next to him, thinking no doubt the same thing he was. What if the body was buried in the pines where they stood?

They didn't dare move, didn't hardly breathe for fear whoever was coming toward them would see or hear them and take off.

The man appeared as a silhouette against the horizon. He walked awkwardly across the uneven ground in the pitch blackness of the cloudy night, the shovel in his right hand.

Just when Cash knew they would be discovered if the man came any closer, he stopped just inside the pine grove, picked up a large rock and threw it aside. Cash heard the sound of metal scrape dirt as the man began to dig.

Cash silently let out the breath he'd been holding, his relief almost as great as his grief. Finally, Jasmine would be found. Whatever Jasmine had done in her life, she deserved to be put to rest. Cash leaned back against the tree to wait.

The digging stopped. The man threw down the shovel and knelt on the ground.

Beside Cash, Mathews motioned it was time. They moved in quickly, weapons drawn.

If the grave digger heard them coming, he didn't have time to react. Cash sprung from the trees, covering the short distance in a matter of a few strides, the shotgun in his hands.

The man was kneeling on one knee next to the grave. Cash pressed the end of the shotgun barrel against the man's right ear. "Freeze! Police!"

Mathews flicked on his flashlight and shone it into the man's face, then into the partially opened grave, the light ricocheting off a skull.

Kerrington blinked, blinded by the light. He let out a sound like a sob and dropped to his other knee. "It isn't what you think," he cried. "I didn't kill her. I swear to God, she didn't fall hard enough to kill her."

Sick to his stomach, Cash pressed the barrel into Kerrington's neck.

"I'll get the patrol car," Mathews said, looking up at Cash, a clear warning in his gaze. "Read him his rights."

"You have the right to remain silent," Cash began.

"You have to believe me. I shoved her. Outside the bar and she fell and hit her head, but she was alive. She was furious because you'd ran into her new car and...because

Sandra had told her that she was pregnant and we were getting married. I told her I wouldn't marry Sandra, but she was so angry. She was hitting me. I pushed her, she fell. I saw that her head was bleeding and I tried to get her to let me look at it but she wouldn't." His voice broke. "I went back into the bar but I was worried about her. She was in such a state. I went back outside. She was sitting in her car, leaning over the steering wheel. I thought she was just upset, maybe crying." Kerrington began to sob. "There was blood all over." He wrapped his arms around his knees, put his head on the ground next to her grave. "I loved her. I would never kill her."

Cash finished reading him his rights. He could hear Mathews coming with the patrol car. "If you didn't kill her, how did you know where she was buried?"

Kerrington wiped a sleeve over his face and raised his head. "I had to do something. I panicked. I shoved her over in the seat and climbed in. When I looked up, I saw the bartender. She'd come outside for a quick smoke. I didn't know how much she'd seen. I hoped she thought Jasmine was just drunk and that I was driving her home. But I knew she'd seen us fighting before that. Maybe even seen me shove her."

"Why did you put her car in this barn?" Cash asked, already knowing the answer.

"She'd had that fight with you. You'd dented her car. I thought…" His voice trailed off. "I wasn't really trying to frame you. After what I did, I couldn't call the cops and tell them where I'd put it. I guess I hoped the car wouldn't ever be found."

"You didn't want to implicate yourself," Cash said. "You were worried that there would be evidence in the car that might incriminate you."

Mathews pulled up, the headlights of the patrol car bobbing across Jasmine's grave.

"Let's go," Cash said and helped Kerrington to his feet before cuffing him and escorting him into the back of the patrol car.

"I called forensics to see about the body," Mathews said and looked over at him as Cash climbed into the front seat. "I've been trying to reach one of my men at your house."

Cash's blood turned to ice. Molly. No.

"No one's answering." Mathews hit the siren and lights as he sped toward town.

MOLLY STEPPED BACK, the counter cutting into her back as Angel slapped Patty, flattening her on the floor. In that instant, Molly had a flash of memory. There was a coffeemaker on the counter, a bear-sheriff cookie jar, obviously a present, probably from Cash's little sister Dusty. An old blender. And the small vase Cash had put her wildflowers in that morning when he'd brought her breakfast in bed.

"Molly," Angel said and grinned. "It is so good to finally see you." There was just enough sarcasm in his greeting to warn her as he swung with his free hand.

He would have hit Molly if she hadn't seen it coming and ducked.

She swung down and around, grabbing the heavy glass of the blender as she came up. She swung it like a club. The blender struck Angel's right hand—the hand with the knife in it—as he dove for her.

He let out a howl. The knife went flying, hit the floor and slid under the stove.

"You bitch," Angel yelled and lunged for her again.

Molly tried to get in position to swing the blender

again, but Angel had moved too quickly. She ducked, flinching in expectation of the pain that would no doubt come from Angel's fury.

"Angel, wait!"

Vince stepped between them. "It's all right, Molly." His voice was soft, reassuring.

She wasn't fooled. She remembered both men only too well and knew exactly what they were capable of from listening in on their conversations when she was fourteen.

She stood slowly, still gripping the heavy glass blender. Patty was on the floor in the kitchen doorway slumped like a rag doll but conscious. Molly could see that her eyes were open and she was still breathing.

"You can put that down now," Vince said in that same quiet deep voice. "No one wants to hurt you."

Molly laughed, a half-hysterical sound. Everyone in this room wanted to kill her. At least Patty would have made it quick.

Vince smiled as if seeing the humor as well.

"You said I could have the bitch," Angel said. He was hunched against the far end of the counter holding his injured right hand. "I think she broke my friggin' fingers."

She could only hope that he wasn't as expert with a knife in his left hand as he was with his right.

"Let's all just calm down," Vince said. "Molly, Molly, Molly." He sighed. "Why would you put the cops on us? You know what we want. Just give it to us and we'll be on our way."

He was lying and she suspected everyone in this room knew it, even Patty who'd never laid eyes on either man before.

"I don't have the diamonds, Vince," Molly said,

knowing he wasn't going to believe her any more than Patty had believed she wasn't Jasmine.

"I told you the bitch would just lie," Angel snapped.

Vince motioned for Angel to be quiet. "I saw Max whisper something to you, Molly."

She nodded, adjusting her hold on the blender. Vince didn't have a weapon. At least not in his hands. Angel had Patty's pistol still tucked into the waistband of his pants, but he seemed to have forgotten about it in his pain. He kept rubbing his right hand, glaring at her.

"All Max said was 'I'm sorry, kiddo. I'll try to make it up to you.'"

Vince stared at her in disbelief. "Are you telling me Max would waste his last words on something so…ridiculous? How could he possibly make it up to you? He had to know he was dying."

"He said that to me every time one of his schemes failed," Molly said, unable to hide her own bitterness. Max was her only family and he was dead because he was always trying to find the easy way out.

"You knew him," Molly said, finding herself getting angry. "You think he ever made my life easy, even once? Max took the diamonds to hell with him. It's obviously the way he wanted it."

"She's lying," Angel said. "Let me get the truth out of her."

Vince just looked at her, then sighed, and she noticed then how much he'd aged. He looked as strong as a bull but his face was gray, his eyes lifeless.

He looked over at Angel and she saw that Vince had given up. He might believe her, but it didn't make any difference at this point.

"She's all yours," he said to Angel and turned, stepping over Patty as he left the room.

"Vince," Molly called, but knew he wasn't going to save her. She heard the creak of the door that opened the bar, heard him pour himself a drink and sit down as if the weight of the world were on him.

It didn't matter if she knew where the diamonds were or not. Vince wouldn't—or couldn't—stop Angel now.

Angel grinned, spittle at the corner of his mouth as if salivating at the thought of torturing her to death.

He took Patty's small pistol from the waist of his pants and tossed it on the kitchen counter with contempt. Then he edged slowly toward her, opening one kitchen drawer after another until he found what he was after.

He drew a large butcher knife from the drawer with his left hand, his grin spreading across his face, making him look crazy. "Lucky for me I'm ambidextrous."

He lunged at her. She swung the blender, but he was ready, catching it with his right forearm. The heavy glass ricocheted off his arm, hit the edge of the counter and shattered, showering them both with glass as Angel grabbed a handful of her hair with his injured right hand and brought his knee up, catching her in the thigh.

She cried out and he dropped her to the floor, her leg cramping in pain, and he was on her, the butcher knife at her neck, his voice in her ear.

"Now, first off I want you to apologize for putting the cops on us," he whispered. "Then I want you to tell me where the diamonds are. And finally, I want to hear you beg for your life. And you will beg, trust me."

MATHEWS HAD THE PATROL CAR up to over a hundred as they raced toward town, the siren blaring, lights flashing.

With growing fear, Cash tried to reach the officers Mathews had left at the house and got no answer on the two-way radio.

Cash looked over at Mathews as they neared town. Mathews cut the lights and siren, stopping up the street from the house. Cash leapt from the car before it completely stopped, the shotgun in his hands as he ran in a crouch toward the house.

The lights were on inside. No cars out front. No one outside either. Nor did the officers appear as he ran toward the front door. Mathews motioned he was going around the back. Molly would have locked the door, but he tried it anyway before he pulled out his key and quietly put it into the lock.

From inside the house, Cash heard a scream.

His fingers shaking, he turned the knob and burst into the house, the shotgun ready.

The first thing he saw was Patty Franklin curled on the floor in the kitchen doorway. At first he didn't recognize her. Her mascara had run and there was a bright red mark on the side of her face as if she'd recently been slapped.

But her face came alive when she saw him.

His forward motion propelled Cash on into the house. Out of the corner of his eye, he saw a large man sitting in the living room. Vince Winslow shot to his feet. He lunged at Cash, but Patty caught his leg, tripping him and biting down hard on his calf. Vince let out a curse and turned to kick Patty.

Cash brought the butt of the shotgun down on Vince's head. He hit the floor hard, out like a light.

Patty motioned to the kitchen and put a finger across

her throat like a knife. Cash went cold. He nodded and stepped into the kitchen.

What he saw almost made him lose control. The short one, Angel Edwards, had Molly on her hands and knees on the floor, a knife to her throat as he leaned over her. There was blood already running down her neck from several cuts. Her eyes were wide. She blinked at him, her expression softening at the sight of him. There was broken glass all around her on the floor. And blood.

"Get off her," Cash said between gritted teeth.

"I'll slit her throat before you can pull that trigger," Angel said, glee in his voice. "You might kill me, but you'll never be able to save her."

Angel hadn't noticed Patty come into the kitchen. Cash had hardly noticed her himself. She moved almost in slow motion, her hands behind her, no expression on her face.

"Now, put down that shotgun," Angel was saying. "Or I'll kill her. Now!" he shrieked, jerking back on Molly's hair.

It happened so fast Cash wasn't even sure he saw it. Molly let out a cry as Angel jerked her head back. Her hands had been on the floor, but now she came up with a large piece of the broken glass. She drove the glass into Angel's calf as she screamed, "Shoot him!"

Didn't she realize he couldn't fire the shotgun—not with her so close?

But the room boomed with a gunshot, then another, and Cash watched in amazement as Patty rushed Angel, firing a small pistol point blank at his head. Where had she gotten that?

Angel had let go of Molly when she gouged him with the broken glass, but he still had the knife in one hand and a fistful of her hair in the other.

That was until he saw Patty running at him, firing the gun he had so carelessly tossed aside. The caliber was too small to put a man like Angel down.

Patty had been shooting over both Angel's and Molly's heads, but when he saw her running at him firing the gun, he let go of Molly's hair and lunged for Patty.

Molly rolled, flattening herself on the kitchen floor. Cash pulled the trigger, the shotgun bucked in his hands. Angel's chest bloomed with blood just an instant before he swung the blade of the butcher knife in his hand toward Patty.

Cash reached for her to pull her back but it was too late. Angel drove the knife into her chest, letting go as he fell to the floor.

Patty stumbled, falling to her knees. Molly was on her feet, rushing to her, catching her and lowering her to the floor as Cash saw Angel reach for the pistol Patty had dropped.

Cash stepped down hard on Angel's hand. He was still alive, staring up at Cash, bloodthirsty to the end.

"I'm not going back to prison," Angel said.

"You're right about that," Cash said and watched Angel die.

Behind him, he heard Mathews come into the room. He was on his two-way radioing for an ambulance and backup.

Cash knelt on the floor next to Molly. She had Patty's head in her lap and she was crying.

"I'm so sorry," Molly was whispering. "I'm so sorry."

Patty's eyes flickered open. She smiled up at Molly. "You're not Jasmine."

Molly shook her head.

"It's all right. I'll be seeing her soon." Patty's eyes glittered at the thought for a moment, then the light went out and slowly her lids closed and she was gone.

Molly leaned over, crying. Cash put an arm around her, drawing her to him as Mathews took the dead woman from her.

"It's over, Molly. It's finally all over. You're safe." Cash held her to him, wishing he never had to let her go.

EPILOGUE

CASH WATCHED MOLLY peer out the plane window and smiled to himself to see how well she was recovering.

"I can't believe this is the first time I've ever flown," she said, her excitement contagious. "Thank you for coming with me."

Past her profile, the Atlantic Ocean shone deep blue as the plane made the final approach to the Miami International Airport.

He'd been in the E.R. waiting room, waiting to hear how Molly was doing from the cuts on her neck, when he'd gotten the call from Frank. Mathews had arrested Vince when he came to and had the coroner pick up Patty and Angel. Vince was back in prison and wouldn't be getting out any time soon.

Kerrington had been arrested for his part in covering up Jasmine's death—and the murder of Teresa Clark. Kerrington swore he hadn't killed the bartender, that Bernard must have done it. Kerrington was in jail in Montana, on no bond, awaiting trial. His wife Sandra had filed for divorce and had moved in with Bernard.

Bernard had confessed, now that Jasmine's killer had been caught. He had admitted that he had been the man the gas station clerk had seen leave with Jasmine. He hadn't come forward because of obvious reasons. He'd said he and Jasmine had talked and then she'd gone to meet Kerrington. He'd said that was the last time he'd seen her and that the bartender had been wrong about him being at the Dew Drop Inn the night Jasmine had been killed.

Bernard had seen that Jasmine was properly buried in Atlanta next to her father.

Mathews was still investigating Teresa Clark's murder, convinced that before it was over, Bernard would be behind bars where he belonged.

Cash had asked for a few weeks off after receiving Frank's call from the FBI.

"Cash, sorry man, I know it's late, but I thought you'd want this news ASAP."

Cash had completely forgotten that Molly's prints were on file somewhere and he'd asked Frank to track them down. It seemed like a lifetime ago—not just hours.

He had started to tell Frank that it didn't matter. He didn't care what she'd done. Or who she was. "Frank, right now isn't—"

"You aren't going to believe this. I tracked down those prints you sent me. Her name's Molly right? It was a kidnapping."

"She's wanted for *kidnapping?*"

"Naw." Frank had laughed. "She *was* kidnapped. Almost thirty years ago. Biological father stole her. Mother never saw her again, later the mother had reason to believe she was dead after the private investigators she'd hired almost caught the father. Found some of the toddler's clothing with a whole lot of blood on it where the two had been staying. Turned out to be the toddler's blood type."

Was that when Molly had gotten the scar on her forehead that she couldn't remember getting? "Is her mother still alive?" Cash had asked.

"Affirmative. That's what makes this case so interesting. This isn't just any kid who was kidnapped. This is the daughter of Rachel Valentine of the Paris Valentines, one of the wealthiest families in Europe."

There had to be a mistake. Molly was a Valentine?

"It gets better. Guess who the father was."

"The Great Maximilian Burke."

"You knew, huh? Well, then you must know about the big diamond heist in Hollywood fifteen years ago. He was shot down by the cops. The diamonds were never recovered. When they took his prints they found out that he was Joe Cooper, the man the FBI had been looking for in the kidnapping of the Valentine baby. But the Valentines paid to keep all that quiet, hoping to find the kid. She would have been fourteen then."

Cash had a feeling he knew what was coming.

"Someone had seen a girl about the right age with Maximilian right before he died, but she disappeared. No one knew what had happened to her. Might not even have been his daughter. According to the guys who were arrested, she *wasn't* his daughter, just some girl he'd picked up to help him with his magic acts," Frank had said. "Whoever she was, she'd just disappeared.

"The thing is," Frank had continued, "the agents really want to talk to this woman. The diamonds in that heist were never found and since she was the last person to see Maximilian alive… Tell me you have her in custody."

"Sorry. Maybe she'll turn up again," Cash had said, afraid he really was going to lose her. "Where'd you say her mother lives?"

"Miami. I can't believe you let her get away," Frank had said and Cash had looked up and seen the doctor coming down the hall toward him.

"Got to go. Thanks, Frank." He'd hung up.

"She's going to be fine," the doctor had said. "Fortunately the cuts were superficial. She might have a couple of light scars, nothing like the one on her forehead. She tell you how she got that one?"

Cash had shaken his head. "She doesn't remember."

"Nasty scar. Must have really bled. I've given her some pain medicine and prescribed some more if she needs it." He'd handed Cash the prescription. "She said she was with you?"

Cash had nodded. "She's with me."

"I'm scared," Molly said now as the plane made its descent into Miami.

He took her hand and squeezed it gently. She squeezed back. He knew it wasn't the landing that had her frightened. It was meeting her mother. Molly had had no idea her mother was still alive. Or that her father had kidnapped her.

"It explains why we never stayed in one place for long," she'd said when he'd told her the news. "Also why he didn't want anyone to know he was my father."

Rachel Valentine had been overjoyed to hear that her daughter had finally been found. And she'd put together the last piece of the puzzle.

"Max sent me Molly's teddy bear," Rachel said, tears in her voice. "I got it in the mail fifteen years ago with a note. All the note said was that he was sorry and that he would someday make it up to me."

The FBI agent Cash sent to check the teddy bear found the stolen diamonds from the heist inside.

The plane touched down. Cash could feel how anxious Molly was—and how worried. Molly and her mother would be strangers. Mothers shouldn't be strangers to their children, he thought, thinking of his own mother.

Except Rachel Valentine hadn't chosen this. She'd spent years and thousands of dollars trying to find Molly. She'd only given up when she'd thought Molly was dead. Later, when Max had been killed, she'd tried again but to no avail. Molly had been running again.

Cash was just thankful that she'd run to him.

The limo that Rachel Valentine had sent for her daughter was waiting as they came out of the terminal. When the chauffeur jumped out and opened the door, a beautiful woman with blond hair and green eyes disembarked from the back. The resemblance between the two women left little doubt that Molly was her long-lost daughter.

Rachel froze at the sight of Molly, her hand going to her mouth, tears brimming in her eyes. Then she opened her arms and Molly stumbled into them.

Cash watched the two hug. They had almost thirty years of catching up to do. He'd promised to come this far with Molly, but now she would be fine on her own. Molly was a strong woman. She'd already survived so much.

He turned to disappear into the crowd. Molly didn't need him anymore.

"Cash?"

He stopped at the sound of her voice, amazed by the effect it always had on him. He turned slowly to look at her. She couldn't have been more beautiful standing there beside her mother.

She smiled at him as she walked to him. "Where do you think you're going?"

"Molly, you don't need me now. You and your mother have a lot of catching up to do. You're finally safe, with family. Who knows, you might decide to stay in Miami."

He looked to the palm trees waving in the sea breeze. "It's beautiful here."

She touched his cheek, drawing his gaze back to hers. "This is just a visit. One of many I hope. For the first time in my life, I've found the place I want to stay, Cash. It's a little town in Montana. Antelope Flats. Ever heard of it?"

"Molly, you don't know what you're saying."

"I spent my whole life running from something I never understood." She touched the scar on her forehead, a head wound from a childhood accident that had bled enough to make her mother stop looking for her.

"I don't want to run anymore, especially from my feelings," she said. "I'm in love with you, Cash McCall. We don't know each other very well, but I was thinking that if I were to hang around Antelope Flats, maybe we could get to know each other."

His heart swelled and for a moment he couldn't say a word. He looked into her eyes, reminded of a spring day in Montana, and thought he caught a glimpse of the future. He pulled her into his arms, closing his eyes and just holding her.

"About that old house of yours," she said when she finally drew back.

"I'll put it on the market when I get back to Montana," he said.

"You bought it because you like old houses, right?"

He nodded, looking embarrassed. "You hate old houses."

She smiled. "I used to, but I have to tell you I've been thinking about your house. It would take a lot of work, but it has…possibilities. Just like you and me."

"Are you sure?" Cash asked, his heart in his throat. "That house has to have some bad memories for you."

She shook her head. "I've run my whole life from bad memories. That house also has some good memories and I'm hoping to make a lot more once I get back to Montana." She smiled. "Which will be soon." She kissed him then, a soft, sweet kiss filled with promise, then she turned and walked back to her mother and disappeared into the back of the limo.

Cash watched her go, turned and, whistling, headed for home. Home. The day he'd bought it, he'd dreamed of someday finding a woman to love and filling that old house with children.

What he'd never dreamed of was a woman like Molly. Some things were even beyond a man's wildest dreams.

* * * * *

HIGH-CALIBER
COWBOY

To my high-caliber cowboy,
my wonderful husband, Parker.

CHAPTER ONE

Saturday night

EMMA INGLES LOVED the night shift. Tonight, she'd fallen asleep watching an old Western on the little TV in the office, her feet up on the desk, her mouth open.

She was a bulky woman, with bad feet and little ambition, who looked much tougher than she was. But she'd found the perfect job for a woman in her late fifties. Well, *almost* the perfect job.

She woke in midsnore. Startled, she sat up, her feet hitting the floor with a slap as she looked around. She muted the movie and glanced at the clock. Just a little after 3:00 a.m.

Listening, she was relieved to hear *nothing,* which was exactly what she should have heard since she was completely alone in the huge old building. At least, she was supposed to be.

Warily, she glanced through the glass-and-mesh window that looked out on the worn linoleum-tile hallway. In the dim light, her gaze wandered down to the chained, locked double doors to the wing that had housed the violent patients, the criminally insane.

Please, not tonight. There were times she swore she heard cries coming from that wing. That's why she kept the TV cranked up loud enough to drown out any noises, real or imagined. The wing had been empty for twenty years now—and locked up tight. If that's where the sound had come from no way was she going down there to investigate—even if she'd *had* a key.

The back-door buzzer went off, making her jump. That must be what had awakened her. But who would be ringing the buzzer at this hour? Her boss, Realtor Frank Yarrow, was in charge of selling the building and would have called or maybe come to the front door if there were an emergency of some kind.

But she couldn't even see him driving up here at three in the morning. The former Brookside Mental Institution was at the end of a winding dirt road, the monstrous three-story brick building perched like a vulture on the mountainside, ten miles from town. Isolated, hidden, forgotten. For sale.

Given the history of this place, the only people who came up here, especially at night, were kids. They'd get a six-pack and drive up from Antelope Flats, Montana, or from Sheridan, Wyoming, which was about fifteen miles farther south.

After a few beers, they'd dare each other to prove how brave they were by chucking a few rocks through the windows or painting some stupid graffiti on the worn bricks. They never rang the buzzer. Probably because few people even knew it existed.

Emma realized she hadn't heard a car, not that she could have over the shoot-'em-up western on TV with the volume turned up.

The buzzer sounded again. Had to be kids. Some punk kids trying to give her a hard time.

Well, she'd set them straight. She hauled herself up from the chair, picked up the heavy-duty flashlight and opened the door to the dark hallway. Scaring kids was another of the perks that came with the job.

There was only one small light on at the end of each corridor to give the place the appearance of not being completely abandoned. She closed her office door, pitching the hallway where she stood into blackness and waited for her eyes to adjust.

Behind her, there was the faint glow of light coming from her office window that looked out into the foyer. But in front of her was nothing but darkness.

She padded down the gloomy hall to where the building made a ninety-degree turn to the left into another corridor that eventually led to the back door. It was an odd-shaped building, with a wing off each side of the entry that jutted straight back, making a U of sorts behind the place where there had once been an old orchard.

The trees were now all dead, the bare limbs a web of twisted dark wood.

Emma made a point of never going around back. The place was scary enough. That's why she was surprised kids would go around there to ring the buzzer.

Well, they were in for a surprise. She'd give them a good scare. Then she'd go back to sleep.

As she turned the corner and looked down the corridor, she saw that the light at the end had burned out again. But a car with the headlights on was parked outside and she could make out the silhouette of a person through the steel mesh covering the back-door window.

The shape was large. Not a kid. A big man, from the size of him. She felt the first niggling of real fear. What could he want at this hour?

The buzzer sounded again, this time more insistent.

Emma had never been very intuitive, but something told her not to answer the door.

Go back to the office, call the sheriff in Antelope Flats.

She told herself that if the man at the back door had a good reason to be here, he'd have called first. He wouldn't have just shown up at this hour of the night. And he would have used the front door.

She started to turn back toward her office to make that call when she heard what sounded like the front door opening. She froze, telling herself she must have imagined it. She'd checked to make sure the front door was locked before she went to sleep.

Cool night air rushed around her thick ankles. *Someone had come in the front door!*

How was that possible? As far as she knew, there were only three keys: one for herself, one for the Realtor and one for the other night watchman, Karl, the man she was filling in for tonight. The Realtor hated to come out here even in daylight. No way would he be here at this hour!

Until that moment, she'd never considered that anyone who used to work here might still have a key since the locks wouldn't have been changed in the vacant building.

She heard the front door close in a soft whoosh and then footfalls headed down the hall in her direction.

Her fear spiked. She couldn't get back to the office without running into whoever had just come in.

From the quick pace of the footsteps, the person headed her way would soon turn the corner and see her. Panicked, she ducked into one of the empty rooms and immediately realized her mistake. The room was small, rectangular and windowless, with no place to hide.

She started to close the door. It made a creaking sound. She froze, even more shaken at the thought of what she'd almost done. The doors locked automatically with no way to open them from the inside. So even if she hadn't left her keys on her desk in the office, she wouldn't have been able to get out.

She could hear footsteps, close now, and didn't dare move even if there had been enough room to hide behind the partially closed door.

Flattening herself as best as she could against the wall in the pitch-black room, Emma held her breath and watched the dim corridor, praying whoever it was wouldn't look this way.

The footfalls hurried past as the buzzer sounded again. She got only a fleeting look at the man. Tall, dressed in a long black coat, a dark fedora covering all of his hair except for a little gray at the side. She had never seen him before.

The buzzer started to sound again but was cut off in midbuzz. She heard a key being inserted in the lock. The back door banged open.

"I thought I told you not to ring the bell," snapped a voice Emma *had* heard before. The man had called a few days ago. She remembered because no one ever called while she was on the night shift.

He'd demanded information without even bothering to tell her who was calling. She hadn't liked his attitude—that sharp edge of authority she'd always resented.

"I'm sorry, who is this?" she'd demanded, and waited until he'd finally snapped, "Dr. French."

He'd asked if anyone was there besides her. She'd told him that was none of his business. Well, did she know what had happened to the patient records? Were they in storage? Or had someone taken them? Could he come up and look for them?

She told him she didn't know anything about any files and no one was allowed in the building at night, that he should talk to the Realtor.

He'd become angry and hung up, but she hadn't forgotten his voice. Or the way he'd made her feel. Small.

"You were supposed to wait," Dr. French snapped at the man at the back door.

"She was starting to wake up and you said not to give her any more of the drug," the other man answered in a deep gravelly voice Emma didn't recognize.

"Get her in here," Dr. French ordered. "Where is the man you said would be here?"

"Karl? Don't know. Haven't seen him yet."

There was a metal clank and then Dr. French said, "You made sure there will be no trace of her?"

"I did just as you said. Got rid of everything. Including her rental car."

Emma didn't move, didn't breathe, but her heart was pounding so hard she feared they would hear it and discover her. They thought *Karl* was working tonight. Because Karl was *supposed* to be working tonight. If she hadn't needed the money when he'd asked her to fill in at the last minute—

"There's a car parked out front," Dr. French said. "It must belong to your friend."

"Guess so, though I thought he drove a truck."

The back door closed in a whoosh, automatically locking. Emma heard another clank and then footsteps coming down the corridor toward the room where she was hiding. Something squeaked as they moved.

Out of the corner of her eye Emma saw the doctor and a large burly-looking man roll a wheelchair past, one of the tires squeaking on the linoleum. The burly man had a bad case of bed-hair, his mousy brown hair sticking out at all angles.

Emma only glimpsed the woman slumped in the wheelchair with her head lolling to one side. She wore a long coat, slacks and penny loafers. Her chin-length dyed auburn hair hid most of her face. She clearly wasn't from around this area.

The wheelchair squeaked down the hall to the echo of the men's footsteps. Emma waited until she heard them turn the corner and start down the hall toward her office before she moved.

Her first instinct was to run down the corridor, out the back door. Except all the doors in the building locked automatically and had to be opened from the inside with a key, a precaution from when patients roamed these halls.

And she'd left her keys on her desk, not needing them to scare away a few kids through the window at the back door.

She would have to hide in the building.

Unless she could get to her keys.

She stole down the corridor, trying not to make a sound. At the corner, she sneaked a look down the hallway toward her office.

The two men had stopped with the wheelchair at

the locked section that had once been reserved for the criminally insane.

The chain and lock on the doors rattled. She watched as Dr. French inserted a key. The chain fell away with a clatter that reverberated through the building. Afraid to move, she watched the doctor hold the door open for the wheelchair.

He had a *key?* Even she didn't have a key to that area and had been told it was only a long corridor of padded, soundproof rooms best left locked up.

Emma waited until the men disappeared through the doors, the burly one wheeling the woman into the second door on the right. The number on the door read 9B. What was it she'd heard about 9B, something terrible. *Oh God.* She had to get out of here.

If she moved fast, she could get to her office, get the keys to the front door—and her car. The doctor had seen it parked out front. He knew she was here. She had no choice. But if she could reach her car and get away...

She hadn't gotten but a few yards when she heard the squeak of the wheelchair; a slightly different sound echoed. They were already coming back!

Panic immobilized her. Down the dim hallway, she saw the burly man back out of the room with the empty wheelchair. She had to move fast. They would be looking for her, wondering where she was, what she'd witnessed. After all, she wasn't supposed to be working tonight.

But where could she go? Not the patient rooms. If they caught her hiding in the dark in one of them, they'd know she'd heard their conversation.

Where?

She caught sight of the ladies' room just a few doors

up the hall in the same direction as the men. *Run!* Except she couldn't run. She couldn't even walk fast because of her feet and years of inactivity. But she managed a lunging shuffle, her heart thundering in her chest—a clumsy, terrifying run for her life.

As the doctor came out of the room and closed 9B's door, Emma shoved open the ladies' room door and stumbled into the windowless blackness. Frantically, she felt her way to one of the four stalls.

Stumbling into the cold metal stall, she closed the door, locked it and, quaking with fear, sat down on the toilet.

All she could hear was the pounding of her pulse in her ears and the echo of panting. She had to quit gasping for breath. They would hear her. The place was old and empty. Every sound echoed through it. If she could hear them, they could hear her. She had to get control, had to think.

She held her breath for a moment and listened. The snick of a lock followed the rattle of the chain on the doors to the closed wing. She let out the breath she'd been holding. It came out as a sob. She clutched her hand over her mouth, breathing fast through her nose.

From where she sat, she could see through the crack along the edge of the stall to the lighter gap under the bathroom door.

The empty wheelchair squeaked down the hall along with the sound of the men's footfalls. She held her breath as a shadow darkened the gap under the ladies' room door. They were directly outside. Had they seen her? Did they know she was in here?

"Looks like Karl's here somewhere," said the burly one. "We interrupted his dinner."

Her sandwich! She'd left it half-eaten on her desk when she'd fallen asleep. She'd also left the light on in her office, the TV on, the volume turned low.

"Karl carries a *purse?*" Dr. French asked in a tone heavy with sarcasm.

Her heart stopped. She'd left her purse on the desk. Her purse!

"Dammit, Davidson, I thought you said Karl was definitely working tonight," Dr. French snapped.

"He *said* he was."

The older man made a disgusted sound.

Emma couldn't hold her breath much longer. Tears burned her eyes. They knew she was in the building. They would look for her. She had to think of something. Some way out of here.

Closing her eyes tightly, she waited. Over the pounding of her pulse, she heard the squeak of the wheelchair growing fainter and fainter as it moved down the corridor away from her.

She waited until she heard the back door close before she moved. Opening her eyes, she forced herself to leave the stall. A dim light filled the gap under the door. No shadows. She pushed open the door.

They were gone.

She leaned back against the wall, weak with relief.

The hallway was empty.

She heard the sound of the back door opening and closing. A car engine revved, the sound growing dimmer.

Her legs were like water and she feared she might be sick as she shuffled back to her office, trying not to hurry in case anyone was watching her. She didn't look behind her down the hall. Nor did she glance toward the locked wing where the men had taken the woman.

At her partially closed office door, she braced herself and pushed. The door swung noiselessly open. Her heart lodged in her throat as she looked to her chair.

Dr. French wasn't sitting in it, as she'd expected he would be.

The office was empty.

The movie was over on the small TV. Her half-eaten sandwich was still on the edge of the desk along with her Big Gulp-size diet cola and her purse.

She began to cry from relief as she hurriedly closed and locked the door behind her. Stumbling to her chair, she dropped into it, her muscles no longer able to hold her up.

She was safe.

They were gone.

She could pretend she'd never seen them.

But could she pretend she didn't know there was a woman locked in one of the padded, soundproof rooms down the hall? And wouldn't the men return for her?

Emma reached for the remote and shut off the TV. She should call someone. The sheriff. But then she would have to stay here alone until he arrived.

Not if she called from home. She didn't live far from here. Just a few miles down the river toward Wyoming.

She picked up her purse and reached for her kitten key chain with the keys to the doors out of here.

The keys were gone.

Panic sent her blood pressure into orbit. She couldn't get out until she found the keys. She bent, thinking she must have knocked them to the floor.

But as she bent over, the hairs rose on the back of her neck.

In slow motion she lifted her head, then turned by degrees to look behind her through the office window to the hallway.

Dr. French smiled and held up her keys.

CHAPTER TWO

Monday night
Two nights later

BRANDON MCCALL couldn't keep his eyes open. He'd driven every road on this section of the ranch and, like all the other nights, he hadn't seen a thing. Not a track in the soft earth. Not a light flickering down in the sagebrush. Not a soul.

Tonight a storm was blowing in. Lightning splintered the horizon and thunder rumbled in the distance as dark clouds washed across the wild landscape, from the Bighorn Mountains over the rolling foothills to the tall cottonwoods of the river bottom.

The first raindrops startled him, hitting the roof of his pickup like hail. He stopped on a hill, turned off the engine and killed the lights.

Taking off his Stetson, he laid it over the steering wheel and stretched his long legs across the bench seat, careful not to get his muddy western boots on the upholstery.

He had a good view of the ranch below him and knew there were a half-dozen other men on watch tonight in other areas, waiting for vandals.

Unfortunately there was too much country, and even

Mason VanHorn, as rich as he was, couldn't afford to hire enough men to patrol his entire ranch.

Something moved in the darkness, making him sit up a little. A stand of pine trees swayed in the stormy darkness. He watched for a moment, then leaned back again. False alarm. But he didn't take his eyes off the spot.

It looked like another long, boring night since he doubted the vandal was dedicated enough to come out in this weather. This was southeastern Montana, coal country, and coalbed methane gas had turned out to be the accidental by-product of the huge, open-pit coal mining to the south. The thick coal seams were saturated with water, which, when pumped out, produced gas that bubbled up like an opened bottle of cola.

With big money in natural gas, thousands of wells had sprung up almost overnight, causing controversy in the ranching communities. Some landowners had cashed in, opting to have the shallow wells dug on their property. Others, like Brandon's father, Asa, would die before he'd have one on his ranch.

The real battles had less to do with traditional uses of the land and more to do with environmental concerns, though. By extracting the gas from the water, something had to be done with all the water, which was considered too salty for irrigation but was being dumped into the Tongue River. The drilling was also said to lower the water table, leaving some ranch wells high and dry.

Mason VanHorn had the most gas wells and was the most outspoken in favor of the drilling. Because of that, he'd become the target of protesters on more than one occasion.

And that was how Brandon McCall had gotten a night

job on the VanHorn spread. He'd been in the Longhorn Café in Antelope Flats the day the new VanHorn Ranch manager, Red Hudson, had come in looking for men to patrol the ranch at night.

Fortunately for Brandon, Red didn't seem to know about a long-standing feud between the VanHorns and the McCalls and Brandon hadn't brought it up. He'd hired on, needing the money. While he worked some on his family ranch at the other end of the river valley, that job didn't pay like this one.

The irony was that his little sister Dusty thought he had a girlfriend and that's why he dragged in like a tomcat just before dawn every day.

He wished. No, this was his little secret. And given the generations of bad blood between the McCalls and the VanHorns, Brandon would be out of a job—or worse—once ranch owner Mason VanHorn found out. He hated to think how VanHorn would take it when he found out he had a McCall on his payroll.

Something moved again in a stand of pines below him. The wind and something else.

He sat all the way up.

A slim, dark figure stood motionless at the edge of the pines. He stared so hard he was almost convinced it was a trick of the light from the storm.

The wind whipped at the trees. Rain slanted down, pelting the hood, pouring down the windshield. He turned on the wipers, squinting into the driving rain and darkness.

This had been monotonous boring work—until last night when several of the wells had actually been vandalized. Nothing serious, just a lame protest attempt, and patrols had been stepped up.

Red had made it clear he wanted the vandal caught at all costs. And now it looked as if the vandal was planning to hit one of the wells in Brandon's section.

The presumed vandal sprinted out from the pines, running fast and low as he wove his way through the tall sage and the rain. He wore all black, even the stocking cap on his head. From this distance, he appeared slightly built, like a teenager. A teenager on a mission, since he had what appeared to be a crowbar in one hand.

The vandal disappeared over a rise.

Brandon slapped a hand on the steering wheel with a curse. If he started the pickup, the vandal would hear it and no doubt take off on him. Brandon needed to catch him in the act.

He had no choice. He was going to have to go after him through the pouring rain and darkness. He'd be lucky if he didn't break his leg or worse, as dark as it was.

Pulling on his coat, he snugged on his Stetson, quietly opened the pickup door and reached back to pull the shotgun from the gun rack behind the seat. Not that he planned to shoot anyone. Especially if it really did turn out to be some teenager with a cause.

But it was always better to have a weapon and not need it than the other way around.

Rain slashed down, stinging his face as he loped down the hillside, winding his way through the sagebrush until he reached the rise where he'd last seen him. In a crouch, the shotgun in both hands, he topped the rise and squinted through the rain and darkness.

At first, he didn't see anything. Coalbed methane wells were fairly unobtrusive. Not a bunch of rigging like oil wells. The wellheads were covered with a tan box about the size of a large air-conditioning unit. The boxes dotted the landscape to the north past the ranch complex, but there were none near the house.

He scanned the half-dozen wells he could see. No sign of anyone. Frowning, he wondered if the vandal might have doubled back, having purposely drawn him away from his pickup. Brandon had been so sure the vandal hadn't seen him where he was parked.

But as Brandon started to look behind him, he caught movement down the hillside toward the ranch house itself and the large stand of pine trees behind it.

The VanHorn Ranch was nothing like Brandon's family's Sundown Ranch, which was family-owned and run with a main house and the barns nearby.

The VanHorn Ranch was run by hired help, so the main ranch house sat back a half mile from a cluster of buildings that housed the ranch office, the bunkhouses and the ranch manager's house.

The rustic main ranch house was long and narrow, tucked back into the hillside and banked in the back by pines. Mason VanHorn lived in the house all alone after, according to local scuttlebutt, his wife had run off and he'd alienated his only two offspring.

The vandal disappeared into the pines at the back of the ranch house, the crowbar glinting in the dim light.

This time of the morning, there were no lights on in the small compound down the road from the ranch house, and few vehicles, since most of the men were out riding the huge ranch's perimeter.

The ranch house was even more deserted since Mason VanHorn had flown to Gillette, Wyoming, two days ago for a gas convention and would be gone for at least another forty-eight hours.

Red had promised a large bonus to any man who caught the vandals or anyone else trespassing on the VanHorn Ranch before the boss got home.

And now Brandon had one in his sights.

A bank of clouds crushed out the light of the moon. Brandon moved, running fast. Had their vandal gone from wells to an even bigger prize: VanHorn's house?

Brandon reached the trees and stopped, moving slowly through the darkness of the dense pines to the back of the house. The guy was nowhere in sight, but Brandon heard the snap of rain-soaked curtains in the wind and spotted the open window.

He thought about radioing for backup, but just the sound of the radio might warn the intruder. At the window, he raised the glass higher to accommodate his height of six-four, and climbed into what appeared to be a bathroom, since he found himself standing in a large tub, the wet curtains flapping behind him in the wind.

Standing perfectly still, he listened for any sign of the vandal. The bathroom door was open and he could see light coming from down the hall.

Moving cautiously, he stepped out of the tub to the doorway. Across the hall, he could see what was clearly a little girl's room. A spoiled little girl's room, from the frilly canopy bed to the inordinate amount of stuffed animals filling the room. It surprised him, since a little girl hadn't lived in this house in years.

He ventured out into the hall, hoping Mason VanHorn didn't come home early and catch him here. He cringed at the thought of the rancher finding a reviled McCall not only in his house, but dripping on his hall rug.

The flickering faint glow of a flashlight spilled from

the last open door on the hallway. He froze, listening. It sounded like someone was opening and closing file cabinet drawers.

He crept toward the sound and the flickering light, moving cautiously, the shotgun in his hands.

As he neared the open doorway, he could hear the intruder riffling through papers, opening and closing desk doors. What was he looking for? Wouldn't a vandal just start tearing up the place? Spray-paint the walls with words of protest instead of going through files?

He stopped as the house fell silent. At the sound of a metallic *tick, tick, tick,* Brandon stepped into the room, the barrel of the shotgun leading the way as he wondered what the vandal had done with the crowbar he'd been carrying. Hopefully he'd left it out in the rain after breaking in through the bathroom window.

The vandal had his back to him, the flashlight beam focused on the dial of a wall safe.

Brandon reached over and hit the light switch. "Freeze!"

The figure froze.

The room was one of those fancy home offices with the massive wooden desk, the expensive leather chair, a nice oak file cabinet and a brushed copper desk lamp with a Tiffany shade. Nice.

The person behind the desk with his back to Brandon was smaller framed than he'd first thought—and from the shape, definitely not a teenager. Nor a man. The hourglass figure was all female and only accentuated by the tight black bodysuit she wore. A long lock of dark hair had escaped the black stocking cap and now hung dripping down her back.

"You caught me," she said in a silken voice as she

turned, one hand holding the flashlight she'd had pointed on the safe, the other empty.

She was in her late twenties to early thirties with wide brown eyes, striking features and the kind of innocence that did something to a man.

"Put down the flashlight. Gently," he ordered.

She gave him a look as if she thought he was being overly cautious, but did as he asked.

"What do you think you're doing?" he demanded.

She blinked. "I was about to open the safe."

"I can see that. *Why* are you breaking into Mr. Van-Horn's safe?" he asked impatiently.

Her face was flushed from exertion and wet from the rain, her errant lock of hair soaked. "I wanted to see what was inside?"

"Do you think this is funny?" he demanded reaching for the two-way radio to call this in.

"No," she said quickly. "I'm just nervous. This is the first time I've ever done anything like this."

His hand stopped shy of the radio. "You're in a world of trouble." More than she knew, once he called the ranch manager....

She nodded, a slight tremble of her lips and an edgy flicker of her gaze toward the door giving away her tension. She *should* have been scared since he was holding a shotgun on her, had caught her red-handed trying to break into his employer's safe and she had no way out.

"Do you have to hold that gun on me?" she asked, her big brown eyes wide with fear. "I'm not armed. You can search me if you don't believe me."

It was a nice offer but he shook his head and swung the barrel of the gun downward away from her. Hell, he could see every curve of her body in that outfit she was wearing. It was time to radio Red Hudson, the ranch manager. His instructions had been quite clear. "No authorities. We handle our own affairs on this ranch."

Resting the shotgun in the crook of his arm, he stepped deeper into the room and unclipped the two-way radio at his hip.

"Please don't call anyone," she pleaded, motioning toward the radio. "I was just out here trying to get a story. I'm a reporter."

He held the radio but didn't press the key to talk. "A reporter?" He hadn't expected that. "Odd way to get a story, by vandalizing and breaking into a man's property."

"I didn't know of any other way since a man like Mason VanHorn, with his kind of power, requires desperate measures," she said. "He can buy all the cowboys he needs to keep his secrets." She gave him a look as if to say he was proof of that.

"Mason didn't buy *me*."

"I thought you worked for him," she said.

"I'm just night security."

She nodded, but clearly believed he was one of Van-Horn's henchmen.

Brandon swore under his breath, upset that she had the wrong impression of him—and yet reminding himself that this woman was a criminal under the law. He didn't have to explain himself to her.

He started to raise the radio.

"What does he pay you?" she asked quickly. "I can't pay you much but—"

"I'm not for hire. Look, if this is your first offense, the judge will probably go easy on you."

She sounded close to tears when she said, "You know if you turn me over to Mason VanHorn, I will never see the local law, let alone a courtroom."

He hated that she was right. VanHorn would take care of this in his own way. Brandon didn't want to think what the rancher would do to this woman.

"I need to sit down," she said suddenly, and swung her hip up onto the edge of the desk before he had a chance to tell her not to move. "I'm sorry. I can stand if you want."

She slid off the corner of the desk, a movement as graceful as a dancer's. A movement designed to distract, to hide her true intention.

He never saw it coming. Never actually saw her grab the brushed-copper desk lamp. Never saw it in the air until he was forced to raise the shotgun to deflect the blow.

The lamp hit the barrel in a loud clash of metals. The bulb broke, showering him in fine glass. He ducked instinctively as the lamp clattered to the floor and he dropped the two-way radio.

He opened his eyes, feeling the broken glass on his cheeks, wanting to brush it off, but resisting the urge.

He darted a look behind the desk. She was gone. Not that he'd really expected her to still be standing there.

He whirled and rushed to the doorway, the shotgun still in his hands. Stopping at the threshold, he looked both ways down the hall in case she was waiting with another weapon.

The hall was empty.

He rushed toward the bathroom. Would she go out the way she'd come in?

The bathroom was dark. The window still open. The

wet curtain billowing in with the wind and rain. He lunged toward the dark opening, determined to catch her. She'd been fast, but he was faster.

He'd only taken a step into the room when he was hit from behind. Pain radiated through his head. She must have been hiding in the room across the hall.

It was his last thought as the white tile floor came up at him just before the darkness.

ANNA HATED that she'd had to hit him and hoped it hadn't been too hard. But he'd given her no choice. She couldn't let him turn her in. Especially before she got what she'd come for.

Hurriedly, she moved back down the hall. She'd found the combination taped under the center drawer of the desk, having discovered a long time ago that men like Mason VanHorn changed their combinations all the time out of paranoia.

But because of that, they had trouble remembering the new combination, had to hide it someplace so it would be handy.

Back down the hall, she stepped around the broken lamp and glass and went to the safe again. She spotted the two-way radio and kicked it behind the curtain.

Starting over after the earlier surprise interruption, she turned the dial, hoping she'd bought herself enough time to finish what she'd started. She began to dial in the numbers she'd memorized.

She'd known she might get caught in the house tonight. There was always that chance. But she'd never dreamed the man holding the gun on her would be Brandon McCall.

She tried not to think about him lying on the floor in

the bathroom. She was angry enough to hit him again. And to think that at one time she'd had fantasies about the kind of cowboy Brandon McCall would grow up to be. Definitely not a cowboy doing Mason VanHorn's dirty work.

The tumblers thunked into place and after a moment, the safe door swung open. She heard a groan from down the hall in the bathroom and was glad he was alive, but sorry he was coming around already. She hadn't wanted to kill him, just keep him out of her hair; if she could just finish here and get away without having to hit him again—or him shoot her.

Standing on her tiptoes, she peered into the safe debating whether to take everything or try to go through it here and chance getting caught again.

The question turned out to be moot. She stared into the cold dark cavity. The safe was empty. Not just empty, but dusty inside except for the spot where there'd been something. Unfortunately, that something was gone.

Another groan from down the hallway.

Tears burned her eyes. Mason VanHorn had moved the papers. She was too late.

She turned, blinded by hot tears of anger and frustration, and started out the door. A thought stopped her. She hurried back to his desk. Earlier she'd searched it, the desk drawers and the file cabinets, but hadn't found what she was looking for.

Now she picked up the phone and hit redial on a hunch. If he'd taken the precaution to clean out the safe, he might have taken other precautions, as well.

After four rings, a voice mail message picked up. "You've reached Dr. Niles French. Leave a number and I'll get back to you."

Dr. French. She clutched the phone, sick to her stomach. She heard stirring down the hall. Another groan. *Move. Get out. Now!* Fear paralyzed her. Dr. French.

A groan down the hall.

Hurriedly, she scribbled down the phone number on the display, her hands shaking. If the last call Mason VanHorn had made was to Dr. French, then she knew she was in trouble.

Suddenly she couldn't breathe. She thought she might pass out if she didn't get out of this room. Out of this house. She could hear more stirring down the hall in the bathroom. He was coming around.

She couldn't go out that way. She moved to the window at the far side of the desk, fumbled the lock open and lifted the frame. Kicking out the screen, she shoved a leg out and climbed up, teetering on the windowsill for a moment, waiting for her eyes to adjust to the darkness before she dropped to the ground.

Footsteps in the hall. *Hurry!* She practically threw herself out the open window, hit the wet slick ground and fell, her leggings instantly muddy and soaked.

Scrambling to her feet, she ran through the pouring rain to the lofty pine trees and the cover they afforded. She streaked across the grassy hillside to the creek bed and the cottonwoods. Following the creek, she ran to where she'd hidden her vehicle earlier. She didn't look back, afraid she'd see Brandon McCall's handsome face—and his shotgun pointed at her heart.

She was soaked to the skin and chilled as she climbed behind the wheel, started the engine and peeled out. All she wanted right now was to get back to the motel and climb into a tub of hot water. She didn't want to think about the empty safe. About the call to Dr. French. She didn't want to think about what she'd learned tonight about Mason VanHorn. Or Brandon McCall.

Her hands were shaking as she drove as fast as she could toward the highway, needing to put distance between her and the VanHorn Ranch.

She shouldn't have been surprised. Not about Mason VanHorn. Or about Brandon McCall. But she was. She'd thought she'd seen something promising in Brandon McCall years ago, but it seemed she had been as wrong about him as she was Mason VanHorn.

Slamming her hand down on the steering wheel, she warned herself not to let this get personal. She laughed at the thought. After years of specializing in digging up dirt, she was good at what she did. She'd written the book on detachment when it came to her job—to her life.

But this wasn't just any investigation. And she could no longer pretend it was. It had suddenly gotten damn personal.

At the two-lane highway, she turned south on the road from Antelope Flats, Montana, to Sheridan, Wyoming. Since her arrival, she'd seen little traffic on this stretch, even in the daytime, except for an occasional coal mine or gas worker, a rancher heading for Sheridan or a fisherman coming up from Wyoming headed for the Tongue River Reservoir. But nobody at this hour of the night.

She watched her rearview mirror expecting to see at least one set of headlights behind her on the rain-slick highway. Instead there was only darkness. At least for the moment. The storm snuffed out all light from the moon or stars, turning the Tongue River to pewter as it followed her over the border into Wyoming.

Her plan had worked, for all the good it had done her. Vandalizing the coalbed methane wells had gotten everyone away from the ranch house. Well, almost everyone.

At least it had gotten her what she wanted—inside the ranch house—inside the safe.

Tears burned her eyes. If Mason VanHorn had cleaned out the safe, did that mean he'd destroyed the evidence? Did that mean she'd never be able to get to the truth?

She rubbed a hand over her wet face and stared past the clacking windshield wipers at the rainy highway. Exhaustion pulled at her. She was wet and tired and cold and discouraged. She'd almost gotten caught tonight, but the fact it had been Brandon McCall made it all the worse.

He hadn't recognized her, she knew she should be thankful for that. But even that hurt. He hadn't remembered her. But she'd remembered him. That should have told her everything she needed to know. Obviously he hadn't been as taken with her as she had been with him all those years ago.

She'd thought about what it would be like to run into him. Just not on the VanHorn Ranch. Not working for the enemy. The long-running feud between the McCalls and the VanHorns aside, she'd expected better of him.

She crossed the river as the highway meandered to Sheridan, Wyoming, fighting her disappointment. Angry with herself for ever thinking he might be different from other men she'd known. Even more angry that, over the years, she'd held him up as the kind of man she would want in her life.

How ridiculous was that? He'd been little more than

a boy. She couldn't know what kind of man he would grow into. But she thought she'd known. Obviously she'd seen something in Brandon McCall that hadn't existed.

She felt sick. Men just kept letting her down. What did that say about them? Or her?

How she would have loved to drive straight to the airport and fly home. But she couldn't leave. Hers wasn't the only life at stake here and this wasn't the first investigation where she'd run into trouble. She was known for hanging in until she got what she was after.

Even if she could have let Mason VanHorn get away with what she knew he'd done, she had Lenore Johnson to think about. When she'd hired the private investigator, she'd warned Lenore how dangerous this was going to be.

Now Lenore was missing. Presumed dead, if Mason VanHorn or Dr. French found out that she'd been asking questions about them.

If Lenore Johnson had failed, Anna knew she had even less chance of finding out the truth. But she had to try to find Lenore, try to help her if she was still alive. How, though, could she find out the truth with every-thing—and everyone—against her?

Along with Brandon McCall, every ranch hand at the VanHorn Ranch would be looking for her now, in-cluding Mason VanHorn himself once he returned from Gillette.

She glanced in the rearview mirror again. Nothing but rain and darkness behind her. The same in front of her. She hadn't been followed. But she wasn't safe. She wouldn't be safe and she couldn't help Lenore until she could get the goods on Mason VanHorn. She desperately needed leverage. She'd thought she would find it in his office safe, that he would keep it where he could get to it, that he needed it as desperately as she did.

If she was right, then the evidence was at the house—just not in the safe. She would have to go back. Tomorrow night, once it got dark.

She'd have to get back into that house, even knowing that they'd all be waiting for her. All the ranch hands and hired thugs. Mason VanHorn, if he heard about tonight—and Brandon McCall.

And if she was really unlucky, the man she feared the most, Dr. French.

CHAPTER THREE

Tuesday

SHERIFF CASH McCALL had just gotten to his office when the phone rang.

"This is Johnson Investigations in Richmond, Virginia," said a woman with a wonderful Southern accent. "I'm calling in regard to Lenore Johnson. She is in your area on an investigation and we haven't received word from her for several days. She had made a prior arrangement to call yesterday afternoon at a set time. She did not call. We have reason to believe she might have met with foul play."

An investigator all the way from Virginia? "I can't file a missing person's report for forty-eight hours on an adult, but I would be happy to take the information," Cash told her.

"We'd appreciate that. Because of the nature of our business, I'm afraid I can't give you the details of the investigation. However, I can tell you where she was staying, the make and model of the car she was driving and give you her description."

"All right." Had she been a tourist, Cash wouldn't even have done that much in the first forty-eight hours. Usually people just lost track of time and forgot to call.

But since she was an investigator… And since he was a nice guy who had taken this job to help people…

"She was staying at the Shady Rest Motor Inn in Sheridan. The rental car was a dark green Dodge Dakota, license MT 3-178649. Ms. Johnson is forty-six years old, five-foot-seven, auburn hair, chin-length, slim build, brown eyes. She was armed."

"This investigation," Cash asked. "She considered it dangerous?"

"Yes."

"And that's all you can tell me."

"At this point. If we haven't heard from her in forty-eight hours, I will be happy to disclose additional information. That will give me time to contact our client."

"Your client? Who you also can't divulge at this point," Cash said.

"That is correct."

He groaned inwardly. "But you'll call me if you hear from her."

"Of course. At once. We greatly appreciate your assistance, Sheriff." She gave him her number and hung up.

Cash called information in Richmond, Virginia, and asked for Johnson Investigations. Same number as the woman had given him.

He had just hung up when he got the call from the Antelope Flats Clinic. He was surprised—and instantly worried—when he heard Dr. Porter Ivers's stern voice.

"You might want to come down here," the elderly doctor said….

BRANDON WAS SITTING UP on the gurney at the Antelope Flats Clinic when his brother came in.

"How's the head?" Cash asked.

Brandon swore under his breath. Dr. Ivers must have called him after Brandon had come stumbling in, bleeding all over the floor.

"Better." His head hurt like hell. But nothing like his pride.

"You weren't in that bar fight out at the Mello Dee, were you?" Cash asked. "I'm looking for the guys who tore up the place last night."

"Nah." If he told Cash about last night, he'd have to tell him about the night security job at VanHorn Ranch. He already knew his brother's response to that.

Nor could Brandon tell him about the vandalisms out there since VanHorn hadn't reported them. As sheriff, Cash would have to pay Mason VanHorn a visit, demanding to know why he hadn't been called—and warning VanHorn not to take the law into his own hands.

Once Brandon's name came up, VanHorn would be beside himself to think he'd had a McCall working for him. Heads would roll. And Brandon—if not shot—would be out of a job. And the VanHorns and McCalls would be at it again.

But Brandon didn't kid himself. None of that was why he couldn't tell his brother. This was about salvaging some of his pride and that meant getting the vandal in his sights again. Hell, he'd been so close to her that he'd smelled her perfume, seen the hint of perspiration on her upper lip, knew the exact shade of her honey-brown eyes.

Unfortunately, he'd fallen for her helpless reporter act and had a sore head to prove it.

If he told Cash the truth, he'd never get a chance to catch the woman. And he *would* catch her. He was counting on seeing her again. His gut told him she hadn't left town, that even though she'd gotten into the safe, she wasn't finished with Mason VanHorn. And this time, Brandon would be waiting for her.

"So how'd you get your head bashed in?" Cash asked. He had his sheriff face on, which Brandon knew meant he'd keep at it until he got the truth out of him. Or something close.

"It was stupid," Brandon said sheepishly, looking down at the floor. He'd perfected this look over the years after getting caught in countless shenanigans. All the McCall boys got into trouble. It was almost a tradition. And as the youngest McCall male, he'd had to sow his share of oats, as well. But at thirty-three, he was taking the longest to straighten up.

He looked at the floor and said, "There was this bull out in a pasture and there was this woman…"

Cash groaned. "You were showing off. This woman have anything to do with why you've been staying out all night for days on end?"

"'Fraid so."

Cash shook his head but smiled. "Our little sister thinks it's serious."

It was serious all right. Just not in the way eighteen-year-old Dusty thought. "Yeah, that Dusty's a real authority on romance," Brandon quipped.

"Doc says you don't have a concussion."

"Just a few stitches," Brandon said, trying to play it down.

"Twelve is more than a few. What'd you hit?"

"Must have found the only rock in the field when I came off the bull," Brandon said. "But, hell, big brother, you had more stitches than that when you were young."

"When I was *young?* I'm only a few years older than you. And I can still kick your butt."

Brandon grinned. "Might have to see about that someday." He quickly changed the subject. "Heard Molly's back from visiting her mom in Florida." Molly was the woman his brother had fallen in love with and from what Brandon had seen, Cash was more than serious about her. "Is that weddin' bells I hear? Bet Shelby's already bought a mother-of-the-groom dress for the wedding."

Shelby was their mother, but after not being part of their lives for more than thirty years and suddenly returning, her five now-grown children couldn't bring themselves to call her mother.

"You tryin' to change the subject?" Cash asked, eyeing him.

"I don't want to talk about my love life, okay?" His nonexistent love life, especially.

"Neither do I," Cash said. "You want me to call J.T. and tell him you won't be doing any work at the ranch today?"

"That would be great," Brandon said, sincerely touched. Cash was offering the equivalent of an olive branch. "You know J.T. He'll think I busted my head open on a rock only to get out of work."

Cash returned his smile. Their oldest brother, J.T., could be a little intense when it came to the ranch. But J.T. had mellowed some since his recent marriage. A woman was exactly what J.T. had needed.

"With Rourke back, they should be able to manage without you for a few days," Cash said.

Brandon grinned, seeing that his brother was getting

him a few days off to recuperate—and spend time with his lady. "You romantic, you. You're okay, Cash, no matter what the rest of the family says about you," he joked.

"I got work to do," Cash said, and turned to leave.

"Thanks," Brandon said to his brother's back. He felt a little guilty about keeping things from Cash. But not guilty enough to confess just yet.

Once he caught the woman from last night, he'd collect his bonus and tell Cash everything. Once VanHorn got wind of everything, the job would be over anyway.

Dr. Ivers came back into the emergency room. He had a frown on his face, as if disgusted with the whole bunch of McCall boys. He'd been stitching up McCall boys from long before Brandon was born. The doc had tried to retire but couldn't seem to make it stick and was only becoming more cantankerous. Kind of reminded Brandon of his father. But then Asa McCall had always been cantankerous and just plain hard to get along with.

That is until recently, when his wife Shelby returned from the dead. Brandon shook off the thought. He didn't want to think about what was going on between his parents.

"You're free to go," Dr. Ivers said, handing Brandon a prescription for painkillers. He checked the bandage on the back of Brandon's head, adding, "I don't want to see you back in here. Don't you have something better to do than get banged up in the middle of the night?" He shook his head again. "Good thing you McCalls are a hardheaded bunch."

"Thanks, Doc," Brandon said, reaching for his cowboy hat. He placed it gingerly on his head, wincing a little.

"You're going to have a scar," said a female voice from the doorway.

"Won't be my first scar," Brandon said with a grin. "Hi, Taylor."

"That's Dr. Taylor Ivers to you," the old doc snapped. Taylor was Dr. and Mrs. Porter Ivers's surprise late-in-life child. She had followed in her father's footsteps, something that Brandon could see pleased the old doc greatly.

Taylor held out her hand. "Hello, Brandon." He took it, not surprised by her firm handshake. She was all business. He hadn't seen her since she was a skinny kid with braces and glasses. She hadn't changed that much, except she had perfectly straight teeth and must have worn contacts.

She'd been one of those gifted kids who went to a special private school, graduating high school at fifteen, college at eighteen and medical school at twenty-two. Last he'd heard, she'd done her residency at some cutting-edge hospital down south.

"You planning to take over for your dad?" he asked her, joking.

"She has bigger fish to fry," Dr. Ivers snapped. "She's not getting stuck here."

"I'll be staying for a while," Taylor said, glancing at her father. "My mother isn't well."

"I'm sorry," he answered quickly.

"I want to be near my parents right now," Taylor said, and turned to her father, "You have a phone call."

"I'll take it in my office." He looked at Brandon. "I'd tell you to take it easy, but I know it would be a waste of breath." The old doc turned and left without another word.

As Brandon slid off the gurney and headed for the door, Taylor busied herself putting away the equipment her father had used to patch him up.

Brandon left with only one thing on his mind—the woman who'd wounded his pride. The flesh injury would heal.

ANNA'S ATTEMPTS to find out if Brandon McCall had been taken to the Antelope Flats Clinic had failed miserably.

As an investigative reporter, she knew a few tricks for getting information. But the woman she spoke to at the clinic, a Dr. Taylor Ivers, wasn't falling for any of them.

Anna hung up, hoping McCall was all right. She'd hit him with a cast-iron cowgirl doorstop. Her disappointment in him aside, she hoped it hadn't hurt him too badly.

She stepped out onto the deck overlooking the Tongue River Reservoir and rubbed the back of her neck, angry with herself for worrying about him. He worked for Mason VanHorn! That should tell her what kind of man he was. More than likely, he deserved anything she gave him.

The morning breeze whispered in the pines and rippled the water's green surface below her into a glittering chop. She could see a half-dozen boats along the red cliffs of the lake and wished she were on the water.

Closing her eyes, she breathed in the smell of the lake and almost thought she felt a memory stir her. She and her father fishing in a small boat, just the two of them, on a summer day, the soft slap of the water against the side of the boat, the steady thrum of the motor, the pull of the rod in her hand.

She knew it couldn't possibly be a memory. She'd never gone fishing with her father. She'd barely known him. At her first boarding school, she'd told everyone that her parents were both dead. In a way, it was true. They were both dead to her.

Going back inside the cabin, she wondered why she hadn't thought to rent a cabin on the lake in the first place. Staying at a motel, even in Sheridan, Wyoming, even miles from the VanHorn Ranch, had been risky. Here on the lake at this time of year, she could blend in.

In a few hours, when it warmed up, the lake would be alive with the whine of boat motors roaring around, the smell of fires from the campground across the water and wonderful sounds of laughter and voices.

And according to the records she'd uncovered, just down the lake was a piece of recently acquired land that was now part of the VanHorn Ranch. Not exactly lakefront property in the true sense. It was swampy, with lots of trees standing knee-deep in the water with the lake up. The land wasn't used for anything except the wild horses Mason VanHorn had collected before there were laws preventing it.

This morning, after a sleepless night, she'd come up with a plan. Unfortunately, she could do little until almost dark and she'd never been good at waiting.

She tried her cell phone and still couldn't get any service in this remote part of the state. Giving up, she picked up the phone in the cabin and dialed the Virginia number.

"Johnson Investigations," a female voice answered.

"I'm Anna Austin—"

"Ms. Austin, I'm sorry but if you're calling for Lenore, she still hasn't called in. As a matter of fact, we have contacted the sheriff in Antelope Flats."

"That's why I'm calling. I wanted to give you my permission to reveal the nature of her business here and who she was working for," Anna said. "I'm worried about her."

"We're concerned, as well, but the sheriff said no missing person's report can be filed for forty-eight hours," the receptionist said. "He has agreed to keep an eye out for her but can do nothing more at this point."

Forty-eight hours. "I'm going to do my best to find her in the meantime." She gave the receptionist the number at the cabin and hung up.

She had hired Lenore Johnson to verify some information she'd received. Lenore had called two days ago to say that at least some of the information was correct. She hadn't wanted to discuss the case over the phone, adding she had another lead to check out before she flew back. Anna had told her she would be flying out and Lenore had given her the name of the motel where she was staying in Sheridan, Wyoming.

But when Anna reached Sheridan, she'd discovered that Lenore had left the motel without checking out, taking everything with her, and hadn't been seen since.

Anna's gaze went to the manila envelope where she'd dropped it beside the phone. The letter inside had been lost in the mail for nine years.

A part of her wished it had stayed lost.

Sitting down, she picked up the envelope and pulled out the single sheet of paper from inside. The barely legible words had been written in a trembling feeble hand. An elderly woman's deathbed confession.

At first, Anna had thought the woman must have been senile. None of it could be true.

But she'd been wrong. At least some it was true, or Lenore Johnson wouldn't be missing.

Carefully, Anna slipped the letter back inside the envelope and, getting up, hid it under the cushion of the chair. She knew she was being paranoid, but it was the only evidence she had. Even if it was worthless in a court of law without proof to back it up, she didn't want to lose it.

Had the private investigator found the proof? Or had she just asked too many questions?

Anna shivered, hugging herself as she thought of Lenore Johnson. Lenore had known going in just how dangerous this was, and she was trained for this kind of trouble. If *she* had failed…

Anna knew she was completely out of her league. Not that she would let that stop her. Nothing could stop her. She would find out the truth, because she knew it was still on that ranch. Too many people had been involved in the cover-up. Mason VanHorn couldn't be sure the others would keep quiet. He would have evidence he could use to ensure they would never talk. He would keep that evidence close to him, so if all else failed, he could get it and destroy it. If it came to that. She didn't think he felt *that* threatened yet.

So the evidence had to be in the ranch house. She had to find it and she couldn't count on him being gone for long. Once he heard about the break-in, he might come back. Or he might just put more guards on the house, assured that he could protect himself and the evidence.

She had to get back into that ranch house. Only this time, she would need a major diversion—something more than vandalizing a few wellheads.

And this time, everyone would be looking for *her* after Brandon McCall told them what she looked like. At least he didn't know her name. Nor would she be easy to find.

As she looked across at the marina, she knew she had just raised the stakes and was about to gamble everything. There was no turning back now, no matter who got in the way. Even Brandon McCall.

She *would* find out the truth. Even if it destroyed them all.

MASON VANHORN PICKED UP the broken lamp in his office and hurled it across the room. It crashed into the wall, dropping with a clatter.

Red Hudson winced but had the good sense not to say a word. The ranch manager had noticed tracks in the mud behind the house, had investigated and called him. Mason had driven home at once, disbelieving that anyone would be stupid enough to break into *his* house. When he got his hands on the bastard—

"They came in through the window in the bathroom," Red said behind him. "Had to know you weren't going to be home."

"They?" Mason turned to look at him. Red was a big man with a shock of bright red hair, thus the nickname. Mason knew he could count on Red's loyalty because he had just enough on the man to ensure Red would never turn on him.

But unfortunately, Red had a little something on him, as well, which meant he couldn't control him like he could the other men. Red could be pushed, but Mason wasn't sure how far.

"I found two sets of tracks coming and going," Red said. "One could be a small man. The other large."

"I thought you hired extra men to make sure the ranch was secure," he snapped.

Red nodded. "But we were expecting the wells to be hit, not the house."

"If that's your excuse—"

"It's not an excuse," Red said, an edge to his voice.

Mason opened one of the file cabinets, then slammed it. "You're saying there are two vandals?"

Red shook his head. "This isn't the work of a vandal. The house wasn't torn up. These guys were looking for something."

Mason didn't look at him.

"Why do I get the feeling you know what they were looking for?" Red swore. "If I'd known the house might be hit, I would have put some men on it. Whatever was in the safe—"

"It was empty."

Red shook his head. "So you knew they were coming."

Mason didn't have to explain himself to anyone. He'd cleaned out the safe as a precaution. He'd never dreamed anyone would actually break into the house. He wanted to turn his fury on Red, to fire him, to send him packing, but he knew this wasn't Red's fault. It was his own.

Moving to the desk, he stared down, suddenly afraid he might have left something incriminating lying around.

Living alone, with no one having access to his office, had made him careless, he realized.

"I want guards around the house until further notice," he ordered. "I want those bastards caught and brought to me."

Red met his gaze. "You think they'll come back?" he asked in surprise.

"Just do it and stop questioning me," Mason snapped.

The ranch manager nodded slowly. "I'll put my best men on the house. But if you really want to catch them, you need to go back to Gillette. If they have a reason to hit the house again, they won't be foolish enough to do it with you here."

Mason couldn't argue Red's logic but he had no intention of going anywhere. "I'll make everyone think I've gone back to Gillette, but I intend to be here tonight when they come back."

"Suit yourself, but it could be dangerous."

Mason laughed. "Only for the bastards who broke into my house."

"It would make my job easier if you'd tell me what they're looking for."

"What makes you think I want to make your job easier? And get someone to clean up this mess." Mason turned and stormed out of his office.

Something caught his eye from down the hall. A drop of blood on the carpet. He felt a chill. Was it possible one of the burglars had been hurt breaking in? He knelt down to inspect the spot. It was right in front of his son's open bedroom door.

He still thought of the room as Holt's even though his son would never use it again. He'd heard rumors that

Holt was in California, Florida, even Alaska. He didn't care where he was as long as he never had to lay eyes on him again. His own son had stolen from him—shamed him.

He clenched his fist at the memory. He'd built everything for Holt, his only son, the heir who would one day take over the vast empire he'd built. Now Holt was gone and Mason had seen to it that his son would never get a penny.

He closed the bedroom door. He should have cleaned it out the moment he learned of Holt's betrayal. Should have had everything in it burned.

He moved down the hall, following the droplets of blood and stopped at his daughter's bedroom door, seeing at once that things weren't as they should have been.

One of the stuffed animals on the bed had been moved. He knew because that rag doll had been in the same place for the past twenty years—exactly where Chrissy had left it.

That stupid part-time housekeeper he'd hired must have moved it when she cleaned the room. He'd have Red fire her.

He stepped to the bed, picked up the rag doll. Honey. That's what Chrissy had called it from the day he'd given it to her. He brought the doll to his face, smelled it as if he thought Chrissy's baby-girl scent would still be in the worn fabric. But of course, it wasn't.

He put Honey back where she belonged—between the teddy bears—and tried to picture his precious daughter in this room, but it was too heartbreaking.

"Mr. VanHorn?"

He turned from the room, practically fleeing down

the hall to where Red stood, giving orders on the phone to whoever was doing the cleanup.

"I found some blood," Mason said the moment Red got off the phone.

The ranch manager nodded. "There's some on the bathroom floor and the windowsill, too. One of them must have gotten injured breaking in."

What had happened here last night? "Who did you have watching the wells behind the ranch house?" Mason asked.

"One of my best men. Brandon McCall."

Mason couldn't speak. He started shaking so hard he thought he was having a seizure. Brandon McCall was working security on *his* ranch? A McCall on VanHorn soil? "Fire him immediately!"

"He's one of my best men," Red said, staring at him in stunned surprise.

"He's a *McCall*." It had never dawned on Mason to tell Red never to hire a McCall. But more to the point, what the hell would a McCall be doing working on this ranch? Only one explanation presented itself. "No. Don't fire him. Bring him to me. Now!"

He stormed back down the hall to the bathroom, stooping to pick up the iron cowgirl doorstop on the floor. As he lifted it, he saw the dried blood. "Get me McCall," he yelled back at Red, feeling as if he still might have that seizure.

HEAD ACHING, Brandon set out to find the woman vandal. He started in Antelope Flats, cruising down Main Street, keeping his eye out for her. Antelope Flats was a tiny western town in the corner of southeastern Montana. Tiny and isolated, just the way he liked it.

He'd been born here and lived his whole life on the family ranch north of town. This was his stomping grounds and he knew this part of the country better than anyone. If the woman was still around, he'd find her.

Not that he expected to see her walking down the street. She was much too smart for that. But he thought he might see her car. He'd picked up an accent last night that he couldn't place, but one thing was clear: she wasn't from around here. That meant she was driving either a car with out-of-state plates or a rental car.

There were a few vehicles in front of his sister-in-law's Longhorn Café, the only café in town. But he recognized all of them. Most were pickups, since Antelope Flats was born a ranching town. A few of the trucks were from the coal mine down the road, tall antennae with red flags on top so they could be seen in the open-pit mines.

Antelope Flats had only one motel on the edge of town, the Lariat. He drove out there, but wasn't surprised to see that the parking lot was empty. Anyone who had stayed here last night was already gone.

He found Leticia Arnold in the apartment at the back of the office making what smelled like corncakes.

She saw him and motioned for him to come into the kitchen. "Want some pancakes?"

"No, thanks." Leticia was his sister Dusty's best friend. After high school graduation, while Dusty had opted to stay and work the ranch, Leticia had taken over running the motel so her elderly parents could move to Arizona. Leticia had been a late-in-life baby, the Arnolds' only child.

"I'm looking for a woman," he said, pulling up a chair

as she sat down in front of a tall stack of corncakes. Leticia was thin as a stick with a wide toothy smile and all cowgirl.

She grinned up at him. "Do you know how long I've waited for you to say that?"

He laughed. He liked Leticia's sense of humor. "I'm too old for you."

"Shouldn't I be the judge of that?"

He reached over and took a bite of her pancakes. "Wow, you're a pretty good cook. Maybe I'll reconsider," he joked.

"You wish. You're right, you're too old for me," she said, trying to sound disappointed.

"You probably have some rodeo cowboy you've got your sights on anyway," he said.

She looked surprised. "Did Dusty tell you that?"

He laughed and shook his head. His sister Dusty never told him anything, but he knew that the two friends had been hitting every rodeo within driving distance and he doubted they were going there for the fried bread.

He described the woman he'd seen last night as Leticia ate her pancakes and then got up to cook a few more.

"She didn't stay here, but there are tons of motels down in Sheridan you could try. What happened to your head?"

"I thought I was smarter than I was."

She laughed. "I could have told you that and saved you a lot of pain." She put the last batch of corncakes onto a plate. "So this woman made a lasting impression on you and yet you don't know where to find her?" She laughed. "A bad-boy McCall chasing a woman? She must really be something."

If you considered a scar on the back of his head a lasting impression. "Let's just say I'm looking forward to seeing her again."

"Then you're going to need your strength," she said, sliding the plate of pancakes over to him. "Dusty told me that you had a woman in your life."

"Did she now," he said, seeing that Leticia was just dying to call his sister and tell her he'd been by asking about a woman. No way around that. Let Dusty think she was right and that he'd fallen in love. Better than the truth.

SHERIFF CASH MCCALL made a few calls to Sheridan about the private investigator. He'd just hung up when he got a call from the Wyoming Highway Patrol.

"We've got a body just over the state line a few feet," the patrolman said. "Looks like she's yours since she's in Montana. Her car's parked along the road. Appears to have fallen down the embankment. Ended up at the edge of the river in the rocks."

"Have you called the coroner yet?" Cash asked.

"Raymond's on his way. He said he would stay at the scene and wait for you. We've got a semi overturned in the southbound lane between here and Gillette."

"Go ahead and respond. I'm on my way. You ID the body?" Cash asked. He hoped it wasn't a local. This was the part of his job he hated. Before the day was out, he could be banging on a door somewhere in the county to inform a relative that their loved one was dead. He also hoped it wasn't the missing Lenore Johnson.

"A woman. I'd say about sixty. The car is locked, keys in the ignition. Her purse is inside along with what looks like a half-empty fifth of vodka. I didn't attempt to open the car—did run the plates, though. The car is registered to an Emma Ingles."

CHAPTER FOUR

HIS HEAD THROBBING with pain, Brandon spent the better part of the day checking motels in and around the town of Sheridan, Wyoming, south of Antelope Flats, Montana.

Few of the clerks could recall a woman matching the description he gave. As luck would have it, he found where she'd been staying at the last motel he checked. Clearly, the woman he was chasing hadn't wanted to be found.

The Shady Rest Motor Inn wasn't an inn. It was barely a motel anymore. The place was on the old highway, too far off the Interstate to get much business other than overflow.

As Brandon walked into the office, though, he was delighted to see that he knew the clerk behind the desk. He'd met her at a party one of those times he'd come to Sheridan to get away and have some fun.

"Hannah, right?"

She grinned, obviously pleased he'd remembered.

They talked for a few minutes about everything but what he'd come for. When she mentioned that the motel owner had gone into town and wouldn't be back for a while, Brandon told her about the woman he'd been looking for.

"Yep, she was here. But she left before I came on this morning."

"I need to find her."

"You know I'm not supposed to do this," Hannah said.

"I wouldn't ask you, but it really is important," he told her. "She's in trouble and I'm trying to help her."

Hannah looked a little skeptical but called up the information on the computer. "She didn't check out, it looks like. She was registered as Anna Austin." Address? A post-office box in Richmond, Virginia. Virginia. That could account for the slight accent he'd picked up. No phone number. Nothing under a business.

"What's with you McCalls? Your brother called here this morning, too, looking for a woman," Hannah said.

"Cash?"

She nodded. "He was looking for another guest from Virginia. Lenore Johnson?"

The name didn't ring any bells. "They weren't in the same room, were they?"

Hannah shook her head. "They weren't even here at the same time." She shrugged. "Probably just a coincidence."

He rubbed his throbbing temples. Right now, there was only one woman he cared about. "Do you remember what Anna Austin was driving?"

"A black Ford pickup with Montana plates," Hannah said.

Why would the woman from last night have rented a pickup truck? She'd looked like a fancy-sedan kind of woman.

He thanked Hannah and left before her boss got back.

The more he thought about the black pickup, the more sense it made. If you wanted to blend in in this part of the country, a pickup would be the way to do it. Especially if your mission was vandalizing coalbed methane wells on the VanHorn Ranch. A pickup wouldn't have raised suspicion like a car, if seen on the ranch.

The fact that she'd probably left the motel in the wee hours without checking out convinced him that she knew he would be looking for her. In fact, she probably figured all of the VanHorn ranch hands and the sheriff's department were searching for her, as well. She wouldn't know that he couldn't go to Mason VanHorn.

So she would try to find some place to hide. In this part of the country, that could be anywhere. Or she'd give up and leave.

His instincts told him she wouldn't give up. Not her.

He had the feeling that she hadn't gotten what she'd broken into the ranch house for last night. The safe had been empty by the time he'd come around. Completely empty. What thief took *everything* in the safe? A thief in a hurry. Or one who found nothing but bundles of money.

Except she hadn't had any kind of a bag with her. He would have seen it as skintight as that Lycra outfit had been. She hadn't planned on taking much with her.

He wondered what exactly she'd been looking for, then. Or if she was even a reporter. He didn't know any reporters who committed vandalism and breaking and entering for a story.

He tried not to think about how she'd hoodwinked him. She'd seemed so scared, so vulnerable, so caught.

And all the time she'd just been playing him until she could get her hands on that lamp to throw at him.

She'd played him for a fool.

He drove back to Antelope Flats, tired, head aching, thinking only of a hot bath. He knew her name and what she was driving. He'd see her again. He was sure of it. Tonight.

One of the VanHorn Ranch pickups was just pulling out of the Longhorn Café. The ranch hand flagged him down.

"Red asked me to find you. He wants you to stop by the ranch to talk about surveillance tonight."

"Sure. Did something happen?" he asked, worried that the break-in had been discovered.

"Not that I know of. I think Red just wants to catch that damned vandal before the boss gets back."

That damned vandal, Brandon thought as he drove out of town again, headed for the VanHorn Ranch.

If things went as he thought they would, he'd catch the vandal tonight. He tried not to think about turning Anna Austin over to VanHorn as he drove south to the ranch.

SHERIFF CASH MCCALL dug the sides of his boots into the steep hillside, sliding in the loose rocks. Below him, coroner Raymond Winters stood next to the river's edge, his hands in his pockets, his eyes averted from the body.

"A trucker saw her from the road and called it in to the Wyoming Highway Patrol," Winters said when Cash reached him. Winters was fiftysomething, a quiet, solemn man who, along with being coroner for Cash's county, owned Winters Funeral Home in Sheridan, Wyoming.

"Thanks for staying at the scene until I could get here," Cash said.

"No problem. She hasn't been in the water long," Winters said. "Twelve hours, tops."

"Cause of death?" Cash asked as he photographed the scene and the body of the overweight woman lying faceup in the water.

"At this point? I'd say a blow to the head."

"Any sign of a struggle?" Cash asked.

"Won't know for certain until I get her back to the lab, but you can see there is some bruising on the fleshy part of her upper arms."

"As if someone had grabbed her, maybe pushed her?"

Winters shrugged. "Women that age bruise easily."

"I heard her car is up the road, locked, keys in the ignition, a half-empty fifth of vodka lying on the floor."

Winters nodded. "I wouldn't be surprised to find her blood alcohol elevated."

Cash looked back up the steep embankment to the highway. "You think she fell?"

"Looks that way. Stopped to relieve herself beside the road, locked the keys in her car, started walking home—she just lives up the road a couple of miles—got too close to the edge, slipped and fell. If she was drunk, it could explain it. She worked the night shift at Brookside and was probably coming from work."

"*Brookside?* I thought that place had been closed for years."

"The state took it over back in the eighties, closed the hospital, but has to have someone up there at night because of the darned kids until it sells," Winters said. "You know kids."

Cash nodded, remembering a night he and his brother Rourke went up there. An old haunted-looking huge building that sat dark and foreboding against the horizon about halfway between Antelope Flats, Montana, and Sheridan, Wyoming. The place scared the hell out of him, partly because of all the stories he'd heard about it. And partly because of the bad vibes he'd felt there that night.

He finished shooting the scene and put his camera away. "Next of kin?"

Winters shook his head. "Widowed. No kids. Lives alone."

"You knew her pretty well?" Cash asked.

"Not really. Just in passing." Winters rubbed the back of his neck. "Okay to go ahead and get her out of the water?"

Cash nodded. "A boyfriend?" he asked, thinking of the bruises.

Winters shook his head. "Highly doubt it."

"Problems with neighbors, work?" Cash asked, still worried about the bruises.

"None that I know of."

Cash glanced again up the embankment. He could see where she had fallen. There were indentations in the loose gravel and blood on the rocks along the river.

"Let me know when you have her blood alcohol levels." Cash figured he knew what would come back. Emma Ingles had drank too much, gotten out of her car for some reason and just lost her footing and fell, her body coming to rest in the water at the edge of the Tongue River.

But it nagged him that she would stop this close to home.

It was a sad end, but no reason to think of foul play. At least not at this point.

Still, Cash decided to put in a call to her boss at the former mental hospital and maybe her co-workers or neighbors. Wouldn't hurt while he waited for the autopsy report.

RED DIDN'T GET UP when Brandon walked into his office on the VanHorn Ranch. The first time he'd seen Red had been outside the Longhorn Café. Red had approached him, having overheard him say he needed another job if he hoped to go to law school on his own—which was the only way he was going.

Brandon wasn't asking his father for money. Because then Asa would ask him about the money he'd been left by his grandfather and he'd have to admit that he'd blown it all. No way.

That day on the sidewalk, he'd known the new Van-Horn Ranch manager hadn't realized he shouldn't be hiring him. Red obviously either didn't know about the feud or didn't realize its magnitude.

Brandon wondered now if Red was wiser, if somehow Mason VanHorn had found out he had a McCall working for him. Or if Red just wanted to see him about security tonight like the ranch hand had said.

On the way into the VanHorn Ranch compound, Brandon had been relieved to see that Mason VanHorn's big expensive car hadn't been parked in front of the ranch house. VanHorn was still in Gillette, so that meant he didn't know about the break-in, right?

The last thing Brandon wanted to do was run into

the man, so he hoped to make this meeting with Red as short as possible. That's why working nights had been so ideal. No chance of seeing the big boss.

"Thanks for coming, Brandon. Sit down," Red said, and at once Brandon knew something was wrong. Before he could get seated, Red asked, "Run into any trouble last night?"

Was it possible someone had seen where the bathroom window had been pried open? Or had someone gone into the house and found the broken lamp in Mason's office?

Red pointed at the bandage on Brandon's head.

He'd forgotten about the injury and since he'd been taught to remove his hat when entering a room, he'd taken if off and now held it in his lap. "Accident after work. Wasn't paying attention. Took a fall."

Red nodded, measuring him, his gaze saying he knew Brandon was lying. "When I hired you, you didn't mention that your family doesn't get along with the VanHorns."

"I didn't think it was relevant," Brandon said truthfully. "I've never had anything against the VanHorns. It's just some old feud that no one seems to know how it got started. Is there a problem with my work?"

"Someone broke into the ranch house last night. Since it falls within your section of the ranch, I thought you might have seen something."

Brandon liked Red—would have liked to tell him the truth. But if he did, he could kiss off any chance of catching the woman. It wasn't just his pride. He owed her.

Before he could answer Red's question a side office door banged open.

Brandon turned, unable to hide his shock as Mason VanHorn stormed into the room. He was a big man, much like Brandon's father, Asa. But where Asa was blue-eyed and blond, Mason was dark.

Over the years, his once coal-black hair had gone from salt-and-pepper to white. Having seen Mason only in passing in town, Brandon couldn't hide his shock at how much Mason had aged—or the fact that he was here—and the ruse was up.

"He asked you why you didn't see this mysterious person who broke into my house," Mason shouted towering over him.

That wasn't exactly what Red had asked him, but Brandon didn't point that out. He could see that he was toast no matter what he said. Surprisingly, his first instinct was to tell the truth. But when he thought of Anna Austin, he knew he couldn't do that. He did his sheepish look. "I fell asleep."

"Like hell," Mason raged. "You were one of the vandals. Who was the other person?"

Brandon shook his head. "I didn't break into your house. I was guarding your wells."

Mason let out a curse that rattled the windows. "What the hell were you doing working on my ranch, anyway?"

"I need the money to go to law school," he said truthfully.

"Why wouldn't you just ask your father for the money? It isn't like Asa couldn't afford to send you to law school."

Brandon rose from his chair, refusing to let Mason VanHorn intimidate him. "It's something I wanted to do on my own, okay? I'm thirty-three. Isn't it possible I want to be my own man?"

"You should have been your own man when you were eighteen," Mason snapped.

Brandon smiled and nodded. "I guess I'm a late bloomer." He was eye-level with VanHorn, matched him in size and had youth on his side. And yet he felt a small tremor when he looked into the man's dark eyes.

If half the rumors about VanHorn were true, Brandon had every reason to be concerned he might never get off this ranch alive.

"You're spoiled rotten, like all the McCalls."

Brandon said nothing, seeing how this could escalate. Also, he *had* been spoiled. And wild. And foolish. And he should have grown up a long time ago.

Also, Mason was spoiling for a fight. "If I find out that's your blood in my house, that you vandalized my wells and broke into my house—"

"I'm not a vandal or a thief. Whatever the deal is between you and my father, it has nothing to do with me." He gingerly put his hat back on his head.

Red handed him his paycheck and he took it.

Mason was still seething. "You're fired."

"I got that," he said, folding the check and putting it into his shirt pocket.

"So now you'll run to Cash the way you ran to Rourke when you lost money gambling with my last ranch manager," Mason said.

So Mason knew that his former ranch manager, Ace, had been fleecing not just the hired hands in the valley, but one of the McCalls.

Brandon felt his face heat. Not with anger but with embarrassment and shame. He'd lost a lot of money by being young and foolish. And now he knew that Mason VanHorn had known.

"I learned my lesson," Brandon said.

"An expensive lesson," VanHorn noted with no small satisfaction.

Brandon smiled. "It certainly was. I'm glad to see at least you enjoyed it. But you know, your former ranch foreman 'Ace' Kelly taught me an invaluable lesson about men who deal off the bottom of the deck. Whatever happened to him anyway? He rip off the wrong cowhand?"

Word in the county was that Kelly had just disappeared. A day later, Red Hudson had showed up and taken his place. Was it possible Kelly had gotten on Mason's bad side? Mason was famous for always getting even for the most minor of slights. Brandon couldn't help but wonder if Kelly wasn't buried somewhere on the ranch.

"I never want to see you on my property again," Van-Horn said as if Brandon had hit a sore spot at just the mention of Kelly.

Brandon tipped his hat to Red, "Thanks for the job," and headed for the door, figuring he got off a lot easier than Kelly.

But now he had a major problem. How was he going to catch the woman? Worse, she had no idea about the trap she would be walking into with VanHorn back from Gillette.

Brandon had no choice. He'd have to sneak back onto the ranch tonight. He couldn't let her fall into VanHorn's clutches. Better to catch her and turn her over to his brother, the sheriff.

Only this time, if he got caught on the ranch, VanHorn

could have him shot for trespassing. But what choice did he have? He knew what he was up against. No way did Anna Austin even have an inkling of how much trouble she was in.

ANNA CHANGED her clothing, putting on her swimsuit under a pair of shorts and a T-shirt. She packed a small backpack with the clothing she would need.

Her thoughts kept returning to Brandon McCall. He'd been the only man who'd ever interested her. She shook her head, smiling at how foolish that sounded.

She'd only laid eyes on him one other time and he'd been years from being a man. But she'd fallen in love with him in an instant. Love at first sight. He'd stolen her heart. And since then, she'd measured every man she met against her idea of him—and they'd come up lacking.

He'd had the cutest, sweetest little grin she'd ever seen. She wondered if he still had it. Now at thirty-three, he'd grown into a heart-stopping handsome cowboy.

It had taken all of her control back at the ranch house last night to hide her surprise at seeing him again. Especially seeing him working for Mason VanHorn.

She'd always pictured him as her hero. So much for that fantasy.

As she walked past the phone on the table in the lake cabin, impulsively she picked it up and dialed the number she'd copied from Mason VanHorn's caller ID screen in his office. Dr. Niles French's number.

She held her breath as the phone rang four times, expecting any moment that she would hear his voice and lose control. An answering machine picked up. An automated voice said, "Dr. French is unavailable. Leave a message and he will return your call at his earliest convenience."

Hang up! The answering system beeped. Silence. She was breathing hard, fighting back tears. "I'm going to get you, you son of a bitch. I'm going to nail you and Mason VanHorn. Do you hear me? My name is Anna Austin and I'm coming after you with everything I have."

She slammed down the phone on a sob and was shaking so violently she had to steady herself against the table. She took deep breaths, trying to hold back tears of anger and frustration. She had to get control. She couldn't let Dr. French and Mason VanHorn get away with what they'd done.

After a moment, her chest quit heaving, her pulse slowed and she straightened. She was still shaky. Knowing what Dr. French was capable of doing frightened her more than she wanted to admit. He was the boogeyman, the monster under the bed. He was her worst nightmare.

In the kitchen she filled a Baggie with sugar cubes, telling herself she shouldn't have called, shouldn't have warned him.

But she knew it was too late for that. She thought of the empty safe. Of the missing private investigator she'd hired. No, Dr. French knew she was after him. By now, Mason VanHorn did, too. But maybe she'd rattle them both and hope that one of them would lead her to the truth.

MASON HAD BEEN anticipating the call.

"I heard you had a break-in last night," Dr. Niles French said, sounding upset.

Mason swore under his breath, wondering who on

the ranch had blabbed. He'd kill him. "It was nothing. A vandal protesting coalbed methane wells."

The doctor sighed. "You and I have known each other for how many years now?"

Mason didn't have time for a trip down memory lane. "What is it you want?"

"I want the records from the sanitarium."

Sanitarium. Mason almost laughed. It was a nuthouse. Loony bin. House of horrors. "What makes you think *I* have them?"

"Because I know you," Dr. French said. "Someone else has been looking for the records. I suppose you don't know anything about that, either."

"Why bring this up now?" Mason asked wondering if Dr. French had hired someone to break into his house for the file.

"I'm finished. I won't do anything else for you. I'm an old man. I'm not proud of things I've done. Especially concerning Helena and you. I would like to die in peace. I don't think that is too much to ask."

"You're not dying."

"Not yet. Mason, after everything I have done for you, grant me this last request. Give me my file. Let me destroy it. I just need to know it will never come out."

"Isn't my word good enough?"

The doctor sighed. "Let me be frank. I have less to lose than you do if anyone should ever find out."

"You aren't threatening me, are you, Niles?"

"Do you want me to come out to the ranch to get the file?" Dr. French asked. "Or do you want to come here?"

What Mason wanted was to tell him to go to hell, but he heard something in the elderly doctor's voice that warned him it would be a mistake. Why was it that when a person reached a certain age he felt the need to bare his soul? To make amends? To tie up loose ends? French didn't think there was a chance in hell that he was going anywhere after death that required a clear conscience, did he?

"I'll need a couple of days to get the file," Mason said. "I don't keep it here at the house."

"You aren't just stalling, are you, Mason?" Dr. French sounded old and tired.

Mason pitied him. "I wouldn't be that foolish. And you're right. It's never too late to end things."

"Yes. On that we can agree." Dr. French hung up.

Mason put down the phone. Hadn't he known this day would come? And yet he hated that it would have to end this way. Why couldn't they have both died peacefully in their sleep? Because neither had lived a peaceful life. Nor would there be any peace beyond this life. Not for the two of them.

CHAPTER FIVE

BRANDON'S ONLY THOUGHT as he drove north through Antelope Flats toward his family's ranch was of Anna Austin. He'd always loved the drive. The road climbed from Antelope Flats, giving him a view of the Tongue River Reservoir. The water glistened as the sun sunk in brilliant orange behind the Bighorn Mountains to the west. The red rock cliffs on the east side of the lake glowed golden just before he lost sight of the water as the highway curved away.

But today he only saw silken black hair, wide brown eyes and a face that would haunt him the rest of his days.

A few miles out, he slowed and turned onto the dirt road that followed Rosebud Creek through rocky outcroppings, thickets of chokecherry trees, willows and dogwood against a backdrop of sage and red rock bluffs and ponderosa pines.

Pulling up in front of the ranch house, he looked up to see his little sister Dusty come out onto the porch as if she'd been waiting for him.

"What happened to your head?" she asked, smiling, making it clear she'd talked to her best friend Leticia. Dusty was all McCall, from her white-blond hair to her pale blue eyes and her need to know everything.

"As if you haven't already heard," he said, and stepped into the house.

She trailed right behind him. "Did you find her?"

"Who?" he asked, giving her his best innocent look.

"You can't fool me, Brandon McCall. You might as well tell me about her."

He shot her a smile over his shoulder as he trotted up the stairs to his room. "Don't hold your breath."

She was grumbling below him. His tomboy sister. She was almost nineteen but she still looked eleven to him. Maybe it was the way she dressed. Jeans, boots, western shirt, her hair pulled back in a braid, no makeup. Nothing girly about her. He felt a surge of love for her as he went into his room, closed the door and headed for the bath.

He showered and changed, dressing in the darkest clothing he had, then sneaked down the stairs, hoping to avoid the rest of his family if possible.

"You're not having dinner with us?" asked a female voice behind him.

He'd almost made it to the front door. Damn. He turned to look at Shelby, his mother. She was beautiful. He could imagine that she must have been stunning when she was younger.

"I'm going camping up in the mountains," he said.

She smiled at that, amusement in her gaze, and didn't ask about the bandage on his head. Obviously, she'd been talking to Dusty. "Maybe some time you could bring her out to meet your family."

The improbability of that made him smile. "Right. Yeah." He glanced at his watch. "I'm running late."

She nodded and waved him off. "Have fun."

Yeah.

Things had been pretty weird at the house since his mother's return. Shelby Ward McCall had been dead to all of them for over thirty years. Then last summer, she'd just appeared at the front door as if returning from the grave.

Except she'd never been dead, no matter what the gravestone said at the local cemetery. Nope. Shelby and Asa had just cooked it up rather than get a divorce. At least that was their story and so far, they were sticking to it.

But Brandon, his brothers and sister hadn't missed that something was going on between their father and mother. Too much whispering, odd looks and times when one of them caught Shelby crying. Shelby wasn't one of those women who cried over nothing, which made them all worry that their parents had a secret between them that would make the others pale in comparison.

He tried not to think about it as he went to his pickup, got his shotgun and the supplies he'd purchased in town, and headed for the barn.

Saddling his horse, he loaded everything, including his sleeping bag, and swung up into the saddle, heading his horse south toward the VanHorn Ranch. The sun was all the way down by the time he reached the first ridge. He stopped to look back on his family ranch, as he always did.

Like his brothers, there'd been a time when he'd tried to run from the ranching life, from the responsibility and the weight of a hundred-year-old tradition, mostly from the feeling that he had no choice in life but to follow in his father's and grandfather's footsteps.

Now, just the thought of leaving here to go to law

school bothered him. What if for some reason—a job, money, a woman—he didn't make it back?

He shook his head at the thought and spurred his horse. It would be dark soon. He wanted to be on the VanHorn Ranch before then.

VanHorn would have all his men looking for Brandon McCall—and his pickup. The only way to sneak back on was by horseback.

He wondered how Anna Austin planned to get back on the ranch. It didn't matter. Whatever she pulled tonight, he'd be waiting for her.

MASON ANSWERED the phone. "What?"

"She called me."

"What? Are you drunk?" he demanded. "Look, Doc, I don't have time for this right now."

"Make time. Did you hear what I said? She called me and threatened me."

Mason was losing his patience. "Who are you talking about?"

"*Anna Austin.* Who the hell do you think?"

Mason felt all the air rush from his lungs. "That's not possible."

"She said she's in town and that she is coming after the two of us. I knew this was going to happen. I just knew it."

"She's not in town." Mason stumbled over to a chair and dropped into it.

"You swore this would never happen. I did everything you asked. You said that would be the end of it. Now do you understand why I wanted that damned file?"

His mind raced. "I'll take care of it. Do you hear me? I'll take care of it."

"Damn you for talking me into this," Dr. French said. "I want the file *now*. I'm not waiting a few days. You get it or else."

"Or else what?" Mason snapped. "Don't forget why you helped me. You needed the money or don't you remember?" he asked, his voice leaden with sarcasm.

"Yes," the doctor said. "I remember. But I'm too old to care now. All I have left is my reputation. I won't let you have that, too, Mason. You took everything else."

"Don't threaten me, Niles. Not if you know what is good for you."

"You can't control me anymore, Mason. If you don't give me the file, you will regret it." He hung up.

Mason slammed down the phone. "I already regret it," he said to the empty room. The old fool had to be mistaken. She didn't know anything about Dr. French. It wasn't possible. Nor could she be in town. He would have known.

Picking up the phone, he called Information for the number at the newspaper where she worked.

He was shocked to learn that she'd left that job six months before. The receptionist thought Anna Austin had resigned to do freelance investigative journalism. No, she didn't know of any other number she could be reached at.

If she had a cell phone, he had no way to get that number. His heart began to pound. He'd always feared that his secrets would get out someday. As he bent to pry up the floorboard and pulled out Helena VanHorn's worn dusty medical file, he prayed to God this wasn't the day.

ANNA TOOK back roads to the marina. She knew all the roads into the ranch would be watched, the house guarded. She had to get everyone away from the house and, at the same time, find a way to get in there herself.

She rented a boat for a week, even though she didn't expect to be in town that long, and left the truck parked in a stand of trees where she didn't think it would be noticed.

Once in the boat, she stuffed her gear under a seat. Then, powering up the motor, she eased away from the dock.

She'd had experience with boats because of the girls she'd met at expensive summer camps and even more expensive private schools. As soon as she was past the No-Wake buoys, she hit the throttle. The motor roared, the bow rising, then dropping as the boat picked up speed.

She couldn't help but smile as the wind and spray hit her face, blowing back her hair. She loved being on the water. There was nothing quite as freeing. She let the craft run full throttle, bouncing over waves from other boats, the sun in her face.

The Tongue River Reservoir stretched for miles from the steep red rock cliffs and pine trees to where the lake turned to river, flat and thick with brush and cottonwoods.

In places along the shore, she could see veins of black coal in the rocks. Up the river, there were coal mines that operated twenty-four hours a day. Sometimes she heard an occasional blast or caught sight of the huge crane at work.

It was getting dark. She watched the shoreline ahead, telling herself she had no choice other than what she was about to do.

IT WAS FULL DARK by the time Brandon stopped on a rise over the VanHorn Ranch complex. He scanned the buildings before him with night-vision binoculars. The ranch house was dark. Mason VanHorn's big car wasn't parked in front of the ranch house and he didn't see anyone guarding it, but he knew VanHorn and the others were there waiting.

And unless someone stopped her, Anna Austin was going to walk right into a trap. He thought about what he would do if he were her. She would have access to maps of the ranch. Several were posted on coalbed-methane-well Web sites. If she really was some famous investigative reporter, she would know where to look. He had to assume she knew the ranch probably better than he did.

She'd used vandalizing the wellheads as a distraction before, but she would know that none of VanHorn's men would fall for that again. It would have to be something bigger, something they couldn't ignore that wouldn't just draw them away from the ranch house, but force them away.

Tonight would be clear, with stars and a full moon. He was betting that she would make her move before the moon came up. And the moon would be up soon.

If he was right about her returning. His gut told him she'd be back. Or maybe he was just hoping. As he sat on his horse in the dark, Brandon smiled to himself at the thought of seeing her again. It was more than just his pride driving him, although he hated to admit that the woman intrigued the hell out of him.

Nothing moved in the darkness. He was beginning to think she'd outsmarted him again. Then he saw it. Down the mountainside, past the highway to Wyoming, past the ranch house. He focused the binoculars on what looked like a boat winding its way through the submerged trees where the creek drained into the lake below him. Hadn't he heard that VanHorn had purchased this narrow piece of swampy land?

"Anna," he breathed, and grinned.

She'd found a way back on the ranch.

Spurring his horse, he rode down the mountainside, following the cover along the creek. Clouds drifted over the tops of the large old cottonwoods as he headed for the lake—and Anna.

As he neared the lake's edge, he heard the *putt-putt* of a boat motor, then silence. Waves splashed at his horse's feet. He reined in and listened, hearing a soft metal thud, the lap of water and then stillness again.

Dismounting, he dropped his reins, leaving his horse to work his way to where he'd heard the last sound. The lake was up, many of the trees in this area now standing in water. He tried not to make a sound as he kept to the dense shadows of the trees.

A light splash, then another. Hunkering down at the base of one of the cottonwoods, he waited.

She came out of the water. Like last night, she wore all black, including the stocking cap covering her dark hair. Only tonight she had on all-black denim—and western boots. To his surprise, he realized she was dressed for horseback riding.

For a moment, he was too surprised to move.

She ran through the trees toward the fence line. An instant later, a half-dozen dark hulking shapes appeared out of the darkness. VanHorn's wild horses?

She didn't really think she could just climb on one and ride it, did she?

He stayed where he was, anxious to see what she planned to do, not wanting to spook her. It would do his pride good to see her lying on her back in the damp soft earth after being thrown—if she even got that far.

He watched her dig out something from her pocket. She was making a sound that had all the horses' ears up. She inched forward. A horse whinnied and stomped the ground.

Behind him, Brandon heard his own horse whinny in answer. Several of the wild horses milled around, a couple shied a little, but came back to where Anna was standing.

He could only see her back, but she hadn't appeared to have heard his horse, didn't seem aware of him behind her, watching. Waiting.

To his amazement, the horses didn't run off as he'd expected they would. It was almost as if she'd been here earlier, the way they'd come up to the fence when they'd seen her. Almost as if they'd been waiting for her.

He saw her hold her hand out, palm down to one of the smaller of the horses. The mare nuzzled the closed hand. Anna didn't move a muscle. The mare nuzzled her hand again and slowly like a flower opening to the sun, the hand turned and opened.

Whatever she'd had in it quickly disappeared. She reached into her pocket for more as she began to stroke the horse's neck.

Brandon edged closer. He could hear her talking softly to the horse and the horse responding.

"Nice night for a boat ride," he whispered when he was within touching distance. He couldn't be sure Van-Horn's men weren't within hearing distance. He wanted to save her—not throw her to the wolves.

She didn't even start, almost as if she'd known he was behind her. Either that or she had nerves of steel. The woman had grit, he'd give her that.

The horses shied, but didn't go far as she slowly turned to look at him. He was close, close enough in the darkness that he could see her face clearly, read her expression. No, he'd startled her, but she was hiding it well.

"Interested in a boat ride? I have a rental. You're welcome to go for a ride if you like," she whispered back.

He smiled at that. "I'm not really dressed for it. For that matter, neither are you. Planning to do a little horse-back riding?"

She turned to the horses that had sneaked back over and dug what he realized were sugar cubes from her pocket. "They're beautiful, aren't they. I've always loved wild horses. They're built so different from domestic horses."

It surprised him. Not just her knowledge of horses, but her obvious love for them.

He leaned over to whisper in her ear. An errant lock of her dark hair tickled his nose. Her hair smelled of smoke, as if she'd been near a campfire. "I know what you're up to."

"Do you?" She didn't look at him as she rubbed the mare between the eyes and dug out another sugar cube.

"Mason VanHorn came home today." He waited for a reaction, but didn't get one. "He's set a trap for you." For us, Brandon thought. "If you try to go back up to the ranch house, he'll be waiting for you."

"I see. And he sent you down here to tell me." She

climbed up onto the fence, straddling it as she sat on the top rail.

"I'm trying to save you," he said and climbed up, as well.

"Oh, I thought your job was security—not protecting women who wander onto the ranch. You save a lot of women, do you?"

He watched her continue bonding with the mare. Several other horses stayed close, curious, but leery.

He knew the feeling as he looked at this woman. "You think VanHorn sent me?" That was so ludicrous it was laughable, but then she didn't know he'd been fired. Or that he was a McCall and shouldn't have been on this ranch to start with.

She raised a brow but said nothing.

The sky glowed golden over the mountains to the east of the lake, warning that the moon would be up soon. "You have to give this up. Whatever it is, it isn't worth getting yourself shot over."

The night air was cool. His boots were wet from wading at the edge of the lake. He could see that her jeans and boots were wet, as well.

"How's your head?" she asked quietly without looking at him.

"Fine." A lie. It still ached. A constant reminder of her. As if he needed another one.

"Have you ever ridden a wild horse?" she whispered.

"One of these brought up from Wyoming's Bighorn?" He shook his head. "And I wouldn't suggest you try to ride one, either, if I were you. I know VanHorn's been breeding them and they might not be as wild as the others, but they sure as heck aren't broken, either."

The peal of a bell filled the night air, startling him. A dozen lights blinked on at the ranch complex. An engine cranked over. Then another. The bell continued to ring. The fire bell!

Anna swung her leg over the fence railing and slipped onto the mare's back as if she'd done it before, earlier. She was going to try to ride that wild horse bareback!

The thought was hardly formed when the horse took off running with Anna hunched over its neck, her fingers entwined in the mare's mane.

She was getting away.

Worse, she was headed in the direction of the ranch house. Headed right into an ambush.

Brandon leaped from the fence and raced back to where he'd ground tied his horse. Damn the woman! He'd tried to warn her. Didn't she realize that VanHorn would have told his men to shoot first and ask questions later? After all, this was Montana and trespassing could get you killed.

Swinging up into the saddle, he took off after her. As the first stars spread a pale glitter overhead, he and Anna streaked across the wide pasture to the thunder of hooves and the peal of the ranch bell. He was gaining on her, but only marginally.

That's when he saw it. A line of orange off the mountain from the ranch house, down not far from the water's edge. A grass fire!

He knew instantly what she'd done. The whiff of smoke he'd smelled in her hair. She'd started the fire as a diversion! VanHorn would go ballistic. What could be so important in that house that she'd get herself killed for it? Or, if she were lucky, only have to go to prison?

He could smell the smoke on the breeze as he raced

across the nightscape. It was a smell every landowner in this part of the country feared. A grass fire could sweep across acres in a matter of minutes. There was nothing more dangerous.

Especially on a ranch with hundreds of coalbed methane gas wells.

As he galloped after her, he could see movement at the ranch complex, men running, tanker trucks roaring off toward the blaze, other vehicles racing from the corners of the ranch as the alarm went out.

He was gaining on her, but she was almost to the ranch house. She'd headed for the back again and the shelter of the tall pines. Brandon could see the line of the fire flickering up in orange waves as the flames rode the light breeze. There weren't any wells for several miles from where she'd started the blaze, but if the breeze kicked up—

With a shock, he realized that he'd underestimated the lengths this woman would go to. Vandalism. Breaking and entering. Now arson? She was looking at some hard time—if Mason didn't get her first.

She rode straight for the ranch house, a deep shadow moving swiftly, her small form almost lost in the horse's silhouette.

One thing was clear. The woman could ride. He spurred his horse, knowing they both could be seen from the ranch house as the moon crested the mountain behind them. Mason VanHorn could have the crosshairs of his rifle on either of them right now.

The moon came up behind them, washing the ranch in shimmering gold. Anna disappeared into the tall pines. He was almost to the dark pines behind the ranch house when her horse came barreling out without her.

"Damn woman," he swore as he swung down from his still-racing horse. The moment his feet hit the ground he was moving. Right into whatever trap VanHorn had laid for them. He wasn't even sure a fire was going to do the trick this time. But he couldn't turn back. He couldn't let her fall into VanHorn's hands. The woman had no idea how dangerous that would be. He was sure she'd never dealt with a man like Mason VanHorn before.

It was pitch-black as he barreled into the stand of large pines, all moonlight extinguished under the wide dark sweeping branches. He didn't see her and sure as hell didn't see the tree limb she swung until it was too late.

She caught him in the chest. The limb wasn't very large. Fortunately for him, she hadn't had much time to find a good one.

All the limb did was knock the air out of him for a few precious seconds. Not long enough for her to turn and run. He grabbed her, swinging her around to face him as he wrenched the limb from her and tossed it aside.

She jerked out of his grip and backed a few inches away from him, as if she knew he'd take her down if she ran. "I can't believe you work for someone like Mason VanHorn."

"*Worked*. He fired me this afternoon."

"I don't believe you," she whispered harshly.

"Fine. Then believe this. You don't have any idea who you're fooling with here. This man will kill you," he whispered back as he stepped a little closer. He could see that if he reached for her, she would fight him like a wildcat. But he wasn't letting her go near that house. "It's a trap," he whispered hoarsely. His chest ached. So did his head. He was getting tired of this woman hitting him. He could hear one of the fire trucks coming back up the hillside. Was it possible they'd already put the fire out? If so, the others would be coming, as well. "We have to leave *now*."

"Not until I get what I came for," she said through gritted teeth.

"Didn't you just hear me? It's a trap. He's waiting for us inside the house."

"Wrong," said a deep male voice behind them. The night filled with the sound of a shotgun shell being slammed into its chamber. "I'm right here."

CHAPTER SIX

BRANDON FROZE AT the sound of Mason VanHorn's voice behind him. He started to turn, the ground muddy from last night's rain, but stopped as he felt the icy cold barrel of a shotgun press into the flesh behind his left ear.

"You've vandalized my wells, broke into my house and now you try to burn down my ranch?" VanHorn's voice rose with anger and contempt. "I should shoot you right now."

"I wouldn't suggest you do that," Anna said, stepping out of the dark shadow of the trees. Her voice sounded strange. Too calm for what was happening here.

The woman had no fear. No sense, either. Brandon looked at her, wondering what he'd gotten himself into. Moonlight filtered through the pines as the moon, huge and golden, cleared the mountains. He could see anger etched into her features. She should have been scared witless. What the hell was wrong with her?

He heard a sound behind him, almost a groan. Suddenly he didn't feel the cold steel of the shotgun. He turned, afraid VanHorn had pointed the gun on Anna. As he spun around, he saw VanHorn slip in the mud and start to fall, dropping the shotgun as he tried to break his fall.

Brandon grabbed the fallen shotgun and reached for Anna.

She stood staring down at the elderly man sprawled in the mud. VanHorn was trying to get to his feet.

"Come on!" Brandon gave her arm a jerk and she seemed to come out of the fog she'd been in. Grabbing her hand, half dragging her, they ran to his horse. He heaved VanHorn's shotgun into the darkness and swung up into the saddle, drawing her up behind him. "Hang on," he ordered, as if he needed to. Her arms were already wrapped around his waist as he spurred his horse and took off up the mountainside. He could feel her shaking now as if in shock.

Behind him he heard the sound of voices. VanHorn's men must have found him. They would be hot on Brandon's trail. He rode hard for the next stand of trees. If he could reach forest-service land, he knew he could lose them. The terrain was steep and wooded. There was no way VanHorn could follow by pickup. And there was little chance of being tracked by horseback until daylight.

His horse lunged up the steep mountainside to where VanHorn land ended and forest-service land began. He'd left his gear at a spot high on the mountainside along a creek. He rode to it as the moon rose higher, making the night almost as bright as dawn.

Ahead, he spotted the old waterwheel, the blades wooden and weathered. Beside it a small shack. He reined in the horse and started to reach back to help Anna off. She slid off with ease on her own and walked toward the creek and waterwheel as if they hadn't been doing anything more tonight than going for a moonlight ride.

"Are you suicidal?" he demanded as he swung down and followed her. He'd bought himself a world of trouble and all because of a woman. One he would probably never understand.

The moon was high, casting a glow over her as he joined her. To his surprise, he saw that she'd been crying. Something softened inside him.

"Are you all right?" he asked, thumbing away a lone tear on her cheek.

She nodded and bit her lower lip as she looked again at the waterwheel. He'd put his pack at the opening to the shack. The small worn structure had no windows or even a door, but it was dry inside, the board weathered gray and soft from wear.

"This is your camp," she said, sounding surprised.

He could see now that she was trembling. She hadn't shown it, but she *had* been scared back there. He was relieved that the woman had a little sense.

"I'll get a fire going," he said. She didn't answer. He'd stacked some wood earlier while he'd waited for it to get dark. Now he went to the fire ring, and lighting a few tiny twigs, got a flame going. Carefully he added larger sticks until he had a good blaze, then put on some logs.

She hadn't moved, her back to him, as if she needed a few minutes alone. He gave them to her as he unsaddled his horse at the edge of the mountainside. Below him, he could see the valley, the Tongue River Reservoir a basin of liquid gold in the moonlight.

If VanHorn's men tried to follow them tonight, he would be able to see them coming. Not that he anticipated that happening. No, VanHorn would wait until first light. If he came after them. Brandon was betting

VanHorn would expect him to go home to the Sundown Ranch where he would feel safe.

Turning back to the fire, he saw that Anna was standing beside it warming her hands. The fire cracked and popped, sending sparks drifting up like fireflies.

"Why didn't you let me get caught back there?" she asked, staring into the flames as he joined her.

"What makes you think you *aren't* caught?"

She raised her eyes to him. All that honey-brown glistened in the firelight. "Why were you working for Mason VanHorn?"

"I needed the money."

"Badly enough to work for a man like that?" she asked.

"The job was temporary. Mason found out I was on the payroll and I got fired. It was bound to happen. The VanHorns and the McCalls have been feuding for years. I have no idea what started it and I don't care."

"If you were really fired, then what were you doing there tonight?"

He took off his Stetson and raked a hand through his hair. "I *was* fired."

She nodded slowly.

"I was there tonight because I wanted to try to keep you from riding into a trap. I had thought you might have the good sense to believe me. I was wrong."

"I'm sorry I misjudged you." She sounded as if she might mean it. "I just assumed that you were still working for Mason. Why would you take a chance like that otherwise?"

"I owed you." He turned where she could see the bandage on his head.

"Sorry. I didn't mean to hit you so hard."

"Uh-huh."

She closed her eyes in a grimace. "And I hit you with the limb, too."

"Uh-huh."

When she opened her eyes they were filled with tears. "I'm sorry I got you involved in this."

"That makes two of us, but it's a little late for that now," he said.

"Not if you give me your horse and let me go. When this is over, I'll make sure Mason VanHorn knows you were never involved."

"When this is over?" He laughed. "No way are you going anywhere without me. I'm up to my neck in trouble *now* because of you, and you're going to get me out of it right away—not when this is over. It's over now. In the morning, I'm taking you to the sheriff so you can turn yourself in. He's my brother. You tell him everything, clear me, confess to your crimes and if you haven't pulled these kinds of stunts before and gotten caught, the judge will probably give you probation."

"If I were to do that, you'd never convince Mason VanHorn that you weren't in on it with me," she said, shaking her head. "Isn't it clear to you that he has something to hide? Until I get the goods on him, neither of us will ever be safe."

"Why do I get the feeling you're about to make me another offer? Just so you know up front, I don't do business with vandals, burglars and arsonists."

She glanced toward the pack he'd left suspended in a tree. "Is there food in there?" She obviously knew there was. This was bear country. Any food had to be put up high enough to discourage the varmints from stealing it. "I'm starved."

He studied her. She was trying to change the subject, stalling. But he wasn't sure he was ready to hear her new offer anyway. Not that she could make him an offer he would accept, he told himself. "I brought some hot dogs."

Her expression brightened. "I can't remember the last time I roasted hot dogs over a fire. Do you have mustard, ketchup and relish?"

"What, no onions?" He laughed as he dragged up a stump for her to sit on. You would have thought he'd offered her a throne the way she smiled in gratitude.

He set about whittling two long sticks, handed her one and got the small insulated bag of food inside his pack down from the tree. He watched as she speared a hot dog on her stick, then carefully held it over the glowing fire, turning the hot dog slowly, the skin blistering and bubbling before turning perfectly brown.

Digging out the ketchup and relish fast-food packets, he handed them to her. "You almost look as if you'd done this before."

"Summer camp."

"Is that where you learned to ride?"

"I've always loved horses," she said. He wondered if she'd dodged his question on purpose. He'd never seen a woman ride like that. She'd obviously ridden more than just at summer camp.

She slid her hot dog off the stick directly into a bun. He watched her lather the dog with ketchup, then squeeze relish onto it. She took a big bite, closing her eyes as she chewed, making an "Mmm" sound.

He couldn't help but smile watching her. In the firelight she was adorable, the light sprinkling of freckles across her cheeks and nose as golden as her brown eyes. He reminded himself just who he was sharing his meal with.

She swallowed a bite and settled her gaze on him across the fire. "You can't turn me in."

He gave her a look that said he could and would. "What did you think was going to happen after everything you've done?"

"Trust me, I have my reasons," she said. "Help me and I promise you won't regret it."

"I *already* regret it."

"Please." The word came out a whisper.

"Save your breath," he said as he speared a hot dog and stuck it directly into the flames knowing it would burn on the outside. He didn't have the patience to cook his the way she did. He told himself he liked 'em burned.

She watched in horrified amusement as his hot dog caught fire, quickly changing her expression when he shot her a look. She'd taken off her black stocking cap and held it by the fingertips of one hand. Her dark hair tumbled in a cascade of loose curls, shiny black in the firelight, down around her shoulders.

She seemed smaller to him. Not the strong, determined woman he knew her to be. She rose and walked to the edge of the mountainside, her back to him. She seemed deep in thought, but he knew she could just as easily be plotting how to get away from him. There was no doubt that she wasn't finished with Mason VanHorn. Clearly the woman had a death wish.

He pulled his burnt hot dog from the fire and rested the stick against a rock. "You might as well make yourself at home. We're not going anywhere until daylight," he called to her.

She turned slowly and came back to warm her hands over the fire, her gaze on the fire, not him. "You don't understand."

"We can agree on that." He picked up the stick with the burnt hot dog, burning his fingers as he pulled off the wiener and dropped it into a bun.

"There are some papers I know he's hidden in the ranch house," she said. "I *have* to find them."

"Weren't they in the safe?" he asked, taking a bite of his hot dog.

She shook her head. "The safe was empty."

He chewed for a moment, watching her, then swallowed. "You just happened to have the combination."

"Men his age change the combination a lot and have to keep the numbers some place they can find them. I found them."

He took another bite before asking, "If these papers are that incriminating, why wouldn't he have already destroyed them?"

"He needs them if he wants to keep the others who were involved in line."

Brandon stared at her. *"Blackmail?"*

"Not exactly. Insurance."

"You seem to know him pretty well," Brandon commented after finishing his hot dog. "Is he blackmailing *you?*"

She shot him a disbelieving look. "You think I would be involved in something—" She waved a hand through the air in obvious frustration. "I told you. I'm an investigative reporter. This is what I do. Find out everything I can about a subject so I know where to look."

"For the dirt?" He hadn't meant to sound so negative about her career path.

"If there is dirt."

He nodded. "You think he knew you were coming after him and that's why the safe was empty?"

"He knew someone was," she said. "I hired a private investigator to look into the allegations."

"And?"

"And she's disappeared."

IT WAS LATE when Sheriff Cash McCall got back to his office. As he walked in he saw that the message light was flashing on his phone.

"Cash, it's Raymond Winters. Call me. I found something interesting during the autopsy."

Cash quickly dialed Winters's number. He answered on the second ring.

"I thought you'd like to know Emma Ingles was sober as a judge," Winters said without preamble. "She hadn't ingested any of the vodka. But you want to hear something odd? There was vodka in her lungs."

"How would vodka get into her lungs?" Cash asked.

The coroner chuckled. "Only one way that I can think of. Someone tried to make it look as if she'd been drunk when she fell into the river by pouring the vodka down her throat. But since she was already dead, it went into her lungs."

Cash swore. "She was murdered?"

"Sure looks that way unless you can figure out how she managed to get that much vodka in her lungs, then walk down the road and throw herself off the embankment, hit her head on a rock and fall into the river—without taking *any* water into her lungs."

"Thanks, Raymond, for letting me know."

"One more odd thing. I found another bruise. This one at the base of her neck. She was hit hard with something."

"You don't think it was during the fall in the river?"

"No."

Cash shook his head thinking about Emma Ingles lying face up in the river. "What killed her?"

"A blow to the back of the head. I'd say it was inflicted before she was thrown off the embankment."

"DISAPPEARED?" Brandon echoed.

Anna didn't answer and he saw that she was crying. Oh, hell. "Don't cry."

"I'm not crying!" she snapped, and sniffed.

Right.

She was crying harder now.

Oh, hell. Being raised by a cantankerous old man and three older brothers, he didn't have a clue what to do when it came to women. Well, at least not the crying part.

This was all Shelby's fault. His mother. If she had stayed around like she was supposed to…

He got up to go around the fire and put a tentative hand on Anna's shoulder. "It's going to be all right."

She shot him a look that told him that was the wrong thing to say since it was an obvious lie.

"Okay, it's not going to be all right." He put his arm all the way around her and she turned into his chest, burying her face in his jacket. "But it could be worse. VanHorn could have shot us both back there."

She wiped her tears with her sleeve, still crying but laughing, too, as she leaned back to look up at him.

"You always see the silver lining in every cloud, don't you?"

Not always, but definitely right now with her in his arms. He held her closer, dropping his cheek to her hair. It still smelled a little like smoke, reminding him just what kind of woman she was. She encircled his waist with her arms and leaned into him as if, for right now at least, she needed someone to lean on.

He hated how good it felt to hold her. He wanted to wring her neck—not comfort her. This wasn't over. VanHorn had seen them. He would come after them.

Not that it mattered at this moment. Brandon remembered his reaction to her the first time he'd seen her. It was nothing compared to having her in his arms. He had the strangest feeling that he'd been here before with her. It made no sense.

Just like the feelings she evoked in him. Just his luck that the first woman who ever made him feel like this was wanted by not only the law but also by his family's sworn enemy.

He touched her long, dark silken hair and thought he felt a shock of electricity shoot through his fingertips. The scent of her wafted up, mixing with the smell of the campfire, the pines, the summer night.

He'd never felt more alive, as if everything was suddenly extra vibrant, the intensity of it making him feel light-headed.

She stepped back, looking a little embarrassed as she wiped tears from her cheeks.

He took a breath, watching her, wondering about her, knowing he needed to back off. It would be a mistake to get involved with this woman. *I'm already involved. Yeah? Not as much as you'd like to be.*

"You never told me what VanHorn did that warranted vandalism, burglary and arson," he reminded her—and himself. His voice sounded a little husky even to him.

"Do we have to talk about this now?"

"Before we go any further here, I'd like to know what I'm involved in." Brandon knew in all fairness that he'd involved himself. He could have radioed Red Hudson last night, let the ranch manager handle it. But he hadn't. And now he had only himself to blame.

"Right now he thinks I'm in cahoots with you," Brandon said. "And given that the VanHorns have always hated the McCalls—"

"That silly feud?"

"Silly? We're talking bad blood for several generations between the families. This little incident is only going to fuel the fires. And I can tell you right now my family will be as angry as VanHorn. No good will come of this."

"I'm sorry but if you had just left me alone, you wouldn't have to be here now," she snapped.

"I was doing my job," he shot back, even though that wasn't quite the truth.

"If you had been doing your job, you would have turned me over to Mason VanHorn. You were working for him. You say you're not working for him, but how do I know he didn't send you to intercept me and find out how much I know? Or maybe to destroy what evidence I have."

Brandon shook his head in disgust. "I haven't lied to you. Don't you wish you could say the same."

"You're wrong," she protested.

He gave her a look, then stepped away from the fire to unroll his sleeping bag.

SHE COULD HAVE kicked herself. She knew he wasn't working for VanHorn. He'd rescued her tonight. Brandon McCall was one of the good guys. She couldn't be that wrong about the blond-haired boy who'd saved her when she was nine. So why was she pushing him away? To protect him? Or herself?

"What are you doing?" she asked.

"Going to sleep. It's late and I'm tired."

"I'm trying to be honest with you. I can't tell anyone until I have proof."

"Uh-huh." He took off his jacket, rolled it up for a pillow, then stripped off his shirt and started to unbutton his jeans. He was more handsome than she had ever imagined he would grow up to be. His back was tanned and muscular and just the sight of him dressed only in jeans and boots took her breath away. It was the first time she'd ever *ached* for a man.

"You might want to turn your head," he said, amusement in his voice as he noticed her staring at him.

She couldn't hide the emotions this man evoked in her, and didn't want to try. She'd dreamed about Brandon McCall since she was a girl. He'd been her fantasy man, one she had idealized in her imagination.

But not even her imagination had done Brandon McCall justice. "Sure you won't share your sleeping bag?" she asked, only half joking. She rubbed her arms, chilled by her own thoughts more than the weather. "It's already getting cold and I'm not use to this altitude."

His gaze locked with hers, burning through her. "I'm not going back to the VanHorn Ranch. Neither are you," he said. "I'm taking you to the sheriff in the morning and there is nothing you can say—or *do*—to change my mind."

He thought she was trying to seduce him? "Brandon, you aren't going to just go to sleep and leave me standing here?"

"Brandon?" He froze, his fingers on the buttons of jeans as he frowned at her. "I never told you my first name. And come to think of it, you never asked."

ANNA REALIZED her mistake the instant his name was out of her mouth.

He stepped toward her. He was shirtless now and she couldn't help but notice the broad expanse of his chest, the soft blond hair like down that disappeared into the space where he'd unhooked the top two buttons of his jeans.

"How long have you known my name?"

"Now look who's suspicious," she said, and saw that he would have an answer or else. "I asked around." Only she'd done the asking when she was nine, some twenty-two years ago.

He stopped just inches from her. His skin was wonderfully browned from working on the ranch without his shirt, his shoulders muscled, his arms strong and well-shaped, just like his slim waist and hips, his long legs beneath the denim.

She recalled being in his arms and the feeling it had evoked.

"Why would you ask around about me?"

This time? "I was worried about you. I thought I might have hit you a little too hard. I called the clinic."

He shook his head. "There is no way they would give out any information on a patient. Try again."

"It doesn't matter how I found out your name, does it?"

"Yeah, it does," he said, stepping so close she could feel the heat radiating off his body. His masculine scent filled her. He let out a low chuckle as if he knew he had her cornered. The sound reverberated in her chest making her heart pound a little faster.

"Just once, I'd like to hear the truth from those lips," he said, his voice low and rough with emotion as he stared down at her mouth.

She licked her lips. "We met once before last night at the ranch."

He leaned closer. "Trust me, I would have remembered."

"You were just a boy. I was sitting on the curb eating a Popsicle on Main Street. Some older kids were giving me a hard time. You saved me from them." She saw his expression. "I guess you don't remember." She tried to hide her disappointment. She knew she was being foolish. Just because he'd made a lasting impression on her—

"How old were you?"

"Nine. You were eleven."

He shook his head.

"It's all right. It wasn't that big of a deal," she said, trying to hide her hurt.

A muscle bunched in his jaw. "Oh, I remember all right."

She smiled sadly. "Sure you do. Then you probably remember that I was eating a grape Popsicle."

"It wasn't grape. It was cherry. You said it was your favorite."

She felt her eyes burn with tears. "You *do* remember." She couldn't help the bubble of joy that rose in her. "I shared my Popsicle with you. You said cherry was your favorite, too."

He stepped back, jerking his hat from his head to rake a hand through his hair. His pale blue eyes were cold with anger. "I remember that little girl. And I remember her *name*. My God, *you're* Christianna VanHorn? Mason VanHorn's daughter?"

CHAPTER SEVEN

ANNA FELT HER heart stop at the look of horror in his eyes. He remembered all right. "Brandon—" She reached for him but he pulled free.

He stepped back from her as if she'd just told him she was the devil in disguise. "Whoa! You're Christianna VanHorn?"

At that moment, she would have gladly denied it. She hated the look of shock and revulsion in his face. "Now you know. Only I go by Anna Austin."

He shook his head, anger in his blue eyes.

"I didn't lie to you."

"No," he said sarcastically. "You've been honest with me from the get-go. It isn't bad enough that the Van-Horns and the McCalls have hated each other for years? I get involved with you?"

"We're not exactly involved," she pointed out, surprised at her own anger.

"Why don't you go by Christianna VanHorn?" he asked. "I mean, that's who you really are."

"Would that make it easier for you?" Anna quickly turned away to hide the tears that that swam in her eyes. Earlier in his arms, she'd thought they'd both felt something. Obviously it was only because he hadn't known whom she was with.

He stepped around her until he was facing her. She

could see that he was still angry. Still shocked as if she had purposely deceived him so he would help her. Hadn't she?

"Why?" he demanded. "Why would you go after your own *father?* Vandalize his gas wells? Break into your own house? Try to burn down the place? Why?"

"Brandon, it's complicated."

"I'm sure it's complicated. You still can't be honest with me, can you?" He turned and walked away from her.

"Brandon? Please."

He stopped, his back to her.

She felt tears burn her eyes again. She'd known he would be shocked when he found out who she was. But it was the look of disgust that was killing her. "I can explain," she said, and reached out to touch his arm.

He drew back as if her touch burned him and shook his head as if warning her to keep her distance. "You should have told me."

"Brandon, this isn't about that stupid family feud, is it? That has nothing to do with you and me—"

"The hell it doesn't. Your father will send out a pack of dogs to hunt me down the moment he realizes I haven't gone to my brother. After last night, he'll think we were in this together."

"That's why we have to stick together, help each other." Her voice broke. This wasn't the way it was supposed to happen. She'd known that one day she would see Brandon McCall again. But not like this.

"I should have turned you over to your father," he said, pulling away from her.

"You couldn't do that," she said to his back.

"Oh, yeah?"

"I know you. I knew the kind of man you would grow up to be. You couldn't give me up to my father and you can't now, just as you had to help me when I was nine."

His broad shoulders slumped, his head dropped, then slowly he turned back around to her, his eyes full of sadness. "Do you have any idea what you've done here?"

"That's why I need your help."

CHRISSY. Mason still couldn't believe it. He'd struggled to his feet in the dim light of the pines to see her and Brandon McCall take off on a horse. Together.

Dr. French was right. But Chrissy wasn't just in town. She was on the ranch. She was after him. She knew.

His worst nightmare had just come true.

Even when Red and a few of the men had come running out to find him muddy and shaken, all he could do was stare after the two as they disappeared into the darkness.

He ignored offers of help as he stumbled into the house and poured himself a stiff drink. "Leave me alone," he barked. Red left with the other men, but Mason knew Red hadn't gone far.

Mason dropped into a chair, suddenly too weak to stand, and took a long swallow of his drink. It burned all the way down. Chrissy. Or Anna Austin, as she called herself for her newspaper and magazine articles.

The ramifications beat him like golf ball-size hail. Shaking, he set the drink on the table and dropped his face into his hands.

His life had been one mistake after another. The only gift he had was making money and now he had more of that than he would ever spend and it meant nothing. He had no one.

All these years he'd thought at least he had Christianna—as long as he kept her thousands of miles away, as long as she never got too close, never found out what demons drove him, consumed him.

But now he no longer even had that. He knew what she was after—and what extremes she would go to to get it. She'd set the ranch on fire! Vandalized his wells! Broken into the house that had been her home!

But that was nothing compared to her ultimate betrayal. She was in on this with a McCall.

BRANDON STARED at Anna in the glow from the campfire, remembering the little girl she'd been. Not so different.

That day on the curb, she'd been holding her own, even against five big kids. She hadn't really needed his help. But she did seem to now.

He hadn't known when he'd shared her cherry Popsicle that she was Mason VanHorn's daughter, Christianna. Would he have helped her if he'd known?

"Why the hell didn't you tell me you were Mason VanHorn's daughter right away?" he demanded, not letting himself think about the freckle-faced girl with the cherry Popsicle or the beautiful woman who'd wanted to share his bedroll.

"I haven't been his daughter for twenty-one years," she said. "He sent me away."

Brandon didn't want to react to the pain he heard in her voice. He thought of his own mother. Gone for over thirty years. But at least he'd had a father. Anna hadn't had either all these years.

He looked at her, his emotions at war. "I can't believe you're Christianna VanHorn."

"Stop saying that like I'm the spawn of the devil. Even if it might be true."

He shook his head. Hell's bells, what had he gotten himself into this time? And more to the point, what had *she?* "You've lied to me from the start, beginning with your name."

"That's not true. Anna is my nickname. Austin is my middle name and my mother's maiden name. It's the name I write under. I never liked Christianna. It was so…"

"Long?"

She rolled her eyes. "Yes, long. Anna's the name my mother called me. She never liked Christianna. It had been my father's baby sister's name, a sister who had died when she was an infant."

He could only stare at her—all of it too much to comprehend. "*Why?* I still don't understand why you would go after your own *father?*"

"Believe me, I have my reasons."

The anger in her voice cooled some of his own. "But he's your *father,*" he whispered.

"I told you, he hasn't been a father to me since I was ten. He put me in one boarding school after another, never letting me return to the ranch that I loved, keeping me at arm's length."

"Why did he do that?" He'd always heard that Mason idolized his daughter.

"Isn't it obvious? He was afraid that some day I would find out what a monster he really was. You have no idea what he is capable of," she said, her voice breaking with emotion. "I do."

MASON HEARD Red come back into the house and lifted his head from his hands, pulling himself together.

"Are you all right, boss?" Red asked.

"It was McCall. He's the one behind all of this."

"Brandon McCall?" Red didn't believe it.

Mason could see it in his face and he knew that if he lied to Red now, he would lose him. He needed Red. Needed someone he could trust. Especially now.

"There was another rider with him," Mason said. "A woman. I want McCall found and brought to me. Make sure the woman isn't harmed. And I don't want anyone to know about this, you understand? *No one.*" From Red's disapproving look, Mason knew he understood only too well.

"I'm not going to harm them, if that's what you're worried about."

"Why not call the sheriff and let him handle it?"

Mason gave Red a piercing look. "The sheriff," he said through gritted teeth, "is Brandon's brother. You think I can get any justice in this town? No sheriff. I'll handle this myself. Just like I always handle things." He could see Red wasn't going to move until he got the whole story. He sighed. "The woman is my daughter."

Red didn't hide his surprise. Or his sympathy. "She's the one who vandalized the wells, broke into the house and probably started the grass fire. Not McCall."

Mason swore. "What the hell is he doing with my daughter if he's not in on it?"

Red shook his head. "I've gotten to know McCall in the weeks he's worked for me. He didn't have anything to do with what is happening here. You fired one of my best men. If this is about that stupid feud—"

"I don't want him with my daughter," Mason snapped,

remembering the day he'd caught his nine-year-old sitting on the curb sharing her Popsicle with the youngest McCall. They'd just been kids visiting on a hot summer day, but he'd had a horrible premonition when he'd seen them together. It was so strong he'd known he had to get his daughter away from Antelope Flats, away from Montana.

And now Christianna was back—and with McCall.

"I need to talk to her. Without him there," Mason amended. "You can understand that, can't you?"

"I can find them," Red said slowly.

"I thought you probably could."

"You want me to start tonight?"

"No, wait until first light when you can track them. I would imagine McCall will head to his ranch. If that's what he does, we'll wait until he leaves it again. We need to get him alone. I'll take care of my daughter."

Red seemed to hesitate, but then slowly nodded.

Mason waited until he heard Red leave before he reached for the phone and dialed Dr. French's number.

ANNA STEPPED AWAY from the fire to the edge of the mountainside again. A cool breeze came up out of the pines and the valley. Lights sparkled in the distance.

The only sound was the crackle of the fire and the gurgle of the creek through the rocks and the broken blades of the waterwheel. She breathed in the sweet smell of pine and the night.

"I don't want to talk about my father," she said without turning around. "Please."

She felt rather than heard him come up behind her. Suddenly the night was much warmer, her skin alive with just the thought of his touch.

"I'm sorry," he whispered, his breath feathering the hair at her right ear.

She closed her eyes, anticipating the feel of him.

His arms came around her, his fingertips making a torturous sensuous trail down her bare arms. He entwined his fingers with hers, drawing her hands back under her breasts as he hugged her to him. She leaned against his solid body and told herself not to trust her feelings—let alone fall for Brandon McCall. She'd seen the way he reacted when he found out who she was.

Yet as he turned her slowly around to face him, her eyes locking with his, she wanted with all her heart to believe in him. To surrender to her feelings. All breath left her as he bent down to brush his mouth over hers. Her lips parted on a sigh. His eyes were the palest blue she'd ever seen. In the moonlight they were like hot flames burning pure. She tried to catch her breath, to hear his whispered words over the pounding of her pulse.

"Anna." He said her name like a caress.

Her skin rippled with goose bumps, her heart galloped as wild as the horse she'd ridden earlier as she'd tried to escape this man. But she'd never been able to escape him, not in her thoughts, not earlier tonight.

And there was no escaping him now.

He lowered his head again and kissed her.

BRANDON DIDN'T WANT to react to the pain he'd heard in her voice. He thought of his own mother. Gone for over thirty years. Did anyone get over that feeling of rejection?

He drew her close, holding her. He wanted her, wanted Christianna VanHorn. Even as he thought it, he knew they had no future. The fact that she was a criminal aside, she was a *VanHorn*. He was a McCall.

And still he kissed her, not surprised by the desire that flared inside him. Or the connection he felt to her, one that had begun with a cherry Popsicle years ago.

He didn't question the bond between them, nor the way she responded to his kiss, her lips parting as a sigh escaped her slim pale throat. He deepened the kiss, wanting her like nothing he'd ever wanted before. Passion sparked between them, like two powerful chemicals that should never be mixed. Not unless you wanted one hell of an explosion.

He pulled back, knowing the inevitable outcome if he continued kissing her and what those actions could cost them.

Moonlight filled her black hair with silver. Firelight danced in her brown eyes with flashes of gold. He looked into those eyes and what he saw there almost dropped him to his knees. A combustible mixture of desire and need.

"I've wanted to do that since I saw you last night," he said, his voice low and rough with emotion as he stared down at her mouth.

Anna pressed her fingers to her lips, her eyes bright with tears. He could see that she was shaken by the kiss. As much as he was.

He nodded and tried to still his raging heart. "You can have the bedroll. I'll be fine by the fire."

She smiled, tears in her eyes. "I'll go to your brother the sheriff with you in the morning if that's what you want. I'll fix things with my father for you. He won't press charges."

He stared at her. She would go to her father for him?

"No, we're in this together now." Whatever the hell it was. "I'll help you."

Tears spilled down her cheeks. She swiped at them, biting at her lower lip as she looked at him. That look could have been his undoing if he touched her now.

But he didn't reach for her. Couldn't. He turned and picked up his shirt, drawing it on without looking at her. He pulled on his jacket, buttoned up his jeans and finally turned to find her still standing in the same spot.

She looked small and vulnerable and his first instinct was to pull her to him again, to hold her, comfort her, make love to her beside the fire. Just the thought of her naked in his arms made him groan.

He turned and headed off into the trees to find some limbs to keep the fire going tonight. Mostly he needed to get away from her for a while.

The fire had burned down to glowing coals by the time he returned. She was tucked into the sleeping bag, lying on her back as if staring up at the stars through the tops of the pines. Smoke curled up from the campfire. Beyond the glow of the coals was nothing but darkness.

"Good night," she said, not looking at him.

He pulled the log stump closer to the fire and stretched out, his back against it. "Good night…Christianna." He watched her close her eyes, her chest rising and falling beneath the thin bedroll. A single tear rolled down the side of her face.

It was going to be a long night.

CHAPTER EIGHT

BRANDON WOKE TO find Anna gone. He sat up, looking first toward his saddle. It was still where he'd left it, but he'd seen her ride bareback. Half-afraid, he glanced in the direction of where his horse should have been, almost surprised the mare was still there. Would Anna have taken off on foot? She could be miles from here by now.

Something splashed in the nearby stream. The day was just breaking through the pines. VanHorn would have his men out looking for them.

Through the trees he spotted movement and the pink glow of bare skin. Another splash. She was taking a bath in an eddy in the creek.

He turned away, smiling to himself. Anna Austin was one of a kind. He quickly reminded himself that she was Christianna VanHorn—no matter what she called herself—or what he'd come to think of her as.

He'd promised her last night that he would help her. That meant trying to find out what had happened to the private investigator she'd hired.

They would have to get moving soon, he thought as he busied himself with breaking camp. VanHorn's men would be after them. No way was VanHorn going to let a McCall get away with running off with his daughter.

But Brandon did wonder what VanHorn would do to Anna.

Now last night made sense—VanHorn slipping in the mud, dropping his shotgun. He'd seen his daughter. He must have been shocked to realize she was the vandal. And to see her with a McCall… VanHorn must be beside himself.

What had happened to make him push his daughter away? Something.

Was that what Anna was trying so desperately to find?

As he finished rolling up his bedroll and stuffing everything else into his pack, he heard her come up from the creek. He promised himself he wouldn't forget who she was. Not again. He would keep his distance. The last thing he wanted was to get more involved with her.

And last night he'd come close. He'd wanted to make love to her. No big surprise there.

No, what worried him was that she seemed to have a hold on him he couldn't explain—and had since the first time he'd seen her on the curb when he was eleven. It was her smile. The girl had been a heart-stealer. The woman…well, she was a heartbreaker.

He turned to look at her and felt all his resolve wash away. Her wet hair trailed down her back in a single braid. She looked all of sixteen with her hair like that, her face flushed from the cold water, her eyes bright.

He looked into her honey-brown gaze and found himself falling. It felt like jumping off a cliff without knowing or caring if there was water below you deep enough that you wouldn't kill yourself.

"Good morning," she said, all business. "Have you changed your mind?"

He shook his head, even though he wasn't sure what it was he was supposed to have changed his mind about. "Good morning, Anna." He couldn't bring himself to think of her as Christianna after he'd seen how much he'd hurt her last night when he'd called her that. "Changed my mind? You mean about helping you? No."

She cocked her head at him. "Is there something else you haven't changed your mind about?" She nodded knowingly. "About the two of us. Frightening, isn't it, just the thought of a VanHorn and a McCall."

She was making fun of him.

"Joke if you want, but can you imagine your father's face if you told him you were interested in a McCall?"

"As a matter of fact, I can. I saw his look when he came upon the two of us on that curb all those years ago," she said and smiled. "I'm not afraid of my father."

"Maybe you should be," he said.

Her smile faded. "Maybe I *should* be." She shivered and he opened his arms, not surprised when she stepped into them.

The bare skin on her arms felt like ice, but soon warmed as he drew her closer, holding her. After last night he couldn't turn her over to the sheriff any more than he could take her—and the trouble they were in—back to the ranch.

He didn't know what to do with her. She wasn't just a criminal, she was a *VanHorn*. He was a McCall. And as much as she wanted to believe that didn't matter, it did.

And yet when she pulled back to look up into his face, he kissed her, not surprised by the desire that flared between them. Or the feeling that he was powerless to prevent it.

He felt the heat of desire rush through his veins—shoving aside rational thought.

She drew back, cocking her head as if to listen, then smiled up at him, leaning against him to kiss him. She had the most wonderful mouth. He lost himself in her mouth, in the taste of her, in the feel of her skin beneath his fingertips as he cupped her face in his hands. He could have kissed this woman the rest of his life.

Suddenly she pulled back, her eyes wide, her breath coming quickly. "I heard something," she whispered.

He listened. He didn't hear anything. Except for the thunder of his pulse in his ears.

Then he did hear it. The sound of a truck engine coming up one of the logging roads below them.

CASH COULDN'T REACH Realtor Frank Yarrow until the next morning.

"Yes, Sheriff, what can I do for you?" the elderly Realtor asked.

"I'm calling about an employee of yours, Emma Ingles. She was a security guard at Brookside?"

"Oh, Emma." Yarrow sighed. "I heard what happened to her. What an unfortunate accident."

"I was wondering if there had been any trouble at Brookside recently."

"Trouble?"

Cash thought he heard something in the man's tone. "Did something happen up there?"

"No. This has nothing to do with Emma. It's just that I went up there the day Emma died to show the place to a woman. She'd been insistent on the phone, so I'd agreed to meet her there. She never showed. It's silly. I can't see that it would have anything to do with Emma. Unless the woman might have gone up there later that night."

"What was this woman's name?" Cash asked.

"I suppose I could give it to you," Yarrow said. "She had a Southern accent. I got the impression she wasn't really interested in buying the place, just curious. I'm afraid I get a lot of those." He chuckled. "When I heard about Emma it got me wondering if she could have gone up there last night, while Emma was working. Silly. It's just that Emma wasn't a drinker. Maybe this woman upset her. Or scared her."

"Her name?"

"Oh, sorry. I do get carried away sometimes. Lenore Johnson. At least that's the name she gave me."

Lenore Johnson. The missing private investigator from Virginia. Why had she wanted to see Brookside?

"We don't need any bad publicity associated to Brookside," Yarrow said, clearing his throat. "I'm having enough trouble finding a buyer for it."

"Then I'm sorry to give you some bad news." Yarrow would read about it in the evening paper anyway. "Emma Ingles's death is being investigated as a homicide."

"Oh, no. If it generates the kind of publicity it did the last time…"

"The *last* time?" Cash asked.

"The last murder. The one that ended up closing the place down for good."

"There was a murder at Brookside?"

"I can't remember all the details. You'd have to ask Abe. Abe Carmichael. He was the sheriff then. Some woman was killed in her bed up there. Pretty gruesome.

They never caught the killer. Everyone just thought it had to be one of the other patients, you know? But after that, the place went bankrupt and the state took over the building."

Cash tried to remember when the institution had closed. He must have been about fifteen.

"Isn't it awful, but I can't remember the woman's name. Just the poor soul's room number. 9B. Was a grisly death. The killer was never caught."

Mason VanHorn woke with a start, and for a moment he convinced himself that last night had been nothing more than a bad dream. Chrissy was in Virginia. She hadn't come to Montana without telling him. She hadn't vandalized his wells, broken into the ranch house or set fire to one of his hay fields. Not Chrissy, his precious daughter.

Not the cute, little sweet cheerful girl he'd known.

But he didn't know Anna Austin, the woman she'd grown into. The woman he hadn't even seen in more years than he wanted to admit.

He'd told himself it was better that way. Better for her to make a life for herself somewhere else. He'd done her a favor, whether she realized it or not.

He padded into the kitchen in his pajamas and made himself a cup of coffee. His hands were shaking as he lifted the cup to his mouth.

"You stupid fool." Dr. Niles French's words echoed in his head. "She's the one who hired that private investigator. She *knows*."

"She just thinks she knows," Mason had assured him last night on the phone. "You just do your part and let me handle her. And make sure you don't breathe a word about this. I don't have to tell you what could happen if you do."

He thought he'd already handled her. When Chrissy had called last week and asked about her mother, he'd just repeated the lie he'd told her since she was a child. A horrible lie, but much better than the truth.

He'd wondered then why she would be asking about her mother now, after all these years, but he hadn't let it concern him. He was so sure that she'd believed the lie. Just as she always had.

But now he knew differently. She had been the one who'd hired the private investigator. And now this. The vandalized wells, the break-in at the house, the fire she'd set. All planned with one thing in mind. To get her father. She'd come after him as if—

He sloshed the coffee in his cup onto the counter as it hit him. She'd come after him as if she already knew the truth. As if someone had told her.

He put down the cup and dropped his head. Suddenly, he felt very old and tired. And afraid.

She had no idea how dangerous this was. She would have to be stopped. As powerful as he was, he couldn't protect her. Not if she continued to dig into the past.

AS THE SOUND of the truck grew closer, Brandon moved quickly. He saddled his horse and slipped to the edge of the ridge, staying in the trees to hide his movements. A stock truck with the VanHorn Ranch logo on the side and two horses in the back. They had tracked him this far already.

Brandon swore and turned to find Anna right beside him. They had only one choice. They'd have to run, and that meant deeper into the Bighorn Mountains, though.

Two men could move faster on two horses than he and Anna could riding double on one.

He glanced toward the snowcapped mountains as he heard a horse whinny on the mountain below them, followed by the sound of the horses being unloaded. They had to move, and fast.

Anna shook her head as if seeing what he had in mind. "We need to double back," she said quietly. "The boat is hidden in the trees and I have a rented cabin on the other side of the lake."

"There's no way we can get past them, especially riding double, and they may have already found the boat."

"Trust me, they won't expect us to come back through the ranch. Why else would they have sent men up here? But you're right. I *do* need a horse. Fortunately, I know where I can find one." She cocked her head toward the horses now being unloaded from the truck below them on the mountain.

"What?"

"You distract them." She gave him a quick kiss on the cheek. "They'll never expect you to ride right at them. Give me a few minutes. When you hear this—" she sounded a bird call "—then come a-ridin'."

She didn't give him a chance to argue. She took off running through the trees. He swore as he hurriedly tied his pack onto his horse and swung up into the saddle.

The woman was going to get them both killed.

Brandon heard the clear call of the bird below him on the mountainside and the sound of the men unloading their saddles and gear. He just hoped they would be busy enough that they couldn't get to their sidearms.

He spurred the horse, riding over the lip of the ridge and dropping straight down toward the truck.

The men looked up at the sound. Anna was right about that much. They were surprised. And distracted. Brandon recognized one of them, a tall, skinny guy called Stick. Stick dove for the cab of the pickup, either ducking for cover or going for a weapon.

The larger of the two seemed nailed to the ground as Brandon barreled down on him.

The two had the horses tied at the back of the stock truck. One horse had a saddle on but not cinched down yet.

Both horses shied. The big man dove out of the way as Brandon shot past. Riding hard and fast, Brandon kept low in the saddle, fearing he wouldn't hear the report of the rifle until he'd already felt the bullet.

The road curved not a hundred yards past the truck. He rounded the corner and dropped off into the creek bed, reining in behind a stand of pines so he had a partial view of the road above him.

He hadn't been there a minute when he heard the sound of horses' hooves headed his way. He stayed where he was until he saw a flash of long dark hair blowing back from the small rider curved into the horse's body as if the two were one.

He couldn't help but smile as he spurred his horse and rode off after her. Behind them, he could hear the truck engine crank over. Anna must have heard it, too.

She dropped down into the creek, then up the other side, riding toward the lake in the distance, leaving the road behind as she took to the lightly forested hillside along the creek bottom. Over a few hills they lost sight of the road—and VanHorn's men.

When he caught up to her, she was grinning, her face flushed with excitement, eyes bright.

"That was one fool thing to do back there," he said. "You could have been killed."

"I could say the same of you," she said, still grinning.

He'd just bought himself more trouble and all for a woman he'd never understand. He was either crazy or... He shook off even the thought as he looked over at her.

Whatever this chemistry was between them, they had a snowball's chance in hell of taking it any further, even if she didn't live in Virginia and him in Montana.

"You're wrong," she said.

He looked over at her. "About what?"

"Us." She smiled. "There's something there, even you can't deny it."

"I'm not denying it. I'm just telling you it would never work," he said as he rode along beside her. "Hell, I don't even know why our families hate each other, do you?" He glanced in her direction when she didn't answer. "You *know?*"

"My father and yours fell in love with the same woman." She rode ahead of him and he had to spur his horse to catch up.

"What woman?" he asked, hearing the fear in his voice.

She didn't answer. He reached over and reined in her horse along with his. "What woman?" he demanded, wishing to hell he'd never brought this up.

Anna sighed, no doubt wishing she hadn't said anything. "Your mother."

He felt as if she'd hit him again, only this time with a baseball bat. "Shelby?" Oh, hell.

"Shelby Ward, now McCall."

All he could do was shake his head. "How do you know this?"

"Before I left for boarding school I found some letters your mother had written my father."

His heart dropped to the pit of his stomach. "When were they…involved?" His mother had supposedly died when he was about three.

"In high school."

He couldn't hide his relief as he let go of her reins and they started through a stand of tall pines, the air cool and moist, sunlight sifting down through the dark green boughs.

"You thought it was more recent?" she asked.

He hated to admit it.

"I heard that your mother…died for a while."

He'd never heard anyone put it quite like that. For some reason it struck him as funny. Or maybe he was just so relieved. "Sorry," he said laughing, "It's just… So we're talking fifteen, sixteen?" His relief made him feel buoyant. "Then it wasn't serious. Asa and Mason were both kids."

"You don't think you can fall in love when you're young?" she asked, an edge to her voice.

"Puppy love, maybe, but not real get-married-have-kids love. Not at that age." He caught her expression. "What?"

She took off on the horse and he had to gallop to catch her. He turned her horse, slowing them both.

"What did I say?" Had he hurt her feelings? "I'm

sorry. Did you fall in love when you were a kid or something?"

"Or something," she said, shooting him a look that said he'd put his boot in it.

"I'm sorry." He reached out to touch her face. She was all soft and vulnerable again and all he wanted to do was kiss her. "*Asa* might have won Shelby, but he couldn't live with her. That's why they've been apart for thirty years. Except for that one moment of weakness when they conceived my sister Dusty," he said, trying to correct whatever he'd said that had caused the change in her.

"It's a stupid feud," she said after a moment. "If Shelby hadn't married Asa, then you wouldn't be here. The same for me if my parents hadn't gotten together."

He heard something in her tone, something he didn't think had anything to do with him or the feud. "I guess it was destined that we be born, huh?"

But it still didn't change anything between them. He tried to imagine what his family would say if he brought home Christianna VanHorn—and quickly pushed the thought away.

Anna grew quiet as they followed a gully down to the lake and followed it as far as the edge of forest-service property. Brandon figured it was best not to say anything. He left his horse where his brother Rourke could pick it up when he called him. Rourke would do it without asking as many questions as either J.T. or Cash.

The boat was right where she said it would be. She slid off the horse she'd just stolen, letting it go on Van-Horn property.

Brandon added horse theft to her other crimes as he

followed her through the thick cottonwoods toward the water and the boat she'd left tied up there.

He'd half expected VanHorn and his men to be waiting by the boat—if they hadn't sunk it or set it adrift.

But the boat was where she'd left it. It seemed she'd been right about that, too.

She untied the boat and waited for him to get in. He could see other boats out on the water, fishing boats, bobbing along in the light breeze.

He climbed in and she pushed them out. At the back of the boat, he got the twenty-five-horsepower motor going. It putted softly as he backed out. He nosed the boat through the shallow water and trees toward open water.

"Where to?" he asked when they were out in the middle of the lake, out of sight of the VanHorn Ranch. Water lapped at the metal sides of the boat, the sun beat down, the air was cool and scented with pine and water.

ANNA LOOKED INTO his face and couldn't help but smile as she pointed the way. There was something so genuine about his expression, his blond hair slightly curled beneath his Stetson, his blue eyes as intense as the sky overhead.

He'd been adorable at eleven. At thirty-three, he was ruggedly handsome. All cowboy. All man. Her body's reaction attested to that.

But their connection was more than physical. She'd felt it that day on the curb. She could still taste the sticky cold imitation-cherry flavoring and remember that strange feeling as if she could see into the future.

"At the cabin I'll tell you everything," she said impulsively.

He met her gaze. She could see the doubt, but he
nodded.

She leaned back, closed her eyes and let the breeze
blow her hair. The sun felt wonderful on her face. She
didn't think about anything but this moment, here with
Brandon McCall. After all these years of wondering
what had happened to him, here she was—risking his
life.

She opened her eyes as the boat slowed and looked
at him, praying she was doing the right thing. Once she
told him everything, there would be no turning back.
He would know too much.

But Brandon was right. He was already involved.
She'd thought she could protect him by keeping what
she knew from him. She saw now that it was impossible.
If she hoped to protect him, he had to know everything
she did. Her father had seen them both last night. Seen
them together. What would he do now? She hated to
think.

Brandon glided the boat into the dock. He watched
Anna jump out to tie it up, then joined her for the climb
up to the cabin.

The sun burned down on them, the lake aglitter with
the bright light. Behind them, boats roared past making
large cresting waves, dogs barked in the distance and
children splashed at the edge of the water in front of the
rows of cabins.

Anna led the way up the stairs from the beach to the
cabin perched on the side of the mountain. It was the
farthest from the water, tucked back in the pines, but
the view was spectacular.

Inside, there were two bedrooms with a stack of bunks in one, a double bed in the other. The kitchen was tiny, but the living room was large with wide windows, much like his family cabin across the bay.

Anna went straight for the table in the kitchen. As she turned, he saw that she held a worn manila envelope in one hand.

He saw indecision in her expression and held his breath, sensing that this moment was crucial for more reasons than he could yet understand.

"Maybe you'd better sit down," she said quietly.

He nodded and pulled up a chair. Was it possible she really was going to trust him?

"I received a letter a little over a week ago," she began. "It had been mailed nine years ago, but had been lost. It was from my former nanny, Sarah Gilcrest. In the letter, Sarah confessed to what she'd witnessed one night when I was three. My mother had been seven months pregnant. The doctor had insisted she stay in bed throughout most of the pregnancy. Late that night, she gave birth early."

Anna stopped, her fingers on the envelope quaking.

"You don't have to do this," he said, seeing how hard this was for her.

"Yes. Yes, I do." She looked up at him, took a breath, and continued, "I trust you, Brandon. The only reason I'm afraid to tell you is that I'll be risking your life even more."

"We're in this together, Anna. You have to realize that. Whatever it was your father did, he will assume you've already told me."

She nodded and swallowed. "Sarah said my father

sent her away when she heard my mother in labor. She was to stay upstairs with my brother and me. She heard a car, assumed it was Dr. Ivers coming to deliver the baby since my father hadn't taken my mother to the clinic in Antelope Flats or the hospital in Sheridan."

She fingered the worn edge of the envelope for a moment. "Sarah heard the baby cry and was relieved. She'd been worried about my mother. She hadn't been well. But that wasn't the only reason she'd been worried. She'd heard my father and mother arguing, my mother saying that the baby wasn't his and as soon as it was born, she was going to leave him."

Brandon braced himself, afraid of where she was going with this.

"My brother and I were both asleep, so she sneaked down the stairs, wanting to see my new baby sister or brother. But as she reached the bottom of the stairs, she heard my mother crying, pleading with my father 'not to do it.' Sarah hid as my father let Dr. Niles French come in. She heard my father tell him that the baby was stillborn and that it was time to take my mother."

Anna stopped and took another breath. It came out like a sob. "Sarah knew the baby hadn't been stillborn. She'd heard it cry. She hurried up the stairs. She didn't hear all of the conversation, just pieces of it because my mother was hysterical, pleading and begging with my father not to send her to Brookside."

"Brookside?" Brandon echoed. "The old mental institution?"

ABE CARMICHAEL had retired a good twenty years ago, but he was easy to track down since he hadn't gone far from Antelope Flats. Cash found the former sheriff sitting on his porch overlooking the river.

"Murder at Brookside? Oh, I remember it well," Abe said. "Hell of a thing."

Cash didn't know why he was bothering asking. What could a twenty-year-old murder have to do with Emma Ingles's murder?

Nothing.

And yet he couldn't let Emma's death go. The only connection was Brookside. But he'd learned to follow any lead that presented itself. His gut told him to follow this one.

"Do you remember much about it?" Cash asked.

Abe chuckled. He was a big man with a head of snow-white hair and bushy eyebrows. "Son, you never forget the cases you couldn't solve. They haunt you the rest of your life. This one was especially tragic. Big news at the time. The woman was murdered in her bed late at night. Room 9B. What made it so sensational was the fact that she was in the criminally insane wing."

"I don't understand."

"That section was locked up tighter than a drum. Only a few people even had keys to that wing. Plus the patients' rooms were also locked—and padded. No windows."

"So it had to be someone who had a key, someone who worked there," Cash said, finally understanding. "That had to narrow down the suspects."

"One of the attendants committed suicide not long after that," Abe said. "He left a note saying he was sorry. Nothing more."

Cash heard it in his voice. "But you don't believe he killed her."

"Never bought it. I think the real killer got away with it, but under the circumstances, without a motive, there was nothing I could do. You see, the woman was a Jane Doe. One of the doctors from Brookside found her wandering down the highway, crazier than crazy, and violent, too. The doctor just put her in that wing for the night to protect her from herself and everyone until she could be identified."

"You never found out who she was?"

Abe sighed. "Never did. She was bludgeoned to death that night. No way to make any kind of ID on her face or dental records."

Cash winced.

"It was a horrible thing. Still gives me nightmares. She's buried at the cemetery as Jane Doe. I go up there every once in a while," Abe said. "Someone's been putting flowers on her grave for years."

CHAPTER NINE

ANNA MOVED TO the window overlooking the lake. Brandon stared at her slim back, too shocked to speak.

"Sarah says she never saw my mother again," Anna continued. "She sneaked back upstairs and pretended she knew nothing. The next morning, my father said the baby was stillborn and that my mother had left. No one was to ever mention her name in the house again or speak of the baby."

Brandon had heard about Anna's mother, Helena VanHorn. The woman was said to have been beautiful, with long black hair and a face like an angel. Obviously that's where Anna had gotten her beauty. But like everyone else, he'd heard that she'd run off. He hadn't known anything about a baby.

"Sarah never breathed a word, afraid of what my father would do to her. She left his employ shortly after that. She was dying when she wrote the letter and said she couldn't go to her grave with the secret. She'd heard I wrote for a newspaper in Maine and sent it there. But the letter got lost and didn't find me until nine years later."

Her story left him horrified. "The nanny's sure she heard the baby cry?"

"Yes. She was in a room directly above my mother's," Anna said.

"What happened to the baby's body?" he asked joining her at the window.

She shook her head. "I can only assume he got rid of it and locked my mother up in Brookside."

"Is it possible she's still alive?" Brandon asked.

"I doubt it. When Brookside closed, my father would have made sure she was never allowed to tell her story and there was no other place for her to go that he wouldn't be found out."

Brandon went cold inside at even the thought that any of this could be true. Mason VanHorn had a reputation for being a bastard and Brandon had seen firsthand how vindictive he could be. But he couldn't imagine the man doing something so heinous to his own wife.

"You don't believe it, do you?" she said, putting the envelope away. He could hear the hurt in her tone.

"I'm sorry, but you have to admit this is one hell of an accusation. You're sure that this woman who wrote the letter didn't get it all wrong? For all you know, she might have been suffering from dementia. None of this might be true."

"That was my first thought. That's why I contacted Sarah's niece, who was with her when she died. Sarah was rational and very much in control of her senses when she wrote the letter. The niece didn't know what was in the letter, but had mailed it at her aunt's request nine years ago. If the letter hadn't gotten lost, I might have been able to talk to Sarah before she died."

Brandon moved around the room, too restless to sit. "My God, do you realize what you're accusing your father of here?"

"Yes. And not just my father. He had to have had help that night."

"Dr. Ivers would never go along with this," Brandon said.

Anna nodded. "I called Dr. Ivers. He said he didn't even know my mother was pregnant. So it must have been Dr. French who ordered the bed rest and delivered the baby. It was right after he left that Sarah said she didn't hear the baby cry again. She never saw the body. She just assumed my father had taken it out somewhere and buried it."

If she was right, Mason VanHorn had gotten away with murder—and much worse. "What about this Dr. French?"

"I gave his name to the private investigator I hired and now she's missing." She looked at him as if to say, how can you not believe me? "Before that, she was able to verify that Dr. French *was* on staff at the Brookside Mental Institution during that time."

"Twenty-seven years ago." Brandon raked a hand through his hair. "Was Lenore able to verify that your mother was a patient?"

"No, unfortunately the hospital was privately owned and when it suddenly closed, the records were lost. At least, that's what we've been led to believe."

"You think someone has them?" he asked in surprise.

"My father would have made sure my mother's medical file never got into the wrong hands. But also to make sure Dr. French never got a guilty conscience and decided to talk."

"That's what you were looking for in the safe."

She nodded. "I know my father has the records. They would implicate Dr. French."

"It would also implicate him."

"Yes. Kind of a Mexican standoff."

"How do you hope to prove any of this without records and the only witness dead?"

"The only witness isn't dead. Dr. French was in the room when the baby was born. I assume my father was also." She shivered. "I used to have nightmares that one day Dr. French would come for me, too."

He took her in his arms. He wanted to tell her that Dr. French would never get his hands on her. But if she was right, if her father had gotten rid of not only a baby but her mother with the help of Dr. French, and now both men knew she was on to them, then her life was in danger.

"Let's go see if we can find that private investigator," Brandon said, wanting to keep moving.

ANNA WATCHED the beach as they crossed the lake to the marina, half-afraid she would see her father or one of his flunkies waiting for them on the other side. Or worse, Dr. French.

But no one paid any attention to them as they tied up the boat, got into her rented black pickup and headed for Sheridan, Wyoming, and the motel where Lenore Johnson had been registered.

"I still think we should go to my brother with this," Brandon said.

"Cash is already looking for Lenore Johnson, the private investigator I hired," she said.

He had the pickup window down, the summer air blowing in. The cloudless day reminded him of cherry Popsicles.

"According to the agency, he will file a missing person's report in forty-eight hours," she said. "I have that long to get some proof."

Brandon couldn't see how after all these years she would ever find the proof.

"They will be running scared now," she said as she drove south down the two-lane. "That's why I called Dr. French and left a message telling him I was coming for him. But they will think they can handle me. They know I don't have any evidence."

"You contacted Dr. French?" he asked in surprise, glancing over at her. "Wait a minute, you're using yourself as bait. You *expect* them to come after you."

She smiled through her tears. "I have to do this. I owe it to my mother and the sibling I lost."

He understood. But how much did a child owe a parent? He thought of his own mother. "She wouldn't want to see you get killed, though."

"I just want to rattle them. It might be the only justice I get. They won't kill me. Not unless they think I really do have something against them."

"Yeah," he said. "That's what worries me." If Van-Horn had gotten rid of a baby he believed wasn't his, and had his wife locked up in Brookside for years and possibly had her murdered when the place closed, why wouldn't he kill again to hide his crimes?

"Did you ask your father about this?"

Anna nodded. "He told me the same story he'd told Sarah."

"I always thought he idolized you," Brandon said.

"When I was little. But something changed. The day I turned ten, he told me I was going away to school. I cried and pleaded with him to let me stay. Maybe the mistake I made was telling him that one day I would marry a cowboy and live on the ranch." Tears welled again in her eyes. "I think I saw it in his face that day. He never let me come back after that. Not even for a visit."

He heard the bitterness in her voice—and the longing. "You were just a kid. Would you have really come back to the ranch if he'd let you?"

"In a heartbeat. I love the ranch. It was the only place I ever wanted to be and he knew that," she said. "I used to think he didn't want me around because I looked too much like my mother, that it hurt him too much to see me."

"And now?"

"Now I think he kept me away so I'd never find out the truth."

Brandon hated the pain he heard in her voice. Damn Mason VanHorn for hurting his daughter—not to mention the other crimes he might have committed.

"If we can find the private investigator you hired…"

She nodded and smiled through her tears. "From that day on the curb when I shared my Popsicle with you, I knew I could count on you."

His gaze locked with hers and he felt desire course through his veins. He wished her eyes weren't that honey color or her hair so dark and luxurious or her body so lush. He wished her lips weren't bow-shaped or her laugh so musical. He wished he didn't want her so badly.

Because no matter how this ended, he could never have her. Not the way he wanted her. Forever.

At the Shady Rest Motor Inn, Anna told him that the motel clerk said she never checked out but all of her belongings were out of the room the next morning. "I was staying at the same motel in case she came back. She never did."

"What about her rental car?" he asked. "I assume she flew into Billings and rented a car there. That's what most people do since there isn't a commercial airport near here."

"I checked with her office. She always rents from the same agency. The car hasn't been returned."

"Okay, what about flights?" he asked.

"She hasn't used her return ticket, her office said."

"Well, maybe we can take a look at the room she stayed in. I know it's a long shot." He opened the pickup door. She was already out by the time he came around to her side, and headed for the motel office.

Anna knew he was hoping that Lenore would turn up safe and sound and provide an explanation for everything—one that didn't involve her father. She felt her own hopes of that slipping away. Lenore Johnson was either in trouble—or way past it. Anna blamed herself for involving the private investigator.

Inside the office, the clerk at the desk let them have the key to the room Lenore Johnson had rented but warned it had been cleaned.

"Were you working when Ms. Johnson was a guest here?" Brandon asked.

The young woman shook her head. "Jo was. She'll be in soon if you want to talk to her."

They took the key and walked down the cracked sidewalk to Room 12. The door creaked as Brandon opened it. Anna stepped inside the room, which was identical to the one she'd rented.

She looked under the bed while Brandon searched the bathroom and small closet. Nothing.

When they returned the key to the office, Jo had taken over the desk.

"Sure, I remember her," the older woman behind the counter told them. "Haven't seen her since Saturday, though, when she came into the office for directions."

"Directions?" Anna and Brandon both echoed.

The woman behind the counter laughed. "You two been married long? Pretty soon you'll be finishing each other's sentences."

"We're not married," Anna said, feeling shy. She didn't dare look at Brandon.

"Oh, sorry. You just seemed like such a perfect couple," the woman said almost dreamily.

"Lenore Johnson asked for directions, you said," Brandon reminded her.

"Oh, yeah. Come to think of it, I thought it was strange." The woman shrugged. "But hey, that's what I'm here for, renting rooms and giving directions." She sighed and looked at them, and must have realized they were still waiting. "She wanted to know how to get to the old Brookside Mental Institution."

SHERIFF CASH MCCALL spent the day working on the Emma Ingles case, as well as trying to track down the Virginia private investigator, Lenore Johnson.

He'd come up empty and was about to give up when he got a call from a friend of Emma Ingles.

Her name was Betty Osborne, she was seventy-six and made the best sweet pickles in the county. She had dozens of blue ribbons from the fair to prove it.

"I was just thinking about Emma today," Betty said,

"and I knew I had to call you. I remembered something she'd said to me after she took that horrible job up there at Brookside."

He waited.

"She only took it because she needed the money. It's a crime what social security pays."

"Something she said to you?" he prodded gently.

"Yes. I don't think she minded the work. All she had to do was be there. She watched a lot of television, you know. I can't imagine being up there alone at night. Gives me chills just to think about it. You know, Emma almost married my second cousin, so we've been friends for years."

Cash was beginning to think he'd have to remind Betty again when she said, "Emma told me she heard voices coming from that wing where that woman was killed. You know, the one who was horribly murdered all those years ago."

"Voices?" He'd heard stories of the place being haunted for years. This was nothing new.

"Hushed voices," Betty said. "Like someone inside one of those padded cells in that disturbed wing. Someone crying out for help."

"I HAVE TO GET INSIDE Brookside," Anna told Brandon as they left the motel office. She could tell that the last thing Brandon wanted to do was go to Brookside. She was dreading it more than she wanted to admit. But if Lenore had been headed there right before she went missing, then maybe the answer to her disappearance was also there.

"Why do I get the feeling that you have a plan?" he asked grinning over at her. "A plan I'm going to hate."

She smiled. "Sorry, but I need you to pretend you want to buy the place."

"It's for *sale?*"

"A local Realtor is handling it for the state. Haven't been many takers, I guess," she said.

"I would assume not. It's just a huge white elephant out in the middle of nowhere," Brandon said.

She figured that, like her, he'd heard the stories about the place. When she'd asked about Brookside, every waitress and motel clerk had a horror story to tell.

Brandon opened the passenger-side door of the pickup for her, but something caught her eye. A headline in a newspaper box near where he'd parked the pickup.

Like a sleepwalker, she moved toward the newspaper box: Brookside Security Woman's Death Ruled A Homicide.

Anna felt Brandon come up beside her. "Do you see that? Do you think it could have anything to do with Lenore's disappearance? It says Emma Ingles worked at Brookside and was killed sometime during the night. That was the same day Lenore went missing."

Brandon sighed. "All roads seem to lead to Brookside."

"According to locals, the place is haunted," she said, and climbed into the pickup.

He slid behind the wheel. "You don't believe in ghosts." He made it sound as if he were waiting for her to reassure him of that.

"If there is something going on at Brookside, it isn't ghosts who are doing it," she said as she handed him her cell phone.

"Cell phones don't work out here."

"Only in some places. Also depends on the phone."

She rattled off the Realtor's number. "He'll believe you want to buy the place quicker than he will me."

She watched him tap in the numbers. "Don't mention me. I want to do some exploring on my own while you keep him busy."

"Great idea," he said sarcastically, then, "Hello, Frank Yarrow? I'm interested in Brookside. I understand it's for sale. Yes, my name is Brandon McCall. Actually, my family is interested in purchasing it."

Anna nodded her approval.

Yarrow agreed to change his schedule and meet Brandon at Brookside in forty minutes.

"That will give us time to look around outside the place," Anna said.

Brandon shifted into gear, heading for the isolated old mental hospital as the sun dipped behind the mountains and the day grew cool and dark.

CHAPTER TEN

BRANDON DROVE out of Sheridan, following the Tongue River as it wound its way north. The road rose into foothills; huge cottonwoods grew at the river's edge, tall gray sage dotted the arid landscape as the land ran from the river toward the Bighorn Mountains.

"I don't like the idea of you alone in that place," he said.

She smiled and touched his cheek with her fingers. "I won't be alone. You and the Realtor will be in there with me. If I need you, I'll holler."

He didn't look convinced, but she knew he would do it. He would do anything for her, she thought.

Even risk his life.

"Thank you," she said beside him.

He shot her a look, his gaze softening. He grinned at her and reached for her hand, giving it a squeeze. "I haven't pulled it off yet. Thank me when you find some evidence that will put an end to this."

"Can you fix the door so we can get back in later tonight if we have to?"

He nodded. That place was spooky as hell in the daylight. He didn't even want to think about going up there at night.

Realtor Frank Yarrow had been beside himself at the thought of selling Brookside. And Brandon doubted it was just for the commission. Yarrow had hesitated a little about showing the place, mentioning that it would be getting dark soon.

Brandon had to smile. Obviously the Realtor didn't like going up there at night, either, but who could blame him?

Fifteen miles out of town, Brandon turned onto the dirt road. There had once been a weathered sign that said nothing more than Brookside, but it had been gone for years.

He looked over and saw Anna gripping the handle on the dash as he started up the winding dirt road. Rock-slides and weeds had narrowed the road to only a single lane in places.

The sun had set. In the twilight, the mountains were purple. Below them, the Tongue River twisted through deep green grass and huge leafy cottonwoods. A flock of geese made a dark V of flapping wings against the horizon.

The highway disappeared behind them as the narrow road rounded the mountain, culminating in a half-dozen switchback curves all headed upward. On one side of the road, there was mountain; on the other, rocky cliffs that dropped down thousands of feet. There were no guardrails. No trees. Nothing to stop you if you drove off the road but the rocky bottom below.

As he came around the last turn, Brookside rose up, black against the dying sunset, a huge looming brick edifice three stories high.

Brandon heard Anna gasp and realized this was the first time she'd ever seen it. Brookside had that effect. Even when you knew the place was just over the rise, it always came as a surprise. Partly because of the isolation. Partly because of the ominous-looking shape of it.

The building was an odd U shape, with the two wings jutting back from each side. The high metal fence had three razor wire strands on top that only a fool didn't know once kept things in, not out.

The iron gate had long since been torn down. Brandon drove through but didn't go up the circular drive, now filled with weeds. He parked a good distance away in a flat spot that was once a lawn.

The windows along one wing had the sun reflecting off them, making them look like golden eyes. The rest of the building was dark. No other cars were parked out front.

He turned to Anna. "Are you sure you want to do this?"

Anna sat for a long moment just staring at the building, trying hard not to imagine her mother locked inside it. She opened her door in answer to Brandon's question and stepped out before she lost her nerve.

Cool shadows pooled around the huge place. Dozens of patients had once lived inside. How many of them were like her mother? she hated to think. This far from everything, few families would ever come to visit. Had that been the idea?

She heard Brandon get out of the pickup as she closed her door and started toward the side. She wanted to take a look out back. The doors would be locked, so she would have to wait until the Realtor arrived to sneak inside. Not that she expected to find anything on the exterior. She'd be lucky to find anything inside.

But she had to confront this horrible place and the fears that had lived inside her since she'd learned about the night Dr. French came to her house and took her mother away.

As she reached the cracked concrete walkway, she heard Brandon come up behind her.

"Watch your step," he warned. "There could be rattlesnakes up here."

Rattlesnakes were the least of her fears.

The broken concrete path led around to the back. She stopped at the edge of the worn brick wall and stared at what had once been an orchard. There were dozens of dead apple trees, their limbs stark and dark against the last of the day's light.

She glanced at the back of the building, a glare keeping her from seeing into the dusty barred windows of the north wing. Had her mother's room looked out on the orchard? Or had she been in the windowless rooms on the south wing?

Brandon walked to the back door. "Look, there's a buzzer." He pushed it and she heard the faint sound echo through the empty building. She was glad he didn't press it again. The sound set her teeth on edge.

"I think I've seen enough," she said.

He nodded and took her arm as they maneuvered along the side.

She would not cry. She would *not* cry. Her eyes burned. She breathed in the mountain air, filling her lungs with it. In the distance, she heard the sound of a vehicle coming up the road, and went to hide.

BRANDON STOOD OUTSIDE Brookside as a fancy new rig rolled up and an older man in a brown suit climbed out. Few people in this part of the country wore actual

suits. Western sports jackets with jeans and boots, yes.
Suits, no.

Frank Yarrow wore a suit that didn't quite fit his squat
body. He tugged at his collar, his thick finger digging
into the flushed flesh of his neck. His toupee was dyed
jet-black and sat like a squirrel on his slick bald head,
the corners lifting in the breeze.

"Frank Yarrow," he said by way of introduction, ex-
tending his hand. "And you must be Brandon McCall.
Heard a lot about the McCalls. Sundown Ranch, right?
Your brother's the sheriff up that way."

"Right." He could see Yarrow already mentally
spending his commission.

"Well, let's have a look inside," Yarrow said with less
enthusiasm. He pulled a ring of keys from his pocket.
"Great space, and quite the view from here." If you
didn't notice the fence.

Brandon followed him, looking around for Anna.
He didn't see her, but he knew she hadn't gone far. It
made him nervous leaving her to her own devices, but
the only other option was breaking in, and he quickly
realized that would be impossible. The place was like
a fortress.

He wished he could have gone to his brother about
this. But there was no chance Cash could get a court
order without evidence.

After digging out a huge key ring, Yarrow opened the
front door. Brandon motioned him to go in first. He'd
picked up a small chunk of wood out back. He took it
out of his pocket now, dropping it as the door closed
behind him but didn't latch.

"This is a great price for this much space," Yarrow
said, waiting for him in the entry, his voice echoing in

the emptiness. The Realtor seemed nervous. Not half as nervous as Brandon was.

"I'd like to start at the top and work my way down if that's all right," Brandon said, following Anna's instructions.

"All right. The elevator—"

"Would you mind if we took the stairs?" Brandon asked. "I have this thing about elevators." They were too fast and he needed to buy Anna as much time as possible.

"All right." More enthusiasm waning. "It is three stories at the center, you realize."

Brandon nodded. "We're in no hurry, right?"

"Of course not. It's just a little hard to see once it gets dark. Not a lot of lighting," he said glancing up the dimly lit stairs as if he was worried what might be waiting up there for them.

ANNA WASN'T ANXIOUS to see the inside of Brookside. The name made it sound like a spa rather than a mental hospital.

She steeled herself for what she might find as she waited until she was sure Brandon would have had time to get the Realtor started up the stairs before she approached the front door. True to his word, Brandon had managed to prop the door open for her.

She stepped inside, assaulted first by the stagnant smell of a long-ago locked-up building, and other smells—she didn't want to know what they were.

The moment the door closed behind her, she heard faint echoes, felt the oppression. It threatened to immobilize her. She tried not to breathe, not to think.

How many years had her mother been in here? Anna

couldn't bear to think what atrocities her mother had been subjected to once she was locked inside this building. Was she just warehoused, a prisoner with a life sentence? Or had her father let them do horrible treatments on her? Just how high was the VanHorn price for being unfaithful, she wondered, raw with pain and anger.

She tried to remember the details of the map she'd gotten from the county as she glanced down the hallway to the south wing. The double doors were chained and locked. She didn't want to know.

The other wing was open.

She hurried down the hallway toward the open wing, past the small enclosed office, the mesh window winking under the dim lights as she passed.

If she remembered correctly, the door to the basement was down the hallway on a corridor in the wing of that side of the building.

She could hear clanking, echoing noises, and would have sworn that not all of them were coming from upstairs where Brandon and the Realtor would be now.

Almost at the end of the hall, she stopped. Nothing but barred or windowless room after room. Could she be wrong? Could the way to the basement be in the other wing? The locked wing?

Her heart fell at the thought. All of this would have been for nothing.

She glanced at her watch. She didn't have much time. The door had to be here. She rushed down the hall, trying not to make any more noise than was possible.

The hallway was long, the linoleum worn and discolored. Doors yawned, open to the patient rooms. She didn't look inside, didn't want to imagine what her mother's life must have been like here.

Almost to the end, she spotted a door that was larger than the others. She could hear voices so faint they sounded like whispers. Let it be Brandon and the Realtor. Not the voices of those poor souls who had walked these worn halls.

The wider door opened into a cavernous dark hole. She flicked on the flashlight and shone it into the darkness. Stairs.

A fetid smell gagged her. She took shallow breaths. The air coming up the stairs was colder, damper, the horrid smell stronger. Not just moldy. Not just stagnant, but something stronger. Something dead.

BRANDON LED THE WAY up the stairs to the third floor, going as slowly as possible, pretending to study the stairwell as he climbed. Frank followed, quickly winded. Clearly, the man got little exercise other than climbing in and out of his car to show real estate.

At the third-floor landing, Brandon stopped to wait for him. Where was Anna? By now, she would be in the building. He hated this more than he wanted to admit. This place gave him the creeps. He could just imagine what it must be doing to her.

Worse, he worried about what she might find. Or what might find her.

"All the floors are almost identical," Yarrow said when he'd caught his breath. He sounded bitter that they'd had to climb the stairs rather than take the elevator.

Brandon smiled and pushed open the door to the third floor. "I guess we're about to see if that is true."

Unfortunately, Yarrow was right. The floor was just a long hallway with bare, uninteresting, windowless or barred rooms off each side. The smell—let alone the thought of who had occupied these rooms and for how long—was enough to make Brandon want to rush through this inspection of the building. He had to keep reminding himself that he was buying time for Anna.

He prayed her information about her mother was wrong. He feared what it would do to her if she found proof that her mother had been housed here out of vengeance.

"As you can see, there are lots of possibilities with something this size," Yarrow said. "It could make a great out-of-the-way hotel. Even a resort."

Right. Yarrow was kidding himself if he thought he could ever dump this place.

"I understand the state owns the building and land now," Brandon said.

"They're very receptive to an offer. They were forced to take it over when it closed. However, there are some restrictions on what can be done with the building," Yarrow said.

"What kind of restrictions?" Not that he really cared. But if he was seriously interested in purchasing the place, it was a question he would ask.

"The building has to be saved if at all possible. It is structurally sound and a historical site."

Brandon stopped walking and looked at the man in surprise. "Why would anyone buy the building and tear it down?"

"One potential buyer was turned down because his plans included razing the site," Yarrow said.

"Really? Anyone I know?"

Yarrow wagged his head. "I'm not allowed to say." He started walking toward the elevator. "The next floor is identical but I'm sure you'll want to see it, as well."

A chill curled around Brandon's neck, as if a cold draft had crept down the hall after him, and yet there were no windows that actually opened.

He hurried after Yarrow, anxious to get out of this place as quickly as possible.

Hurry, Anna.

"You don't mind if we take the stairs, do you?" he said, and held open the stairway door for the Realtor.

ANNA TRIED the light switch at the top of the stairs. Nothing. She shone her flashlight down the concrete steps to the bottom. Slowly, she descended the stairs, forced to keep the light on the steps ahead of her rather than the darkness beyond it.

At the bottom, she stopped and shone the flashlight beam around the room. Other than for support beams, the huge space appeared to be almost empty except for some old bed frames, a few mattresses and some metal chairs against one wall.

The smell was much stronger down here. She covered her mouth with her free hand, her eyes stinging.

At a sound, she swung the flashlight beam in that direction. Pipes. She held her breath, listening. *Drip.* A water leak. *Drip.* Nothing more. But she kept the light on the pipes for a moment as she tried to calm herself.

She shone the light around the perimeter of the room again, hoping she might find a filing cabinet. Or boxes. Or something that might hold old files. She knew there was little chance the files would be down here. The place had been closed for years. Any evidence had long since been lost. Or taken.

As her flashlight beam skimmed along the outer walls, she saw that several of the basement windows had been broken. No bars. Access if she had to come back. The light skittered along the wall. She stopped. Behind one of the bed frames she saw the top of what could be the outline of a door frame.

Cautiously, she stepped off the last stair onto the concrete. If the files had been stored down here, who knew what kind of shape they might be in, even if she did find them.

But she had to hold out hope. If she was right, her mother had spent the last years of her life in this building.

She had to put the flashlight down on the concrete floor, the beam aimed at the bed frame as she tried to pull it away from the doorway. The bed frame was heavy—dense metal and awkward to move.

It finally budged. She scraped the bed frame across the floor far enough that she could see she'd been right. A door.

Picking up the flashlight, she shone the light on the door. Her fingers closed over the knob. She held her breath, saying a silent prayer as she tried it. The knob turned in her hand, the door swung open with a groan and Anna blinked in shock as she found herself looking into another smaller room—this one filled with rows of old gray metal filing cabinets.

BRANDON STARED DOWN the second-floor hallway. It was indeed identical to the floor above. He couldn't stall much longer. Yarrow kept looking toward the barred windows. Twilight had turned the mountains deep purple. Huge pools of darkness hung in the pines. It would be full-dark before they got out of here at this rate.

"The first floor is all we have left to see," Yarrow said. "That's where the office is and the north wing, which was once used as a dormitory for nurses and students."

As far as Brandon could tell, the place had been completely cleaned out. He doubted there was anything to find. He heard sounds on other floors and wondered if Yarrow heard them, too. Maybe Anna wasn't making the noises. Now there was a frightening thought.

Yarrow held open the first-floor stairway door.

Brandon couldn't put it off any longer. He headed down the stairs. At the bottom, he looked around for Anna and fortunately didn't see her.

"What's down that wing?" he asked, seeing the chained and locked double doors.

"Patient rooms. Why don't we go on down to the basement first while there is still a little light?" Yarrow said. "I brought a flashlight."

"Do you mind if I see this wing first?" Brandon asked. "I'm trying to get a feel for the size of this place."

Yarrow obviously did mind, but he tried not to show it. "There is nothing down there but rooms. The basement contains the boiler, a storage room. Plenty of room for a laundry."

"You have a key to this wing?" Brandon said, stepping over to pick up the chain and inspect the padlock.

Still Yarrow hesitated. "That wing was where the

criminally insane were kept. The rooms are padded. Soundproof."

"Interesting," Brandon said, thinking it was the last place on earth he really wanted to go. "Why is it still locked up like this?"

"Kids. They're like ghouls. Same with some of the security people. Just best to keep the curious out of here," Yarrow said. "A bit morbid, if you ask me."

"You have a key?" Brandon asked again. "I might as well see it all." Was this the wing where Dr. French had brought Anna's mother?

With obvious hesitancy, Frank pulled out the keys and dug through until he found one that fit the lock attached to the chain.

The padlock opened, the chain fell away and he pushed open the double doors, motioning Brandon to go first.

Brandon looked down the dim hallway of padded rooms. A thought struck him. What if, when he stepped through those doors, Yarrow locked them behind him? It was so ridiculous he almost laughed. Almost.

RUSHING TO the filing cabinets, Anna jerked open the first drawer. The moment she felt it slide toward her, she knew. It was empty. She tried another and another. All empty. Her heart sank. Nothing.

She stumbled back a few feet, letting the light flicker over the old metal file cabinets, fighting the urge to cry. The evidence *had* been here. How long ago had the files been cleaned out? If the state hadn't taken possession of them, then who had? Maybe they had just been destroyed. Maybe there was no possible hope of ever proving her mother had been here.

But she knew in her heart that her father had the file she was looking for. Still, she'd hoped there might be something....

She opened each file cabinet drawer. Empty. Empty. Empty. Her fingers felt grimy. She wiped them on her jeans as she moved to the last of the file cabinets.

Time was running out. She couldn't keep looking. Brandon would be making his way in this direction with the Realtor.

Why was she wasting her time? All the file cabinets were empty. There was nothing here. She started to open the top drawer, already hearing the empty clank as she touched the handle. She froze. Then slowly, she shined the light on what had caught her eye.

Something had fallen between the last two metal filing cabinets. Not a file. She could see that. But what looked like a thin bound ledger.

Laying the flashlight on top of one of the other file cabinets, the beam angled away from her eyes, she shoved the last file cabinet aside, then moved the next one until there was space enough to reach in.

Retrieving the flashlight, she shone it into the space before she bent to retrieve the dusty ledger and, with trembling fingers, opened it. At first, she didn't have any idea what it was. The only numbers seemed to be times and dates. On the left were names, then times, then signatures.

Her heart leaped to her throat. It was a log book. Visitors had been required to log in.

Hurriedly, she checked the dates. This book could have been used during the time she believed her mother was incarcerated here.

But if no one knew her mother was alive, then she

wouldn't have had any visitors. Her heart fell at the realization.

She started to close the book when something caught her eye. Room 9B. Only the initials: HV. Helena Van-Horn? Her gaze shot over to the signature of the person who'd visited the patient.

All breath rushed from her. She grabbed the edge of the file cabinet. Spots appeared before her eyes and she thought she might pass out.

She'd seen this almost illegible signature on the checks she'd received for spending money from the time she was ten until she completed college and began returning the checks—uncashed—in an envelope with nothing else. The same way the checks had arrived.

The signature was Mason VanHorn's.

CHAPTER ELEVEN

ANNA STARED AT the signature. He'd come to visit her mother? She quickly thumbed through the book and found more entries. Why would he visit her? Just to taunt her?

A noise overhead startled her. She had to get out of here. She turned and, clutching the ledger to her, made her way to the door to the huge room.

The smell was much stronger in this room. She glanced toward the mattress against the wall and thought she heard the scurry of small feet. Mice. She cringed at the thought of what might be living there—worse, what had died there. That corner was definitely where the smell was coming from.

She shone the light in that direction. There was something back in the corner under one of the mattresses. She stepped closer, suddenly afraid. There was more room behind the mattress than she'd first thought. Enough room for a body. A body would decay quickly down here.

Her mind recoiled at the thought. The smell was overpowering now. She moved a little closer, bracing herself as she reached out to draw back the mattress.

THE WING for the criminally insane was worse than anything Brandon had seen. The rooms were padded, dark, small, windowless. They instantly gave him claustrophobia and made him sick to his stomach at just the thought of being locked in there.

He tried not to show the panic he was feeling just being in this wing. Sweat broke out on his forehead despite how cool it was. He wiped at it. "It's hot in here," he said, seeing that Yarrow had noticed.

"Have you seen enough?" the Realtor asked.

"What's in there?" Brandon asked at the closed door of Room 9B.

"Just another room," the Realtor said, trying the door. It was locked. The small window in the door had been covered over, making it impossible to see inside.

Anna was somewhere in the building looking for the lost files. Was it possible they were in this room? Why else lock up the wing with a chain and padlock and this room? And cover the window? "You have a key for this room?"

"I'm sure it's just another room like the others," Yarrow said, sounding more than ready to get out of here.

Brandon couldn't have agreed more. But he wanted to see what was in this room. He had to, for Anna's sake. Then he just wanted out of here.

He needed fresh air so badly it was all he could do not to take off at a run for the front door.

Yarrow smiled to cover his irritation and began to go through his keys. He tried one after another. "That's funny. I don't seem to have a key to this room. But I'm sure there is nothing in there."

As Anna pulled back the corner of the mattress, she saw what at first appeared to be a pile of rags. Her heart jumped to her throat, choking off her startled cry as she saw the head.

It was dark, the hair matted, the eyes lifeless. She let go of the corner of the mattress and stumbled back, covering her mouth and nose with her hand.

A coyote. It must have been sick or hurt, came through one of the broken windows at the back and curled up and died here.

A door slammed overhead, making her jump. She could hear footfalls above her. She'd been down here too long. If she didn't get out now, she would be caught leaving the building.

She turned and ran to the stairs, slowing to hide the sound of her footsteps as she ascended the steps to the first floor.

As she carefully pushed open the door, she heard Brandon's voice. Her spirits buoyed at just the sound. He and the Realtor were at the other end of the building.

She practically ran down the hallway toward the front door. She tried not to look in any of the rooms, tried not to let herself imagine what it would have been like for her mother spending the rest of her life locked up here.

As she turned the corner in the hallway, she saw Brandon and the Realtor in the far wing, their backs to her.

She sprinted down the hall, past the vacant office to the front door. She slipped out and gasped for air, suddenly crying. The sobs rose from deep inside her, racking her body.

Her mother had definitely been in Brookside. She had no idea how many years she'd been imprisoned there. Or what had happened to her once inside. But her father couldn't lie to her any longer. She had the ledger. She knew!

She climbed into the pickup, curling onto the seat and closing the door softly behind her, unable to stanch the flood of tears. She cried for the mother she'd never really known, for the pain her mother must have suffered, for justice and finally for her father's soul.

Her cell phone rang.

She fished it out of her pocket in surprise. There was cell-phone service in Sheridan, but not around the lake or Antelope Flats. But apparently there was out here on this mountaintop.

She glanced at the number on the tiny screen, foolishly hoping it was Lenore Johnson, her private investigator.

It wasn't, of course.

It was her father, Mason VanHorn.

MASON VANHORN had gotten her cell-phone number from Anna's former boss. He held his breath, praying he could get her to meet him, praying he could convince her to stop this horrible vendetta against him. He had to convince her. The alternative was too horrible to even consider.

He was surprised when her cell phone rang instead of telling him she was out of the calling area or had her phone turned off.

He was even more surprised to hear her voice on the other end of the line.

"Christianna," he said on a surprised breath.

"I go by Anna now," she said, her voice cold and clipped.

"Anna." Why had she changed her name? Didn't she know how much that hurt him?

She *wanted* to hurt him. If she had her way, she would destroy him. The realization came with less shock than pain. His Chrissy. He'd done so many things wrong with her. Just as he had his son. He should never have had children. He realized that now. But he never dreamed he would have to raise them alone, never dreamed how his actions over the years would harm them.

He took a breath. Now that he had her on the line, he didn't know what to say. "Where are you?" He prayed she'd say Virginia.

"I'm at Brookside."

His heart lunged in his chest, knocking the breath from him.

"What? Nothing to say? I know you put my mother in here and I can prove it."

"We need to talk." He said, finally able to speak.

She laughed. The sound cut him like a blade. "So you can lie to me again?"

He closed his eyes, wiping his free hand over his face. "I lied to protect you."

"The way you protected my mother?"

"Chris— Anna, if you come out to the ranch, I will tell you the truth. I should have a long time ago, but I couldn't bring myself—"

"I'm going to expose your lies. You and Dr. French. If you think you can stop me the way you did the private investigator I hired, you're wrong. What did you do with her? Did you really think you could get away with it? Or are you planning to get rid of me, too?" Her voice broke.

He felt sick. "You have to know I would never hurt you."

"You have already hurt me. I'm going to destroy you the way you did my mother and the child she gave birth to. You killed them both. The baby quickly, my mother more slowly to punish her for her affair. Or are you going to try to deny that she had an affair and that the baby was another man's, the way you've denied everything else?"

He heard the pain and anger in her voice. It broke his heart. "No, I'm not going to deny it. Your mother did have an affair and became pregnant with another man's child."

He heard what could have been a sob on the other end of the line. "But I didn't murder anyone." As he said the words he'd said to himself so many times over the last almost-thirty years, he heard the lie in his voice.

"Anna, please, if you don't want to come out to the ranch, then meet me somewhere. We have to talk."

"Meet you so you can dispose of me the way you did my mother? Or the private investigator I hired?"

He didn't think his heart could break any further, but he was wrong.

She was crying now, her words almost lost in her tears. "Turn yourself in. Don't make this any worse." The line went dead.

When he tried to call her back, she'd turned off her phone.

Realtor Frank Yarrow nervously wiped his full upper lip. "Sorry, I guess I don't have a key for this room. The wind probably caught the door and when it shut, automatically locked it."

Right. A gust of wind in a wing where there were no windows?

"Wait a minute," he said. "Here it is." He slipped the key into the lock and turned it. The door to Room 9B swung open.

Brandon held his breath, half-afraid of what he would see.

"There, I told you. Just like all the other rooms," Yarrow said.

He stared at the small padded cell. Empty. Just like all the others. But the room had an odd smell. Almost like…perfume. He recoiled at the scent, not wanting to know about the woman who must have lived in 9B. How odd that the smell would still be here after all these years.

"When was the last time this room was occupied?" he asked Yarrow.

"Twenty years at least," the Realtor said. "Shall we check out the other wing?" He sounded anxious to get this over with.

"Did you notice the smell of perfume?" Brandon asked, unable to let it go.

Yarrow gave him a pitying look. "No."

Brandon followed him back through the double doors. He could see through the entry windows that it was dark outside. Behind him, he heard Yarrow start to padlock the chains together again.

"Is that necessary?" Brandon asked. "I mean, why keep that wing locked up?"

Yarrow looked down the long empty hallway. Clearly, he liked keeping it locked, probably for reasons he didn't even understand himself. He snapped the padlock into place. "The night security guards like it locked."

He just bet they did.

The other wing was nothing but empty rooms, a men's restroom and a ladies', each with a few stalls or urinals.

"This was the nurses' office," Frank said. The door to the office was open. It was the only room Brandon had seen that had furniture in it—and heat. There was a small television perched on a filing cabinet.

Brandon opened the filing cabinet. Empty. "Emma Ingles worked here?" he asked, trying the other drawers. All empty.

Yarrow cleared his throat. "Yes. Of course, her death had nothing to do with Brookside."

Of course.

"So there is a security guard every night," Brandon said, hoping he and Anna didn't have to come back, that she'd found what she was looking for. Or at least realized it wasn't in this drafty old horrible place.

Yarrow coughed. "Well, with Emma's unfortunate demise and Karl quitting without notice… Of course, I will get more security hired just as quickly as possible. Don't worry about that. No one can get in. The place is locked up tight. Have to be careful not to get locked in."

"I really don't need to see any more," Brandon said. Yarrow looked more than relieved.

They walked to the front door. It was dark outside, shadows moving in the breeze. Brandon held the door open. Yarrow rushed through almost at a trot. Brandon closed the door, the small piece of wood keeping it from locking just in case they had to come back. Or Anna was still inside.

"Well, thank you for showing it to me. I'd like to

give it some thought. I'll get back to you." He shook Yarrow's hand.

"I think it could be a good investment for you and your family," Frank said as he started to get into his car. "Definite possibilities."

Brandon nodded, still unable to imagine what anyone would do with Brookside, given its history. But didn't all buildings come with a history, usually one the owner had no way of knowing?

Wisps of clouds brushed across the dark sky. A rim of gold shone over the mountains to the east where the moon would be rising. The air felt cold for this time of the year, but then they were at least a thousand feet higher up here than down by the lake.

Brandon pretended to study the hulking dark shape of the building as Yarrow drove off. The moment the Realtor was over the first hill, Brandon headed for the pickup. He opened the driver's-side door, the light coming on in the cab.

Anna was hunkered down on the seat in the darkness. She sat up and he saw her face.

Oh, God. "What happened?"

ANNA HALTINGLY TOLD HIM about the dead coyote she'd found and her father's phone call.

He pulled her into his arms, holding her tightly. "All I found was a locked room in the padded cell wing. At first Frank didn't have the key and I thought... But then he found it and the room was empty like all the others."

She pulled back. "What was the room number?"

"9B."

Anna thought her heart might stop. "That was my

mother's room." She fumbled the ledger out from under the seat where she'd hidden it, opening it to the page where she'd found her mother's initials, pointing to the room number next to them. And her father's signature.

Brandon stared down at the ledger in obvious shock. "You found this in the building?"

"Dropped between two file cabinets in the basement. The files were all gone, but this proves that my mother was here."

"And that your father came to visit her." He sounded astonished, much as she had. He looked out through the windshield at Brookside. "Do you mind if we get out of here?"

She shook her head, closing the ledger as he turned off the dome light and started the truck.

As Brandon pulled away, she glanced back only once at the massive brick building and felt a chill quake through her. They'd left the door partially ajar. In case they had to come back.

MASON SAT IN THE DARK knowing what he had to do. Chrissy was with Brandon McCall. Who knew what lies McCall had told her? His daughter. He was going to lose her, too.

He closed his eyes and felt the burning tears behind his lids. He couldn't remember the last time he'd cried. Then he realized that, too, was a lie.

It was the night his beautiful wife gave birth to another man's baby.

He opened his eyes, wiped angrily at his tears as he picked up the phone and dialed Red Hudson's extension.

"Get up here!" he snapped, and hung up.

He had to stop Christianna before it was too late. But first he would have to separate her from Brandon McCall. No matter what it took. The McCalls would love to see him destroyed. Especially Asa.

He heard Red come in the front door without knocking, heard the rapid thud of his footfalls and knew he'd made Red angry again. He wondered if he'd hired the wrong man for the job. He was about to find out.

Red's large frame filled his office doorway. "You drunk? Or just forgot how to turn on a light?"

Mason reached over and snapped on his desk lamp.

Red's expression changed from one of irritation to worry. "What's wrong?"

"You still haven't found McCall?"

Red shook his head. "Stick and Bubba found the camp where the two of them stayed last night. But they got away. I have men out looking for them."

Mason studied the man. The problem with Red was that he had scruples. But there'd been a time when he hadn't. And that was the leverage Mason had on the man. Unfortunately, Red was determined to change his life.

"Find out if they've gone to the McCall ranch. If not, then they have to be staying around here somewhere. Check motels and rentals. I need McCall out of the way."

Red raised a brow.

"All I want you to do is detain him. Put him in that old storage bin on the south end of the ranch. Make him comfortable. But make sure he doesn't leave until I give you the word."

Red said nothing.

"My daughter and I need to talk—without McCall. So I need you to find him. Turn over every rock in the county if that's what it takes."

"You're that sure she's still around?"

Mason nodded. He could see Red was wondering what she'd been doing in the house, in the safe. "I wasn't a very good father. She wants to hurt me."

Red shifted on his feet, obviously uncomfortable with Mason's confession.

"Maybe McCall tried to stop her and she hit him with that iron doorstop," Mason continued, knowing he had to get Red on his side. "Now he seems to be sympathizing with her. Or at the very least, trying to protect her from me."

Red shot up a brow. "Is that necessary?"

"She's my daughter. I love her more than my own life," Mason said without hesitation.

Red nodded. "I'll try to find them myself. You do realize, though, that such an action might be considered kidnapping?"

Sarcasm. "Yes, I'm aware of that, but I don't think McCall will press charges. He was trespassing on my land just last night and helped a known vandal. Also, I think you might be right about him."

Red smiled but still looked skeptical.

"Just get McCall away from her. I'll take care of the rest."

Red stood for a moment, as if considering everything he'd been told, then slowly nodded. "I'll find them. But if anything happens to either of them, you're on your own."

Mason nodded. "Let me know as soon as you have him. Make sure my daughter is protected."

He watched Red leave. If anything happened to Brandon McCall, Red would go to the sheriff. Now Mason knew how much he could trust Red Hudson. Not very damned far.

But Mason wasn't worried about Red. No, his concern was with Niles French. The doctor was running scared and that made him dangerous. Very dangerous.

Dr. French would be looking for Christianna. Mason had to find her before he did.

CHAPTER TWELVE

THE LIGHTS FROM the pickup cut through the darkness as Brandon started down the narrow winding dirt road.

The night was black, the clouds low and dark. Behind the pickup, dust rose like ghosts chasing after them.

He tried not to drive too fast, but at the same time he wanted to put distance between them and Brookside.

Anna leaned back against the seat and closed her eyes. "I don't know what to think."

She'd found what appeared to be evidence that her mother had been in the institution. But even more disturbing was finding out that her father had visited Helena during that time.

"Are you all right?"

"Mmm," she said in answer.

He reached over to cover her hand with his free one. He gave her fingers a light squeeze.

A lone tear coursed down her cheek. He lifted his hand to thumb it away. He'd noticed earlier that she'd been crying, her face flushed, eyes red.

He hadn't said anything, not knowing really what to say. Just as he didn't know what to say now. The ledger seemed to confirm that her mother had been in Brookside—just as she'd feared. They still didn't know for how many years she was locked up there, or even if she still might be alive somewhere.

But the big question the ledger raised was why visit a woman Mason VanHorn supposedly hated so much he'd had locked up?

Brandon glanced back almost as if he thought some intangible evil might be chasing them. The set of headlights surprised him. Frank Yarrow had gone down first. And since there were no turnoffs and the road ended at Brookside, where had the vehicle come from?

There hadn't been another car at Brookside. At least not when they first got there. Was it possible someone had driven up while they were inside?

In the rearview mirror, he watched the lights growing brighter and brighter as the vehicle grew closer, coming up fast behind them.

Brandon touched his brakes, hoping the driver could see the flash of his brake lights through the dust. The car didn't slow. It was headed right for them.

"What is it?" Anna asked. She was sitting up, staring at him. She glanced back. "There's someone behind us?"

"Hang on!"

"He's going to ram us," Anna cried.

The cab filled with light as what appeared to be a black SUV smashed into the back of the pickup with a jarring crash.

There was no way to pull off the road or get away from the other vehicle. Brandon fought to keep the truck on the road as he went into another hairpin turn.

The SUV slammed into the pickup again, this time making it fishtail. The back tires slid toward the edge of the cliff. Brandon turned the wheel and righted the pickup, hitting the gas, hoping to put a little space between them.

Through the headlights, he could see another sharp curve coming up, remembered it from earlier, knew that was where the vehicle behind them would hit again.

On one side, he had the mountain; on the other, a cliff that dropped in a tumble of rocks.

He couldn't outrun the vehicle behind them and it would be suicide to try.

But the curve was coming up quickly and if he was hit from behind while in that tight curve— He had only one chance. He glanced over at Anna. "Brace yourself."

He punched the gas, spinning the rear wheels as he sped up, churning up as much dust as he could. The SUV's headlights disappeared behind them in the cloud of dust. He was almost to the curve. He couldn't see the SUV behind him but he knew it was there, probably coming up fast behind him again. The driver knew the road. He wasn't trying to scare them. He was trying to kill them.

Right before the curve, Brandon cut hard into the side of the mountain. Along with the initial impact came a shower of dirt and rocks that flew up over the top of the pickup.

"Hang on!" he yelled over the thunderous roar as the pickup dug into the mountainside, coming to rest precariously, leaning to one side. If it rolled, they were both dead. An instant later, they were struck from behind, only a glancing blow as the vehicle clipped the back bumper and scraped along the side of the truck as it careered past, taking the side mirror with it.

Anna let out a sound. Not a scream, but a cry as the other vehicle shot past, barely making the curve.

Brandon only got a glimpse of the dark-colored SUV, then it was gone.

"Are you all right?" he cried, looking over at Anna as dust and darkness settled over the pickup.

She nodded, her eyes wide in the lights from the dash. He reached over and cupped her pale face in his palm. "My God, you're hurt."

"It's nothing. I just hit my head on the window," she said. "Is he gone?"

Brandon nodded. "He's in front of us. He'll take off, afraid we'll come after him." He opened the glove box and pulled out a packet of tissues. "Here." He pressed several into her hand. "It's not bleeding badly, but I'm taking you to the clinic to have you checked out anyway."

He hurriedly shifted the pickup into reverse. The tires spun for a moment, then caught as he backed up onto the road and sat for a moment, trying to collect himself. That had been too close a call.

"He tried to kill us," she said, her voice growing stronger.

Brandon got the pickup moving, thankful he hadn't blown a tire or worse. He just wanted off this mountain and away from Brookside.

"MY FATHER DRIVES a dark-colored SUV," Anna said when they reached the highway. There was no sign of the vehicle that had tried to run them off the road.

Brandon looked over at her. "A lot of people drive dark-colored SUVs around here. Anyway, he had no way of knowing we were at Brookside."

She bit her lip, her eyes swimming in tears. She wiped at them. "When he called me, I told him where I was. He wanted to see me. He said if I'd meet him, he would tell me the truth."

Even in the dim light from the dashboard, she could see his shock.

"Don't jump to conclusions," he said. "Frank Yarrow could have told a number of people he was showing me the building. I don't believe the person driving that SUV was your father. He's in his sixties."

"And strong as an ox," she said.

"But he wouldn't try to kill you," Brandon said adamantly.

She wished she could be so sure.

At the clinic, he helped Anna inside against her protests that she was fine.

"Is Dr. Ivers here?" Brandon asked the receptionist. "Can you call him?"

"I'm here," said a voice behind them. Brandon turned to see Dr. *Taylor* Ivers. "What seems to be the problem?"

"She hit her head," Brandon said.

"It's nothing," Anna protested.

"Step in here, please," Dr. Taylor Ivers said as she drew back a curtain in the small emergency area. She let Anna pass, but stopped Brandon. "*You* may wait out there."

She closed the drape in his face.

The woman was as obstinate as her father, Brandon thought with a curse. He couldn't sit in one of the half-dozen chairs in the small waiting area. He paced.

Fortunately, Anna appeared in only a few minutes, a small bandage on her temple. "She said I'm fine, just as I told you." She glanced back. "I liked her. Didn't you say her father was a real curmudgeon?"

He laughed, letting out the breath he'd been holding. Anna was fine. "Taylor has his bedside manner."

"She was very nice to me," Anna said. "She was telling me she might stay here in Antelope Flats and continue her father's work in infertility." Anna cocked her head at him. "Maybe it's just you she doesn't like," she joked.

Brandon glanced back. Dr. Taylor Ivers watched them leave, a frown on her face. He figured it was for him. Anna might have something there. The woman certainly didn't seem to like him.

Brandon drove back to the marina. The small fishing boat she'd rented was tied up at the dock. She didn't see any of her father's men waiting for them as they climbed into the boat and started across the lake in the darkness.

The lake was quiet. Lights glittered along the shore. Campfires flared from in the pines, and she could smell the smoke and the water. She heard the murmur of voices around the campfires and music carrying on the summer night air, the sound broken only occasionally by laughter.

They were both silent on the ride across the lake, both lost in their own thoughts. Brandon pulled into the dock in front of the dark cabin, tied up the boat and led the way up to the porch.

"Let me make sure we don't have any company," he said, and left her on the porch to go inside.

A few moments later, several lights came on inside and the door opened. She looked at him framed in the doorway and threw herself into his arms—just as she had wanted to do all day.

He cupped her face in his hands and dropped his mouth to hers again.

She sighed as he deepened the kiss, her arms wrapping around his neck, her lips parting in response to the heat of his kisses. "Brand," she whispered against his hot eager mouth. "Make love to me."

Brandon pulled back to look at her. The sounds of the warm summer night wafted around them. She smiled. "Yes," she whispered. "Please."

He laughed softly and kissed her with the longing that had been building up inside him all day. Then he swung her up into his arms as he carried her inside.

She tossed his hat aside and kissed him as he worked his denim jacket off and tossed it onto the floor. Her kisses were teasing, her fingers tangled in hair at the base of his neck as he worked her jacket off.

She slowly began to unbutton her shirt. He watched, mesmerized. The fabric fell open, exposing skin that had never seen the sun. Her white breasts rose and fell with each breath, the dark peaks hard against the silk of her bra.

She grasped the front clasp with both hands and in one swift movement, the bra parted and her breasts were free.

He pulled her to him, his thumbs flicking over the already hard nipples. She let out a groan and pressed against him as he cupped her wonderful breasts in both hands, bending to kiss the rosy tips.

She slithered out of her boots and jeans as he suckled one breast, then the other. She moaned, her head back, her silken white neck exposed.

He kissed her, caught up in the glorious feel of her body, her mouth, her long dark hair tangled in his fingers as her fingers worked the buttons on his shirt, then his jeans.

When he lifted his lips from hers, they were both

naked. He held her at arm's length to look at her, soaking up every inch of her luxurious body with his gaze. Goose bumps rippled over her skin, her eyes radiating desire.

She pulled him to the floor, to the bed of clothing and jackets.

His skin was wonderfully browned from working on the ranch without his shirt, his shoulders muscled, his arms strong and well-shaped just like his slim waist and hips.

She trembled as he drew her against him. Her skin felt on fire, his touch a flame that burned across her, setting her center ablaze. She'd dreamed about this moment, but never in her wildest imagination had it been this amazing.

He touched her face as he lay beside her on the floor, his fingers trailing from her cheek, down her throat to her breasts, his gaze locked with hers. His fingertips moved across her stomach.

She could feel the heat radiating off his body. His masculine scent filled her. He let out a low chuckle as if he knew he had her cornered. The sound reverberated in her chest, making her heart pound a little faster.

She closed her eyes as his fingers found her center. He gently spread her thighs. She caught her breath, then let it out in a pleasured sigh as he made love to her.

Her senses rose with each touch, each caress, until she was soaring higher and higher. He leaned over her and she looked into his face. She trusted Brandon McCall with her life. But with her love?

She met his pale blue eyes and at that moment she knew she was about to surrender her heart to him, as well. That surrender came with no promises. She knew

B.J. DANIELS
413

he didn't believe they stood a chance in hell of being together. She might never be able to change his mind.

"Anna?" he whispered.

She smiled up at him, wrapping her arms around him as he gently filled her. She stared into his eyes, matching his wonderful rhythm as he took her higher and higher until she thought she couldn't stand any more. And then he released her.

She cried out, the pleasure so intense, her body quaked under his. He wrapped her in his arms and kissed away the wetness on her cheeks, smiling down at her. She hadn't even realized that she'd been crying.

It took a few minutes to catch her breath. During that time, he gazed down at her as if memorizing her face.

"I used to dream about what it would be like to kiss you," she said, feeling suddenly shy. "I never dreamed…" She sighed. "Brand."

He kissed her, curling against her on the floor. "We could go to the bed," he whispered.

She laughed. "I'm sure we will. At some point."

And she fell asleep in his arms, as if that day on the curb, when they'd shared the cherry Popsicle, they'd also shared this destiny.

BRANDON WOKE, shocked to see that it was early afternoon. He was starved and tried to remember the last time he'd eaten. They'd picked up a couple of burgers on the way to Brookside. That had been almost a whole day ago. No wonder his stomach was growling.

He rolled over in the double bed and looked at Anna. He couldn't believe they'd slept so late, but then they'd been up half the night making love and talking.

He stared at her. Last night in her arms, he thought

everything had changed. But as he looked at her, he knew nothing had. They'd been kidding themselves. They'd needed each other. Fear did that to people. When she opened her eyes this morning, she would see that he was right.

It was time to go to Cash, to tell him everything, to let the law handle this. It was time for Anna to go back to Virginia and the career she obviously loved. He would be on his way to law school in the fall.

Her face was soft in the warm summer light. She looked like an angel, her dark hair spread out around her face. Even knowing how foolish it was, he wanted desperately to kiss her.

Don't fall for this woman, he warned himself as he slipped from the bed and followed the trail of dropped clothing, picking up each piece until, by the time he reached the living room, he was dressed. He checked Anna again to make sure she was still asleep, then closed her door. He would run across the lake to the store by boat and be back before she even knew he was gone. He might even have time to stop by the sheriff's office.

But if he did that without her, he would feel like he was betraying her.

He glanced out the window and saw children already splashing at the edge of the water. Opening the door, he heard the hum of boat motors. The air smelled of pine and water; summer smells. He breathed it in, remembering last night and Anna in his arms. He'd never felt so close to anyone before in his life.

He started down the steps when he saw movement off to his right. An instant later, he felt the pinprick of the needle in his arm. He tried to turn, tried to fight off the men who caught him before he hit the ground. Their faces were the last thing he saw before darkness. VanHorn's men.

ANNA WOKE to a sound. She opened her eyes, forgetting for a moment where she was. With a rush, she remembered the lake cabin—and Brandon. She smiled and started to close her eyes when she realized that the spot next to her on the bed was empty.

"Brand?"

No answer. She sat up. "Brand?"

Maybe he was out on the porch. Or down by the lake.

She got up, drawing the blanket around her as she walked into the living room and stopped cold.

A large redheaded man was sitting in a chair by the window. From his reaction, he'd been waiting for her to wake up. She'd never seen him before, but she knew from the look of him why he was here.

"My name's Red. Get dressed. Your father wants to see you."

"Where is Brandon?"

"You should ask your father about that."

She picked up her clothing, keeping an eye on the man. He watched her, his face expressionless, as she backed into the bathroom with her clothing in hand and shut and locked the door.

The window over the tub was too small even if she'd wanted to escape. But she was ready to face her father. She had to. He had Brandon. Turning on the shower, she stepped under the spray, trying not to think of what her father might have done to him. She had to stay strong. Her father could smell weakness.

For years, she'd let Mason VanHorn feed her lies. Worse, he'd kept her from the ranch she loved. She hadn't put up a fight.

Now he had Brandon.

Her father didn't know it yet, but he was in for the fight of his life.

She showered, dried and dressed quickly, berating herself for not realizing that Mason VanHorn would use every resource available to him to find her. And his resources were many. She'd known they weren't safe, wouldn't be safe until this was over.

Stepping out of the bedroom, she looked to the large redheaded man still seated where she'd left him.

"I'm ready. Take me to my father."

BRANDON WOKE with a headache and a horrible taste in his mouth. His arm ached where the needle had gone in. He wondered what they'd given him.

Opening his eyes, he blinked in the cool darkness, disoriented and still feeling the effects of the drug.

He pushed himself up, his eyes slowly adjusting to the lack of light. He was in a small old building of some kind—four rough-hewn log walls, a heavy wooden door, no windows.

Anna. Where was Anna?

Stumbling to his feet, he lumbered to the door and tried to open it, not surprised to find it barred from the outside. He leaned against it, waiting for the nausea to pass, then slammed his shoulder into it. The door didn't budge. He cursed under his breath as he rubbed his aching shoulder and listened.

A little light leaked through the cracks in the logs. He

leaned against the wall and started to check his watch, but it was gone. How long had he been here?

Pressing his eye to one of the wider cracks, he peered out, surprised at how dark it was. He found a wider crack and peered out, trying to figure out where he was.

It was afternoon, but not as late as he'd first thought. Dark clouds hunkered on the horizon, making it seem later. A thunderstorm was headed this way.

He couldn't see much through the crack in the wall. Just the corner of another building, but he recognized the red-and-white barn. He was on the VanHorn Ranch.

His head began to clear.

He'd known it had been VanHorn's men who abducted him but he hadn't expected them to bring him to the ranch. Why had they? He would have thought they'd have taken him to Mason. Or taken him out somewhere and either shot him or just dumped him.

Instead, he'd been put here as if on hold. What were they waiting for?

In an instant, he knew.

Anna. VanHorn had Anna.

He slammed into the door again with the same result as the first time. Swearing, he looked around the shed. He had to get out of here. Anna was with a monster. There was no telling what the man might do to her. It didn't matter that she was his flesh and blood, his only daughter. Look how he'd treated her all these years. And now she was on to him—and he knew it.

MASON VANHORN was waiting for her in his office. "Thank you, Red," he said without even looking up at them from his desk.

Red left, closing the door behind him and she was alone with her father. "What have you done with Brandon?"

He lifted his head slowly.

For a moment, she was too stunned to speak, amazed at how much he'd aged. She'd always remembered him as being big and powerful, his hair black like her own, his face tanned and strong.

His hair was almost completely white now, his face sallow and lined, but it was his eyes that made her wince. They were dull and dark, lifeless.

She had wanted to see this man suffer, had come all the way out here to make sure that happened. But one look at him told her he already had suffered more than he ever would at her hands.

"Please sit down."

She shook her head and remained standing.

"I have no idea where McCall is," he said.

"You're lying."

His eyes darkened. "Brandon sold you out," he said quietly. "He went back to his family. He doesn't want any part of this."

She shook her head. "He wouldn't do that." She hated the lack of conviction she heard in her voice. Wasn't that her greatest fear? That she could be wrong about him? Just as she had been about her father?

"Wouldn't he? Then where is he?"

She stared at her father. "I know you did something to him. If you hurt him—"

"Don't be ridiculous," he snapped. "You act as if I had him killed."

"Isn't it easier after the first time?"

He let out a heavy sigh. "Chrissy, what are you do-ing?"

"Don't call me that. My name is Anna now. Anna Austin."

"You changed your name just to hurt me?"

She laughed but the sound held no humor. "Every-thing is about you, isn't it? Why did you have me brought here?"

"I don't understand your anger at me," he said, sound-ing genuinely confused. "What have I done to you?"

"Give it some thought. It will come to you."

Mason wagged his head sadly. "McCall put you up to this. He's the one feeding you these lies."

"McCall? I should have known you'd blame him. He tried to stop me from finding out the truth about you. I knew this would be a waste of time. All you're going to do is lie to me again. Well, save your breath. I don't believe anything you tell me because I know what happened to my mother. I have proof you put her in Brookside."

All the color drained from his face as he reared back as if she'd slapped him.

"I know you put her in there to punish her. I know what a heartless bastard you really are."

He rose from his chair and started toward her.

Her heart lunged in her chest. She couldn't help but step back, the look in his eyes terrifying her.

He stopped as if shocked. His face seemed to crum-ble. "Chrissy, I wouldn't hurt you. You can't believe that I would hurt you."

The ridiculousness of his words struck her as funny. She let out the breath she'd been holding. It came out on a laugh. "You killed my little brother or sister, then sent my mother to an insane asylum because she cheated on you. And you don't understand why I'm afraid of you?"

He stared at her, his face a mask of white. "Where would you get the idea…"

"Sarah Gilcrest, my nanny. She heard it all from the room upstairs."

He stumbled back, dropping into the chair behind his desk. He seemed small and she wondered why she'd been afraid of this man only a moment ago. "I don't know what she told you—"

"*She* told me the truth. She heard the baby cry. It wasn't stillborn. She heard my mother begging you not to put her in that place. She heard the doctor take my mother away."

He shook his lowered head without looking at her. "Sarah misunderstood what she heard."

"Like she misunderstood the next morning when you told her the baby was stillborn and my mother had run away?"

He raised his head. "This is why you've done the things you have? Because you believed…" He waved a hand weakly through the air. "Oh, Chrissy— Anna," he corrected. "I see that I should have told you the truth years ago. I swear on everything I hold dear that isn't what happened."

"Everything you hold dear?"

"You hate me." He seemed surprised by that.

"I don't know you," she snapped. "You sent me away when I was ten. I begged you to let me stay here.…" Her voice broke. She looked away, hating the tears that burned in her eyes. She would not cry.

"I was trying to protect you."

"Or protect yourself?" she snapped back. "You have a habit of getting rid of things you don't want."

His dark eyes swam in tears. "Is that what you think? That I got rid of you because I didn't want you? Please sit down. I will tell you everything. No more lies."

She knew she couldn't believe him, but she wanted to and that's what frightened her. "I know about Dr. French."

He looked up at her, something in his eyes saying more than she knew his words ever would.

Guilt. She saw the answer. She stumbled back, spinning about to run out the door, out of this house, out of this state. Red stepped into the doorway, his broad chest blocking her escape.

"I can't let you leave until you hear the whole story," her father said flatly.

Anna felt the hair stand up on the back of her neck as she turned to look at him. His expression told her he meant every word.

But once she heard the whole story, what then? He couldn't let her go. He had to know she would go to the sheriff. He couldn't let either her or Brandon go. He had too much to lose.

THERE WAS NO WAY to break down the door, Brandon realized as he looked around the empty space. Nothing to use as a battering ram and he wasn't foolish enough to try again with his shoulder.

The walls were thick square logs. He doubted dynamite could blow through one of them.

He looked up and saw what looked like dim light coming through a corner of the roof. He moved closer.

The roof appeared to be the original—only single-thickness sheets of wood nailed across the rafters.

Unless his eyes were playing tricks on him, one corner of the roof had leaked, the wood rotting enough to let in a little light.

The rotten corner was a good ten feet above his head, though, and there was nothing to stand on to reach it.

He looked around for a spot where the chinking between the logs had worked out and climbed up into the open rafters. Clinging precariously from one of the rafters, he swung back and forth until he had enough momentum, then he kicked at the corner of the roof. The wood gave a little.

Hope soared through him. He swung again. And again. The wood broke away at the corner. He could see daylight, smell the storm headed this way. Lightning flickered, thunder boomed. The storm just might hide the noise he was making. If only he could make a hole large enough to get out before he was discovered.

Another thunderous boom overhead. He stopped for a moment, his hands burning from swinging on the rafter, his legs aching. Just a little more.

He heard the crunch of footsteps. Someone tried the door.

"PLEASE, SIT DOWN," Mason VanHorn said, motioning to a chair. "Red, would you close the door?"

Anna pulled the chair to her, putting as much distance as she could between them. Her father saw the movement, knew what she was doing. The pain in his expression gave her no pleasure. He was holding her here against her will. Just as she knew he was holding Brandon. She just prayed he hadn't hurt him.

"Your mother was never strong."

She told herself she wouldn't believe anything he told her but the moment he started to speak, something in his voice told her she was finally about to hear the truth.

"It started before—" he waved a hand through the air "—before her affair, before her pregnancy. Then, when the baby was born… The baby was horribly deformed. When your mother saw it, she just…lost her mind."

"What did you do with the baby?"

"The doctor wrapped him in a towel—" His voice broke. "I couldn't bear to look.…"

"You didn't see him?" Anna asked.

He shook his head. "I took him out and buried him in the VanHorn graveyard on the hill. At the very last moment I parted the towel and looked into his face. He was beautiful. Just like your mother."

As hard as she tried not to, she started to cry.

"Helena had been hanging on to reality by a thread. After that…" He looked down at his hands. They were weathered and covered with age spots. The hands of an old man. "She fought me, throwing everything she could get her hands on. I tried to console her but she…" He shook his head and she saw that he was crying.

Anna had never seen her father cry. It was a shocking sight. She didn't want to have any sympathy for him. "How can I believe you?"

He didn't seem to hear her. "She'd been seeing Dr. French. For her…problems. That night…there was nothing I could do. I couldn't let you and Holt see her like that. I was afraid that she might…" He looked up and she saw the fear in his face. He thought she might hurt her other children? "Dr. French took her to Brookside."

Anna sat motionless. "How long was she at Brookside?" she asked into the silence that followed.

"Until she died. When you were nine."

Anna had known her mother had to be dead but still, it hit her hard. She was too stunned to speak for a moment. "That's why you sent me away?"

"I wanted to protect you."

"Does my brother know?"

"Holt?" He shook his head.

"Why did you lie all these years?" But the moment the words were out of her mouth, she knew. "The baby was alive at birth, just like Sarah said. You had the doctor kill it."

AT THE SOUND of someone at the door, Brandon froze, hanging from the rafter. An engine fired up nearby. He used the sudden noise to cloak the sound of his boots hitting the floor as he dropped down and curled back up on the floor.

He heard the lock click. The door opened a crack. Someone called out. A truck door slammed. The door closed and whoever had opened it locked the door again and moved away, his footfalls retreating. The truck motor revved and then there was silence again.

Climbing back up the log wall, Brandon grabbed the rafter and kicked again at the roof, praying he could get out of here and to Anna before it was too late. Unless someone had just taken her away in that truck.

The roof splintered under his boot, the hole large enough that he should be able to wriggle through.

Climbing across to the end rafter, he reached an arm out and grabbed the corner of the overhang. Holding on, he shoved his shoulder and head through the hole, then worked his other shoulder out.

Bracing himself with both hands on the remaining roof, he pushed upward until he was sitting on the roof.

He could see the ranch complex up the road. Mason VanHorn's car was parked in front of the ranch house.

Jumping down, Brandon ran along the back side of the buildings, headed for the ranch house. If anyone knew where Anna was, it was Mason VanHorn.

"ANNA, YOU HAVE TO understand—"

She was on her feet again. "You were covering up a murder."

"I didn't kill that baby. He was so badly deformed that he only lived a few moments."

"Then why lie?"

Her father rose from the chair but didn't come toward her. Instead, he moved to the window at the rear of his office and stood with his back to her. "I am ashamed, but the truth is I couldn't bear for anyone to know about your mother. I didn't want her…sickness to make people in town treat you and Holt differently. There is so much about mental illness that we don't understand. It was worse thirty years ago."

"You shut her away in that place because you were embarrassed?"

He turned to look at her. "You don't understand. She was violent. She—" His eyes filled again with tears— and a look that froze her blood with horror.

"No," Anna cried. "My mother killed the baby!"

CHAPTER THIRTEEN

CASH PUT DOWN the twenty-year-old Jane Doe murder file next to his notes on the Emma Ingles murder.

He could find no connection. Not that he'd expected to find one.

But he'd discovered when he talked to the motel clerk where Lenore Johnson had been staying that his brother Brandon had been asking about her, too. Lenore had also asked for directions to Brookside the last night she was seen.

Cash had been trying without any luck to find his little brother. He couldn't wait to ask him what he'd been doing at Brookside with Frank Yarrow and why he'd let the Realtor believe the McCall family might be interested in buying the place.

Brandon was also seen with a dark-haired young woman.

Yep. Cash couldn't wait to get his hands on his brother. Whatever Brandon was up to, he just hoped it had nothing to do with Emma Ingles's murder.

Molly had called earlier and was holding dinner for him. Just the thought of her made him close the file and reach to turn out his light.

The phone rang. A 911 call forwarded to his number. He picked it up. "Sheriff Cash McCall."

"Help me. Please help me." The whispering voice

of a woman made him sit up straighter. *"My name is Lenore Johnson. I don't have much time before he comes back."* Her words were slurred, he could barely hear her. *"I'm being held at Brookside. I think he's a doctor. He—"*

The line went dead.

"Hello? Hello?"

Cash hung up the phone, his heart pounding. He quickly picked up the receiver again and dialed his home to tell Molly dinner would have to wait.

THE LOCK on the bathroom window behind the Van-Horn ranch house was still broken, just as Brandon had suspected. Mason's men either hadn't had time to fix it or had left it hoping to catch the vandal.

Carefully lifting the window, he slipped inside. He could hear voices coming from down the hall.

At the door, he looked out. He hadn't seen any of VanHorn's men. Not even Red. Maybe he'd sent them all off, wanting to be alone with his daughter. The thought chilled Brandon.

The hallway was empty, the door to VanHorn's office closed. He could hear voices behind the office door. Mason was talking quietly, almost reassuringly.

Brandon moved silently down the hallway and put his ear against the door. He couldn't hear what was being said but it sounded as if Anna was crying and Mason was trying to soothe her.

He knew he would have hell getting Anna out of here without a fight and unfortunately, he had no weapon. Playing hero now could just get them both killed.

But there was no other option. He could call his brother but it would take Cash too long to get here.

He gripped the doorknob, listening.

"ANNA, I'M SO SORRY that I didn't tell you the truth before," Mason said in a monotone, his head down. He looked horrible, as if reliving all this had aged him more.

Anna didn't know what to say. Or what to believe. If he was telling the truth… "What about my mother?"

He raised his head to meet her gaze and she knew at once that she didn't want to hear this. "She's dead."

"You already told me that." She bit her lip. "Where?"

He looked away and she knew he'd had to cover up her death, as well—with Dr. French's help.

She sighed. "So many lies. Was it worth it?"

A spark lit in his dark eyes. "To protect you and your brother? Yes. I would do it all over again."

She stared at him. How much of it had been for her and Holt? And how much for her father? "Who was the man?" she asked, thinking about the feud between her father and Asa.

He shook his head. "Just one of many cowboys."

Anna felt sick. "She died at Brookside?"

"Twenty years ago."

That long? She knew she should feel relieved that her mother hadn't suffered for years in that place.

"She was starting to get better," Mason said. "She knew who I was and she even asked about you and Holt." His voice broke.

The phone rang. He jumped as if it were a rattle-snake on his desk. It rang again. He seemed to be trying to ignore it and something in his expression made her suspicious.

"Go head, answer it," she said as it rang again. "Isn't that your private line?"

It rang again. Clearly, he wasn't going to answer it.

Before he could stop her, she stood, reached over and picked up the phone. All she wanted was to see who was calling, to verify her hunch on the caller ID.

"Dr. French's number." She hit Talk but said nothing, her gaze going to her father's.

The answering machine started to pick up. "Mason, it's Niles. I know you're there. You have to get up to Brookside. You have to stop—"

Her father grabbed the phone from her before French could finish.

Anna stumbled backward toward the door, tears burning her eyes. "It was all a lie, wasn't it?"

"No," Mason cried. "I told you the honest-to-God truth. You have to believe me."

She was shaking her head, moving away from him, wanting to run. For a while there, she'd believed him. "Where is the private investigator I hired? What did you do with her? Is that why you have to get up to Brookside? Who is it you have to stop? Lenore Johnson, the woman I hired? Or me?"

"Chrissy, listen to me." He slammed down the phone and grabbed her arm. She tried to break free.

She heard a sound behind her and spun around to see Brandon framed in the doorway.

"Let her go," Brandon ordered, and reached for her.

"I could have you arrested," Mason snapped at Brandon, but he let go of Anna. She grabbed up the set of keys from her father's desk, the keys to his SUV.

Brandon pulled her to him, drawing her close, his arm around her as they backed out of the room. "Don't try to stop us."

"Chrissy, if you leave here, I can't protect you. I'm afraid of what Dr. French will do once he knows that I told you everything."

BRANDON PUT HIMSELF between Mason VanHorn and his daughter. "I'm taking her to Cash," he said. "I've already called him. He knows that you had me abducted. He knows Anna is here. If I don't call him back soon, he will come out here with the state police." It was all a lie, but one that seemed to be working.

VanHorn stumbled back, dropping into his chair, his face slack with defeat.

"She'll be safe with the sheriff," Brandon said. "It's over."

"Yes," he said, not looking at either of them as they left.

Brandon rushed Anna out the front door to her father's expensive SUV parked outside. She slid into the passenger seat as he swung behind the wheel and started the motor.

He'd expected Mason to send out an alert to his men but as Brandon spun the SUV around and headed down the ranch road, he didn't see anyone coming after them.

"Are you all right?" he asked, putting his arm around her and pulling her closer. One look at her face told him she was far from all right.

When he reached the highway, he headed toward Antelope Flats. The thunderstorm raced across the landscape, clouds low and dark, lightning flickering and thunder a drum in the distance.

She filled him in, including Dr. French's phone call.

"I lied about calling Cash, but I have to now," he said to Anna, afraid she might want to argue.

She didn't. She nodded, still looking numb, her face pale.

He stopped at the phone booth in front of the Decker Post Office. Decker, Montana, consisted of the post office and a couple of houses. At one time, there'd been a bar but it had closed years ago.

"I'll be right back." He got out and stepped into the phone booth as the first drops of rain began to fall. They pelted the phone booth. Brandon looked through them to the empty highway, afraid Mason would have a bunch of his cowboys hot on their trail.

"Brandon?" Cash said the moment he came on the line. "What the hell is going on? Frank Yarrow called me wanting to know if my family was still interested in buying Brookside. He said he gave you a tour."

"It's a long story. Where are you?"

"The dispatcher patched you through. I've got a lead on Lenore Johnson."

"At Brookside?" Brandon asked in surprise.

"I'm not sure how you're involved in all this—"

"Cash, Mason VanHorn just got a call from a Dr. French. Something is going on up there. I'll tell you everything when I see you."

"Stay away from Brookside. There have already been two murders—"

"*Two?* I saw the story about Emma Ingles—"

"There was another one twenty years ago in Room 9B."

All the air rushed from Brandon's lungs. "9B? That was Helena VanHorn's room. We'll tell you everything when you get to Brookside." He hung up before his brother could argue.

"WE'LL TELL YOU everything? Brandon!" Cash swore as he sped out of town, siren and lights blaring, headed for Brookside, wondering how deeply his brother was involved in this.

Lightning flickered on the horizon as dark clouds swept toward him. He raced down the empty highway in the growing darkness as rain pelted the windshield as hard as gravel. He turned on the wipers as the storm became a downpour and visibility dropped.

Just a few miles outside of town, he saw a set of headlights flash on from a side road. Even with the rain, Cash knew the driver had to see him coming with the lights and siren on.

The next instant, the car pulled out in front of him. He swerved, realizing too late that the driver had pulled out on purpose. The patrol car went into a skid on the wet pavement.

It happened fast. One moment he was on the highway, the next, he was sliding across the pavement, hitting the graveled edge of the road and was airborne.

BRANDON HAD JUST climbed back into the SUV when he saw a set of headlights in his rearview mirror. A vehicle was coming up the highway moving fast. He recognized the rig as it sped past. Red's pickup. Only Red wasn't driving. Mason VanHorn was.

Mason didn't seem to see them, his attention on the highway at the high speed he was traveling.

"That was my father," Anna said, sitting up to stare after him. She looked over at Brandon. "Follow him."

Brandon nodded, pretty sure he knew where VanHorn was headed. The same place Cash was. Brookside.

"I believed him," Anna said as Brandon took off after the pickup. She shook her head. "I actually believed him. Until Dr. French called."

"Cash is on his way to Brookside. He said he had a lead on Lenore Johnson."

"Oh, my God!" Anna cried. "That must be why Dr. French was calling my father, telling him he had to come to Brookside. He said, 'You have to stop—' Stop something. Or someone?"

THE SHERIFF'S DEPARTMENT patrol car slammed down, tires digging into the side of the ditch, and rolled in a shower of mud and rain and weeds.

Cash lost track of time as he crashed down into the deep ditch beside the highway. He'd lost his sense of direction as the car rolled. He wasn't sure which side was up or down.

Then everything stopped. He hung from his seat belt for a moment in stunned silence. He was alive. The patrol car had landed upside down in the ditch. He'd been wearing his seat belt and the airbag had deployed. Nothing hurt, at least that he could feel.

He unhooked his seat belt and dropped to the roof of the car. For a moment he just lay there, trying to get his bearings. He tried the door. It opened about ten inches before getting stuck in the mud. He reached over and tried the passenger side door. It swung open and he crawled out into the rain and darkness. He couldn't see the other car, only the glow of the headlights above him on the road.

He hadn't hit the other car but he couldn't be sure the

other driver hadn't wrecked, as well. Or was the driver just waiting to finish the job he started?

Cash drew his pistol and started up the steep embankment. It was slick and he had to scramble in the wet, loose dirt. He didn't see the man until he was almost on top of him.

At the rim of the embankment, Cash blinked through the rain and saw the large dark figure for just an instant before he saw the gun in the man's hand. The man seemed just as surprised to see him and drew back his boot, kicking at Cash's head.

Cash managed to dodge the worst of the man's kick, catching a glancing blow to the shoulder. But his pistol went flying as he fell backward down the embankment.

A bullet zinged past as he tumbled back to the bottom of the ditch. Scrambling to his feet, he ducked behind the patrol car and reached inside for his shotgun as a shot ricocheted off the roof.

Glancing back up toward the highway, he saw the man silhouetted against the blurred headlights. He hadn't gotten a good look at him at the top of the embankment. Just a feel for the man's size—and intent.

The man hadn't wanted to kill him or he would have shot him—not kicked him when he had the chance. Did that mean he was only trying to detain him? Is that why he was taking potshots at him, trying to hold him down here? Until what? Until someone took care of Lenore Johnson at Brookside?

Cash swore and looked down the road a ways to where the embankment wasn't quite as steep. He waited after a bolt of lightning flashed above the highway for the darkness that followed, and then took off running.

Scrambling up the embankment, he ran to the man's car and hunkered down next to it. The car was a black SUV, some foreign job. The side was scraped, as if the driver had already been in an accident.

The man was still standing at the edge of the embankment looking down. Thunder boomed overhead. Cash saw the man jump back as if he thought he'd been shot at. He turned and started toward his car.

Cash waited until he was close enough, then rose up, pointing the shotgun at the man's chest. "Freeze!"

The man raised his gun and fired a wild shot. Cash pulled the shotgun's trigger. Light flared in the rain. The man dropped to the wet pavement.

Cash moved quickly to him, kicking away the man's weapon before he looked down at his face.

A pair of vacant eyes stared blankly up at him. "Josh Davidson?" Why the hell would the orderly from the clinic run him off the road and try to keep him from getting to Brookside?

BRANDON DROVE the narrow road up the mountain, his headlights cutting a swath through the low dark clouds of the storm. Lightning flashed. Thunder boomed on its heels. He was already jumpy after the last time they'd come up this road. For all he knew, Dr. French or Van-Horn might be waiting just around the next corner. Only this time, French or VanHorn might succeed in forcing them over the cliff.

Anna sat staring ahead, her hands clenched in her lap. He could see the fear on her face. What would they find at Brookside? He hated to think.

As he rounded the curve, Brookside rose up like a monster on the dark horizon.

Several large raindrops splattered against the windshield. Brandon jumped, his nerves raw. The rain came hard and fast, blurring everything as he pulled up to the front door—directly behind Red's pickup, which Mason VanHorn had been driving.

The driver's-side door of the pickup was standing open, Mason no longer behind the wheel. Something large and dark moved through the rain, disappearing into the inky black shadow of the building.

There were no other vehicles in the lot. No sign of Cash's patrol car. He should have been here by now. Brandon realized with a start that something had to have happened to keep him from beating them here.

Anna let out a cry. "Did you see that? I saw someone at a window on the third floor."

He looked up through the windshield in the direction she pointed. He saw nothing but darkness.

"I'm going in," Anna said, and reached for her door handle.

"We should wait for Cash," Brandon said beside her.

She looked over at him. "He should have been here by now. Lenore's in there. I can't let him kill her." She opened her door and slipped out. She didn't even feel the rain as she ran toward the front steps.

She wished she had a weapon, anything. But there was little chance for finding something she could use in the rainy darkness. She could hear Brandon behind her, but she didn't look back as she topped the steps and felt her breath catch.

From inside the dark building came the clank of an elevator door opening.

A bolt of lightning cut a brilliant white ragged tear in the sky illuminating Brookside. In that split second of blinding light, she saw that the front doors stood open. Clearly someone had been expected. Her father? Or her and Brandon?

Anna felt Brandon's hand on her arm. He pointed to the front doors. She could see the worry on his face. It matched her own. But she couldn't wait. She had to go inside. Her father was in there. With Dr. French? And what about Lenore?

Anna had gotten the woman into this. She had to help her. If it wasn't too late.

She stepped through the double doors into the entryway. The cold silence of the building settled over her. The office was dark. So was the hallway past it. Her gaze fell to the worn linoleum floor. Wet footprints.

The footprints were headed in the opposite direction—not toward the office corridor—but toward the wing for the criminally insane.

"Wait," Brandon whispered next to her.

She turned to watch him go into the office. He came back out with a large heavy-duty flashlight. He flicked it on. The battery was low, the light dim. He shone it down the hallway past the office. Empty.

When he shone it the other way, the light caught the wet footprints before shining on the open double doors of the wing that had once housed the violent, the criminally insane. Her mother, Anna thought with a horrible jolt. The light illuminated the number on the door of 9B.

Past it, the corridor was pitch-black. She thought she heard footfalls somewhere in the building, the echo making it hard to determine from where. But all her instincts told her that the figure she'd seen in the third-floor window was now on this floor.

She started in that direction when she heard a door open behind her and the creak of a sole on the floor. She spun around as a slight dark figure came stumbling out of the ladies' restroom, a piece of galvanized pipe clutched in both hands. Even as dark as it was, Anna could see that the woman's eyes were wild and she was breathing hard.

Brandon started to launch himself at the woman. "It's Lenore!" Anna cried.

Lenore only got a few steps before her legs gave out under her. Brandon caught her before she hit the floor, gently laying her down and prying the pipe from her fingers.

"It's all right," he whispered, and glanced at Anna. "She looks like she's been drugged."

"Have…been…drugged," Lenore slurred and tried to focus her gaze as Anna knelt beside her.

"Lenore, it's me, Anna Austin. You're all right now. You're safe."

Lenore shook her head. "Dr. French…" She closed her eyes, licked her lips and whispered, "Still here."

Anna looked down the hallway in the direction from which Lenore had come, then shifted her gaze to the wet footprints. They had to be her father's. Then where was Dr. French?

Anna picked up the pipe Brandon had taken from Lenore and the flashlight. She rose and shone the light in the direction of 9B. The wet footprints glistened in the light. She moved toward the wing for the criminally insane.

"Anna, wait. Don't."

She barely heard Brandon's words.

The chain was no longer on the doors to the wing, but hanging down, the padlock on the floor.

She stepped through the doors. Ahead, the wet footprints disappeared at Room 9B. The flashlight went out. She shook it. The light flickered on. She stepped to the open door of 9B. The flashlight went out again.

She stopped, swallowed back the fear that made her palms damp, her heart a thunderous ache in her chest, and took a step into the dark room. Her ankle brushed up against something. Her heart stopped.

She shook the flashlight. The light flickered on and she let out a cry as she stared at the body at her feet.

CASH HAD no choice. He rolled Josh Davidson's body off the road and, taking the man's keys, ran to the SUV.

Because of the isolation in this part of the state, Cash didn't have a full-time deputy. Didn't really need one. The few instances he'd needed help, he'd call the state investigators in Billings and they'd sent down someone.

Unfortunately, Billings was two hours away. No time for anyone to drive down. He was on his own.

The front of the vehicle had been badly crushed. One headlight was cocked at an odd angle. What the hell had Davidson hit? Cash didn't want to think.

He leaped behind the wheel and started the car, glad to hear the engine turn over on the first try. He didn't know how much time he'd lost. His greatest fear was that

Brandon would reach Brookside before he did. Lenore's call scared him. Someone had been holding her at the old mental institution. But what scared him the most was the way her call had been cut off.

The rain fell harder, the sky was even darker, as he turned onto the dirt road to Brookside. There were other tracks. Brandon's. But also several other vehicles'. Cash swore and gave the SUV more gas, fear driving him up the mountainside.

He just prayed it wasn't too late.

ANNA HEARD Brandon's running footfalls behind her. She turned away from the body on the floor.

Brandon took the flashlight from her. "Oh, God," he said as he shone the light on the body.

Out of the corner of her eye, she watched him kneel down to check for a pulse. "He's still warm. He hasn't been dead long."

Anna looked again at the body, unable to hide her shock. "It's Dr. French," she said, her voice coming out in a hoarse whisper. But how could that be? If he was the killer… His eyes bulged, his face was blue, a rope was tied so tightly around his neck that it cut into his flesh. There were horrible scratches on his throat where he'd fought to tear the rope away to no avail.

"My father killed him," Anna cried.

Brandon put his arms around Anna. She pressed her face to his chest. "Let's get out of here, okay?"

Lenore had joined them. She stumbled up and leaned against the door for support. "We have to get out before he comes back." Her eyelids were heavy and it looked as if it took everything in her to stay on her feet.

Brandon released Anna to shine the flashlight on the body. "Dr. French is dead. He won't be coming back."

Lenore looked down at the body lying just inside Room 9B. She blinked as if trying to focus. "That's not him."

Brandon exchanged a look with Anna. "This isn't the man who locked you up here?"

Lenore shook her head.

"But that's Dr. French," Anna said.

"I might be higher than a kite but I know the face of the bastard who did this to me," Lenore spat. "He said to call him Dr. French…but that isn't the man. The other one must have killed him."

"The other one?" Brandon asked, afraid of what Lenore was going to say. If Anna was right and her father had killed Dr. French—

"He must have lied about his name," Lenore said and turned to look behind her. "That's the man."

They all turned to see the tall man in the dark coat standing in the dim hallway behind them holding the gun.

"I'll take that flashlight," Dr. Ivers said. "And please put down that pipe, Ms. VanHorn. We've had quite enough drama for one night."

The authority and calmness in his tone sent a chill through Brandon as he handed over the flashlight, the light shining on the floor at their feet.

Brandon shot Anna a look. Her face was ghostlike in the eerie light, but she looked strangely calm as she dropped the length of pipe to the floor.

It clattered at her feet. "So if you aren't Dr. French, then who are you?" Lenore Johnson asked.

"Dr. Ivers," he said as he pushed them back toward the door to the room. He stooped, keeping the gun trained on Brandon, to pick up the pipe. "I have been known to use Dr. French's name, though, when the need arose." He motioned with the gun for them to step back into Room 9B. "If you would, please."

He sounded exactly as he always had at the clinic, all the years he'd stitched up Brandon and his brothers.

"What the hell is going on?" Brandon asked.

Dr. Ivers gave him a look that said he didn't like swearing. Or being talked back to. "I think you're smart enough to figure out that I'm going to lock you in that room for a while."

"Why?" Brandon asked, seeing something in the elderly doctor's eyes that frightened him more than the gun.

Ivers sighed. "Please don't be difficult, Brandon. I tired of you and your brothers' antics long ago."

"You can't keep us all locked up here," Lenore said. "Give it up, old man. It's over. Whatever it is that you're trying to hide, the cat is out of the bag."

Anna had been watching the doctor, trying to understand how Dr. French could be dead, why the kindly Dr. Ivers had pretended to be French and, more important, why he was now holding a gun on them.

Then she knew. "You delivered my mother's baby," she said. "That's what this is about, isn't it? My father let me believe Dr. French must have delivered the baby."

He smiled forlornly. "Your father used to tell me what a bright girl you were. He was always bragging about your articles, all those awards for investigative journalism. He was so proud of you. What a shame you had to use all that skill to try to destroy so many lives."

"This is more than covering up a baby's death," Anna said. "Or my mother's confinement here. You and my father made some kind of deal. Why else would you go along with it otherwise?"

Dr. Ivers looked over his shoulder. Was he expecting someone? "Why couldn't you have just left it alone?" he demanded. "My wife of sixty-two years is very sick. She doesn't have much time left. I won't have her distraught by all this. Do you understand?"

"Distraught, my ass," Lenore said. "You kill us and I promise your wife will be more than distraught when she finds out."

"My Emily only has a few days left," he said.

"What about your daughter?" Brandon asked. "Taylor."

"My daughter, yes." He glanced over at Anna. "I won't be able to protect Taylor. But I can at least spare my wife any further pain. I owe her that much."

"Don't you at least owe *me* the truth?" Anna said. "You delivered my little brother. What happened to him?"

"He was stillborn, just as your father told you."

She shook her head. "My nanny heard the baby cry. Did my mother kill the baby?" she asked with a sob.

Dr. Ivers furrowed his brows. He seemed distracted and she could tell he was listening for something. A vehicle? "Your father had feared she would. I let him believe she had. Your father was already so upset, he would have believed anything I told him but the baby was stillborn just as I said. I sent him off to bury it."

That moment of hesitation. "The nanny *heard* a baby cry."

Dr. Ivers looked startled as if her words had finally sunk in.

"The nanny was in the room right upstairs." Anna let out a gasp at a sudden realization. "There had to have been *another* baby. Twins. That's why you told my mother to stay in bed during the pregnancy."

"Enough," Dr. Ivers snapped. "Step into the room."

"No. Tell me the truth. There was another baby, wasn't there? What did you do with it?"

Brandon swore. "He kept it. Earlier at the clinic when I saw you and Taylor together I thought how much—"

"I don't want to shoot any of you, but I will if I have to," Dr. Ivers said, suddenly agitated. "All of you into the room."

"Taylor is my *sister?*" Anna cried. She remembered the competent doctor at the clinic who'd bandaged her head. The woman had dark hair and eyes like Anna's mother. Like Anna. Taylor, the only child of elderly parents.

Anna heard a car coming up the road, the whine of the engine a faint buzz. Cash? Was it the sheriff?

Or was it someone else? Whoever Dr. Ivers was expecting?

The doctor tilted his head. He heard the sound, too. "Time is up." He pulled the trigger. The report echoed like a cannon through the hallway. The bullet lodged in the padding in Room 9B.

Anna jumped back.

"I'm not going back in that room," Lenore said, standing her ground. "You can just shoot me."

"Have it your way," Dr. Ivers said and pointed the gun at her.

Brandon stepped in front of the private investigator. "You don't want to kill anyone. Think of Taylor. She is going to have to live with whatever you do here today."

Dr. Ivers shoved Brandon backward, knocking Lenore back, as well. Lenore stumbled over Dr. French's body and started to fall. Anna caught her. The doctor reached to close the door.

Anna saw movement behind him. Her father. He staggered up behind Dr. Ivers, his white hair wet from the rain, his expression pained. Blood ran down one side of his face. He had a gun in his hand. He pointed it unsteadily at the doctor's back.

"I can't let you do that," Mason VanHorn said. "It's over, Doc. It's finally over."

"Sorry, Mason, but this time I hold all the cards." Dr. Ivers swung around, leading with the pipe her father couldn't have seen in Ivers's hand.

"No!" Anna yelled as the pipe struck the gun in her father's hand and sent it skittering across the worn tile floor.

Dr. Ivers pulled the trigger. Anna saw her father stagger backward and fall. Before the doctor could get off another shot, Brandon hit Ivers from behind. Ivers stumbled forward, fell toward the opposite wall, caught himself and then kept going down the corridor at a run.

"Get him!" Lenore cried. "The bastard is getting away."

But Anna could have cared less about Dr. Ivers. She ran to her father and knelt beside him. His shoulder bloomed red with blood. She hurriedly stripped off her jacket and put it on the wound. His eyes were closed. She quickly checked his pulse. It was faint.

"Brandon, get help!" she cried. "We have to get him to the hospital."

"Ivers won't get far," Brandon assured Lenore as a vehicle pulled up out front; a car door slammed. He ran down the hall and called back to them, "It's Cash." Turning to his brother, he cried, "Call 911."

CHAPTER FOURTEEN

"YOUR OLD MAN saved our lives," Lenore said, sitting down next to Anna on the floor as they waited for the ambulance. "Go figure."

Anna held her jacket to his wound, clutching his hand with her free one. "You're going to make it," she whispered. "Damn you, don't you leave me now."

Brandon put his arm around her. They could hear the sound of the ambulance siren in the distance.

Cash waited for the ambulance. As the attendants loaded Mason into the back of the ambulance, he asked Brandon, "I'm going after Dr. Ivers. Where will you be?"

"With Anna. Christianna VanHorn. At the hospital."

Cash looked at Anna standing next to Brandon. "So you're Christianna VanHorn." He glanced at his brother, a questioning look that said he was going to be demanding some answers. "I'll want to talk to you both. You'd better take Ms. Johnson to the hospital with you. Who knows what the doc had been giving her drugwise."

Brandon nodded, his hold on Anna tightening. "I'll take care of them."

Cash smiled and dropped his hand on his brother's shoulder as he left in the familiar-looking black SUV with the dents.

"I wonder what that's about," Brandon said, more to himself than to Anna. She was watching the ambulance pull out. He walked her and Lenore to Mason's SUV and followed the ambulance to the Sheridan hospital.

The doctors admitted Lenore for observation against her protests—and took Mason right into surgery.

"You don't have to stay," Anna said as he waited with her.

"I'd like to. If you want me here," he said.

She nodded, tears in her eyes. He put his arms around her. She leaned into his chest, and they waited several hours until a doctor finally came out to tell them the news.

"He should make it," the young male doctor assured Anna. "He has a slight concussion from a blow to the head and he's lost blood from the head wound and the gunshot but no vital organs were affected. He's strong for his age and in good shape. Now it just comes down to a will to live."

"May I see him?" Anna asked.

"He's sedated. But you can go in for a few minutes."

BRANDON WAITED outside as she went into the room. Her father looked so old against the white of the sheets, his face pale and haggard. She stared down at him for a long time, not knowing what to say.

"I love you. I've always loved you." She touched his weathered hand, remembering how he'd been when she was a girl. If only she could find that man in this one. If only she got the chance.

"Please come with me home to the ranch," Brandon said when she came out of her father's room.

She wiped her tears and looked at him in surprise. "Are you sure they'll want a VanHorn under their roof? Especially after they hear what happened?"

Brandon had been the one who'd said they had no chance because of their families and the feud. "I was wrong," he said. "Come on." He reached for her hand.

She smiled through her tears and took his hand.

At least he hoped to hell he was wrong about their families, because right now he wanted her with him and there was only one place he wanted to be—on the McCall ranch.

CASH DROVE Davidson's SUV up to the front door of Dr. Porter Ivers's house. All the lights were on. Dr. Ivers's car was in the drive. He'd half expected the doc to run. Ivers had had plenty of time. Cash was a good forty-five minutes behind him, but he hadn't been able to leave until the ambulance got up the road and he was sure the others were safe.

Cash was worried. He didn't have the whole story yet. Brandon had filled him in on some of it, but Cash still had three unsolved murders—Emma Ingles, Dr. Niles French and Helena VanHorn, the Jane Doe in Room 9B at Brookside.

All Cash knew at this point was that Dr. Ivers had shot Mason VanHorn, held Lenore Johnson captive and threatened his brother and Christianna VanHorn.

That was enough to pick him up and arrest him until all of this could be sorted out.

He didn't see Taylor Ivers's car and wondered if she was still at the clinic—or if her father had taken her car. Cash climbed out of the SUV, weapon drawn, and approached the house.

Dr. Porter Ivers lived in one of the large old homes in Antelope Flats. He'd come here right after he'd married his wife Emily and took over the clinic after Dr. Neibauer retired.

Cash recalled talk around town that Dr. Ivers and his wife had hoped to fill that huge old house with children. When Emily couldn't get pregnant, the doctor had become interested in infertility.

He'd helped other infertile couples, including Leticia Arnold's parents, have children. At least that had been what Cash had believed.

But as Cash walked up the steps to the front door, he had a bad feeling about how the doctor had "delivered" those babies.

The door was standing open. He looked through the screen into the lit living room. Everything was neat. No sign of anyone, or anything out of place. No sounds at all.

He knocked on the door frame, waited and knocked a little louder. He couldn't help but remember walking by this house on a summer evening and seeing Doc and Emily sitting on the porch trying to catch a cool breeze. No one who'd seen them together would ever doubt the devotion they had for each other.

Cash knocked again. No answer. A bad feeling settled over him as he pushed open the screen door and stepped inside.

"Dr. Ivers. It's Sheriff Cash McCall. Please come down."

No answer.

He checked the lower rooms, then started up the stairs, afraid of what he would find.

BRANDON DROVE HOME to the Sundown Ranch through the growing darkness. The lights were on inside the ranch house as he parked out front and glanced at his watch, surprised it was only eight-thirty. It felt like midnight.

He opened his door and Anna slid out after him. He took her hand, felt the tension in her. She was the one who said it didn't matter how their families felt about them being together. She'd lied and now he knew it.

"It's going to be all right," he tried to assure her.

She gave him a look that said she highly doubted that.

"Your father is going to get better," he pointed out.

"And go to prison for his crimes, whatever they all are." She shook her head. "I hate to think that you were probably right about our families."

He squeezed her hand. "It doesn't matter."

She smiled up at him sadly. "Yes, it does."

As they started up the steps, the front door opened. Shelby stood framed in the doorway. "Brandon? Who is that with you?" She turned on the porch lights.

"Mother, this is Christianna VanHorn," he said.

Shelby blinked in surprise. Either from the fact that a VanHorn was standing on her porch, or that he'd finally called her Mother.

"I prefer Anna," Anna said.

"Anna." Shelby extended her hand, taking in the dirty, blood-stained jeans. "Come in, please."

Anna let Shelby draw her into the house. Brandon followed. He could forgive his mother everything at that moment. He'd been lying to himself. He was worried as hell what kind of reception they would both get.

Of course, there was still his father. Asa could be a

hard, unforgiving man. And while having Shelby back had softened him, he was still a force to contend with sometimes.

"Oh, dear," Shelby said, looking them over once inside the house. "What has happened?"

"It's a long story," Brandon said.

"Have you two eaten?" Shelby asked. "We were just having a late dessert, but I can have Martha fix you both a plate from dinner. You look like you could use it."

"That would be great," Brandon said.

Anna nodded. "Thank you."

His older brother J.T. came out of the dining room. He seemed surprised to see Brandon with a woman. Brandon realized he'd never brought one home before.

"Come on in and meet the rest of the family," Brandon said, his gaze locking with J.T.'s.

"Anna, would you like to freshen up?" Shelby asked. "There's a powder room right down the hall. Dusty's about your size. I'm sure we can rustle up some clean clothes."

"Thank you," Anna said as she looked down at her jeans. Her fingers went to her father's dried blood on her pant leg.

"Dusty," Shelby called. "Get a pair of your jeans, a blouse and a brush for Anna."

"I should clean up some, too," Brandon said, but he hated to leave Anna down here alone with his family.

"She'll be fine," Shelby said with a fierce motherly look that made him grin. "You don't have to worry about her."

"I'll be right back." As he took the stairs to his room, he heard Shelby giving orders to Martha to set plates for the two of them. Then he heard his mother go into the dining room and announce that Brandon and Christianna VanHorn would be joining them.

"What the hell?" Asa bellowed before someone closed the dining room door, drowning him out.

When Brandon came back downstairs, Anna was dressed in a pair of his little sister Dusty's dungarees and western shirt. Her hair was brushed, her face no longer smudged with dust.

She smiled as he joined her in the dining room.

His father showed the most surprise as Brandon sat down. Asa started to speak, but Shelby put a hand on his shoulder.

Martha served them both plates heaped with roast beef, mashed potatoes, gravy, fresh corn from the garden and sliced tomatoes.

They ate as Shelby kept a light conversation going. Brandon felt himself smiling at his mother, appreciating her more than he ever imagined.

"Are you sure you're both all right?" she asked when they'd finished their meals and dessert.

"It was wonderful, thank you," Anna said.

"Now are you going to tell us what the hell is going on?" Asa demanded.

Shelby shot him a warning look.

"I think we'd all like to know," J.T. said.

Brandon nodded and looked over at Anna. He covered her hand with his own and smiled reassuringly at her. "Like I said, it's a long story. And as far as we know, it doesn't have an ending yet."

CASH FOUND Dr. and Mrs. Porter Ivers in the master bedroom. Like all the other rooms, this one was spotlessly neat. The window next to the bed was open, the curtains billowing on the night breeze, the air fresh after the rainstorm.

Dr. Porter Ivers lay on the bed, his wife Emily in his arms, the two locked in an embrace.

Cash didn't need to check their pulses to know that they were both dead, but he did before he picked up the phone beside the bed to call Coroner Raymond Winters.

Beside the phone was an empty bottle of pills. Next to it was a glass half full of water. Propped against the night side lamp were two envelopes—one with the words *Sheriff Cash McCall* written on it, the other with simply *Taylor*.

CHAPTER FIFTEEN

ANNA SPENT THE night in the guest bedroom at the Sundown Ranch. Dusty brought her a white cotton nightgown.

"I'm sorry about your mother," the youngest McCall said as she gently laid the nightgown on the end of the guest bed, smoothing the fabric with her fingers. "I didn't have a mother, either." She turned and looked at Anna. "Well, until recently," she said with an eye roll.

"It's tough growing up without a mother," Anna agreed. "But you have one now."

Dusty shrugged. "Just like you have your father now. Aren't you mad at him, though, for what he did?"

Anna nodded and sat down on the edge of the bed, moving the nightgown so Dusty could join her. "I *am* angry. Part of the reason is that he lied to me for so long and I still don't know the truth."

"Yeah," Dusty said, then lowered her voice conspiratorially. "My parents told us why they did what they did to protect us. But we all know there's more. Like why she came back *now,* you know?"

Anna nodded.

"And how can I tell if they are telling me the truth now after they lied to me my whole life?" Dusty asked, sounding miserable.

"I guess all we can do is start somewhere. I want to

know my father. I know there is good in him now. And he's family. You're lucky to have such a large family."

"But it sounds like you might have a sister," Dusty said.

Anna nodded, wondering how Taylor would take all of this. She hated to think. "I just know I don't want to waste any more time hating my father."

Dusty nodded and let out a long sigh. "It's just been so embarrassing, everyone in town talking about us." She mugged a face, then brightened. "But I guess they'll be talking about your family now." She caught herself, her eyes widening in horror. "Oh, I didn't mean—"

Anna laughed. "It's all right. If it takes away from people gossiping about your family, then something good has come out of it." Until the town got wind that Christianna VanHorn was with Brandon McCall. Even temporarily.

BRANDON COULDN'T sleep. He checked on Anna. She was tucked into the guest bedroom, asleep, breathing softly, reminding him of the nights they'd spent together; his sleepless one in the mountains and the amazing one at the lake cabin.

"I need to check on Cash," he told his mother. "Would you keep an eye—"

"On Anna? Of course." She seemed to study his face. "How serious is this, Brandon?"

He took a breath and let it out slowly. "On my part? Or hers?"

His mother nodded as if the answer was only too clear and patted his arm. "Go check on your brother."

He looked at her, seeing how beautiful she was now,

thinking how pretty she must have been when she was even younger than Dusty.

"In high school," he began, "when Dad and VanHorn were both in love with you…" He swallowed.

"Was I in love with Mason?" she asked.

He nodded.

She smiled and seemed to choose her words carefully. "It was always Asa. Always. But if there hadn't been an Asa…" She sighed and met his gaze.

He let out the breath he'd been holding. "All right." He backed toward the door. "Thank you for tonight."

"She's a beautiful, smart, capable young woman," Shelby said.

"Yeah, she is that."

ALL THE LIGHTS were on inside the sheriff's department. Brandon parked out front next to several state patrol cars. Several men were leaving as he walked in. Cash stood behind his desk, his back to the room.

"Did you get Ivers?" he asked.

Cash turned and nodded slowly.

Brandon could see by his face that something horrible had happened.

"He and Emily were dead when I got there," Cash said. "He left a confession."

"Does it clear Mason?" Brandon asked hopefully, thinking of Anna.

Cash nodded. "How are you?"

"Fine. Mason came out of surgery. Anna's out at the ranch."

"The Sundown?" he asked in surprise. "Asa must be beside himself."

"He took it pretty well," Brandon said. "But I don't

think he'd be wild about having a VanHorn for a daughter-in-law."

"Not that it matters what he wants. Is that something he should be worried about?"

"Anna and I..." He waved a hand through the air. "She thinks she wants to live on the home ranch. I think she won't last a month before she's ready for the city and her life back there."

"So it's like that," Cash said.

"Truthfully?" Brandon asked as he straddled a chair across from his brother's desk. "I don't know what it's like right now. So much has happened. I guess only time will tell."

"Have you told her you love her?" Cash asked as he pulled out his chair and sat down.

Brandon looked up at him in surprise.

"It's a place to start, little brother," Cash said with a smile. "Now, tell me what the hell's been going on."

Brandon started at the beginning with his job as night security on the VanHorn Ranch. Cash only interrupted a few times, usually just to swear or say, "What the hell were you thinking?"

From the job to the vandal to meeting Anna to finding out who she was and why she was in Montana, Brandon told him everything, including why Asa and Mason hated each other in the continuing feud of the McCalls and VanHorns.

"Mother?"

Brandon smiled and nodded. "She said if there hadn't been an Asa..." He told him about Anna's nanny and the deathbed confession, up until the part where Cash walked into Brookside.

"The nanny thought it had been Dr. French who delivered the babies and took Helena to Brookside," Brandon said. "The two were built the same, even about the same age, and Dr. Ivers said he used Dr. French's name when it suited him."

The phone rang. Cash answered it. "That was the hospital," he said after he hung up. "I can talk to Mason now. I still want a statement from you and Anna." He glanced at his watch. "Can the two of you stop by in the morning?"

THE NEXT MORNING, Anna left Brandon outside her father's hospital room while she went in.

Mason looked up, obviously surprised to see her. She went to him and planted a kiss on his weathered cheek. A tear rolled down. She brushed it away.

"I thought you would be gone back to Richmond," he said quietly. "I thought you would never want to see me again."

She pulled up a chair and sat down, taking his hand in both of hers. "I need to know the truth," she said, meeting his gaze. "No more lies."

He nodded and repeated the story he'd told her. "Ivers let me believe your mother killed that little baby."

"So you took it out to bury it," she said. "You didn't know she was having twins?"

He shook his head and looked down. "But when I came back in Ivers had called Niles French. French pulled me aside, I guess, so I didn't see Ivers leave. He was carrying something in his arms. I heard it cry. I knew there had been another baby...." He broke down for a moment. "God forgive me, but I didn't want that baby. Not a baby your mother had with another man, and

I knew she wasn't able to take care of the two children we already had."

"So you knew Taylor was my sister?" Anna asked.

"No, I had no idea. I should have seen the resemblance, but Ivers let everyone believe his wife had been pregnant and had the baby early while staying at her sister's. Since the baby was a fraternal twin, it would have been premature."

Anna thought about her sister for a moment. "Dr. French took my mother to Brookside that night?"

He nodded. "I visited her every week. She didn't know who I was and sometimes she wouldn't even look at me, but I would talk to her and take pictures of you and Holt." Mason stopped, cleared this throat. "She was getting better...." Tears filled his eyes. "I adored your mother but she was always fragile."

"Cash says she was murdered in her room, 9B," Anna told him.

"Dr. French told me she was killed by another patient. He covered it all up, saying she was a Jane Doe he'd picked up off the highway and put in Brookside for the night. I still visit her grave and put flowers on it. Oh, Anna, I'm so sorry. I was a coward. If I'd only told the truth from the start...."

She squeezed his hand. "Did you kill Dr. French?"

His face hardened. "I realize now that Ivers killed your mother. She was getting better. She might have remembered the twins being born, she might have asked about the daughter who had lived."

Taylor. "His world was crumbling, his wife dying, me digging into the past," Anna said.

"He would have done anything to protect his daughter," Mason said. "I can understand that." He swallowed.

"Your mother, in the days before she died, would look at the pictures I took her." He smiled through his tears. "She would touch the one of you and say how beautiful you were."

"I look like her."

He nodded. "I realize now it was the reason I pushed you away. I was afraid that I'd made Helena the way she was. I feared…" He lowered his head, broke down.

She stood, leaning over him to press her lips into his hair. "I'm so sorry for all the horrible things I thought about you."

He wiped at his tears. "I am a hard man. Helena was the part of me that was soft and gentle. When I lost her…"

"Cash says you will probably get probation."

"I'm not worried about me." He drew back to look at her. "What will you do now?"

"I want to stay here." She met his gaze.

"McCall." He said it softly, then chuckled. "I guess I knew that day I saw the two of you sitting on that curb on Main Street. I thought if I sent you away…" He shook his head. "I thought the ranch and me made your mother sick. I wanted to free you from all of it. I guess it's always been your destiny."

"I hope so," Anna said.

BRANDON PUSHED OFF the wall where he'd been pacing back and forth as Anna came out of her father's room. There were tears in her eyes. "Is he all right?"

She nodded and bit her lower lip as Brandon reached for her. She came into his arms and he encircled her, burying his face in her dark hair. She smelled like sunshine and rain and summer. He thought about what Cash had said. But this wasn't the place where he wanted to tell her he loved her.

The idea of telling her frightened him more than he wanted to admit. But he knew he had to do it, no matter the outcome. He couldn't let her leave Montana without knowing how he felt.

"I told Cash we'd stop by his office and give him our statements," he said.

She nodded against his chest, then pushed back, drying her eyes and taking a deep breath. She let it out slowly. "I'm ready."

CASH WAS on the phone in his office. They waited until he hung up to take the chairs he offered them.

"That was Lenore on the phone. She can't wait to get back to Richmond. She says she'll call you," Cash told Anna.

"I feel bad about what I put her through," Anna said.

"It comes with being a P.I. I'm sure she told you that." Cash leaned forward, turned on the tape recorder and took their statements. When they'd finished, he turned off the tape recorder and nodded. "Your stories fit what Dr. Ivers left in his confession and what Mason VanHorn told me."

"Have you talked to Taylor?" Anna asked. "Is she all right?"

Cash nodded. "According to Taylor, her father had been planning to take his wife's life and his own. That's why she came back to Antelope Flats."

"But she just learned that her father was a murderer," Anna said.

"No," Cash corrected her, "Taylor just learned that her father was Mason VanHorn."

Anna stared at the sheriff. "But my father said—"

"Your father was wrong. Taylor had suspected for some time that she wasn't Porter and Emily's biological daughter. It didn't add up. Mason was in the clinic a few months ago for a checkup. He showed both senior and junior Dr. Ivers a photograph of you, Anna. Taylor saw the resemblance—and the way her father reacted. She took some DNA when she did your father's checkup."

Anna was flabbergasted. "So my mother hadn't had an affair. But my father believed—"

"Your mother was very sick. I think Dr. Ivers knew the truth," Cash said. "That's why he was so afraid when a private investigator showed up asking a lot of questions. The night security woman saw Dr. Ivers and Josh Davidson bring Lenore into Brookside; she didn't know Ivers's real name. He'd told her it was French. But after she'd seen him lock Lenore in 9B... It wasn't her night to work. The other security watchman became suspicious when Davidson asked him a lot of questions about when he would be working and asked Emma Ingles to fill in for him. He later quit and left town. But it cost Emma her life."

Brandon reached over and took Anna's hand. "But you think Mason will get off with probation?"

"Probably," Cash said. "He and Dr. French did cover up your mother's death and your little brother's, as well as keep her stay at Brookside a secret. But the real crimes were committed by Dr. Ivers."

"Ivers killed Dr. French?" Brandon asked.

Cash nodded. "French wanted to come clean. He had been trying to get Helena's file from your father,

Anna. He needed it to prove what had really happened. I guess he had cancer and wanted to confess all before he died."

"And Dr. Ivers couldn't let him," Brandon said. "Why did he just keep Lenore at Brookside and not get rid of her permanently?"

"Ultimately, Ivers was buying as much time as he could with his wife. I don't think he wanted to kill anyone." Cash leaned forward, putting his arms on the desk. "You might as well hear this from me. It will soon be common knowledge in Antelope Flats the way the gossip mill works here. Taylor wasn't the only baby Ivers took. You remember the Arnolds, Brandon?"

"Leticia's mom and dad?" Leticia was his sister Dusty's best friend.

"They wanted a baby desperately. I guess Leticia's mom was an unwed teenager," Cash said. "There are other babies Ivers stole. We're not sure how many."

"Does Leticia know?" Brandon asked.

Cash shook his head. "She doesn't know yet. It's one of the things I have to do before the day is over. Are you all right, Anna?"

She nodded, surprised that she was.

"Taylor says she'll stay in Antelope Flats and take over the clinic," Cash said. "I think in time she'll be glad she has a sister."

"Maybe someday," Anna said. "Right now, maybe I can just be a friend. She's going to need someone."

"That day at the clinic," Brandon said. "I saw her frowning as we left. I thought she was frowning at me, but she knew then that you were her sister."

Anna nodded. "I remember while she was checking my injury that she kept staring at me. Funny, but I did notice her eyes and thought how much they were like mine."

The phone rang. Cash answered, "Sure. Okay. All right." He hung up and looked at Anna and Brandon. "That was Shelby. She has called a family dinner. To-night. Everyone is to be there." He raised a brow. "Who knows what's up now? But she said you're to bring Anna."

BRANDON DROVE Anna out to the lake to get her things. She was quiet on the drive. As they started up the steps of the cabin, he stopped her.

"Let's take a walk down by the lake first," he said, not wanting to see her pack her bags. Not yet, anyway.

She looked a little surprised, but agreed.

The lake was glass, the morning sun golden in a cloudless blue sky. The air smelled of pine and water and summer. He breathed it in, reminded of the summers he'd spent on the lake with his dad and brothers—and eventually his little sister. This was where he wanted his children to be raised. This was home—this valley, this life.

As he walked with Anna along the sandy beach, he realized that not long ago he'd wanted to escape it. To go to law school, knowing he probably wouldn't be back.

How could things have changed so much for him in a few days? He knew the answer. He'd never been in love before, didn't realize what a strong pull it exerted over him. Now he wanted to make new roots, to build a family, to make a life for himself here.

"There's something I have to tell you," he said and stopped to take both of her hands in his. He looked into her dark eyes, startled at how beautiful she was. "I love you."

The words were out so quickly, he surprised himself. He chuckled. "I had intended to say it more eloquently than that."

"Oh, I thought that was wonderfully eloquent," she said, her gaze locked with his.

He let go of her hands to pull off his Stetson and rake a hand through his hair. "I know this is sudden."

She laughed. "Sudden? You call twenty-two years sudden?" She cupped his face in her hands. "I fell for you that day on the curb, Brandon McCall. Do you know my father saw us together? It's another reason he sent me away. He was afraid I'd end up a ranchwoman."

"Oh." He felt all the wind come out of him.

She shook her head. "I told you that stupid feud wasn't going to keep me from what I wanted. I told you what I've always wanted. You, and to get back to Montana. Ranching is in my blood. Anyway, my father knows how I feel about you."

"And?"

"And," she said smiling, "he said it must have been destiny."

"Destiny?" Brandon laughed. "I'm not sure that's what Asa is going to say."

"Don't worry, I'll win him over," she said and put her arms around him to gaze up into his face.

Brandon sighed. "Well, I guess tonight will be the night."

CHAPTER SIXTEEN

ANNA SPENT THE afternoon in Brandon's arms inside the cabin. They made love, talked, made love again, and talked some more. Suddenly, it seemed there was so much they had to say.

Until finally she laughed and said, "We have time to learn everything, don't we?" He hadn't asked her to marry him. And the one thing they seemed to have avoided talking about was her family ranch. She wondered if she was wrong about the two of them being able to overcome the feud between their families.

She wanted desperately to live on her ranch. That's how she'd thought of it since she had been a girl, when she used to ride her horse across the far reaches of it with her father. No one understood better than she did that feeling of ownership. Land was something solid to build on.

She knew she couldn't bring up the subject herself because she still had to talk to her father about what she wanted. He knew she wanted this way of life. He didn't know she wanted the ranch. Not yet, anyway.

"Could we stop by the hospital on the way to dinner?" she asked. "I need to see my father again."

MASON VANHORN was awake, sitting up a little in his bed. His face brightened to see her walk in. He glanced toward the door. "You can bring McCall in with you. I won't bite off his head."

She smiled at that. "I wanted to talk to you alone. It's about the future. I don't want to go back to Richmond. I want to stay on the ranch."

He nodded. "You want to marry Brandon McCall and stay on the ranch."

"Yes."

"Even knowing how our families have battled for generations?" he asked.

"It was a silly feud." She regretted the words when she saw his pained expression. "You loved her, didn't you?"

"Your first love is hard to get over," Mason said.

Didn't she know it.

"I can't forgive Asa for taking her and making her so unhappy she left and lied about her death," Mason said.

"You don't know what happened between them," Anna said. "They're together now. I've seen them. They're happy."

He studied her a moment. "And you're happy with... Brandon."

She smiled at the way he said *Brandon* because she could see him coming around. "What were you going to do with the ranch if Holt didn't come back?"

"Holt isn't coming back. He's never had any interest in the ranch."

"So you were going to leave it to posterity?"

He laughed. "That does sound like me, doesn't it." He shook his head. "I was going to leave it to you. I didn't like to think what you would do with it. Sell it, I suppose." He met her gaze. "You want it, though."

B.J. DANIELS 469

She nodded. "More than almost anything else in life."

"Except Brandon McCall."

She smiled. "Except Brandon McCall."

"I liked building it up better than I ever liked running the ranch. It's yours, Anna. Lock, stock and barrel."

She couldn't hide her joy as she planted a kiss on her father's cheek.

"I'll have the papers drawn up right away," he said.

"I'd like it as a wedding present."

He raised a brow. "You're that sure this cowboy of yours is going to ask you to marry him?"

"Yes," she fibbed.

"I guess we'll see if McCall has any sense," Mason grumbled. "There is a great spot on some land to the north for a house."

She smiled. "You get well. I'm going to need you to walk me down the aisle. Only you won't be giving me away. You'll be welcoming me home."

Mason's eyes welled with tears. He cleared his throat. "Well, don't leave this man of your dreams out in the hall. Tell him to come in here."

"He hasn't asked me to marry him yet," she said quickly.

"Don't worry, I won't embarrass you," Mason said.

Anna called Brandon into the room. He looked gunshy but who could blame him?

"Brandon," Mason said. "I wanted to thank you for taking care of my daughter. She's really something, isn't she?"

"Yes, she is," Brandon said.

Mason nodded, watching the two of them.

"We really need to get going," Anna said. "We're having dinner with Brandon's family."

Mason raised a brow. "I'm sure you'll let me know how that goes. I'd say give Asa my best—"

"Let's not go there," Anna said, dragging Brandon back into the hall. She laughed at his expression.

"He hates me," Brandon said in the hallway.

"No, he doesn't," she assured him.

"Right. And now we have to face my entire family. You could probably use a stiff drink."

"It's going to be fine," she assured him.

He just nodded and she could tell he was worried. "Let me tell you about McCall family dinners. The last one my father called us together for, right in the middle of it, my mother showed up from the dead."

She laughed and hugged him. "I'm sure tonight will be fine."

He didn't look convinced.

BRANDON WAS RELIEVED that when they reached the Sundown Ranch house, everyone else had already arrived. Clearly, his mother had briefed them all on Anna.

A few were on the porch. Brandon made the introductions. "This is my brother Rourke and his wife Cassidy." Cassidy was very pregnant and more beautiful than he'd ever seen her. Cassidy had made the announcement of their happy news not too long ago.

"You've already met J.T.," Brandon said. "This is his wife Regina."

"Reggie," Regina corrected and grinned at her husband. "It's wonderful to meet you, Anna. Do you ride?"

"She's a wonderful horsewoman," Brandon said, everyone hearing the pride in his voice—including Anna. She blushed and looked embarrassed.

"I'm still trying to learn," Reggie said. "Maybe someday you could give me some pointers."

"I'd like that," Anna said.

"Does that mean you're staying in Antelope Flats?" J.T. asked.

Brandon looked at Anna. She smiled. "Yes," she said.

Inside the house, Dusty greeted Anna like a long-lost sister, and Shelby swept Anna away to the kitchen.

Asa and Cash had been sitting in front of the fireplace. Brandon was surprised to see that there was a small fire burning. The house felt hot, but Asa was in the chair closest to the blaze. Brandon felt a stab of worry.

"Hello, son," Asa said and motioned to a chair near him. "Cash was just telling me about old Doc Ivers. Isn't that somethin'? Who would have ever suspected him of such things."

Unlike Mason VanHorn, Brandon thought. "It was a horrible set of events. Especially for Mason. And Anna."

"Yes," Asa said, his eyes narrowing. "You brought her with you to dinner?"

"Mother insisted," Brandon said carefully.

"Mother, is it now?" Asa said, then nodded. "I'm glad to hear it."

Cash got to his feet and, turning his back to their father, inclined his head as if to say, "Talk to him."

"I need to check on Molly. I think Mother has

her cooking something. A frightening thought," Cash said.

"Your brother never has been subtle," Asa said as he watched Cash leave. "So what is it you want to talk to me about?" he asked, turning to look at his youngest son.

"I'm in love with her," Brandon said simply.

"Any fool can see that. But do you know what you're getting into? She's a *VanHorn*." Asa shook his head. "No good can come of it."

Brandon heard the familiar words and found himself smiling. "I've heard that all my life when it came to the VanHorns and the McCalls. But you're wrong. I love her and I'm going to ask her to marry me. If she says yes, then I'm hoping to make you and Mason grandfathers. What do you think about that?" Brandon demanded, leaning toward his father, daring him to say the wrong thing.

To his surprise, his father began to laugh. "I wondered how long it would take you to be your own man. It's about damned time." He reached for his son's hand and shook it, his grip not as strong as Brandon remembered it.

"Dinner's served," his mother called from behind them.

When Brandon turned, he saw tears in her eyes. She quickly brushed them away and reached for his hand. She pressed something into it and whispered. "It belonged to my grandmother."

Everyone filed into the dining room. Brandon hung back, staring down at the small velvet box and the pretty simple diamond ring inside.

He looked up at the sound of Anna's laugher. She

came down the hallway from the kitchen, joking with Molly. She stopped walking when she saw him.

"Sit by me at dinner," Molly said, and gave Brandon a grin as she entered the dining room. Everyone else was inside except Brandon and Anna. The double doors were open and he could see them all pretending not to watch.

"I have no idea what my mother plans to announce tonight at dinner, but I know what I'd like it to be," Brandon said as he looked into Anna's dark eyes.

Taking a breath, he pulled off his Stetson and dropped to one knee. "Would you marry me?"

Anna's eyes filled with tears as he held out the diamond.

"It belonged to my great-grandmother, I'm told," he said.

Anna blinked, then brushed at her tears and sniffled as she threw herself into his arms. "Yes, oh, yes!" she cried, knocking him over backward.

The dining room erupted in applause.

For a few moments, Brandon lay sprawled on the floor with his future bride. Then he slipped the diamond onto her finger—not all that surprised when it fit perfectly. Some things really were destined.

He kissed her, losing himself until he heard his father clear his throat.

Getting up, Brandon helped Anna to her feet. They brushed themselves off and entered the dining room as if nothing had happened.

When they were seated, his mother looked over at Asa and started to speak, but Asa took her hand and shook his head. "Tonight, we celebrate."

She looked at her husband for a long moment, then nodded and smiled as she glanced around the table.

"Is there something going on we should know about?" J.T. asked, looking worried.

"We don't have enough of these family dinners," Asa said, sounding a little choked up. "You kids always think something is going on. Everything is wonderful," he said, looking around the table. His gaze lighted on Anna. He looked worried for a moment, then cleared his throat and said, "Welcome to the family."

"I GET TO HELP with the wedding," Dusty said eagerly as everyone raised a glass to the engaged couple.

Martha appeared in the doorway. "Ty Coltrane is here. He just wanted you to know he left the horses you bought in the pen, Asa."

"Tell that boy to come in here and have some dinner," Asa hollered. "Martha, get another place setting."

"Sir, I didn't mean to interrupt your dinner," said the lanky, good-looking young cowboy in the doorway. "I should be getting home." The young man's gaze went straight to Dusty. His mouth fell open a little at just the sight of her.

"Dusty, make some room for him," Asa ordered. "Brandon, get another chair. Of course, he's joining us."

Dusty glared at her father. "He just said he couldn't stay for dinner."

"Nonsense," Asa said. Dusty was his last. She was young and stubborn. All she needed was a good man. Not that he would ever say that to Shelby. She'd have his hide.

"Well, thank you, sir," Ty Coltrane said. "I wouldn't

mind joining your family for dinner if you're sure it's not an inconvenience."

"None at all." Asa smiled at his wife. She was giving him one of her warning looks. He'd never listened to good advice in all his years. No reason to start now.

Dusty was giving him her don't-do-it-or-you'll-regret-it look. Asa smiled as Ty enthusiastically drew up a chair next to Dusty.

"Now," Asa said as he looked around the table. "Let's have dinner."

Dusty shot him the always-popular teenager's I'm-never-speaking-to-you-again look. He chuckled to himself. He could use the peace and quiet.

Shelby reached over, took his hand and squeezed it, shaking her head as if he were the most incorrigible man she'd ever met. He sure as hell was.

He squeezed back, savoring this moment in time. He had tonight and he was damned sure going to enjoy it. "To the McCalls," he thought to himself, and raised his glass in a silent salute.

* * * * *

Harlequin® A *Romance* FOR EVERY MOOD™

PASSION

For a spicier, decidedly hotter read—
these are your destinations for romance!

Silhouette Desire®
Passionate and provocative stories
featuring rich, powerful heroes and
scandalous family sagas.

Harlequin® Blaze™
Fun, flirtatious and steamy books
that tell it like it is, inside and outside
the bedroom.

Kimani™ Romance
Sexy and entertaining love stories
with true-to-life African-American
characters who heat up the pages
with romance and passion.